PRAISE FOR DAWN METCALF

"This exhilarating story of Ink and Joy has marked my heart forever. Dawn Metcalf, I am indelibly bound to you. More!"
—*New York Times* bestselling author Nancy Holder on *Indelible*

"[Metcalf's] rich physical descriptions create a complex fey world that coexists uneasily with the industrialized human one. An uneven but eventually engaging story of first love, family drama and supernatural violence."
—*Kirkus Reviews* on *Indelible*

"Dangerous, bizarre, and romantic, *Indelible* makes for a delicious paranormal read, and I for one can't wait to see more of the Twixt."
—*Bookyurt* on *Indelible*

"Fans of fae fantasy, YA paranormal and modern fantasy will adore this novel and find themselves willingly trapped within the Twixt. Read. This. Book!"
—Serena Chase, *USATODAY.com*'s *Happy Ever After* blog on *Indelible*

"Romance fans will melt for this new tale of the Twixt."
—*Booklist Online* on *Invisible*

**Books by Dawn Metcalf
available from Harlequin TEEN**

The Twixt series

(in reading order)

INDELIBLE
INVISIBLE
INSIDIOUS

DAWN METCALF

INSIDIOUS

• THE TWIXT • BOOK THREE •

If you purchased this book without a cover you should be aware that this book is stolen property. It was reported as "unsold and destroyed" to the publisher, and neither the author nor the publisher has received any payment for this "stripped book."

Recycling programs for this product may not exist in your area.

ISBN-13: 978-0-373-21165-4

Insidious

Copyright © 2015 by Dawn Metcalf

All rights reserved. Except for use in any review, the reproduction or utilization of this work in whole or in part in any form by any electronic, mechanical or other means, now known or hereinafter invented, including xerography, photocopying and recording, or in any information storage or retrieval system, is forbidden without the written permission of the publisher, Harlequin Enterprises Limited, 225 Duncan Mill Road, Don Mills, Ontario M3B 3K9, Canada.

This is a work of fiction. Names, characters, places and incidents are either the product of the author's imagination or are used fictitiously, and any resemblance to actual persons, living or dead, business establishments, events or locales is entirely coincidental.

This edition published by arrangement with Harlequin Books S.A.

For questions and comments about the quality of this book, please contact us at CustomerService@Harlequin.com.

® and TM are trademarks of Harlequin Enterprises Limited or its corporate affiliates. Trademarks indicated with ® are registered in the United States Patent and Trademark Office, the Canadian Intellectual Property Office and in other countries.

Printed in U.S.A.

For S.L. & A.J.
I love you more than all the words!

ONE

JOY OPENED THE DOOR WITH A MIX OF NERVOUSNESS, excitement and dread. She smiled at her boyfriend, who stood in the hall looking human.

"Ink!" she said, giving him a kiss on the cheek. He smelled like spring rain. "Just act normal," she whispered by his ear.

Ink blinked in confusion. His glamour made his all-black eyes look brown.

"I am not normal," he said.

Joy hooked his arm and squeezed. "Aaaaaand that's what I love about you." She steered him into the condo. "Ink's here!"

"We can see that," Stef said, coming up behind her. "We have eyes. Two of them, in fact. Both in working condition." He gave a toothy grin. "Imagine that."

Joy frowned. Her brother didn't mention that Ink had stabbed her in the eye six months ago when he'd discovered that she had the Sight—the ability to see the Folk like him in the Twixt—but he didn't have to; it hung in the air like an unspoken threat. The kitchen light flashed off of her brother's glyph-scribbled glasses.

"Stef—" Joy warned.

He pointed to himself. "Older brother," he said. "It's part of the job. With great power comes great scrutiny."

"Stef." Their father's voice came from across the kitchen. "Are you harassing our guest?"

Joy said, "Yes!" just as Stef said "No!"

Mr. Malone shook his head. His girlfriend, Shelley, chuckled while untying her apron. "Let's all sit down," she said soothingly. "Dinner's ready."

Stef stepped aside. Joy marched Ink in.

We can do this, she thought. *No problem. It's not war, it's not life-and-death—it's just dinner with my family. And my boyfriend. My inhuman, immortal, usually invisible boyfriend.* She patted Ink's arm. *Okay, remember: one conniption fit at a time.*

"Have a seat." Joy's father waved at the table. "Glad you could make it, Mark." Mr. Malone refused to call Ink by his nickname, which was funny since "Mark Carver" was his human alias—everyone in the Twixt called him "Indelible Ink." His True Name was written as an unpronounceable symbol, a *signatura*. Names were powerful things in the Twixt, and the Folk had learned to take precautions against human entrapment.

"I'm glad to be here," Ink said, careful to use contractions. Joy had coached him that he sounded more human that way. Joy guided Ink to the chair next to hers. It was the one she'd been sitting in when he'd first traced her ear, exploring the tiniest details of what it meant to be human...and accidentally learning what it felt like to fall in love.

She saw him remember. Two dimples appeared, and Joy felt her cheeks warm as she smiled.

Stef sat down and began heaping chicken and green beans onto his plate. Joy grabbed the platter out of his hands.

"Guests first," Joy said through clenched teeth.

"That's right, Stef," Mr. Malone said as he offered Ink a large bowl of roasted red potatoes. "You know the rules."

Picking up the salad, Stef scooped out big chunks of feta and black olives. "Whatever happened to 'you snooze, you lose'?"

"Some rules are meant to be broken," Mr. Malone said. "Like free Wi-Fi privileges while you're home if you don't start acting more civil. Got it?"

Stef stared at his plate and nodded. "Got it."

Mr. Malone sighed. "Sorry, Mark," her dad said, reaching for the salad. "The unofficial family motto is what got this family through puberty. These two grew up eating everything in sight."

Shelley leaned forward with a stage whisper. "My advice? Watch your fingers."

Ink clutched the bowl closer, eying Joy and Stef warily.

Joy swallowed. "Ha-ha," she said. "Just a joke. Very funny." Given the variety of monsters who lived in the Twixt, Joy could well imagine that some of them ate fingers. She served a portion of chicken to Ink and kept the platter moving. Ink slowly relaxed, loosening his grip on the potatoes. She nudged his knee and rolled her eyes toward her dad.

"Joy has been talking about the big trip this weekend," Ink said, reciting his opening line like a pro. "How long will you be gone?"

Mr. Malone grinned. "Three days," he said and clapped a hand on Stef's shoulder. "One last camping weekend before this one goes back to college."

Stef didn't respond as he chewed, but Joy suspected it was less about his bottomless appetite and more about avoiding talking directly to Ink.

"Will you be visiting Stef on campus?" Shelley asked Joy.

Joy exchanged a look with her brother. Both frowned. "No. Why?"

"Oh, well, I didn't know if U Penn was on your list," Shelley said as she stacked three cucumber slices on her fork. "I asked your father, and he said he didn't know your plans."

"Plans?" Joy said.

"It's your senior year," Mr. Malone said. "I know we sent off a bunch of college applications, but I haven't heard anything since."

Joy was speechless. College applications had been the last thing on her mind. After Mom had left, she had quit gymnastics and joined Dad's swan dive into a sea of depression, axing her dreams of becoming an Olympian, which was all she'd ever wanted since age six. She'd become a numb, moping black hole. Shaking it off had been largely thanks to her best friend, Monica, a night dancing at their favorite club and unexpectedly getting stabbed in the eye. A lot had happened since January. She'd forgotten all about college.

"Um..."

"I know it's been a tough year," her dad said. "And I didn't want to push, but you really need to start thinking about what you want to do next fall." He saw her squirm in her seat and gave a slight nod, acknowledging Ink. "We can talk about it more during the trip."

Joy untwisted her fingers from the edge of her shirt. "Yeah. Okay."

"And what do you do, Mark?" Shelley asked Ink. Joy had told her father that Ink was a kind of exclusive tattoo artist... it had not gone over well.

"I mark people," Ink said.

Joy almost snarfed her lemon water. She grabbed her napkin, and Ink looked mischievously pleased as he continued, "I like to say I get paid to draw on people's skin." Joy marveled at the single dimple tucked into his half smile like a smirk. "It's not exactly glamorous," he said. "But I never want for work."

Joy pressed her napkin to her mouth, trying not to laugh. He'd told the truth! *Not exactly glamorous"—but it had more than paid for his glamour!* The wizard's spell had been insanely expensive, but it was the only way her friends and family could see Ink without the Sight. He wore the magical projection like a suit, a perfect picture of himself, but with human-looking eyes and a tattoo of Joy's *signatura* on his left arm.

"But that's not a long-term thing, right?" Stef said, looking smug. "What do you want to do when you grow up?"

Joy picked up the serving spoon, debating its heft.

Shelley paused over the dressing. "I thought only the chicken was getting grilled tonight," she said and winked at Joy. Joy sent her a smile of thanks. At least Shelley had her back.

"You're just lucky I didn't invite Monica," Dad said. "She would've brought the thumbscrews."

Ink glanced at Joy. "Thumbscrews?"

"He's kidding," Joy said, patting Ink's hand. "Seriously. Kidding."

Ink's eyebrows twitched under his long, black bangs. "'Seriously kidding'?"

Stef and Dad exchanged glances. Joy's heart beat double-time and she waved at Ink to forget about it. She'd try to explain later. *If they made it through this dinner alive.*

"So, Ink, where do you live?" Stef said with a wicked, knowing grin.

Joy drained her drink and slammed down her cup. "Anyone need more water?"

"You sit. I'll get it." Her father got up, snagged the empty pitcher and went to the fridge, filling the room with gurgles and the crack of the ice maker.

Shelley looked at the glares across the table and sighed. "I'll cut some more lemons," she said and joined Mr. Malone where they could talk quietly by the sink.

"Have some more ice water," Joy whispered to her brother. "Then take the hint and *chill out!*"

"I'm testing a theory," Stef whispered back, pointing a fork at Ink. "I thought that his kind couldn't lie."

Ink looked up, surprised. "I cannot lie."

"Oh, really, *Mark Carver*?"

Joy hissed, *"Stef!"*

"Ah," Ink said, cutting his roll neatly in half. "I see your mistake. That name is not a lie—more like a time-honored tradition." His voice skimmed low over the table, crisp and clear. "I did not change my name, I simply named my glamour 'Mark Carver.'"

He grinned and took a bite. Butter wet his lips.

Joy beamed in relief, and Stef laughed despite himself. "Clever," he said.

Mr. Malone thunked the water pitcher on to the table, cutting off their conversation. He and Shelley sat down.

"Now, where were we?" he asked, setting his napkin on his lap.

"Grilling," Ink said.

Stef snorted.

Joy lunged for the earthenware bowl. "More potatoes?"

Ink spooned out three roasted potatoes and watched them wobble across his plate. He poked at one with his fork, painting a long trail of rosemary and oil. Catching a piece of herb on a tine, he examined it curiously, turning the fork over and over, watching the bit of leaf glisten under the lights. His face was a mask of pure fascination. Joy put a hand on his leg. Startled, he looked up with a smile.

"This looks delicious," Ink said.

"It is," Mr. Malone said. "It's Shelley's recipe. She's a great cook."

"Oh, stop," Shelley said and patted her red hair into place. "It's an old family recipe. The secret is to crush fresh herbs and garlic and store it in the olive oil overnight."

Ink put the potato in his mouth, chewed carefully and swallowed.

"I have never tasted better," he said. Joy grinned. Besides being polite, Ink was telling the truth: he had only recently begun to taste things because he'd only recently begun to eat. It was fun watching him talk circles around the others, hiding the whole truth behind words that were one hundred percent true.

Joy's phone rang. She glanced at her purse in the hall.

"Don't you dare," her father said without looking up from his plate. "Whoever it is can wait."

No phones at the dinner table was a new household rule. Dad was trying to reinstate the sacredness of family dinners before everyone split up again. Joy didn't recognize the ringtone so it wasn't Monica or Kurt or Graus Claude or Luiz. It might be one of the other Cabana Boys, which made her feel nervous and guilty. Ink's sister, Invisible Inq, had a tribe of mortal lovers who supported one another through thick and thin, like an extended family of hot male models that stretched across the globe. Even if Joy technically wasn't Ink's *lehman* anymore, she was still considered one of them—a mortal who loved one of the Folk—and a call from one of the boys meant something important. Joy sat on her hands as the call flipped over to voice mail.

"Thank you," Dad said. "Now can you please pass the—"

Joy's text messaging pinged. And again. And *again*. Dad sighed. Stef rolled his eyes. Ink looked up, curious. Joy took a shy bite of green beans. Shelley passed Dad the pepper.

"Where will you be camping?" Ink asked as he sliced a potato in half. Joy was glad that he could handle subject changes as easily as a fork and knife.

"Lake James," her father answered and took a drink of water. Ink took a drink at the same time, mimicking her father's movements, watching him with the same intensity he used while watching Joy. Ink was still learning the subtleties of how to act human. His efforts made her smile. Stef glared at his green beans as he chewed.

"It's a great place," Dad said. "We used to do a lot of family camping trips—" he swerved to avoid the words *before Mom left* and continued smoothly "—when the kids were little." The subject of Mom didn't hurt like it once had—they'd all grown used to the weekly calls and video chats. Time healed things without meaning to, whether you wanted it to or not. "How about you?" he asked Ink. "What does your family do on vacations?"

Ink put his fork down, and Joy twisted her napkin over her thumb. This was what they'd been rehearsing ever since Dad suggested that Joy invite Ink over for dinner. Her nervousness reminded her of how Monica had felt about her boyfriend, Gordon, meeting her parents, but Ink wasn't a different race, he was a different *reality*. As a member of the Twixt, Ink, like Joy, could not lie...but the Folk could be rather creative with the truth.

"I never knew my parents," Ink said and smiled to take the sting out of his words. "But I have a twin sister, and she's all the family I can handle."

Joy laughed. Stef didn't. Mr. Malone looked apologetic.

"I'm sorry," he said. "I didn't know."

Ink shrugged and made looping swirls in the ketchup. "It's all right," he said. "She and I are very close. We've traveled a lot, met lots of interesting people, seen many amazing things together—over the years, we have created our own family."

"That's good," her father said, nodding. "Family's important."

Mr. Malone glanced over at his son and smiled. It was only recently that Stef had come out as gay, and Joy had forgiven their mother for the divorce. The past two years hadn't been easy for anyone, but they'd made it through as a family—albeit a different one from the original. A lot had changed, but they still loved each other, and that was something.

Shelley turned in her chair, sniffing.

"Did we leave the stove on?" she asked. "I smell something burning." She got up and walked over to the oven.

Joy could smell it, too—a whiff of smoke like a burnt matchstick. She recognized the odor: vellum and ash. *Filly.* It must have come from the pouch the young Valkyrie used to send Joy messages. Now Joy knew something was wrong. Ink did, too; his body tightened, tense and alert. Joy put down her fork, trying to think up some excuse to grab her purse and go check.

That was when she saw the face in the window.

She almost screamed but bit her lips together. It was a tiny face, different from the monstrous Kodama that had scared her that first time. The small, winged creature pressed its bulbous nose against the glass, hair and beard a wild halo of tangles. It waved to get their attention. Joy couldn't move, but she couldn't look away. Ink casually traced the silver chain at his hip to the wallet in his back pocket where he kept his blades. Joy held her breath as Shelley walked right past the creature on her way back to the table. It watched her pass, its wild eyes bulging with curiosity. Stef's face was carefully neutral, his fingers white-knuckled on his knife. Joy wasn't sure what any of them could do with Dad and Shelley present.

The creature pointed emphatically at them.

Under the table, Ink pointed to himself and raised his eyebrows like a question.

The tiny creature shook its head and pointed again, tapping the glass.

Shelley glanced at the window. "Do you hear pecking?"

"It's the birds," Mr. Malone said without turning around. "There's one of them trying to build a nest in the window box. I keep meaning to install a mesh lid."

Joy lifted her napkin to hide her hand and pointed at herself. The little creature nodded, wagging its tail. Joy dabbed her lips. *Great. Now what?*

The winged Folk hooked its tiny toes into the sill, licked one of its long fingers and drew a word reversed on the glass. Its saliva was brown and sticky-looking, the letters gooey and smeared.

call now

It made a big show of licking its finger again, a dribble of drool stuck to the hairs on its chin.

bring ink

Joy felt light-headed. This was how it had all started: strange messages left on her window and phone for a mysterious someone called "Ink." She glanced at him across the table. He kept his eyes down and nodded as if in thought. It was enough confirmation for the little creature, who flipped backward, wings unfolding, and hovered in the air. Stef rolled up his sleeve, and Joy wondered if he was going to draw wizards' symbols on his forearms with the butter knife. She shook her head. Her brother glared at her and picked up his unused spoon.

"You need to wash it off," Stef said, shoving it at her, pointedly not looking at the window. Joy swallowed. He was right—even if Dad and Shelley didn't have the Sight, there was a chance they'd see the words written on the glass in ooze.

"Stef—" Mr. Malone said tiredly.

"No, he's right," Joy said, grabbing the spoon and standing up. "It was my turn to do the dishes. My bad." She hurried over to the sink, blocking the view of the kitchen window with her body. She turned on the water and scrubbed the spoon, mouthing to the creature, *Wash it off!* She made a scrubbing motion with the sponge and lifted the water nozzle. The little face scrunched up in confusion. Joy pointed at the letters. *Wash. It. Off*, she overemphasized with her lips.

The creature suddenly smiled and nodded, its big eyes glinting merrily through its bristly mane.

Joy gave it a wave of thanks and returned to her seat, handing back the spoon to her brother. "There," she said. "Better?"

There was a drizzling, trickling sound like rain against the window. Joy peeked over her shoulder. The incriminating words dribbled down the glass as the little creature flew around, peeing on them. Stef changed his snort into a cough, and Joy pushed her plate aside, having suddenly lost her appetite.

Ink looked at Joy's father. "More potatoes?"

Mr. Malone shook his head and patted his stomach. "Portion control," he said. "Don't tempt me."

Shelley shook her head. Stef did, too. "Pass."

Ink lowered the bowl slowly. He touched his chest, rubbing the dip at his breastbone, the space above his heart where he now felt things like love and pain and fear. He looked disoriented, confused.

Joy touched his arm, "You okay?"

Ink didn't say anything. He turned around in his chair and stared at the door.

Someone knocked.

Joy went cold.

"That's odd," Mr. Malone said, standing up. "Who could that be?"

Joy couldn't decide whether to stop him or not, wondering if he'd even see anything should he look through the peephole. Stef and Joy exchanged glances. Joy reached for Ink's hand. Stef picked up a steak knife and the salt.

Mr. Malone opened the door...and there was Invisible Inq.

The resemblance between the two Scribes was unmistakable. Even wearing their glamours, they both had the same spiky black hair, the same long, lean bodies and the same youthful faces with liquid eyes that wobbled when wet. Mr. Malone didn't need to ask who she was, but it was eerie having her stand there so still.

"I'm sorry," she said, and Joy was startled to hear that she really sounded sorry—no snark, no sly wit, no smoky insincerity. Inq glanced at the table. "Sorry to interrupt. I see you're having dinner. With my brother—" she looked at Ink, eyes pleading "—I need to talk to him. And Joy."

"It must be a twin thing," Shelley whispered.

"Come in," said Mr. Malone. "Would you like to sit down?"

Ink stood up. "What is it?" he said, but everyone heard *What's wrong?*

A smile warred with a frown on Inq's face as if she couldn't quite decide which was which. Her eyes swam, pools of fathomless black.

"It's Enrique," she said.

And Joy knew even before Inq could say the words.

TWO

WANDERING THROUGH THE FUNERAL PARLOR, JOY examined the photos on display—Enrique sailing ships, climbing mountains, posing with friends laughing, clinking glasses at a bar, windsurfing at Cape Hatteras, showing off an octopus in both hands, hiking somewhere in the rain forests, riding a camel through the desert, snorkeling in the Great Barrier Reef and haloed against a gorgeous sunrise at the top of Machu Picchu—Enrique's life had been one amazing adventure after the next. It was hard to believe that he was dead.

People milled about in black dresses and crisp suits, talking in low voices and hugging one another in tissue-soft arms. Joy could hear the whispers between them, words like *aneurysm*, *what a shame* and *really knew how to live*. Joy inhaled the sweet scent of lilies. The flowers crowded the reception tables and flanked the heavy-looking urn. Inq welcomed guests, looking glamorous in a little black dress and a choker of pearls. She smiled and nodded and thanked them all for coming. Luiz had saved Joy a seat with the rest of the Cabana Boys, who looked unusually somber in the front row. Joy remembered that Enrique had said that he had no family, so she figured that these were his friends, his business colleagues and a few dozen invisible people.

Joy sat down gingerly, self-conscious about joining the

row of beautiful men who had known Enrique best, but she didn't know anyone else here. The murmurings and gentle noises slid around her, not touching, not comforting, barely real. Unlike Inq, she didn't know what to say, and the silence felt as black as her dress. Beside her, Ilhami took her hand and squeezed. She squeezed back. With all that was unsaid between them, they understood each other perfectly.

"Sorry, Cabana Girl," he whispered. "No booby doll today."

He'd surprised a smile out of her. "That's okay."

He shrugged, looking uncomfortable in his expensive suit. "Where's Ink?"

"In some hospital in Darfur," Joy said. "He said he'd be here soon."

Ilhami tugged his cuffs over his tattoos. "Better save him a seat."

She placed her purse on the empty seat to her right and tried to remember the sound of Enrique's voice, the way his eyes twinkled when he was being clever, or her first impression of him—a South American James Bond. She tried to hold on to the things that he'd told her, that family was important and that they were both very lucky and how sorry he was for bringing her deeper into their world of danger and politics. He'd tucked her into a coat and kissed her forehead and given her coffee before he'd sent her into a drug lord's den on the edge of the Twixt in order to rescue Ilhami. Later he'd driven the getaway car at high speeds and ensured she'd made it back home in one piece. A tightness welled in her throat, and Tuan offered her a box of tissues. She took one and twisted it around her fingertip.

She didn't remember calling in to work. She didn't remember what excuses she'd given. She had told her father that she was going to the funeral of her boyfriend's sister's boyfriend, which was close enough to the truth that it hadn't hurt to say it except for the usual hurt of having to say such things aloud.

That morning, Nikolai had picked her up in Enrique's customized Ferrari and handed her a cup of coffee as they'd driven together in silence. His full lips had pinched as he'd hit the hidden switch, slipping them instantly through time and space to arrive just south of the funeral home.

Joy glanced out the window. She had no idea where they were—probably New York City, which was where Enrique had worked when he was in the States. It was green and leafy outside, unfamiliar, with an open, airy sky that didn't *feel* like New York, but they could be anywhere. It didn't really matter. Enrique, the eldest Cabana Boy, was gone, leaving behind friends and tears and photos and ashes. Joy stroked the inside of her palm, tracing the damp lifeline.

This was where all adventures ended. This was what it meant to be mortal.

Even with Folk blood in her veins and her own *signatura*, Joy Malone was not immortal.

The service washed over her in a buzz of condolences, Bible quotes and expensive cologne. Words wafted through her ears, unremarkable and unimportant. Joy fixed her gaze on the dark metal container in the center of the dais. She had a hard time reconciling how anything so small could possibly contain Enrique, who had lived so large. It was too small, too ordinary, too quiet to be him. Without seeing a body, Joy found it hard to believe that he was dead.

He could be faking it—staging his own death. Living under the radar, off the grid, leaving his old life behind in order to live in the Twixt. Maybe Inq helps him do it. Maybe he's older than he looked and has to make a new life somewhere every sixty years to throw people off the scent. There are movies like that, right? It makes sense. It could happen. It could be a bluff...

But she knew, in her heart, it wasn't.

It had taken Inq several tries to convince Joy that her *lehman's* death had been due to natural causes, a sudden burst in the brain, and not some kind of mistake, and even *more* convincing to assure her that he hadn't been a victim of Ladybird or Briarhook, Sol Leander or any one of their other enemies in the Twixt. Enrique's death hadn't been murder or revenge—it had just been time.

"He was mortal," Inq had said. "Mortals die."

It had happened. It was real. And there was nothing Joy could do. Humans were mortal. There were some things not even her magical scalpel could erase.

Sometimes there are no mistakes.

Joy shuddered and pulled her shrug closer.

She didn't have a lot of experience with death, having been six or seven when her last grandparent died. She didn't know how her Folk blood might affect how long she'd live and what would happen to her afterward. She knew what she was *supposed* to believe, but her brief stint in Sunday School had never prepared her for being part-Twixt. Did Folk go to Heaven? Did their half-human descendants, those with the Sight? Or did they go somewhere else? Where was Great-Grandmother Caroline now? Had she died young, for one of the Folk, or had she been old for a human? Joy glanced at Inq, dry-eyed and poised, knowing few could see the pale glyphs flying over her skin in silent fury.

A dark, long-haired woman offered Inq a tissue, which she politely refused. Joy stared at the Scribe. Would Ink be this calm when Joy was the one in a box?

The scent of lilies became cloying, and Joy pressed the tissue to her face.

When her eyes cleared, Ink was beside her.

She didn't know when he had arrived, whether he'd

walked through the door or if he had appeared out of thin air, but she quickly took his hand in hers, twining their fingers together. *He's here. We're both alive. We're together. I love you.*

Ink was handsome in his black suit; only the silver wallet chain hanging by his leg looked slightly out of place. She leaned closer, breathing in the fresh rain scent of him. He sat comfortably, open-faced, listening to the speeches, taking cues from her and those around him, immersing himself in what it meant to be mortal, to experience loss, to be part of her world, even as his sister walked up to the podium to say a few words.

She ignored the microphone and stood straight in her heels. "Thank you for coming," she said in her crisp, clear voice. She didn't need an amplifier—even her whispers sliced through sound. "I loved Enrique, as did all of you." She tipped her head to the side. "Well, maybe I loved him a little bit more." There were some appreciative chuckles, Joy's among them. Ink ran his thumb gently over her wrist. "And while I loved his beautiful body—" a few eyebrows rose, Joy's included "—I mostly loved his soul—his funny, warm, incredibly generous, fiercely competitive, adventurous, wondrous soul." As she smiled, her black eyes grew bigger, shining with bright flashes of hot pink and green. Joy wondered what those without the Sight could see in them. "And I will miss him, as do all of you." Inq lowered her chin, taking a moment to breathe. "But I might miss him a little bit more." Her smile was wreathed in sadness; her voice wilted as she gestured toward the urn. "This was just his body. His soul will live on—that funny, warm, incredibly generous, fiercely competitive, adventurous, wondrous soul. We all knew him once, and therefore, when we live life to its fullest, strip it naked and pour it to the brim, rich and overflowing, then he will live on in each of us, until we meet again."

The priest stumbled on the "Amen," but Inq was already leaving the podium.

Antony and the long-haired woman helped escort her to her seat as the priest gave instructions about where the reception would be held. The other guests rose and gathered their things. More kisses. More talking. More handshakes and hugs. Joy was surprised to see that many of the Cabana Boys had brought someone with them, often female, but then again, she knew that Inq wasn't big into monogamy. There was lots of comforting. Joy squeezed Ink's hand again, and he pressed a gentle kiss to her temple.

"Are you all right?" he asked.

"No," Joy said and dabbed her eyes. "But I will be." Ilhami offered her a last tissue. She took it. "Thanks."

Ilhami nodded, eyes red-rimmed, and Joy wondered if he was crying or high. He sniffed and straightened his lapels.

"I'll see you at the funeral," he said.

Joy frowned. *Definitely high.* She tried not to be angry with the young Turkish artist. Enrique had loved his brother *lehman*, despite his habits, but Joy still hadn't forgiven him for the terrifying trip to Ladybird's. "We're *at* the funeral," she said quietly.

Ilhami sniffed again with a little laugh. "This? For Enrique? I don't think so." He nodded politely to Ink and tapped Joy's shoulder. "See you there."

He walked down the row only to be grabbed by Nikolai, who hugged him so fiercely, he nearly lifted the smaller man off the floor. They pounded on each other's backs as Ink helped Joy to stand.

"Thirty-seven," Ink said.

"What?" Joy looked up.

"Types of hugs," he explained as the Cabana Boys embraced. "I have been counting subtle differences as separate variations." He tilted his head to one side. "Why do they hit each other?"

"I don't know," Joy said, wiping her eyes. "But don't try that one with me."

"How about this one?" Ink gathered her around the shoulders. Her arms circled his body, and she leaned against him, warm and solid. She took several deep breaths of him and calm, life-giving air. She was alive. Ink was alive. He was here, holding her.

She rocked in his arms for a long moment before whispering, "Which one is this?"

"Number sixteen," he said. Joy smiled.

"It's perfect."

He breathed into her hair. "I am learning," he said, drawing her closer, sounding sad and lost. "But I wish I did not have to learn this lesson so soon."

Joy said nothing as they slowly broke apart, and she picked up her purse. "Come on," she said and made her way toward Inq, who was accepting a hug from an older couple, the last stragglers in the room. As they left, Joy stepped forward and gave Inq a hug, too.

"I'm sorry," she said, because that was what people said at funerals.

Inq nodded. "I'm sorry, too." Her smile seemed to wobble as she tucked a stray bit of brown hair behind Joy's ear. "Stupid fragile humans." She laughed a little and slid her fingers along her string of pearls. Her gaze switched to Ink. He gave his sister a kiss on the cheek, and they rested their foreheads together for a long, quiet moment. Inq blinked and raised her head.

"Thank you," she said, although Ink hadn't said anything at all.

"Ink?"

The long-haired woman crossed the room and took Ink into her arms like an old friend. He hugged her politely, not at all like he'd held Joy. He *was* learning, but his hand lingered on the small of the woman's back. Joy figured they still had to work on exits.

"Joy, this is Raina," he said. "Raina, I would like you to meet Joy."

Raina was stunning—all long limbs and shining black hair and deeply tanned skin. Her smile was winning, radiant, haloed in shimmering gold lipstick.

Joy smiled timidly and held out her hand. "It's nice to meet you."

Raina ignored the hand and hugged her, comfortably and sincerely. Her copious hair smelled warm and tropical, as if she'd just flown in from someplace exotic. It parted over her shoulder in a long, glossy sheet, like in a Pantene commercial.

"It is a pleasure to meet you, Joy," she said, pulling back, yet still holding both of Joy's hands. "I am only sorry that it is under such sad circumstances."

Joy's brain struggled to remember where she'd heard the woman's name before while politely trying to extricate her fingers from the strong, lingering touch. Raina seemed to sense her discomfort and let go as she reached out to stroke Inq's shoulder. Raina stood very close, as if oblivious to personal boundaries.

"Enrique was the finest among us," Raina said. "A true treasure."

Joy felt a frown, but didn't let it show. *Us?* Joy could see that Raina was human, her Sight able to pierce things like glamours and the veil. Was Raina being figurative? Or was she like Mr. Vinh, someone with a foot in both worlds? Joy glanced between Ink and Inq, trying to guess. *How much does this woman know?*

Inq smiled and smoothed a hand over Raina's hair. "He was a handsome boy with the shiniest toys and was a lion in bed, and I will miss him greatly." Raina gave Inq's hand a squeeze, eyes full of sympathy.

"I'll see you after the reception," Raina said, and she slipped her arm smoothly into the crook of Ink's elbow. Joy stared at it. Then stared at them. They made a striking couple. "Mind walking me to my car?" she asked, steering him down the aisle. Raina smiled warmly over her shoulder. "It was nice meeting you, Joy."

And together, she and Ink walked out of the room.

Joy stared numbly—dumbly—after them.

What just happened?

"I need to talk to you," Inq said, taking Joy's hand and tugging her closer to the urn. The smell of lilies was overwhelming. Joy's brain was trying to keep up.

"But..." Joy tried to catch a glimpse of where Ink had gone—with Raina—outside, rewinding time in her mind, sifting through facts like Ink, Enrique, death, numbered hugs, black hair, white lilies and hooked elbows. She struggled to find the puzzle piece that made everything fit, the missing key to making this moment make sense. It wasn't working.

Joy sneezed.

"Hello? Earth to Joy?"

Grabbing another tissue, she turned to Inq. "What is it?"

Inq lowered her voice. "I want you to kill someone."

THREE

IT TOOK A MOMENT FOR THE WORDS TO SINK IN. JOY ran through them a second time just to make sure she'd heard Inq correctly.

"Um, I don't think you can talk about killing someone at a funeral," Joy said, checking discreetly for witnesses. "I'm pretty sure there's some rule against it."

Inq sighed. "Look, this sad, sorry ritual has reminded me that we haven't got much time together," she said. "I'd forgotten how short human lives can be, and if I'm going to use your help, then we've got to act fast."

Joy gently but firmly removed her arm from Inq's grip. "I have no idea what you're talking about."

Inq grinned slyly. "Yes, well, you do and you don't. That's why you're perfect for the job." She plucked a flower from the arrangement and twirled it slowly in her hands. "I know what you can do, and *you* know I know what you can do—so don't disappoint me by being difficult." She handed the lily to Joy, its stiff petals curled over her palm. "Even without your armor, you're still a wildflower with bite."

"Yeah, but I don't..." Joy's mouth turned dry, her tongue fat and swollen, the next words solidified, lodged in her throat. She couldn't say *I don't kill people!* because that wasn't true, and Joy, being part-Folk, could not tell a lie. The fact was, she had done more than kill someone—she had erased one of the

Folk completely out of existence. And Inq had seen her do it. It was a secret Inq had agreed to keep "just between us girls."

"I'll explain later," Inq said at normal volume. "Still *so* much to do! And *so* little time—isn't that the theme of the day?" She scooped up the urn in both hands. "See you at the funeral!" she cooed as she skipped down the stairs.

"You mean the reception," Joy said dully.

Inq waved a hand dismissively over her head. "Oh, don't be silly," she said as she strolled down the center aisle. She patted Ink's arm as she passed through the doors. "See you both later!" She snagged a thin wrap from the coatroom and strutted to the waiting limousine parked out front.

Ink approached, fingers absently sliding along his wallet chain.

"Joy?" he said. "What happened?"

She looked at him blankly. She couldn't say, exactly, what had happened. *Had she just been blackmailed into being Inq's assassin?* Joy couldn't figure out how to tell him what Inq had said because it didn't make sense, but she couldn't lie. She hadn't told him what had really happened to the Red Knight, and she couldn't bring herself to ask him who Raina was or why he'd gone with her or what Ilhami was talking about or what Inq was up to this time—it all felt strangely surreal, like an illusion. She shook her head. *Only Aniseed could be so cruel.*

Joy remembered being trapped in an illusion of her kitchen by the ancient dryad as bait for Ink. Aniseed's hatred for humans had fueled her plans for worldwide genocide and an imagined "Golden Age." Joy had been the one to stop her, erasing Aniseed's *signatura* and the poison within it. She shuddered at the memory of the eight-petaled star of eyes on her skin. Joy was glad that Aniseed was dead.

She leaned over and put her arms around Ink.

"Can I have another number sixteen, please?"

He slipped his arms around her and they stood together, Ink rocking Joy gently against his chest. She blinked a few times as her breath fluttered. She felt as if she were running in circles while standing still.

"Are you ready to leave?" he asked.

"Yes," she mumbled gratefully into his shirt.

He stroked his fingers through her hair and whispered, "Come with me."

Taking her hand, he led her into the tiny coatroom and shut the door behind them. Joy's eyebrows shot up.

"This is hardly appropriate," she said, wondering if funerals brought out the weirdness in Scribes. Maybe immortals didn't do well when faced with death? Both he and Inq were acting very strange.

Ink smirked as he twirled his straight razor in one hand, looking much as he had when he'd first tossed a jug of milk into the air, slipped thousands of miles away, then stepped through the breach to catch it a mere moment later. It was a mischievous, slightly naughty little-boy grin.

"Follow me," he said. Slashing a quick line, he peeled away the edge of the world halfway through a set of empty hangers and the floor. A wild darkness shot with colored light pulsed beyond the rift.

Joy hesitated. "I thought we were going to the reception."

"That is for humans," he said mysteriously. "Not for us."

Joy didn't know what to say to that, so she took his hand, warm and smooth, and stepped through the void, stumbling into the sudden dark. It took a moment for her eyes to adjust. She stepped onto the lip of rough stone and looked all the way down.

Then Joy understood.

Below the rocky ledge was a cavern full of bonfires. Shadows of wild, frenetic dancers moved to tribal music throbbing with heavy percussion and rattles and horns. Folk were laughing, drinking, spinning, eating, dancing. They gathered in groups of threes and fives tucked into natural nooks and along the edges of the crowd. Knotted roots covered the sloping walls like tapestries in reverse, the veins of different minerals shimmering in the light of many fires; pinks and grays and greens and blues with flecks of mica winking in the bedrock like stars. Things resembling balloon-animal, crystal chandeliers hung suspended in the air, made up of individual twists and tubes of glowing glass. There were whispers of melodies and rhythms that seemed familiar mixed with earthy, primal songs and high-pitched undulating cries. There was no smoke, but the smell of roasting meat, rich and bubbling and basted in wine, filled the subterranean fête. There were tables of food absolutely everywhere, and the noise fizzed like champagne bubbles, effervescent and overflowing.

Joy looked down at the carnival in the stone basin. "Where are we?"

"Under the Hill near the Wild," Ink said. "That is where Enrique said he wanted his ashes buried."

"As well as the North Pole, Sri Lanka, Maui, Budapest, Mount Everest, Taiwan, Rio, Portugal and the dark side of the moon," Inq said, sidling up to the pair in distinctly less than her funeral attire—in fact, it didn't look like she was wearing much more than body paint. "I've just gotten back from honoring his wishes, with a short delay on that last one because there isn't another space flight scheduled at present, but I've got time." She looked over the two of them, frowning with a pout of her lower lip. She smelled of wine and dusty roses. "Why haven't you changed?"

"We just got here," Ink explained.

"No excuses!" Inq said and yanked off Ink's coat. "This is Enrique's celebration, so start celebrating!" She threw the suit jacket away. It hit the wall. "Less clothes, more music! Honor the spirit! Enrique loved to dance!" She spun and ran down the incline, jumping off the jagged ledge. Joy's heart lodged in her throat as she watched Inq fall, but the hands of many strangers rose up to meet her; a hearty cheer of triumph erupted as they caught her body in its trust-fall landing. Together, they lowered her to the ground. Inq broke away, laughing, and ran to join a circle of dancers stomping and clapping and throwing handfuls of powder into the air. When the dust hit the bonfires, the flames changed color and spat out twirling, whistling sparks.

Ink stepped closer. Joy felt him on her skin.

"Is she okay?" Joy asked.

"Do not worry about Inq," Ink said, undoing the top buttons of his shirt. "Everyone grieves differently."

"Uh, yeah." Joy gaped at the spectacle. "This is...?"

"Enrique's funeral," Ink said. "The way the Folk celebrate it."

Joy shook her head in wonder. "Wow. It's..."

"Bacchanalian?" Ink said.

"No. It's beautiful," Joy said. There wasn't a sad face in the crowd. It was bold and boisterous, lively and wild—just like Enrique. "It's perfect."

"The Folk do not ritualize death as humans do," he said, leading her down the incline at a much safer stroll. Joy removed her heels, and Ink carried her shoes. "Being immortal means that death is possible but not inevitable. So we celebrate a life well lived. Enrique certainly did." Ink gestured to the revel. "Now those who knew him gather together to honor that and remember. We grieve the body, but honor the spirit."

Joy smiled. It felt a lot better than tears. "So, what do we do now?"

Ink lifted two glasses from a table and handed one to her. "We eat, we drink, we dance, we talk, we tell stories, we reminisce." He stepped toward her and looked up at the swirls of crystal colors and light. The spots of brilliance reflected bright sparkles in his eyes. "We remember." He smiled at her. "We celebrate life."

"To Enrique!" someone shouted from deep in the hall.

"To Enrique!" the gathered crowds screamed as many whooped and drank.

"To Enrique!" Inq shouted giddily. "And the Imminent Return!"

"To the Imminent Return!"

Joy lifted her glass along with the rest. "What's the Imminent Return?" she asked.

"It is an old toast," Ink said. "To friends long forgotten but still in our hearts."

Joy clinked her glass against Ink's. The liquid inside swirled. She paused.

"Can I drink this?" she asked.

Ink considered the wine. "Why not?"

She twirled the stem, watching the liquid hug the sides of the glass. "I've read stories where if a human eats or drinks something from Fairyland, then they can never go back." The deep purple liquid smelled of cherries, oak and fire. "Or maybe it was the underworld? Something with pomegranates? I forget."

Ink cocked his head. "This isn't Faeland," he said. "And you are not human."

"Good point," Joy said and sipped her drink. It barely had a taste, more like a vapor of old forests and honey that filled her head and slid down her spine. She hadn't realized she'd swallowed, it was so smooth. It burned, slow and sensuous, inside her. Joy put the glass down carefully. "Aaaaaand that's enough for me."

Ink placed his glass next to hers and curled his arms

around her middle, his chest pressed against her back, his chin resting on her shoulder.

"What would you like to do?" he asked. "Dance? Sing? Sculpt?"

"Sculpt?" Joy asked, and Ink pointed. Like a weird reception line, there were Folk picking soft, translucent balls out of a tall basket, which glowed like a kiln. Each person molded whatever was in their hands, fashioning the clay with fingers and claws, small tools or stones spread out on the floor, crafting shapes lovingly, delicately, or banging them hard against the wall. As the Folk worked, the stuff began to glow from within, growing brighter the more they tinkered with it until the shapes became too bright to see, illuminating faces like miniature suns, hardening into crystal.

"What are they?" she asked.

"Memories," Ink said. "Emotions. Wishes. Watch."

Joy hushed as a thin man with dragonfly wings lifted the glowing crystal over his head and opened his hand slowly, letting it go. Joy followed his gaze as his creation floated gently upward while a small, shaggy thing with flaring nostrils snuffled around his ankles and whipped its finished crystal angrily at the sky. Both lights eventually slowed as they rose the great distance to the high ceiling and slid into place among the other luminous shapes that hovered in midair. That was when Joy realized that the chandelier was actually a mass of memories—the collective thoughts about Enrique by those who knew him best. It made her heart swell.

"The memory crystal holds on to those thoughts, those memories, like dreams under glass," Ink said. "We can visit them anytime to free our thoughts and remember so that our loved ones will never be forgotten."

"That's beautiful," she murmured.

"That is immortality."

She turned and faced him. A powerful heat sparked between them, trickling up the soles of her feet, wrapping around her knees and thrumming in her teeth. She tapped her fingers on the drum of his chest as her body swayed in Ink's arms. The music and magic were a warm glow in her veins.

"I want to dance," she said.

It was ridiculous, but it was true. When she felt so much more than her body could hold, she wanted to *move*—to run and trick and flip and kick. She was kinetic, kinesthetic. It was as necessary to her as breathing, like living, like flying. The shiver up her legs was an urge, a push. The energy in the room was stronger than the wine. She wanted to leave everything that had happened at the dreary human funeral behind. Ink looked at her, eyes sparkling, as if he understood perfectly.

"Come," Ink said, taking her hand and leading her across the room, weaving expertly between Folk who unconsciously moved out of his way. He could always part a crowd with ease. Joy followed, feeling the heat of bodies and bonfires burning all around her. The music hummed in her rib cage, an anticipating crackle under her toes. She wanted to dive into this like Inq into the crowd, swim above it, through it; she wanted to feel that freedom Enrique had loved during all of his adventures all over the world.

He'd said that she was an ordinary girl who'd been given an extraordinary life. She'd known that, intellectually, but this was where she *felt* it for the first time—what it meant to be part of this world, paired with someone who loved her.

Blackmail and jealousy and damp tissues could wait. This was about Enrique, and they were going to *dance*!

Joy squeezed Ink's hand as they wove between circles and dodged couples shouting over the music. Someone bumped into her, smearing her black dress in blue paint.

"*Perdóneme*," the figure said and then stopped dead. "Joy?"

"Luiz?" Joy almost laughed. She would never have recognized the young *lehman*. He was painted in bright colors from his wavy hair to his toes, save for what looked like a loincloth and a spattered necklace of metal beads. He was dripping with sweat; rainbow rivulets ran down his chest. He flashed his butter-melt smile and gestured at her dress.

"I'd hug you," he said, "but it'd only make things worse."

"I'll risk it," she said, and he squeezed her in his strong arms, swirling her around and laughing—but it was laughter that she understood; it was mortal and tight, and there were tears behind it. Humans grieved differently than Folk. Luiz was drunk with glee and sorrow. He let her go, peeling himself away in primary splotches. She laughed at herself smeared in red, blue and gold. He gestured to the whole of the room.

"Do you like it?" Luiz said, waving all around. "Enrique loved things like Burning Man and Carnival. Honor the spirit, right? Well, trust me, he would've *loved* this!" He turned to Ink, arms wide. "May I?"

"Number four?" Ink said with a shrug. "Of course."

Luiz swept forward and picked up Ink, twirling and laughing with him just the same, smearing his pristine dress shirt a mottled tie-dye of yellow and purple and a shocking lime green. Luiz dropped him, and Ink staggered back, a rainbow riot. Joy laughed so hard, she cried.

Ink grinned with deep dimples as Luiz patted his back.

"Ditch the shirt," Luiz advised and glanced at Joy. "And the shoes. Let's dance!"

He grabbed Joy's hand as she grabbed Ink's, and they swung into the circle of rhythmic dancers swirling around the flames. Stomping feet became clapping hands, and whirling contras slid into hand-off marches, grasping forearms, passing partners, smearing paint on arms and cheeks. Beads were looped around strangers' necks, shells clattered, rattles shook, feathers blurred and fur rippled as trinkets passed from hand to hand to hand. Ink threw his stained shirt into the flames to a collective cheer. Joy kept her dress on, inviting teasing and laughter. Soon she was festooned in ribbons and crystals and mad swirls of paint. Ink matched her, bare-chested, wearing smeared handprints and a lei of teeth. Both of them laughed, running and twirling, spinning and leaping, and it wasn't long before Joy was lost to the music, her body vibrating with heartbeat and the thunder of sound.

Thump-THUMP. Thump-THUMP. Like a wordless chant, the glow inside her built like a clenched fist, power eking through the cracks, an almost-pleasure-pain...

Too much. Too much!

When it crested, Joy launched, her legs fueled by the sound, the fire and the deep, driving light—Ink caught her, tethering her to this world and the ground. She split-kicked as Ink held her aloft, arms locked, solid and strong. She tilted her head back and spun under the chandelier, its crystal labyrinth filling the ceiling as more and more people poured out their joy and grief.

The strange, wondrous feeling poured through her limbs, shivering down her arms and out the soles of her feet. It might have been grief, but it felt like magic. This was her tribute. This moment. This memory. *This.*

Joy slowly bent her knees and came down to applause, feeling vulnerable and proud, energized and spent. Ink twirled her around, a wild excitement in his eyes.

"It is you!" he said. "Can you feel it? This is joy!"

Another swing in the music and several drums joined in, tumbling over one another, beating faster and faster, like outrunning death. Joy and Ink became separated as twin circles of dancers raced around the fires. The flames began to lift and swirl into snapping plumes. The mob became a percussive instrument—a living, flashing Kodo drum, a sword dance of flying feet and clapping hands without blades. Scarves and ribbons streamed like banners. Sweat ran through paint. Joy's hair flew over her shoulders and into her face. Adrenaline coursed through her body, pounding her heart and slamming her feet, smacking her soles against the hard-packed ground, driving the defiant beat harder, faster. The music spun, twirling random partners together and apart in the maelstrom of motion, a rave on fire—*this* was where she lived: this body, this earth, with Ink and the rhythm of her blood in her ears. This was life. This was living. This was alive. *This.*

The music stopped abruptly. Panting, Joy beamed, holding a stranger's hand.

"You?"

She registered the shock of white hair and the gray-green eyes, chest heaving under a familiar feathered cloak. His smile was fading fast.

It was like déjà vu in reverse, the way the strange young man stared at her, exposed on the dance floor, surprised at being seen; but this wasn't Ink at the Carousel—this was the young courtier who'd stood by Sol Leander, a member of the Tide, the faction that had hired the Red Knight to kill her. She was too surprised to do anything but stare.

His shock turned to revulsion as he yanked his hand out of her grasp and swept away with a dramatic swirl of his cloak.

"Joy?" Ink appeared behind her.

"Ink!" she whispered as they stepped away from the fires. It was colder now—much colder—and fear brought goose bumps to her skin.

"Hoy, Joy Malone!" Filly bounded over, wearing her usual leather vambraces and short cape of bones, as brash and bold as ever despite the scandalous smears of blue paint down her front and the crown of ivy wilting atop her head. The young warrior turned to watch the feathered cloak swirl away between the dancers and licked the blue tattooed spot beneath her lower lip. "Problem with your dance partner?" she quipped.

"I think the problem's mutual," Joy said. She was grateful to have the young Valkyrie near—Filly was both a true friend and crazy good in a fight. "What is *he* doing here?"

Ink curled his arm around Joy and spoke close to her ear. "Perhaps he knew Enrique," Ink said. "All who knew him are welcome here." He brushed back a wet curl from her face. "Despite being human, Enrique was well-known for his adventuresome spirit, and that made him quite popular." He gestured around the room with a pink-and-orange hand. "Normally the Folk do not acknowledge Inq and I or our associates, but Inq has gone out of her way to make herself difficult to ignore." He lifted his chin toward his sister, who was crowd surfing, carried aloft by many loving hands. She swam in the decadence, a blissful smile on her lips. "The fact her *lehman* were allowed to attend such an event is a testament to how high the Folk hold her and Enrique in their esteem."

Or her skill in blackmail, Joy thought as she watched the pale-haired man cross the room. When he glanced back, it was with thinly guarded fury. She looked away, feeling strangely guilty, then angry at herself for feeling anything of the sort. The Tide wanted her dead! They claimed that she was a threat to the Twixt—the most dangerous human in the world: one who had the Sight and could also wield power over their True Names given form. Only the Scribes were allowed to draw others' *signaturae*. But once Joy had claimed her birthright, she'd become one of them—one of the Folk, a member of the Twixt, the Third Scribe—protected by the Council and therefore, sacrosanct. The Folk were too few for infighting, but that did not mean that she had been forgiven. Her near-escape and new status did not make her popular—it made her infamous.

And the Folk had long memories for revenge.

"Is his master here?" Joy had trouble even saying the words *Sol Leander* without feeling sick.

"Ha!" Filly barked. "I doubt you'll see any of the Council down here. Not even your overdressed toad in his finest silks."

"Most of the Folk would not honor a human in this way," Ink said. "Sol Leander in particular considers humans to be the enemy and we Scribes to be mere tools, barely more than animated quills—we do not register as 'alive' to him, so he would hardly acknowledge the death of one of our *lehman*."

Joy nodded dully. While the words made sense, she couldn't ignore the creepy chill that now colored her mood. She felt every flaky inch and prickle of dried paint on her skin. She began walking away. *Away is good.*

"Let's go," she said. "Let's get out of here."

"Leaving so soon?" Filly said, surprised. "They haven't even cracked the casks open yet! The night is young, and blood beats hot!" She grinned and gestured to the bonfire plumes. Firelight turned her horse head pendant gold. "Come dance and remember! Dance and forget! That is what we are here for—to dance ere we die!"

"No, thanks," Joy said, taking Ink's hand. "I'm going home."

Filly grinned wider. "There are other kinds of dancing."

Ink tugged Joy closer. "Well said and well met."

The young horsewoman raised a goblet and snorted. "Good morrow, then, as you shall surely enjoy a good night!"

They made their way up the incline, leaving Filly and the feast and the Folk behind. Collecting her discarded shoes and purse, Joy stepped onto the jutting overhang where they'd first come in, safely distant from anyone who might blunder into Ink as he sliced open a door through the world. Joy cast a last glance around the revelry, trying to spy familiar faces in order to wave her goodbyes, but her attention snagged on a feathery cloak illuminated in the light of the basket kiln.

She watched as Sol Leander's young aide opened his hand, allowing the crystal spire he had wrought to slip free. The look on his face was reverent as his eyes followed the delicate sculpture up-up-up, glittering like a tiny star climbing toward the light.

"Joy?" Ink said. He held a flap of nothing at all.

She turned her back on the spectacle, took Ink's hand and stepped quickly through the breach.

They appeared in her room, just inside the door, and Joy found herself suddenly in Ink's arms, his lips hungry on hers. She kissed him back gratefully—thankful to be alive, to be together, safe and finally alone.

He cupped her face as he kissed her and ran his hands through her hair, combing out stray feathers and glitter. She felt his bare arms and shoulders, his smooth, muscular chest pressed flat against hers. Paint flaked off under her fingertips. She wiped her hands on her dress and laughed into his mouth.

"Your poor shirt," she said between kisses.

"I can get another," he said and kissed her again—over and over as if he could not get enough. Joy was convinced he was addicted to kissing. Ink paused, his lips grazing hers. "Graus Claude has a very good tailor."

She laughed and squirmed under his touch. He'd driven all bad thoughts away. It was getting hard to keep standing. She twisted a finger in his wallet chain and tugged him closer. His fingers traced the zipper down the back of her dress. Joy hadn't realized he knew about zippers.

"We're covered in paint," she whispered next to his ear. He breathed a warm line down the length of her neck. Her fingers tightened in his hair. He kissed her collarbone and lifted his fathomless eyes to hers—they were dark and drowning.

"I don't care," he said.

She smiled at his rare contraction. "You 'don't'?"

He shook his head; only the tips of his hair moved, black eyes unblinking. "No."

Joy backed up, pulling him along by his chain. He followed. She pressed herself against the wall by her headboard and wrapped one arm over his shoulders, drawing him into a long, luxurious kiss. He groaned against her, one hand flat by her ear. She distantly heard his fingernails scratch against the paint. She tapped her palm beside her hip.

"Can you make a door—" she tapped the wall again "—here?"

Ink withdrew an aching inch, looking where she'd knocked.

"Where do you want to go?" he asked.

"Just through the wall."

He grinned like a little boy, all dimples. "Oh? Why?"

Joy tugged the silver chain again and whispered in his ear, "Come see."

He needed no further encouragement. Reaching behind him, Ink pulled the straight razor from his wallet and snapped it open with a practiced flick. Staring into her eyes, he drew a line directly over Joy's head. He then carefully traced a long loop past her shoulder, her elbow, her hip, her knee, and then sliced along the baseboard, nudging Joy to one side. He stood, pocketed the blade and pushed the breach open like a door. His eyes twinkled as he gave a small bow. Joy grinned in delight and kissed him as they walked through the wall with the taste of limes in her mouth.

Then she was kissing him in the bathroom, the sound of their breaths a tiny echo against tile. Joy tasted his lips and curled her toes in the thick bath mat. She caught his bottom lip gently in her teeth—she had to be careful with teeth; last time, he'd bitten her.

"Shh," she whispered as she released him and reached through the shower curtain to twist the knob. The room exploded in splashing applause. High-pressure water rained against the bathtub and the air slowly turned misty with steam. She brushed her bangs from her eyes and touched the flaky handprints on his chest.

She looked down at his feet on the bath mat and then up. "Ditch the shoes," she all but mouthed. Joy smiled. Ink stared at her mouth, his fingers gone still.

She drew him toward the shower, holding his forearm as she pushed the curtain aside and stepped in. The water was hot and she adjusted the temperature as he took off his boots and stepped in beside her, both of them still clothed. Paint began spilling in rivers down his chest, pooling at the waistband as water soaked his jeans.

Joy stood under the showerhead. Rainbow colors slid down her body, dripping off her elbows and swirling around her feet, her black dress plastered against her thighs and her back. She wiped water from her face and blinked at Ink through wet lashes. He absorbed her every movement, his gaze coursing over her like the water itself, hugging her curves and caressing her skin.

She leaned forward and kissed him, her mouth slick and wet. Ink kissed her curiously. She stepped back. He licked his lip.

"It is different," he said. "It is like kissing you in the rain."

"You can feel the difference?" Joy asked.

"Yes. Warmer, less friction." He touched the drop at her chin. "Wet."

His eyelashes were speckled with watery pearls. His black hair drooped in long, damp tendrils over his cheeks. Joy's dress was completely drenched as she ran a hand from his neck to his belly button, admiring that tiny detail. *We did that.*

She picked up a bar of soap and began lathering it in her hands. Ink watched the bubbles form with kittenlike interest. The foam turned pink and gray and blue.

"Feel this," she said and spread a smear of soapy bubbles over his chest. Ink gasped and stepped back awkwardly, contained in the narrow tub. Joy held on to his wrist, his skin sliding against hers. She squeezed, slipping her fingers over his long muscles, massaging his arm. He stared, fascinated. She watched him feeling every inch of the new sensation. Joy pushed soap up to his shoulder. Froth cascaded down his back. Ink held on to the wall and exhaled with a hitch in his breath.

Joy smiled, spreading her slick hands over his chest, fingers swimming through the suds, rubbing slow circles, washing the paint from his skin. The foam turned red and purple and yellow and green. Joy wiped away the colors and cupped her hands under the showerhead, splashing his front, trickling clean.

Ink touched a hand to his chest, splayed fingers wide. There was a flicker in his throat, and his eyes brimmed full of mist and stars.

"Again, please."

Smiling, she did. Running the soap through her fingers, she kissed him as she slid her hands over his back. His spine arched toward her, and he held on to her shoulders, kissing and gasping with one shared breath. She tugged him under the spray—now hotter—rinsing him off as she squeezed her eyes shut, her hair a dark curtain running all over her face. She squeezed past him, letting the shower hit Ink full in the chest. His head tipped back, and his arms loosened as his eyes slipped closed. She turned him around by the shoulders so that his back was to her. Water slid off his wallet chain.

His *signatura* flashed in the dark. Joy touched the ouroboros under the water, watching the dragon-swallowing-its-tail circle spin, wondering if his mark was sensitive to temperature and emotion like Inq's. *Like hers?*

She smoothed her palms over his shoulders and up the sides of his neck, thumbs pushing into his hairline. She smiled, hearing him sigh.

His head lolled forward, and he flattened his hands against the wall, warm water coursing down the back of his head. A tiny stream ran down the length of his spine, bisecting the ouroboros and her circle of soap. Joy traced it with her fingers and pushed the heels of her hands into the muscles of his back. He steadied himself and murmured, a sound crisp and clean through the splash; although she didn't understand the words, she got the meaning loud and clear.

Pushing her knuckles into his lower back, she kneaded upward and inched her thumbs slowly up either side of his spine. Ink arched again, lifting his head and turning to face her. His hair was drenched flat. His eyes were cavernous. Joy had the odd thought that he looked taller when wet. She stopped moving, her heartbeat loud in her ears, wondering what, exactly, would happen next.

Ink slowly took the soap from her hand. Running it smoothly between his palms, he gazed at her, unblinking. Soapy bubbles dripped down his forearms, off his elbows, and hit the floor. His voice was a sort of whisper.

"Now you."

He took her wrist and slid his thumbs up the inside of her forearm, squeezing gently as he soaped her to the elbow. Joy's mouth opened, trying to catch enough breath, hot and misty and clean on her tongue. He cupped her shoulder, pushing the bubbles down her collarbone, suds dripping along the scooped neckline of her dress. His fingertips followed, drawing long, slow circles, working off smears of orange, blue and black. Joy's eyes fluttered under his strong hands. One of his palms rested over her heart, fingers spread across her breastbone, his pinkie slipping under the shoulder strap of her bra. Joy's pulse thudded in her chest, a thick beat through the foam. Ink's hand slid up her neck, behind her ears. Her eyes opened as he brushed a dab of paint from her cheek.

He looked into her eyes for a long moment, breathing.

Joy reached over her shoulder and pressed his fingers to the tiny metal pull at the back of her neck. Ink pinched it in his finger and thumb. He watched her face, mesmerized, as he slowly unzipped her dress.

She felt his hands slide over her bare back, and she made a small sound in her throat. He pushed the heels of his hands into the muscles above her hips, kneading upward as she had, running his thumbs along either side of her spine. Joy arched into him, meeting tongues and lips and wanting. He was following her every motion, mimicking her lead, and it was driving her crazy.

"Ink," she said, almost dizzy with heat.

He slid her body against his. She gasped in his mouth.

"Joy," he said.

Kissing him deeply, Joy pulled her arms through the straps and let the sodden weight of the dress hit the drain.

She shrieked as the water turned ice cold. Ink plastered himself against the wall, gaping in shock. Joy twisted out of the bathtub and yanked the water off. Wrapping a towel around her shivering shoulders, she saw the last twinkles of a spell fade.

"Take the hint," Stef's voice said through the crack in the door. "And *chill out*."

Joy's teeth chattered. She was shaking, mortified.

Ink and his boots were already gone.

FOUR

JOY JUMPED OUT OF BED AND TRIPPED OVER THE SOGGY pile of clothes. Picking up her shoes, she sighed. The multicolored scuffs on the heels looked deep, and she wondered if it was even worth trying to salvage the dress. She ran a hand over the smears of paint and smiled despite herself. She'd dreamed of lilies, dancing, feathers and fire. *And Ink. So much Ink.*

She reminded herself to punch Stef in the face.

After stuffing the dress into her trash bin, she tossed her shoes into the closet, pulled her hair into a ponytail and changed for work. The summer was almost over and then her hours at Nordstrom Rack would be cut in half. Dad was right—she should be thinking about colleges or work or what she wanted to do after her senior year, since she obviously wouldn't be training with a private gymnastics coach in Australia come next July. She couldn't say that she wanted to travel around the world with her boyfriend—not only did that sound bad, it wasn't entirely true. She unwound her finger from the twist in her shirt and smoothed out the wrinkles. *What do you do when your lifelong dreams change?*

Joy wandered into the kitchen with a head full of thoughts. Stef was still snoring in his room. She debated waking him with a glassful of ice water, but Dad was already at the table, so her best-served-cold revenge would have to be served sometime later.

"Morning," she said sleepily.

Dad looked up from his laptop. "Morning," he said. "I didn't hear you come home last night."

"It was late," she said as she poured herself some cereal and sliced a banana into the bowl.

"I didn't realize funerals ran late on Monday nights." Her father tried to sound nonchalant but only got as far as "parentally concerned" with a dash of "gently warning his daughter that he'd noticed the time."

"Yeah, well," Joy said, fishing the milk out of the fridge. "This wasn't your average funeral." *Massive understatement.* "And Ink and I went out afterward." *Massive understatement squared.* She grabbed a spoon and sat down, quite pleased with her almost-deceptions. She was getting better at this. Maybe it ran in the genes.

"Well, we've got two days to pack, load up and head out to Lake James," he said around his last mouthful of eggs. Joy saw that the buttered toast was absent. Twelve more pounds to goal weight—he kept a total on the fridge. "We have this one last hurrah before Stef's back at U Penn, and I want to make the most of it, so I don't want to spend a lot of time on Friday dithering."

Joy chewed and swallowed, still thinking about bonfires and chandeliers.

Her father frowned. "Joy?"

"Check," she said. "No dithering."

"I'm serious, Joy. Stef's already packed."

"Of course he's already packed. He's going back to college next week." Joy's flippant comment fell flat in her lap. She hadn't fully realized the truth until she'd said it aloud. Only a few more days with Stef, and then it was back to just her and Dad. And Shelley. Joy liked her father's girlfriend, but her dad had been spending a lot more time out with Shelley and less time around the house—which was good—but with Stef gone, the condo would fast become dark and lonely again with Joy home all by herself. She didn't want a repeat of the Year of Hell, the one following her parents' divorce when her father had become a smelly zombie hermit and she'd quit the gymnastics team to match. She poked a bit of banana into the milk with her spoon. It had been nice having her big brother home—cold showers aside—and it had been handy to have him save her life with wizard's magic once in a while. She mumbled into her cereal bowl, "I'll be ready, don't worry."

"Being a father, I worry," he said. "Being the father of two teenagers, I've learned to take precautions." He wiped his mouth and balled up the napkin. "Be fully packed by 5:00 a.m. Friday, or I'm taking your phone for two weeks. Got it?"

He was pulling out the big guns. Joy swallowed. "Got it."

"Okay, then. I'm off to work," he said. "When do you have to punch in?"

"Nine o'clock."

"Don't be late." Joy rolled her eyes. Her father prided himself on being punctual, reliable, loyal and hardworking—to be in all ways indispensable. It was the one thing he'd held on to throughout the rough years, and it had finally paid off. He'd gotten a promotion, which came with a decent raise and had done worlds for his confidence. Her father slipped on his jacket and grabbed his new leather briefcase. "And see if you can't get Stef out of bed before you leave. He's been staying up nights and sleeping half the day."

"Sounds like college," she said around her last spoonful of cereal.

"Sounds like lazy," her father said and paused at the door. He was staring at her feet. "Wait—no mismatched socks?"

Joy shrugged. "It's against the dress code."

He frowned a mock-sad-clown face. "Is the big, bad capitalistic corporation squishing the individuality out of my baby girl?"

She grinned over her spoon. "I wear mismatched earrings."

He pumped his fist. "Stick it to the Man, sweetheart! I'll see you tonight."

"I'm meeting Monica after work," she reminded him.

"Okay, but tonight's Stef's special smorgasbord send-off. Don't forget." He checked his watch. "Got to go."

Joy waved as he closed the door, then washed her bowl in the sink and watched as he hopped into his Accord and drove away. She inspected the kitchen window for monsters or message pee and did a double-take when she saw the white sports car drive around the corner. Joy leaned over the sink, trying to follow it with her eyes, trying to convince herself that she'd imagined it—*it couldn't be!*—but hope caught in her throat. She almost dropped the bowl when it pulled up to the gate: a white Ferrari 458.

There was a buzz from the intercom. Stef groaned in protest. Joy ran over to the call box and hit the button.

"Yes?"

"Joy?"

She didn't recognize the male voice, husky with sleep. *Could it be...?*

"Yes? Who is this?"

He's alive!

"It's Ilhami." Joy's heart stuttered. Not Enrique—just his car. She started breathing again, but the air felt too thin. She almost missed the next words. "You left something behind last night."

Disappointment colored her voice. "I did?"

"Yes," Ilhami said. "I brought it over. Want to come down and get it?"

She hesitated, her finger on Call. "Hang on," she said. Joy

released the button, checked the call box for glyphs and dug inside her purse. Grabbing her scalpel, Joy opened the door and marched outside into the moist August heat.

She kept her hand on the blade as she walked down the stairs. She couldn't remember leaving anything behind at the funeral or the celebration. Her senses were on orange alert. She remembered Inq's bizarre request, and she didn't trust Ilhami. Enrique had once called the young Turkish artist a "tortured genius," but Joy hadn't forgotten what had happened in East New York, fleeing the cops at high speed and making an enemy of Ilhami's drug dealer, Ladybird. She'd had to pay three drops of blood for a dose of Ladybird's powerful Sunset Dust in order to take down the Red Knight. Joy had no idea why Ladybird had wanted her blood and was fairly certain she didn't want to find out. So the question now was whether Ilhami was up to something, obeying orders from Inq or Ladybird, or if he was being used as bait to flush her out of her house and its protective wards. Either way, between Ink's scalpel and Inq's gift—a little *push* glyph on her palm—Joy wasn't going anywhere unprepared.

When she crossed the parking lot, she saw Ilhami leaning casually against the gleaming Ferrari parked on the grass. His head was freshly buzzed to a millimeter fuzz, his tattooed arms bare in a muscleman shirt, and his thumbs tucked into the belt loops of his jeans. He gave an easy smile.

"'Morning, Cabana Girl," he said.

"Good morning," she said warily. "I didn't see you at the celebration last night."

"Oh, I was there." He smirked. "I hooked up with some pixie chick with a wicked sense of gravity. Talk about a headrush!" Joy rolled her eyes. Ilhami shrugged. "What? Honor the spirit. Enrique *loved* hooking up!"

"Anyway...?" she prompted. "What did I forget? Is it bigger than a bread box?"

"I'd say so," he tapped the car door and threw her something. She caught it, heavy in her hand. Keys. He winked slyly. "It's all yours."

Joy gaped. *"What?"*

Ilhami wiped an imaginary speck of dust off the hood with his thumb. "Enrique wanted you to have it," he said. "He felt bad about you losing your wheels. Said you needed your own way to get around. I had it detailed and everything. Nik may be pretty, but he smells like beans."

Joy looked at the keys, the car and her second-floor kitchen window, praying that nobody could see her. This was the last thing she'd expected.

"I can't have a car like that!" she said under her breath. "Seriously. I'm a senior in *high school*. People would ask questions...people like my *dad*! I can't say I got it from some nice older gentleman who died and left me his car." Joy shook the keys in her fist. "Cuz that sounds *really, really* bad!"

"Whatever. I haven't even told you about the special features, yet," Ilhami said, opening the driver's door, dropping into the seat and pointing at the dash. "You already saw how the slip-drive works. I changed the GPS coordinates to this spot so you can park it without blocking the driveway. It's got a short-range auto-drive feature—like Cruise Control for Dummies—treated windows, voice-activated phone, glyphs on the safeties and securities, and a warded buffer field." He tapped the door again. "Enrique hated getting it dinged. It's not like he could take it into the shop. Oh, and press the blue button on the fob."

Curious, Joy did. The car disappeared. Ilhami smiled from the half-open door suspended in nothing.

"Cloaked parking feature," he said. "Very slick."

Joy shook her head. "You have *got* to be kidding."

Ilhami climbed out of the invisible car and shut the door. "The engine's tricked out—runs on pure water. Filtered, not tap," he warned. "The Folk seriously frown on fossil fuels."

"But..." Joy stammered. It was a dream car—an impossible, invisible, luxury dream car. "I can't *drive* it!"

Ilhami snorted. "So what? Give it to Ink—it'll be his excuse for wheels," he said. "If he's going to start coming over for family dinners, he can't keep ripping his way through thin air, right?" He leaned forward, grinning ear to ear. "Right?"

"Right," Joy said weakly. Enrique had given her his car. She couldn't refuse it. "Um...thanks."

Ilhami shouldered his backpack, which had been behind the bumper and was fully visible now that the car was not. "Hey, I'm just the messenger," he said. "No thanks necessary. And besides, you shouldn't thank me—you still have to wait until you're twenty-one to get your part of the inheritance." He laughed at the look on her face.

"Inheritance?" she squeaked.

"Oh, yeah. Enrique had *bank*, but he had no parents, no children," he said, spreading his arms to embrace the summer sky. "We're his family, Cabana Girl, and for some people, family is everything."

Joy shook her head. She stammered, "I *can't*..."

Ilhami waved her off. "Pfft. Whatever. Luiz got the yacht, but I'm not complaining." He climbed into a sharp-angled Lamborghini parked on the curb. It looked like an enameled shark. Joy squinted down the street. *How did it get here?* He kissed his fingers and waved, a gesture she recognized from Nikolai. "*Arrivederci*, Cabana Girl! Remember, life's short—have fun!" he howled out the window, gunned the engine and roared unapologetically down the street.

Joy stared after him, feeling silly and stupid as she tucked the keys into her purse. His visit had nothing to do with Ladybird or with Inq's weird request. She had no idea what to think. She checked her phone for the time. Swearing, she turned her back on her magic sports car, running at top speed to catch the bus.

She was ten minutes late for work.

"Hey, wage slave!" Monica chirped. "You almost done?"

Joy stopped folding the light sweaters and sighed in relief. Just seeing her best friend brought a wave of much-needed sanity after a long day of stock work.

She dropped her tag gun. "If there is a God, then, yes."

Monica adjusted her shoulder strap. "As a churchgoing girl, I'd say you're free and clear, but you might want to check with your boss first." She stroked her dark hand over the autumn-colored cashmere. "Ooo. Pretty. Do you think I'd look good in orange?"

Joy collapsed a cardboard box with a practiced snap. "Honestly, I'm not a big fan of orange." The color reminded her of fox fur, mahogany eyes and malice. Joy still had nightmares and scars on her skin, both gifts from Aniseed. "I vote red."

"Mmm. Gordon says red *is* my color," Monica said. "Passionate, vibrant, smoldering hot..."

Joy gathered up the extra security tags, smiling. "Whatever happened to him bringing out your softer side?"

Monica shrugged and smoothed her slicked bangs. "I got over it."

They laughed as Joy punched out, swapping directions to the closest decent restaurant they could find via GPS. Once they'd nabbed some chips and salsa at the nearby cantina, Joy started feeling half human again.

"Remember to breathe," Monica said. "Aren't you having another family dinner thing in a couple of hours?"

"It's just Stef's last excuse to pig out on Dad's tab," Joy said and pointed to herself as she chewed. "And, hello? Hypoglycemic, remember?" She slurped a chunk of tomato off her chip. "My metabolism needs food every four hours. The doctors say I have to keep up a base caloric intake or I'll turn into a stick."

Monica snapped a chip in half. "I think I speak for all dieters everywhere when I say *pfbthth*!"

Joy drank her water, ignoring the raspberry. The ice cubes clunked against the glass and her teeth. She speared a piece of ice with her straw and crunched on it as they waited to order—she had picked up the less-than-genteel habit from the normally genteel Graus Claude. She had been surprised not to see the Bailiwick last night, but then again, Filly had been sure that he wouldn't show. Joy had no idea if the Bailiwick knew the Cabana Boys personally, but she didn't think he would stay away because of bigotry, like Sol Leander; Graus Claude knew that the Scribes were people. The only difference was that they were made, not born.

"So," she said while fishing her straw around for another cube. "What are you going to do while I'm gone?"

"Pine," Monica said, scooping more tomatillos onto her plate. "Waste away to nothing without my bestie." She pressed the back of her wrist to her forehead and swooned dramatically against the seat. "Or, on the other hand, I could curl up with my sweetie and watch a mindless movie marathon. It's a close second."

Joy snickered. "Did you just call Gordon 'my sweetie'?"

Monica snagged the last chip. "Didn't I just."

"I think I feel ill."

"That's the salsa talking," Monica said. "But I was wondering if I could borrow your MGM Classics collection. I remember you got the set for your birthday."

"Sure. I think it's still shrink-wrapped," Joy said. It had been a gift from her mother back when Joy wasn't speaking to her.

Things had changed, slowly but surely, but she hadn't had time to watch late-night movies. Her nights had been filled with secret trips to London, Glasgow, Rome and Belize. She'd gone anywhere and everywhere with Ink and Inq and Inq's horde of gorgeous guys and felt supremely guilty about not sharing any of it with her best friend. Joy's mood slipped when she thought about Enrique and veered into extra-nervous when she thought about his invisible car parked on her lawn. Joy poked her straw around the glass, letting the sound mask her silence.

"Sounds like somebody is becoming a homebody," Joy teased.

"As if," Monica said. "I'm still up for dancing the night away whenever you get your skinny butt in gear—you just say when."

Joy smiled, remembering her last dance—the pull and the heat of it. "When."

"Seriously?" Monica said, surprised. "Tonight?"

"No," Joy admitted. "My feet are killing me. But soon. Maybe when I get back? Last fling of summer?"

Monica and Joy clinked spoons. "It's a date."

Their server apologized for the wait and took their order. Joy felt a twinge of sympathy for the woman bussing her own tables and the two families with toddlers who were making a huge mess. She made a mental note to leave an extra-large tip. She'd been on the other side of the napkin, and it wasn't pretty.

Monica handed back their menus as their server disappeared into the kitchen. "Can I ask you something?"

Joy chewed more ice. "You look beautiful."

"No," Monica said and leaned forward. "Are you ever going to tell me what went down at the hospital? Because, FYI, I would really like to know."

Joy glanced at her friend's face, the bald scar in Monica's eyebrow a telltale remnant of their encounter with the

Red Knight, the invincible, invisible assassin who had been sent to kill Joy. While Joy had been protected by Inq's glyph-wrought armor, Monica had not, and she'd suffered a glancing blow from his massive sword. Joy's attempts to erase the scar, and her guilt, had nearly cost her Ink and her place in the Twixt. Now every time she looked at Monica, that scar was a reminder of what was at stake, what really mattered and what she'd almost lost forever. And, if Joy looked more closely, she could still see the *signatura* etched there—the angled arrow of Sol Leander's True Name like a gruesome slash on Monica's face. Her best friend lived under the auspice of Joy's greatest enemy in the Twixt.

Monica misunderstood Joy's silence. "You have to tell me eventually, you know."

"I know," Joy said.

"I covered for you," Monica said. "I lied to my parents."

"I know."

"You know," Monica repeated back at her. "You're just lucky that my mom believed that crazy story about Aunt Meredith. Her sister was *seriously* into some weird voodoo." Monica shook her head, setting her gold hoops swaying. "I mean, what am I supposed to do when the woman sends me an ox-bone knife for Confirmation? I mean, seriously? But she's family, right? I couldn't just throw it away." She brushed the edges of her razor-cut bob. "I use the thing for a letter opener."

Joy laughed. Monica's eyes grew serious. "Joy, you've *got* to tell me what really happened—Mom said you had a knife over my head, and the police said that no one saw anybody attack us at the mall."

Joy's insides burned hot, then cold. She held her breath and concentrated on Monica's chin as she kept talking. "There was a whole lot of weird reports that day—things flying around, stuff breaking, lights smashed—but no one could explain it, not even the security tapes, not even the shrinks." Monica's ebony fingers curled over one another, turning her knuckles pale. "I know you'd never hurt me, and you know you can tell me anything," she said earnestly. "*Anything*, right? So why don't you?"

Joy squirmed, staring at Monica's burgundy nail polish. Monica was her best friend—Joy owed her the truth—but she couldn't tell her the truth, and she couldn't lie. The risks were bigger than both of them, and she refused to place Monica in danger again.

"It's...hard to explain," Joy ventured. She couldn't say that she *couldn't* tell Monica, because, physically, she *could*—she just knew that she shouldn't, for both of their sakes. Joy squinted up at the overhead lights. "I'll tell you once I can wrap my brain around it." *Which could easily be never.* She tried to act brave as she made eye contact, ignoring the accusing welt in her friend's arched eyebrow. "But I'm not ready," Joy said. "Not yet."

Monica could've been angry, but she wasn't, although her eyes were cool and distant. Monica would accept that there was a reason, and that it was important, and that what Joy needed was time. Joy loved her for it—but it made her feel worse for not telling her outright: Joy was the reason that Monica had gotten hurt. The guilt burned hotter than jalapeños and brought a flush to her face.

Monica might not understand why Joy wouldn't talk, but they weren't best friends for nothing. She simply said, "Why not?"

Joy smiled weakly. "Because, remember—No Stupid."

Monica took a deep breath, wide nose flaring. Joy tried to look earnest. It felt fake even though it was true.

"Okay," Monica said finally. "Okay. I can deal with that. But someday?"

Joy's breath was tight in her chest. "Yeah," she said, "someday."

"Promise?"

Joy shook her head. "No."

Monica jerked like she'd been slapped. Joy twisted her napkin and tried to explain.

"Look," she said. "I won't promise you something that I can't guarantee." Joy leaned over the tabletop, voice low. "If I promise you something, I will *always* mean it, because you deserve that," she said. "I won't lie to you. Ever."

Their server appeared with impeccable Waitress Timing, dispersing the tension of too much truth with a double order of large veggie quesadillas. Monica wordlessly spread her napkin in her lap and tapped her fingernails on the table before picking up her knife.

"But you *will* tell me," she said slowly. "When you're ready?"

Joy sighed, caught. Monica was right—that was what she'd said. Joy could easily understand how the Folk—tricked by countless centuries of humans who could twist their words against them—had needed to develop better protections against mortals. Using *signaturae*, unspoken True Names, now made more sense to Joy—it was hard to get tangled up in words when the most important things couldn't be said.

"Okay, yes," Joy said. "I'll tell you when I'm ready."

Monica nodded. "I'll hold you to that. Pass me the hot sauce."

"Hot sauce? On quesadillas?"

Monica waved a manicured hand. "I have sophisticated taste."

Joy gave her the small orange bottle and welcomed the silence of eating good food. She didn't know how she was going to settle things with Monica and the Twixt, but for now she could enjoy a *quesadilla grande* with her best friend and pretend that things were normal, the way they used to be before everything went crazy.

Joy folded a triangle of cheese and peppers in half and wondered when, exactly, crazy had started feeling normal.

FIVE

Your presence is required at 9am EST. Training will begin promptly. I will send the car to collect you. Prepare to take notes. —GC

JOY DELETED THE TEXT AND KISSED HER DAD GOODbye as she prepared to meet the Bentley. She'd woken up Stef with an ice cube in his ear and sprinted out the door when he'd screamed. She hoped that her manager didn't call home to see how she was feeling after she'd taken an emergency sick day; Joy suspected Stef wouldn't cover for her.

"Are you packed?" her father asked as she headed for the door.

"No. Not yet."

He frowned. "Are you pack*ing*, as in, 'in the beginning stages of getting packed'?"

Joy laughed and grabbed her purse. "I'm on it. Don't worry."

"I'm your father," he said. "It's my job to worry."

"Later. Gotta go!"

Joy's hand was on the doorknob as she spied her brother in the hall. He didn't stop her or berate her, but he knew where she was going. The silence hung between them, filled with unsaid things. Stef despised the Folk, the "Other Thans," who had hurt their great-grandmother so long ago, but he loved his little sister, and he knew that she loved Ink. That was probably what made it so hard for him to see them together, and why it was so hard for her to tell him that he was one of them—part-Folk—which was probably why she hadn't yet.

It was another secret standing between them.

It was amazing how close secrets were to lies.

Joy tried not to think about it as she opened the door, crossed the courtyard and the street, and stood waiting at the corner of Wilkes and Main. She tried not to dwell on it as she watched the vintage car take the turn, and attempted to put it out of her mind as she settled into the buttery leather seats, letting sleep overtake her in its customary way as she slipped from Glendale, North Carolina, to Boston town.

She tried very, very hard, but she felt guilty all the same.

Joy blinked awake as the Bentley slowed to a stop in front of the grand brownstone, and she waited politely for the driver to open her passenger door. Wiping the gunk from her eyes, she scraped her heel against the edge of curb just to convince herself once again that this was real—she'd traveled hundreds of miles in a matter of moments during a spell-induced catnap. She'd never get used to it.

Joy climbed the stone steps and rapped the old-fashioned brass knocker twice. She had her tablet under her arm and a new pair of shoes, but she still felt unprepared for her meeting with Graus Claude.

Kurt opened the door and ushered her in with one whitegloved hand. The fact that the other wasn't tucked into his jacket over the bulge of his gun made her feel better—what did it say about her that she felt comforted by the fact that this *wasn't* one of those times when someone was actively trying to kill her?

Joy stepped into the foyer as the Bentley rolled away in a hush of white-rimmed tires. She followed Kurt as he walked through the cream-colored foyer, down the long hallway toward the great double doors of the Bailiwick's office.

"Any hint of what I'm in for?" Joy whispered.

Kurt said nothing, only knocked upon the ironwood doors and then opened them both at once. He was in butler mode—silent, efficient, precise, unhelpful. Joy sighed and walked inside.

"Ah, Miss Malone." Graus Claude got up from his enormous, thronelike chair and stood behind the great mahogany desk. The grandiose amphibian stood eight feet at the shoulder, his hunchback somewhat lessened under a tailored pinstripe suit with extra-wide lapels. All four of his arms ended in crisp cuffs folded back from his manicured claws, and his smile was full of sharp teeth. "Please, have a seat." He gestured to one of the chairs facing him with two of his hands; the third clicked the wireless mouse and the fourth flipped open a pocket watch on a chain. "We have a lot to go over in a regretfully brief time, so I shall begin my duties as your sponsor in the Twixt with all due haste." The gentleman toad's icy blue gaze swept over her. "I would advise you take notes," he said. "Starting now."

"Right," Joy said, flipping her tablet and attaching the keyboard. She placed it on the edge of the desk and clicked open a new document.

"Now then," the Bailiwick said, lumbering out from behind the desk. "Since you have already accepted your True Name, there is no need to go into a detailed synopsis. Your unique sigil will protect you from undo harm and direct spell manipulation, save from those to whom you give it willingly." He paused, giving weight to his words. "This is something I do not recommend." Joy underlined the sentence in her document as he continued. "However, my research indicates that your case falls neatly between two known categories—

that of a changeling and that of a halfling." He threaded two clawed hands together while the others gestured as he spoke. "A changeling is a Folk child, disguised as a human child, who is switched shortly after birth for the human mother to raise out of infancy—" He paused at Joy's look of horror. "This practice rarely occurs anymore."

Joy rolled her eyes. "Why? Did somebody finally figure out that it was *wrong*?"

Graus Claude's head stilled as his eyes narrowed. "There has not been a birth in the Twixt for over a thousand years. It is considered a *sensitive* subject."

Joy blinked. "Oh."

The Bailiwick smoothed the gold watch chain against his side. "As I was saying," he continued, "halflings, on the other hand, are the product of a Folk-human pairing." His palsied shake returned as he circled the stone basin of floating lily pads. "While, technically, you would not be a halfling—I might estimate closer to a two-to-the-sixth-power-ling—if we theorize that those with the Sight are descendants of mixed heritage, then this category would most aptly suit your situation. In fact, it serves our purposes nicely as halflings traditionally make their way back to the Twixt by their own means, like hatchling turtles making their way home to sea." He gave a solemn nod. "We can use this to explain your unusually dramatic and unanticipated arrival Under the Hill."

Joy finished typing and looked up at Graus Claude's expectant expression.

"Okay," she said. "Great."

"O-kay," Graus Claude rumbled and took a deep, bellows breath. "As you know, the Folk are few and thus bloodshed is highly discouraged." She all but felt the Bailiwick's stare touch her shoulder, the place where her Grimson's mark burned. Inq had put it there after Joy had killed the Red

Knight; her act of self-defense was only considered acceptable because the assassin had broken the Edict. "Indeed, this is one of the reasons that the Scribes were created—to take on the risks inherent in marking humans claimed by the Folk without putting any of our own people in danger."

"But Ink and Inq are your people," Joy said, turning in her chair. She rankled at bigotry in either world. "They are part of the Twixt, too."

Graus Claude shifted his elephantine feet. His shoes were topped in immaculate peach spats. "Technically, Master Ink and Mistress Inq are not Folk, per se," the Bailiwick said. "They are homunculi, constructed instruments that attained consciousness over time. While they are, indeed, part of the Twixt, they are not, strictly speaking, part of the Folk. They were made, not born."

"So it's okay to put them at risk," Joy said hotly. "Sort of like stealing babies?"

The Bailiwick sighed. "Miss Malone, this is not an ethical debate. Please, try to stay on topic." Joy chewed the inside of her cheek and typed *The Council Sucks!!!* in bold font. Graus Claude either didn't see it or chose to ignore it as he ambled past. "This paucity of numbers has created a symbiotic network among the Folk, a web of alliances, threats and favors that have ensured the collective safety and status of practically everyone within the Twixt. That network must now adapt to include you." He paused by her chair as if to emphasize the point. Joy felt a warm breath puff her hair. She kept typing. "The Folk must find a place for you and will attempt to weave you into their matrices like so many spiders spinning their webs. They will wish to sway you to their favor, bow to their behest, absorb your resources into their positions of power—in essence, the Folk will jockey to claim you under their influence." He brushed away a line of imaginary dust. "This will be cloaked in etiquette at best and intrigue at worst. My charge is to educate you on the finer points of protocol and proper behavior so that you may forge your own alliances wisely and not place yourself in any undo danger by giving offense."

"Danger?" Joy said, looking up from the keys. "What danger? I thought you said that the Folk can't off one another."

"Well, certainly they *can*—" he said with a casual flip of one hand. "The Red Knight was an excellent case in point. By triggering fresh incarnations after the Council's initial binding spell was cast, the new Knight was not included under the Edict and therefore was unaffected by the rule, free to hunt without recrimination. In essence, the spell did not call him by his True Name, and therefore, he was not bound to obey it. A neat little loophole you closed up nicely." The Bailiwick tapped the basin's edge. "But do not make the same mistake that many mortals do—just because you cannot be killed outright does not mean that you cannot die due to injury, foolishness or being maneuvered into a less-than-desirable position." He smiled, all teeth. "It is one of the finer diversions of a prolonged existence, the subtle art of abiding by the rules that govern our world whilst applying a deft hand to their creative interpretation." He raised one manicured claw. "If you were to change an enemy into a tree or a fly or bury them a thousand feet underground, then, technically, you would not have killed them, but it can make life considerably inconvenient for the offender, not to mention quite brief." Joy stared at the giant toad's beatific smile. He noticed her expression and lowered his head to hers. "Therefore, the most prudent thing to do is *not to offend*." They locked eyes for a long moment. Graus Claude tapped her screen. "Write that down."

She did.

For the next several hours, she dutifully typed everything that the Bailiwick dictated about the Council, its representatives, the Hall and Under the Hill, the Glen—the First Forest, which was how the town of Glendale got its name—as well as outlining several key Houses and Courts that divided the Folk into categories based on their origins or common alliances. Some of them were familiar, like Water, Earth, Forest and Aether, others had strange names like the Middle Kingdom, the Fortunate Isles or the Silver Ley Axis, but whenever she tried asking about them, she was immediately shushed and ordered to keep typing.

"When you are greeted by your given name, you must respond with grace, with thanks and in kind," he said. "If you do not know a person's given name, then they have you at a disadvantage and have asserted themselves into the superior position. This can be counteracted if you know their proper title, address or that of their superiors..." Graus Claude paced the room as he orated, recollecting details and nuances and innumerable ways one could possibly offend someone or attempt to avoid domination, sometimes mumbling vague complaints under his breath.

"By the swells, this is going to take forever..."

"Sounds painful," Joy muttered as she typed.

Graus Claude stopped. "What was that?"

"Sorry," Joy said and cracked her knuckles over the keyboard. "I know this is serious. I'm just getting punchy staring at the screen."

"No." The hunchbacked frog drew closer. "What did you *say*?"

Joy swallowed, wondering if she had already given some offense. Graus Claude hadn't covered Folk swearing. "Um... I said, 'Sounds painful' having the swells." She tucked her hands under her lap. "'By the swells'? Get it?"

The Bailiwick examined her face, staring into one eye, then the next. "You should not have heard that," he said, grimacing, eyes narrowing to icy slits. "He said you were not Water, but then how...?"

Joy was growing increasingly uncomfortable under his close scrutiny and the proximity of his many teeth. "Who said?"

Graus Claude made a sound like waves crashing together, driving flotsam into the undertow. Joy was surprised that she recognized it.

"The hippocamp?" Joy said. "Oh. He said I had an *eelet*."

"An *eelet*?" Graus Claude said, surprised. "Where did you get an *eelet*?"

"From Dennis Thomas," she said. "Before he turned me over to Aniseed, back when he'd asked me to deliver a message to Ink. He tipped me a seashell, which evidently had a *thing* inside it that went into my ear—" Even talking about it made Joy want to stick a finger in her ear and fish it out. "It lets me hear Water Folk." She debated trying to pronounce the water horse's name but quickly ditched the idea. "The hippocamp told me that this *eelet* was some royal, deep-water breed."

Graus Claude rose up, nearing his full height, and stared down on her.

"You always bring me the most unusual surprises, Miss Malone," he said. "As your sponsor, I imagine that I shall grow to expect them over the years." Joy wasn't certain if this was meant to be a compliment. He reached one claw out and tapped the tablet. "Keep typing."

Joy's hands were stiff and the pads of her fingers pink and swollen by the time Kurt entered with a rolling tea tray and a carafe of freshly squeezed orange juice. Joy inhaled a tall glass in several gulps. She had begun to feel the effects of going too long without food, but hadn't wanted to risk annoying Graus Claude despite the growing headache and winking lights on the edge of her vision. Kurt was both aware of her blood sugar and possessed excellent timing.

She poured herself another glass. "If having the Sight means that I am part-Folk, then why haven't any others been found out before now?" Joy asked her question while the Bailiwick sipped his tea so that she could not possibly be accused of interrupting him again. It was sneaky, but she was desperate for answers.

"Well," Graus Claude said, warming to the topic, "I must admit that I do not know how many humans born with the Sight were ever marked, let alone had experienced prolonged involvement with the Twixt or were otherwise affected by such a wide variety of individuals from our community as have you." He wiped his lips with several napkins.

Joy scoffed, "That's because you blinded them first."

"Which, logically, would place them under Sol Leander's auspice," Graus Claude mused. "They would be survivors of an unprovoked attack."

"Ugh! I couldn't stand being under his auspice," Joy said and tried not to think too hard about how Monica, her best friend, had Sol Leander's mark—a mark she'd all but put there and one that she could have erased...but hadn't. Guilt still burned like a slow coal in her gut. The idea of Sol Leander watching over her made her ill.

"Fortunately, this was a fate you were spared by becoming *lehman* to Master Ink," the giant toad said. "Still, if those with the Sight are, indeed, descendants of our bloodlines, then one would think that, as survivors of an unmitigated assault, they would have been claimed by Sol Leander and discovered for what they were. And, if not, why not?" He pursed his olive lips. "It would be a closed loop to both abide by the rules and yet refuse to acknowledge claims. Hmm. Perhaps the base theory is flawed..." The Bailiwick settled himself back into his chair. "There are a great number of Houses that account for all the denizens of the Courts, as well as old families, oath societies, political factions and formal alliances that make up the modern Accords. Any one of them might have records about a circumstance resembling yours, yet none have come forward." He spread his four hands. "Therefore, it is all a matter of where you fit into the Twixt."

"So where *do* I fit?" Joy asked. "What House do I belong to?"

Graus Claude placed his teacup in its saucer. "Usually that is a matter of the maternal or paternal progenitor stepping forward and acknowledging their claim," he said. "However, since we have only recently entertained the possibility that those with the Sight share a common ancestry, I would not imagine the Malones have been registered as being under Folk scrutiny."

"The McDermotts," Joy said. "I inherited the Sight from my mother's side, not my father's."

"Hmm. It is good to be aware of such things," he said as he applied a pat of rich butter to his bread with even strokes. "The Folk take pains to keep track of their progeny, else the past has ways of catching up when it is least expected and most inconvenient." Graus Claude lifted another one of his covered plate lids and began dicing a huge steak into pieces with the dance of four hands. "In any event, we can simply wait to witness your change," he said casually. "Then your genealogy should become fairly evident."

"Change?" Joy said. "What change?"

The Bailiwick lifted a polite finger to wait as he skewered four pieces of steak into his mouth. He swallowed. "Once you manifested your True Name and accepted your place within the Twixt, the change would have begun," he said simply.

"Hence why I described you as being betwixt categories, as it were—halfling and changeling." He dabbed at his wide chin. "Essentially, after taking on your True Name, you will take on your true nature as one of the Folk."

"*What?*"

Graus Claude blithely ignored her outburst as he stabbed more cubes of steak. "The change is already under way," he said. "I suspect it began when Master Ink first marked you, alighting the magic in your blood." He tapped one of his skewers against the side of the plate. "It is my theory that if those with the Sight are marked by one of the Folk, it ignites the latent, recessive genes into activity. The *signatura* ritual brings it to the surface, completing it. Or, perhaps, it is triggered by heightened physical response—panic, elation, fear, desire." He gave a double shrug. "As this has never happened before, I can only hazard an educated guess, but you ought to be experiencing some of the effects by now."

Like heat and light and a glow in her veins—the elation of dancing and the pain of grief. She'd felt…something. *What happened at the funeral? Has it already begun?* Joy hugged her arms to keep herself from shaking.

"But I don't *want* to change!" Joy said with spiky terror, her mind racing through the myriad of misshapen creatures that she'd met inside the Twixt. "I don't want to grow feathers or claws or whatever—" a horrific thought struck her "—I don't want to be *invisible* to my parents!" Panic scrabbled inside her, roiling acid hot and squeezing her voice thin. "I want to go to college! I want to graduate and have kids someday! I want to be seen on TV!" Joy didn't know where all the words were coming from; they were bubbling out of her mouth in a rush. She thought she might throw up. "I'm still *human*—part-human—and I want to keep that!" She pressed a hand to her chest. "I want to keep being *me!*"

Graus Claude gave one of his deep-chested sighs. "Miss Malone, I feel that we keep returning to this same conversation, ad infinitum," he said. "You, yourself, were the one who chose to exercise this option, and now you are having some difficulty accepting its outcome." His gaze grew sharp. "Did you think this is an honor we bestow upon a mere human? Your choice—and here I must emphasize the word *choice*—was to join *this* world. And you have—or you will—when the change is complete." He lifted an enormous, fluted glass filled with water in two hands. "Those are the rules, Miss Malone, not guidelines or suggestions—they are the very words that created this world. They *are*."

"Rules can be changed," she said. "Rules can be broken."

"Not by you," Graus Claude said dangerously. "And not by me. Nor by anyone on the Council or anyone in this world—and they would all tell you the same." He huffed like a sneeze. "Human laws can be changed, Miss Malone, minds can be changed, fates may be altered, and fashions might fall out of favor, but the rules that created our world were the ones that cleaved order from chaos, light from darkness, and forged rational thought out of the wild abyss. They are absolute. They *cannot* be changed." A contemplative quiet passed over his features, which faded as he set down his glass. "Even the human world recognizes the power of words that set the wheels of life into motion. Do not presume that you are an exception."

"I've been one before," she said, which earned her a darker glance. "Even you admit that my circumstances are unusual."

The Bailiwick's expression didn't change in the slightest. "I can hardly contain my astonishment that the word *unusual* would be closely associated with your person, Miss Malone. In point of fact, during our brief association, I find that adjective to be most appropriate." He sat back in his chair, which settled with its familiar, wooden groan. "But not this time. Despite circumstantial evidence, it would seem likely that you will follow the pattern woven into the very fabric of life in the Twixt. Best accept that inevitability as the choice you have made."

Joy sputtered but couldn't help remembering Ink's advice when she'd first encountered the Bailiwick. *Respect him. Always.* She counted to ten in her head. Then upped it to twenty, clamping her fingers under her armpits to keep herself still. She could buy a glamour if she had to, right? She could look the same. But she would know the difference—she and all the Twixt. She couldn't imagine looking into a mirror and seeing an unfamiliar face any more than she could imagine looking into a mirror and seeing nothing at all.

"What is going to happen?" Joy asked. "What about me is going to change?"

Graus Claude sat back, his ire abating as he wove his double set of fingers over his chest. "The changeling acclamation can affect any number of characteristics, depending on one's genealogical source," he said. "Once you adopted your *signatura*, you placed yourself within the magics that make up the Twixt, the last vestiges of magic on Earth. Just as you accepted the Twixt, now the Twixt must accept you." He leaned forward slightly. "You must adjust yourself and your expectations to the rules that bind our world—the rules that will shape and govern the rest of your life—and that, I suspect, will be the thing that will change you the most."

Joy tried to follow the implications of his pretty speech. "I'm becoming *magic*?"

Graus Claude looked askance. "You *are* magic, Miss Malone," he said. "All humans and places who have a modicum of magic are the very people who are chosen by the Folk and thereby claimed under an auspice, subsequently marked by one of the Scribes. You were marked by Master Ink, therefore it is no wonder that you should have originally possessed some of that magic in the first place, having been one with the Sight, and now that magic has been activated, either instigated by his hand or by your own actions during your latest display in the Council Hall." His browridge quirked. "Indeed, given your history, we should have expected something like this."

Joy marveled at the ever-widening definition of *something like this*.

There was a knock at the door, and Kurt entered bearing a silver tray with a single calling card. The Bailiwick wiped each of his four hands on cloth napkins before taking it primly in his claws. Graus Claude squinted at the words, and two hands pushed against the arms of the chair as he heaved himself up, still staring at the piece of card stock. One hand folded the napkin over his plate as the fourth brushed crumbs from his suit.

"Let him in," Graus Claude said.

Kurt bowed and departed. The Bailiwick eyed Joy, who had stopped eating.

"Remember what I told you," he said quietly.

Before she could reply, Kurt opened the door and Sol Leander walked in.

Joy's stomach flipped as he strode across the room, his sunken eyes sharp and ferret-bright beneath his dramatic widow's peak. The cloak of starlight wheeled about his legs in a haughty sweep, and his arms were tucked into bell sleeves that made him look like a rather severe-looking monk or a vampiric Jedi knight. He bowed to the Bailiwick, who inclined his head in return.

"Welcome, Sol Leander," Graus Claude said magnanimously. "To what do we owe the pleasure of this visit?"

The Tide's representative stared right past Joy and rendered what he must have thought was a smile. It looked like it hurt.

"I am pleased to find you both here," he said. Joy privately suspected that he had spies watching her and had known that she was here all along. When he spun to face her, she flinched. "I came to bid you welcome, on behalf of the Council." He raised his hands in grandiose greeting. "Welcome, Joy Malone. Welcome home to the Twixt!" He slid his hands together, tucking them once more beneath his sleeves. Joy was surprised that his voice held not a hint of mockery. Sol Leander was very, very good at this game.

She, on the other hand, was new at it. Dangerously so. Joy could feel the Bailiwick's eyes on the back of her head. She'd just written this down. *Respond with grace, with thanks and in kind.*

"Thank you, Councilex Leander," she said with a bow.

"Very good," Sol Leander said as he turned to her sponsor. "She can be taught! You are to be commended, Graus Claude. Proper manners and etiquette will, of course, be essential for her upcoming debut."

Graus Claude's left eye gave an infinitesimal twitch.

"Debut?" he inquired politely. "What debut?"

"Why, the one to welcome Miss Malone, of course," Sol Leander said as he produced an envelope from one sleeve, signed in elaborate script. He handed it to the Bailiwick. "You were right, Councilex Claude—this is a rare and exciting opportunity that should not be challenged, but celebrated! It's been far too long since we welcomed an addition into our world, and we have suffered far too much loss as of late— don't you agree?" His smile was reptilian. "What better way to revive our community spirit than a gala?" He gave a small nod to Joy, who stood transfixed by the exchange. She had never seen Graus Claude struck speechless before. "I am here to extend a formal invitation to yourself and Miss Malone. The festivities will be in your honor, of course," Sol Leander said to Joy. "You are to be presented to the Council and then to your people, the entirety of the Twixt, in order to take your place among them." His eyes flicked over her shoulders and knees. "Proper attire is required. Masks are optional, although there will certainly be no need to hide *your* face—" his dark eyes glittered "—*you* are the reason all of this is happening, after all." The pointed double meaning wasn't lost on Joy. She pressed her fingers together to keep them from twisting into childish knots.

"I see," Graus Claude said softly, his tone hinting that he comprehended far more than what was actually being said.

"Yes," Sol Leander said. "I imagine so." He gave a bow to the Bailiwick and then to Joy, his eyes hard. "The gala promises to be an event that will equal your esteem." He inclined his head. "Formal attire. In your honor. In three days' time."

"Three days?"

Joy wasn't sure whether she or Graus Claude said it first. Sol Leander looked mildly surprised.

"Naturally the Council wished to make immediate reparation for the unfortunate circumstances concerning Miss Malone," he said. "Therefore, it was deemed urgent in order to put all of this sordid business behind us and continue forward as a people, united. You, yourself, Councilex Claude, called for such action before regarding Miss Malone's necessary Edict and referendum." Sol Leander lifted his shoulders and stood straight as an obelisk. "It is a matter of honor."

The Bailiwick sat back in his chair, the groaning wood sounding like a threatening growl. He passed the invitation from hand to hand until it rested quite neatly in the center of his desk.

"Quite," he said, over-enunciating the *t*.

Sol Leander stepped back with a flourish. "Until the Imminent Return," he said with a bow.

"Until the Imminent Return," Graus Claude answered.

Casting a last, parting glance at Joy, the Tide's representative bent neatly at the waist as if to speak to her in confidence. "And I would advise that you keep your friend Miss Monica Reid well away," he said with more than a hint of warning. "Her safekeeping is in everyone's best interests. We are allied in this, at least, Miss Malone." And without another word, he swept through the door, his starlight cloak a swirling flick of finality.

The office doors clicked closed.

Graus Claude leaned heavily to the side, one hand over his eyes. Joy wet her lips, her mind whirling in mad, panicked circles.

"What's that about the Imminent Return?" she said, finally. It seemed strange for Council members to part with a toast.

The Bailiwick ran two of his hands over his face as the two others cleared away any trinkets on the desk. "It's an old expression that hearkens to a mythical 'someday' when we won't have to play these sorts of games any longer." He sighed deeply and considered the invitation. "Well, that's done it nice and neat," he said, tapping a claw against the seal. "I could not have designed it better myself."

Joy wound the edge of her shirt around her thumb. "I take it this gala isn't a good thing?"

"Oh, a welcome gala is a marvelous thing—all finery and majesty, with riches to dazzle your every sense, opulence and decadence beyond anything imaginable. A parade of marvels and magics set upon a stage of high drama, low morals and clandestine affairs," Graus Claude said, smiling. "However, three days…" He shook his head. "Three days? It's unconscionable. And they *agreed*?" His many claws clicked against the desk. "Certainly, as your sponsor, I have only myself to blame. I suspect Maia is behind it. She entertains a particular delight in seeing me squirm."

Joy waved a hand to get the Bailiwick's attention. "Excuse me?" she said, leaning forward. "What are we talking about here? Because it sounds to me like this is just an elaborate excuse to let me fall on my face and make you look bad."

"Precisely." Graus Claude beamed. "Very well done!" He seemed genuinely pleased, which was strangely flattering. "Sol Leander has successfully woven a rope of many threads and expects you to tie the noose and hang yourself with it." The Bailiwick squeezed a single fat fist. "Therefore, it is our job to make certain that he is the one who chokes on it instead." He sounded positively vicious.

"Lovely," Joy muttered. "So what do we do?"

"What, indeed?" he said. "There is simply no way to teach you all that you need to know before being presented formally to the community at large. A proper gala to welcome a new member into society takes months, years—perhaps he convinced them on an expedient time line given your mortal nature. More likely, certain favors changed hands. In any case, it is an effective way to make your introduction uncomfortable in the least, and virtually guarantee a number of long-term social casualties. Formal etiquette is very strict, and many in the Twixt are easily offended—they'll use it as an excuse to cause all sorts of trouble. 'Bridges burned wound lurking trolls,' as they say." He paused at Joy's baffled expression. "Another old saying," he explained. "Like the Imminent Return. Regardless, you will be expected to know how to present yourself accordingly and demonstrate your ability to establish your status in the pecking order, selecting your supporters and spurning your detractors in equal measure. Your presentation must be staged with precision and care, for among the Folk, impressions are everything and memories are long." Two of his hands smoothed down his lapels as he came to a sudden realization. "Good heavens, I'll have to contact my tailor..."

"Hello? Newbie halfling here who will be out of town those three days and currently hasn't a clue what's going on." Joy pointed to herself. "I can't go."

"Correction—you *must* go," Graus Claude said. "It is a welcome gala being held in your honor, after all—it will probably be the event of the century. To snub this invitation would cast yourself as a social pariah, which, trust me, is not a viable option." His hands wove themselves together in pairs. "And you have nothing to worry about concerning distance or time. Indeed, there are far more serious things to worry about."

"Like if I'm going to grow wings?"

"Don't be absurd." Graus Claude sniffed. "You would have sprouted fledgling nubs by now."

Joy dropped her head into her hands and felt sick.

"Now, now, don't fret overmuch—these things take time and, considering how dilute your lineage, you may be long in the tooth before you develop fangs." Joy shot him a look. "Or gills," he amended. "Actually, you might be quite fetching in spots."

"Stop," Joy said, closing her eyes and rubbing her hands over her knees. "One conniption fit at a time, okay?" She took a deep breath through her nose and out through her mouth. "If there's no way that I can possibly learn everything before I immortally offend someone and smear both our reps, what options does that leave us with?"

Graus Claude gave one of his wide, toothy smiles.

"That's simple," he said. "We cheat."

* * *

Joy picked up a pearl from a small pile spread across the Bailiwick's desk. He was inspecting each one carefully, comparing their size and color and hue. It was hard for her to imagine Graus Claude ordering her a dress to match. *Ball gown*, she reminded herself, *for my welcome gala*. It was too ridiculous to take seriously.

"Is this really necessary?" she said.

"Trust me, Miss Malone, I believe this is our best option, given the current situation." He opened his hand expectantly. Joy placed the pearl into his palm.

"I don't understand what this has to do with my learning enough proper etiquette in time for the gala."

Graus Claude grinned. "Leave it to me."

"So I can stop typing?"

"Very droll," he said while rolling the pearls between two plates of smoked glass suspended over a mirror. Joy couldn't quite see how the thing held itself together, but Graus Claude stared intently at each pearl with a jeweler's eyepiece jammed under his brow and several thin instruments in each of his hands. Long tubules ran from what looked like a brass coronet on his forehead to a nest of bulbs at its base. The emerald lamp shone close to his chin, highlighting every crag of his face in white gold. "You continue your work and I shall continue mine." The Bailiwick went back to tinkering and muttering. "Think they can outsmart me, do they...?"

Figuring that she was still hearing him through the *eelet*, Joy decided not to comment. She turned back to the long list of official acknowledgment protocols on the tablet in her lap. *Eye contact is mandatory excepting when bowing or curtseying to those greater than two stations above your current rank, whereupon eyes are lowered and lifted prior to attaining an upright position...*

bend at the knees, ankles parallel...hind in, chest out, don't swallow as it is considered lewd...

A flicker of movement caught her eye. She stopped typing, grateful for the interruption—*any* interruption—Joy would have willingly hugged Hasp for the chance to escape. The outcast aether sprite may have been an evil toady for Briarhook, but an unexpected kidnapping certainly wouldn't be dull! She wasn't sure if her eyes, her back or her hands hurt worse.

Kurt opened the door and stepped inside without so much as a knock. *That's strange.* Joy felt a prickle of premonition.

Inq marched into the room, lifting her hand to her eye as the four-armed toad glanced up, brow furrowing in confusion. She spoke before he did, crisp and sharp.

"I demand entrance to the Bailiwick of the Twixt."

Graus Claude froze. His icy blue eyes glazed over, growing milky like cataracts, his wide mouth open in midbellow. His great jaw yawned with the weight of gravity, unhinging with a tiny *clack* and opening impossibly wider, lips peeling back from the rows of sharp, pointy teeth. Joy watched in fascinated horror as the giant amphibian's tongue curled back upon itself, pale pink and gleaming, and adhered to the roof of his mouth.

Beneath the Bailiwick's tongue were stairs, going down.

"Guard the door," Inq said without looking at Kurt. He moved to obey. She placed one boot on the edge of the bottom lip and gestured to Joy. "Follow me."

Joy gaped, attempting to make sense of what was happening, what she was seeing. She knew her eyes, at least, could be liars.

"Are you kidding me?" she asked, looking at Inq, then Kurt. "I mean, are you *freaking kidding me*?" The Bailiwick showed no awareness of any of them, or, for that matter, anything at all. He didn't look alive any longer—it was as if he'd become a statue, a piece of furniture, like a wardrobe with its doors thrown open, exposing his insides to the world. Joy waved at his maw. "What did you *do* to him?"

"I've invoked his raison d'être," Inq said simply. "And I'm entering the Bailiwick, as are you. I want to show you something."

Joy looked to Kurt. "Is this normal?"

The muscular bodyguard did not so much as twitch. "He is the Bailiwick," Kurt said, as if that explained everything. Which it didn't.

Joy pointed behind her. "There is a *stairway* under his tongue!"

Inq smiled slyly. "Precisely," she said. "Follow me."

And she stepped over his bottom lip, which zipped a line of blue fire just behind his teeth.

"Don't worry," she said. "It always does that." Inq winked. "Watch your step!"

And she marched down, down, down into the Bailiwick's throat.

Joy looked desperately around the room. Kurt stood in front of the office doors, staring ahead, politely averting his eyes. She wondered if Kurt was there to keep people from coming in or to keep her from running out. She edged closer to the gaping maw—widened to the full height of a man—and tentatively placed a foot on the first step. It was solid stone, worn slightly smooth in the center, and was the first of many going down into darkness.

Joy hesitantly shifted her weight, trying not to think too much about her head passing under the frog's upper lip, stepping into his mouth, under his tongue. The line of blue fire zipped by her feet, changing to ruby red as it passed. Joy stumbled and nearly tripped on the stair. Her hand shot out to steady herself. Her fingers gave under the moist inner cheek.

"Ew," she muttered and wiped her hand against her jeans.

"Come on," Inq's voice coaxed from somewhere down below. "It's safe." Inq's words rose up, unseen. "In fact, it's probably the safest place in the world."

"Small comfort," Joy muttered as she swallowed her fear and took the next step down.

The stairs descended into a dark tunnel with a yellow, misty light at the end. It didn't smell like a dungeon and didn't feel like a trap, but the stairway itself felt very old and the air was very still. The passageway brightened as she continued down the steps, growing slightly warmer, friendlier and smelling faintly of grass.

Joy blinked as she walked into a verdant green meadow that spread out to the horizon under a soft, sunny sky. She and Inq stood on the edge of an ancient wood, shaded by towering trees and twisting, leafy vines. The ground smelled loamy and rich and brown. A clear, sparkling brook chuckled over smooth stones. There was a hushed whisper as a breeze tickled the grass and clapped the leaves, but Joy could not feel the air on her skin. Despite what her eyes were telling her, everything felt like a held breath.

Inq squatted next to a patch of periwinkle flowers. She looked truly happy for the first time...ever. It was the look on her face that made Joy feel that it was okay to take those last, few steps into the impossible grove. She crossed the last riser and blinked up at the hazy suggestion of a sun.

"Where are we?" Joy asked. "And don't say 'inside the Bailiwick.' That doesn't explain any of this."

"Doesn't it?" Inq chirped, rising to stand. "The Bailiwick isn't a title like a bailiff or a duke—it's a *place*. The Bailiwick is the comptroller of the space between worlds. Specifically, this space." She ran her flawless fingers over the tops of the grass. "Imagine this is a pocket sewn inside the Twixt. A little pocket universe, a tiny closet in space and time."

Joy turned around in a circle. The base of the stair floated behind them with meadow fading out in all directions into an indistinct blur. The horizon was the exact color of the sunlight overhead. It was as if the whole world bowed at the edges and slipped under itself like tucked-in sheets. The slippery perspective made Joy's head swim. She squeezed her eyes shut momentarily. She could only manage one word:

"Why?"

Inq's face grew serious. The pink-and-green sparks in her eyes flickered like flames. "To protect a door," she said. "A door built between worlds—and shortly afterward, we had to use it to protect something else."

Her eyes flicked over Joy's shoulder. Joy turned and saw a tall woman standing by a tree. She was dressed in a long, flowing gown belted low on her hips, and her arms were covered in purple-black glyphs, her hair long and black and shining. Her eyes were as old as centuries. And when she smiled, two dimples appeared over a tiny, button chin.

"Hello, Joy," she said. "My daughter has told me so much about you."

SIX

JOY STARED AT THE TALL WOMAN STANDING ON THE edge of a forest inside the belly of Graus Claude. Many things slid into place, but too many others slipped away, defying reason and sanity.

"You're..." Joy began, but wasn't sure how to finish. "Ink and Inq," she tried again. "You *made* them?"

The woman drew her fingers down the bark of a tree. Calligraphy shimmered under her touch. "Yes, but they are their own persons now. Just as I designed them to be." She gestured to Inq, who hurried forward and tucked herself into the crook of her mother's arm, resting her heart-shaped face against her shoulder. The family resemblance—if that was what Joy could call it—was unmistakable.

"You're their mother," Joy whispered. *Inq and Ink shaped themselves to look like her.* Joy glanced at Inq. *No*, she remembered, *Inq was the one who shaped them both. She was older. She'd been first. She'd known all along.*

Joy swallowed, heart hammering. "Does Ink know?"

Inq shook her head. "No."

The words echoed in her ears, boring into her brain.

"What do you mean, 'No'?" Joy snapped. "You can't tell me you're hiding Ink's *mother* in a pocket universe for his own good!"

"Of course not," Inq said. "She's hiding here to save her life."

Joy found herself strangely unwilling to take another step. She was trapped along the edge of this world in a secret corner of the Twixt, all but feeling her skin bubbling with nerves. She felt lost, caged, betrayed by both her frenemies and by her own, changing body, afraid that any one of her reactions might trigger something new.

"Okay, stop. Just stop." Joy took a deep breath and let it out slowly. "Look, I've had a long, strange day, but this is beyond too much," she said, rubbing her hands against her jeans. "We are *inside the Bailiwick*."

Inq nodded. "Yes."

"Why?" Joy crossed her arms. "Why bring me here?"

The woman drifted forward. "I am told that you can help set us free."

"Oh," Joy said, as if that explained everything. Which it didn't. "Okay." She glanced at Inq. Joy noticed that her eyes were the color of her mother's sigils—a deep indigo-black. So were Ink's. *A family trait.* "Can you elaborate?"

"It's complicated," Inq said.

"Really?" Joy said. "Try me."

Inq's mother stepped to a nearby laurel tree and folded herself gracefully into its cradle of branches, curled to form a perfect seat. "It started years ago, back when our people and yours began forgetting their obligations and grew increasingly at odds." She tilted her head back. "Many of our people had been enslaved, tricked into servitude. Retributions were swift and the death toll was rising, birthing a mutual sentiment of distrust and fear." Joy glanced aside—it was a familiar story throughout history. "So the King and Queen decided to strategically withdraw, taking the bulk of our people out of harm's way."

"Wait a minute," Joy said. "What King and Queen? The Folk are ruled by the Council."

The statuesque woman turned her head. Unlike Ink and Inq, her eyes looked human, but they still had that cavernous, fathomless quality that she'd given to the Scribes. Joy felt like she was falling into them. "The King and Queen rule over the Twixt, the land which they cleaved from the elemental wild." Her answer left no room for doubt. "When they chose to leave, they left behind a skeleton crew of loyalists in order to maintain our obligations and uphold our honor, fulfilling our pledge to sustain the magic inherent in the world and look after our own. They created a Council to rule in their stead, to be their voice while they were in exile." Her smile faded like the sun slipping behind a cloud. "They chose a courier who would visit the door and ferry messages back and forth between worlds, bringing the King and Queen's wisdom to their Courts." Her words grew heavy. "The courier would also serve as the gatekeeper, the one who would tell them when it was time to come home." The woman looked wistful. Her gaze lifted to the branches waving in a tousled breeze that Joy still could not feel.

"Where did they go?" she asked.

"They fashioned a door," the woman said. "A door between worlds, and escaped to a safe haven on the other side."

Another world? Joy wanted to ask more, but Inq interrupted her thoughts.

"The Council was supposed to open the door when it was safe to return," Inq said from her perch in the grass. "Or, if the humans ended up killing all of the Council members, the strongest and wisest of the Folk, then the door would open automatically and the King and Queen would return to avenge their people." She looked at her mother, fierce with love. "But the courier stopped coming," she said. "And then there were whispers of a coup—that those who remained here could govern themselves and no longer had need or want for a king and queen."

"I suspect they were bitter," Inq's mother said softly. "They felt abandoned and afraid. It was not easy to stay behind in this world."

Inq swiped her fingers along the fluffy tops of weeds. "Just so, their loyalty should have been absolute." She glanced at Joy. "Graus Claude and I decided to hide her inside the Bailiwick, the entrance to the hidden doorway, until we could identify the traitors and end the coup."

"I don't understand," Joy said to the regal woman lounging in her throne of branches. "What does this have to do with you?"

The woman smoothed her dress over her knees. "Of all of my family, I was the only one who chose to remain in the Twixt," she said. "And while I was not a full member of the Council, I was a convenient figurehead—the youngest descendant of my parents' rule."

Joy coughed on her spit. "You're a *princess*?" she said. *Of course. I'm supposed to help rescue a princess of the lost King and Queen. How perfectly fairy tale.*

The tall woman smiled. "In a sense," she admitted. "I felt that, of all my sisters, I could do more good here." She gestured with her rune-painted arms. *"Ca'cleuth me teer po'ur,"* she murmured. "I write to remember." Her dark eyes—deep, brown eyes—lifted as she gazed at Joy. "When the King and Queen prepared to leave, we were already investigating the possibility of *signaturae*—binding the magic of our True Names to symbols which could not be said aloud and, thus, would keep us safe from those who would abuse us. I was in the process of creating both Inq and Ink for the purpose of delivering those marks in our stead and thought that it would only be a little while until we were reunited with our people once again." She caressed the tree bough, leaving a trail of fading cursive, and slid her fingers over new leaves, each one lit up with spring-green script. "I thought that by remaining behind, I could help hasten their return."

Joy glanced between the two in the moment of stretched-thin silence. "But something happened," she guessed. "Something went wrong."

"Yes," the princess said softly.

"When we discovered that there was a plot against the royal family, I brought her here, in secret, so she could be outside the bounds of the Twixt," Inq said. "That way, no spell could touch her, let alone find her. No one else would know." She glanced back up the stairs. "The only ones who came here were the courier and the other members of the Council—those who could locate and open the door between worlds—the traitor *had* to be among them. The Bailiwick and I thought that her disappearance would lure the culprit out or, at the very least, it would keep her from harm until we identified the conspirators." Inq's voice grew hard. "I waited here, certain that I would see the villain for myself, but no one came." Inq drew her fingers through the water. "When I went back to report to Graus Claude, I returned to find that the coup had ended."

Joy frowned. "But that's a good thing, isn't it?"

Inq looked at Joy as if she were an idiot. "There was no coup because suddenly no one remembered the King and Queen—or that there ever *was* a King and Queen—or nine princesses, or the rest of their people, or a hidden door between worlds. It was as if they'd forgotten everything but the Council!" Her voice hinted at old frustrations and anger. "And, worse than having forgotten, they *could not* remember. They could not be convinced that the King and Queen had ever existed. I could not convince the Bailiwick of his function, I could not find anyone who remembered the royal family or that there were thousands of our people sequestered somewhere else, in secret. Worst of all, if the traitor had forgotten about it as well, the crime would be wiped as clean as their memory—the conflict was neatly ended." She glared at Joy with her startling eyes. "I could not risk anyone finding out that I still retained my memories, in case the traitor was still out there." She looked at her mother. "I am her only eyes and ears outside of this alcove, out in the world. We have been searching for this traitor since before the Dark Ages. The crime itself has been long forgotten, we have no allies and the trail is cold." Inq stepped closer to Joy. "Now you understand why I cannot risk being silenced or made obsolete or killed for making mistakes." Her voice was a whisper. "She depends on me."

Joy thought back to how all of this started—her being labeled a *lehman*, Ink's chosen mortal lover, to cover up the fact that Ink had made a mistake in failing to blind her; that they had to keep up the pretense that the Scribes were infallible, able to be relied on to deliver *signaturae* without flaw or question, so that neither of them would be considered defective and in need of being replaced. Everything Joy had experienced in the Twixt during the past six months was with the single purpose of keeping the three of them alive. Joy looked again at the princess of the Twixt. *Not just the three of us—four. As well as thousands more lost behind a forgotten door.*

Her head spun with implications.

"Okay, wait, I understand that someone wanted to overthrow the King and Queen after they left with most of the Folk, and that you worried that they might go after your—" Joy gestured at the princess and struggled to use the word "—mom, and then everyone else seemed to have forgotten all about it and can't be forced to remember. With you so far," Joy said and took a deep breath. "But I don't understand how come *you* weren't affected or why you're telling me."

The princess rose to her feet. "Inq and Ink were not affected because they are not Folk," she said. "I made them with my own hands, my own magic, my own words—I am a Maker, like my family. My words have power. Everything you see here, every whorl of wood, every stone, every leaf, every drop of water and each grain of sand I have made while I have been imprisoned here." Joy's eyes drank in the whole of the pocket world, trying to imagine every detail created by hand. She tried to step off the grass that curled underfoot as if she were accidentally crushing someone's art.

"Whatever affected the entirety of the Folk left the Scribes untouched." The princess considered Joy with interest. "Humans were not affected, either—you've retained your memories, unlike the rest of the Folk." She paused, then amended, "Although I imagine that that is also true of those who escaped—the treachery was limited to the confines of this world, the world of the Twixt. It is why we can have this conversation at all," she added. "Inq said that, being part-human, you would be able to remember."

Joy frowned. "I don't know anything about any King and Queen," she said. "Or any lost Folk, for that matter. This is the first I've ever heard of it."

"Not you," Inq said. "Your stories—your myths and legends and literature passed down through the ages. I've read them. I know that they're there." She counted on her flawless fingers, "Genesis, Exodus, Homer, Shakespeare, Spenser, Chaucer, Yeats, Grimm, Oberon and Titania, Zeus and the Titans, Persephone and Hades, Enki and Ereshkigal, Osiris and Isis, Yul-ryeo and Mago, Inti and Mama Kilya, Dagda and Lugh." She gasped for more breath. "Tam Lin, Olorun, King

Arthur and Gwenhwyfar, Seelie and Unseelie fae, the fairy courts, the Snow Queen, Queen Mab, Morgan le Fey—any of this sound familiar?" Inq gestured at the expanse created by the Maker-Princess in her caged closet world. "Humans *remember* the past in a way the rest of the Folk cannot. It lives in your stories, which means it lives in you. That means that you can help me, you can *do* something."

Joy knew exactly what Inq wanted her to do.

"You want me to help you find the traitors," she said quietly. "And kill them."

"If it comes to that," Inq admitted. "Of course, I suggested simply killing everyone on the Council years ago and forcing the door to open," she said with a smile. "But it's hidden down here from all but the Council, and we don't know where it is. Besides," she added, "Mother didn't like it."

"I do not approve of killing innocents, no," the princess said. "Even if there is a wickedness among them. It was the reason I chose to stay behind in the first place—too many innocents had suffered death on both sides." She glanced at Joy. "I understand that you and I share this respect for both worlds." She knelt and drew her hands through the brook, cupping them together, merging twin handfuls of water. "Once our peoples were one—that, too, has been forgotten. This was our world, a shared world." She let go with a splash. The liquid clung to her fingers and fell like real water, the light sliding and splashing as she shook droplets from her nails. But the next moment, her hands were instantly dry. It was eerie and somehow horribly sad, how unreal and imaginary it all was. "I would like it best if we could identify the traitors, force them to undo that which they wrought, and thereby locate the door to our King and Queen so that the rest of our people can come home." She opened her hand to Inq, and they linked their fingers together. "I would like to reunite my family, to see my mother and father and sisters again."

Joy squirmed around the all-too-familiar fantasy, the tug-of-war, love-and-hate dream of her mother and father getting back together, forgiving and forgetting and becoming a family again. Hers could never really be like that, but she understood the longing. But did someone have to *die* to make it happen? Worse than death—erased from existence as though they'd never been? Joy winced at the memory of falling into the hollow briar patch and realizing what she had done to the Red Knight.

"Why not forget about ousting the traitors and seeking revenge and concentrate on finding and opening this door?" Joy asked. "It's got to be somewhere in here, right?"

"The courier alone knew its location," the princess said. "And no one but the Head of the Council knows the courier's identity, which was chosen in secret in order to protect and balance the Twixt's many fractal loyalties. Whoever it was abandoned that task or forgot about it long ago. No one aside from myself and Inq has been here since."

Joy sighed. "But if you *could* find the door, you could open it."

The princess shook her head. "The door cannot open until either the Council members unanimously agree to open it—decreeing that it is safe for the others to return—or it will open automatically when all those on the Council have perished, allowing those on the other side to return to have their revenge."

"Return?" Joy said. "You mean like the Imminent Return?"

The princess smiled. "It is one of the few memories that remain," she said. "The old saying may have lost all meaning, but the words cannot be undone. Our traditions are endemic and still contain hints of the truth. Whatever happened to erase their memories, it could not undo it all. In our hearts, we know that our King and Queen will come back to us someday."

"Returning to Earth from somewhere behind a locked, lost door," Joy said.

The princess touched the glyphs at her breast. "Those are the rules."

The words made Joy's blood pound. She was *sick* of rules! "Whose rules?"

"Theirs—the King's and Queen's," the woman said. "They created the Twixt by making the rules."

A cold splash shivered down Joy's spine, her mind suddenly clear. "The King and Queen made the rules?" she asked. "They were the ones who made the rules of the Twixt?"

The princess nodded sagely. "Yes," she said. "Of course. That is why they are our King and Queen, the greatest Makers, and why all the Twixt must abide by their rules." She gestured with a graceful hand. "We surmised that the only way the traitors could have conspired a coup was to somehow negate the First Edict, to forget their loyalty to the King and Queen—you cannot be loyal to that which you do not know exists."

"So find the traitors, find the door, open the door," Inq said, counting them out on her fingers. "Presto! Instant Imminent Return."

"But if no one remembers them..." Joy began, then stopped at the expression on the tall woman's face. It was a look of pain and loss and hope and despair that she remembered during her own Year of Hell, reflected a hundredfold. A wrenching war of *What if?* and *What then?* A prickle crawled over her skin, peppery and uncomfortable.

"They will be able to set things right," the princess said.

"They can revise the rules once they return. Only, we must find the way to bring them back."

But Joy was no longer listening, her attention riveted by that one sentence: *They can revise the rules.* Hope blossomed, fierce and fiery, blotting out everything else. She wouldn't have to change. She could keep her body. She could get out of whatever Sol Leander had in store for her, whatever the Twixt was doing to her, whatever was brewing in her veins—it could stop.

If she could find the King and Queen, then they could change the rules.

"Okay," Joy said softly before she knew it. "I'll help." She turned to Inq. "But on two conditions. First, no assassinations." She couldn't say "no killing" because even Joy knew not to bind Inq that much. The female Scribe nodded, and the princess looked on with approval. "And second, you have to tell Ink."

Inq's face crumpled. "What?"

"You have to tell Ink *everything*," Joy insisted. "Tell him everything you've told me. No secrets. No loopholes. You have to introduce him to his mother. You have to bring him here and let him see the truth."

"No," Inq said, watermarks flying over her skin. "No, Joy—you don't know what you're asking." She looked to her mother with desperate, wide eyes. "He doesn't know. He's *never* known. It's kept him safe..."

"It's kept him *out*," Joy said. "It's kept him alone."

Inq's face flushed, a swimming montage of watermark glyphs. "No," she said, looking close to tears. "That's not true. He's had me..."

Joy shook her head, adamant. "That's not enough," she said. "It's not enough and you know it. Not when she's here, now, and he doesn't know. "

Inq spun angrily away, her hands curled tight into fists. Joy guessed that perhaps this was one of the few things Inq had kept for herself—the identity of their creator, their mother, who depended solely on her daughter to be her one confidante, her link to the larger world. Inq had kept the secret for her mother's safety, but also for herself, something precious that made her unique, individual, different from Ink. But that was no excuse.

"I mean it, Inq," Joy said, pushing the point. She thrust out her hand. "Everything. Do we have a deal?"

Inq scrunched up her face, petulant, stubborn. "I get to say how," she said. "And I get to say when."

"But it will be soon," Joy said.

"*Soon* is a relative term," Inq said. "But it will be before the Imminent Return."

It sounded as if that had always been Inq's intent, but she'd never dared to think it could be this close. Joy mutely shook her outstretched hand. Inq finally took it. "Deal," she said, giving Joy's knuckles an extra squeeze, and then she suddenly brightened and beamed at her mother—the transformation was startling. "See? I *told* you she would agree," Inq chirped, winking at Joy. "You're so refreshingly simple." She smiled and skipped toward the stairs with a spring in her step. "Now come along. Let's get you up to speed before the Bailiwick's tongue dries out."

It was a long moment before Joy figured out she'd been played.

"We'll return with news," Inq said to her mother. "And some new company."

The princess smiled. "I look forward to it. Go, and be safe, both of you." Inq and Joy left her standing at the edge of the stair as they climbed.

Joy welcomed the familiar burn in her muscles as she followed the sound of Inq's footsteps, catlike in the dark.

"So you're blackmailing me to help you find and kill an unknown traitor in order to free your mother, the princess, and reunite the Folk with their King and Queen," Joy said aloud and shrugged. "You could have just asked."

Inq laughed, bell-like and genuine. "Now you know why I was so upset that you undid all my hard work when you took on your True Name," she said. "That glyph armor I made for you was a great piece of work and your best protection against the rest of the Folk, including whoever is the traitor. Now my greatest weapon is both unprepared and unprotected, sworn to abstain from wearing any armor at all—brilliant. We could be up against just about anyone in the Twixt."

Joy refused to feel badly about the choice she'd made; the sacrifice of her magical armor was a small one compared to giving up Ink or her eyes. "Do you have a list of suspects?" she asked.

"Kurt and I have some theories."

Joy paused. "Kurt knows?"

"He's originally human, remember," Inq said matter-of-factly. "Now he's mostly human-with-benefits, but, yes, he does remember. And he's twice as cautious as me."

Joy snorted. "Only twice?" she said. Inq smirked. "Why don't you have him kill whoever it is? He'd do anything for you, and you know it."

"Everything except go against the Council," Inq said. "It is part of his contractual servitude to the Bailiwick, else he would have killed Aniseed years ago. Besides, we're not talking about killing someone—you can *erase* them. I figure that's got to be the best way to make sure that whatever was done is undone as completely as possible...if they don't agree to undo it themselves, of course." Inq said, acknowledging their terms of agreement. "No killing unless strictly necessary." Joy felt a small pat on her arm. "Thank you for helping us, Joy."

Inq was haloed in the light at the end of Graus Claude's tunnel, giving her a strangely benevolent glow. She looked unlike herself, something holy, divine. Joy averted her eyes.

"You were threatening to blab my secret," Joy muttered. "What choice did I have?" Joy didn't like having the fact that she'd erased the Red Knight hanging like a Sword of Damocles over her head.

Inq smiled knowingly. "You always have a choice," she said. "But, knowing what you know, you would've said yes, anyway."

"Yeah," Joy said, continuing to climb. "Probably."

Of course, Inq didn't know that Joy had her own reason for agreeing to find the King and Queen and open their secret door as soon as possible.

Joy was about to change the rules.

Inq stepped gingerly over the edge of Graus Claude's teeth. Joy followed close behind, carefully keeping her hands away from the walls. She tried to ignore the creepy, freakish feeling as she stepped off of the deep stone stairwell onto the fleshy lower lip. Another ruby-red line of fire zipped past her feet. She shuddered as she hurried out onto the rug—the safe, normal, perfectly ordinary rug. Joy had never been so thankful to stand on a rug in her life.

Kurt stood rigidly at his post like a soldier.

"Take a seat, Joy. Breathe a little," Inq said. "What is it my brother always says? 'It only takes a moment?' Time does funny things when you fold it over twice."

Inq walked with a self-satisfied strut that carried her across the room, where she stopped briefly to press a hand to Kurt's cheek. Only his eyes moved, but they spoke volumes as she smiled.

"Be sure she gets out okay," Inq said. Dropping her hand, she spoke over her shoulder. "I formally withdraw from the Bailiwick."

Graus Claude's mighty jaw trembled and began to contract. His tongue detached from the roof and slid like a pink python over his teeth. Kurt crossed the room in swift strides and took Joy by the arm, setting her quickly in her chair. He tapped the tablet, waking the screen, adjusted the keyboard, set the jeweler's loupe in one set of his master's slack fingers and strode back to the doorway, grasping both door handles in his hands. Before Joy had a chance to collect her thoughts or speak, he was gone.

The jaw reset with a click. Graus Claude's eyes faded from milk to ice-blue. He blinked like a yawn and set the eyepiece back near his face. Joy jumped in her seat as Kurt swung the doors open as if in midmotion. Graus Claude rolled a pearl between his fingers and palmed it as Kurt gave a perfunctory bow.

"Yes, Kurt?" Graus Claude said without looking up.

"Apologies for the interruption, sir, but the hour grows late," he said in his surprisingly soft tenor. "Miss Malone said that she had an appointment this evening."

Joy nearly dropped her tablet. Her brain scrambled, trying to sort out what was real. Then she remembered: Kurt was human. He knew everything. And he could lie.

"Oh, very well," Graus Claude said with a huff and set down his jeweler's loupe. "Ready the car. Miss Malone, I expect that you will commit your notes to memory as I will endeavor to commit my memories to these." He gestured at the piles with two hands. "Pearls of Wisdom," he said slyly. "Let them be not before swine."

"Excuse me?" Joy stammered, still collecting her swirling thoughts.

"Matthew 7:6," he said with a sigh. "I wonder whether I should abandon all literary references not pertaining to the funny pages."

Joy stood up quickly, stuffing the tablet and keyboard into her purse. Her fingers shook. She couldn't even look at Graus Claude without imagining what lay under his tongue. *And who.* She forced a smile. "When you start quoting Harry Potter, then I'll be impressed."

"J.K. Rowling is a visionary of her era," he said primly.

"Now you're talking. Gotta go!" She shouldered her purse and nearly ran for the door, but stopped at the threshold. *Respect him. Always.* "Thank you, Graus Claude."

His voice rumbled ominously. "You do not have cause to thank me yet, Miss Malone."

Joy ran out of the brownstone and down the stairs, looking for the chocolate-caramel Bentley and its nougat-colored wheels. Instead, she saw a young man with sea-colored eyes standing on the edge of the walk glaring up at her through his snowy hair as if she'd done something stupid.

"Are you?" he asked.

Joy wasn't certain if she should grab her scalpel, bang on the door to get back in or run as fast as she could. Instead she said, "Am I what?"

"Are you truly one of us?" the young aide asked. "One of the Folk? A descendant of mixed blood born with the Sight?"

Joy sighed a tight exhale and adjusted her bag. "Yes," she said, slightly annoyed. "I am. You were there in the Hall when it happened. You saw."

The young man nodded, his eyes hooded, suspicious. His cloak of feathers rippled gently in the wind. He glanced up at the brownstone. "I am supposed to follow you," he said. "And report your actions to my master."

Joy arched her eyebrows as the Bentley rounded the corner. "Oh?"

He nodded stiffly. "Yes," he said. "But I do not think it right nor fair to spy on our own, so while I will not disobey a direct order or dishonor my position, I wanted to inform you of it." His lips thinned as the car slowed. "You deserve to know."

"Really?" Joy said, mildly curious now that she was fairly certain that he wasn't about to attack her here on the sidewalk. "Why?"

He stepped away from the curb as the Bentley slid to a stop. "Because if you are one of us, then all Folk are welcome within the Twixt," he said. "No matter what their origin or circumstance."

The Bailiwick's driver stepped out, adjusted his uniform jacket and opened the door for Joy. She took the last steps and paused before getting in, her stomach queasy, her senses alert.

"Why tell me this?" she asked. "I thought you worked for the Tide."

The tiniest flush colored his face, a creeping pink tingeing his neck and cheeks. "The Tide stands for all of its citizens. It is Sol Leander who wants you to fail," he said. "He will use any means to achieve that end, and the gala presents him with the perfect opportunity."

Joy hesitated. "What would happen if I 'failed'?"

The courtier placed his hand firmly on the door like a wall between them. Joy settled herself on the leather seat and he shut the door with a slam. She heard his last words muffled through the glass. "Mark my words, Joy Malone—do not fail."

SEVEN

JOY SKETCHED OUT A PLAN IN HER HEAD AS SHE SORTED her pre-packing laundry. The first thing she had to do was to find out how everyone in the Twixt had managed to forget about the King and Queen—not just "not remember." Inq said that they were actually *unable* to recall something that should have been impossible to forget. If Joy could figure out what had happened, then she'd be one step closer to finding the culprit and one step closer to finding the door. Joy was fairly certain Graus Claude would help her petition for a slight change in the rules as a reward. One thing she knew for certain: the Bailiwick was very, very good at negotiations and always came out ahead.

She scratched the back of her hand, the skin pink, scaly and raw. It was probably her allergies, seasonal eczema, but she couldn't stop imagining her body changing somehow. Was there something hiding below her skin? Feathers? Fur? Scales?

Joy emptied her basket and fled the room.

Normally she might be worried that if Inq and Kurt hadn't come up with a way to solve this mystery by now, she never could, but Joy had learned that being human gave her a fresh perspective—like the way she'd seen Aniseed's *signatura* on all of the Scribes' clientele while they'd been oblivious—and now Joy had a few advantages that they did not. Not only could she erase *signaturae* should it come down to it, but she also knew something about magic. She knew that there was a difference between glyph magic and spell magic; what the Folk considered magic and what humans considered magic was as different as 80% Lindt was from Cadbury milk.

If it had been spell magic, it was unknown to the Folk—a carefully guarded secret among wizards—but Joy just so happened to have a man on the inside.

"Sounds like a blanket spell," Stef said as he stuffed more shirts into his duffel bag. "In order to spread an effect without requiring line-of-sight on all intended targets, you'd have to define the boundaries based on geographical parameters, or in this case, magical ones." He spoke over his elbow as he cleaned out another drawer. "A spell that affects everyone in the Twixt? One that no one knows about? That would have to be a Class Ten, at least. Way beyond anything I know, or anyone I know would know, for that matter." He sniffed a sweatshirt at the pits. "Why do you ask?"

Joy couldn't say "Nothing," but she couldn't lie, either. It wasn't like she had a school report on spell classifications due anytime soon.

"Something happened, Stef, and it's affecting everyone except Ink and Inq. I know you don't like it, but that world's a part of me now." *And it's a part of you, too.* This was the perfect time to say it. Here. Now. Right now. *Stef, people with the Sight are part of the Twixt. We are descended from Folk. We have a drop of faerie blood in our veins.* But she didn't want to say it. He wasn't like her; he didn't have someone like Ink. He didn't love the Folk—he hated them. She didn't want him to hate that part of himself, any part of himself. It was weird trying to protect her older brother when he'd always been the one protecting her.

"I have an obligation," she said instead.

"No, you don't," he said, rolling pants into logs. "It sounds like Other Than politics to me. Best to stay out of it."

"Stef, we could help..."

"'We?' No. I'm not getting involved," he said. "And neither should you. Do you remember the last time you got mixed up in one of their plots?"

"Um, I stopped a magical disease from killing off most of humanity?"

"No. You almost got killed when an assassin tried to drown you in your car!"

"Oh," Joy said. "You mean the *last* last time."

Stef paused, adjusting his glasses. "Wait. What was that first thing you said?"

Joy blanched. "Never mind."

"No! Not 'never mind,'" her brother said angrily. "Exactly what's going on?"

Joy shook her head. "Please, Stef, you don't understand." She had to say something. *Something! Now! Say it!* "It...has to do with the rules of the Twixt," she blurted out. Joy twisted her thumb in her shirt. "Do you know about the rules?"

Stef glared at her through his rectangular lenses, knowing she was editing herself. "I know about the Accords, the written agreements between the Council and our world, I know about the Edict that protects us, I know about having the Sight, and I know more than a little bit about wizardry and spellwork—proper magic, not glyph magic, that's for Folk and druids," he said, fiddling with his red thread bracelet. He tossed another shirt into the bag. "That's more than enough rules for me."

"Yeah, well, someone's messing with the rules that created the Twixt, and that can affect both worlds," she said. "You, me, all of us."

Stef flung his stuff down on the bed. "Joy, what is going on?"

She couldn't say "I can't tell you" or "I don't know" or some other throwaway phrase because that would be a lie. *Argh!*

"It's a secret," she said, which was about as close to the truth as she dared.

Her brother fumed for a long moment and then wiped his lenses on his shirt. "Yeah, well, secrets don't tend to stay secret forever."

Joy didn't say anything to that. It was true of her mother's affair, her father's first girlfriend, Stef coming out and her own *signatura*. There were no secrets that *stayed* secret. There was no use trying to hide the truth.

She took a steady breath and looked him straight in the eye. "Stef..."

"Listen," he interrupted. "I'm headed back to school soon, and I want you to promise me that you won't go seek out my master anymore."

That threw her completely off track. Joy frowned. "Your 'master'?"

He sighed. "Mr. Vinh."

"Mr. Vinh is your *master*?" she said. "The Wizard Vinh?" Had she known the manager of the C&P was her brother's teacher? Or had she forgotten? Had Mr. Vinh known about her when she'd appeared that first time with Inq? How much did Stef know? Her ears rang. She was deep into information overload.

"Don't look so surprised," Stef said. "I said I was a wizard's apprentice, and you knew he was a wizard. How hard can it be to connect the dots? He even said you'd gone to see him about a glamour."

Joy shook her head. "That was for Ink."

"And you bought one?" Stef asked angrily. "With what?"

She was obscenely glad that Stef didn't know anything about her trade with Ladybird. It didn't take a genius to know that paying three drops of blood to a drug dealer was bad.

"With nothing," she said. "I didn't end up buying one. Ink did! Because he knew I wanted you guys to meet him."

Stef blew out a long breath. "Fine. Well, that's a relief," he said as if it were one more thing to check off his to-do list. "Just promise me you won't go to the C&P for anything other than convenience store crap."

Joy hedged. This was getting perilously close to lying territory.

"That's why I came to *you*," she said earnestly. "You could help me."

"You? Yes. You, I can help. Here's my helpful, brotherly advice—stop whatever it is you're doing or whatever it is you're *thinking* of doing right now. End sentence. As far as helping *them*?" He snapped a pair of his jeans in the air with a sharp *smack*! "I'm *not* helping any Other Thans."

Joy stepped back, stung.

Tell him, she thought.

"Stef..."

Tell him!

Their father's voice called from the den. "What are you two doing?"

Stef shouted, "Joy's not finished packing!"

"Joy!" Dad barked. "What did I tell you?"

"No dithering!" she shouted back and, with a last glance at her brother, went to her room and started yanking open drawers and throwing stuff on her bed. Stef might not want to help her out, but he'd just helped her enough to make a start.

She might not know what a Class Ten blanket spell was, but she knew a few people who did.

Shoving a last fistful of underwear and socks into her pack, Joy hit the auto-dial and waited for the click. Monica picked up on the first ring.

Joy said, "When."

"You serious?" Monica said. "Aren't you heading out in two days?"

"I am," Joy said, grabbing her hiking shorts and ratty jeans. "But the feet want dancing now."

"You packed yet?"

"I'm pack*ing*," Joy said. "As in, 'in the final stages of getting packed.'"

"Hmm. You know your Dad'll kill me if I spring you before you're through, and I have this crazy, personal attachment to breathing."

"Aw, c'mon," Joy begged, folding T-shirts into thirds. "One last night of fun? It'll be special—we could double date."

"Double date?" Monica said suspiciously. "You mean like you, me, Gordon and your invisible boyfriend? Or are you planning on bringing a Ken doll in your purse?"

Joy snorted. "Ha-ha," she said. "You in or not?"

"In," Monica said. "Seriously in. What time are we talking?"

"You name it."

"Gimme till nine," Monica said. "I have to pick out an outfit and call Gordon and everything."

Joy grinned. "Nine it is."

"And dare I ask where this party will go down?"

"The Carousel," Joy said, putting her plan into motion. "Where else?"

Ink appeared for their date through a rift in the wall. Joy checked the clock.

"Right on time," she said.

"I received your message." He touched the carved box he'd given her on her birthday. Joy found that a scribbled note placed inside would disappear. A response would appear later. They sent little love notes back and forth at all hours of the day and night, tiny scraps of paper that made every day a surprise. Joy had a small collection of her favorites stashed in her drawer. It was *way* better than email!

He tugged his shirt across his chest self-consciously. "How do I look?"

Joy chose not to say the first word that jumped to mind. *Scrumptious* wasn't perhaps the subtlest of adjectives.

"You look great," she said. "Really." And he did. As nondescript as his tight black tee and skinny blue jeans were to human eyes, they hugged his long, lean muscles, and his smooth, boyish face made him look anything but ordinary. The silver wallet chain only added to the clean-cut Goth vibe, coiled and cool. Joy remembered thinking that he had an intense, animal grace when she first saw him across the floor of the Carousel. Admittedly, that was *before* he'd tried to cut out her eye. Theirs was not a case of love at first Sight.

"You are remembering," he said, reading her face.

Joy blushed. "I am."

"The first time or the second time we were at the Carousel?"

The first time, he'd tried to cut out her eye. The second time, they'd danced as close as a second skin in the middle of the crowded floor where no one else could see him. Joy felt the hot memory trickle along her ribs, warming the sides of her neck and tightening her chest.

"Well, I *was* thinking about the first, but now I'm thinking about the second."

Ink leaned close enough to whisper, "Third time's the charm."

Joy laughed and stepped back, wondering where he'd learned *that* line. He smiled, pleased with himself. She could tell because both dimples were there. The secret of his mother and the door inside Graus Claude burned inside her. She'd promised Inq that it was her decision, but the look on his face made her want to tell him everything. He was so open, so trusting and so handsome standing there just like a normal boy. Joy consoled herself that after tonight, everyone would be one step closer to the truth.

"However," he continued, "I suspect our going out tonight is not to reminisce."

Okay, maybe not *that* much truth. Not yet, anyway.

"You're right," she said. "We're going to share Date Night with Monica and Gordon, and then I have to see a guy about a spell." She glanced back at him. "Got your glamour on?"

He twisted his hand, activating Mr. Vinh's spell. Having the Sight, Joy couldn't tell the difference, but she recognized the on/off gesture. "Ready to go," he said.

"Joy..." Her father stopped in her doorway, staring at Ink. "Oh. I..." Her dad glanced back at the hall. "I didn't hear you come in." His brow furrowed. "Did you come in? I was in the den..."

"We were just heading out," Joy said, grabbing Ink's hand. "We're meeting Monica and Gordon at the Carousel."

Dad sighed. "Have you packed?"

"Yes. Packed. Done," Joy said as she led Ink down the hall. She didn't want to get caught in any questions she couldn't easily dodge.

"Fine. I'll walk you out," Dad said, grabbing his keys.

"What?" Joy said. "Why? I mean, what for?"

"I need to get some bungee cords and things for the tent."

"I can get them," Joy volunteered, standing in front of the door. She didn't need Dad witnessing their exit. "We can pick them up. You can text me a list."

Dad wavered. "Nah. Thanks for the offer, but I know I'll forget to write something down, and then I'd have to go out again later. I'll just haul my keister out to the store and maybe force myself to hit the gym while I'm out." He smiled at Ink and clapped him on the shoulder. "Come on, Mark, I'll walk you to your car."

Ink looked curious but smiled. "Okay."

Closing the door, Joy thought she was going to have a heart attack and die.

They walked down the stairs and out to the parking lot. Joy grabbed the keys from her purse and double-clicked the fob as they turned the corner. She was relieved to see that Enrique's car had appeared right where Ilhami had left it. Her father approached the Ferrari with a low whistle.

"This is your car?" he said.

Ink tucked his thumbs in his belt loops the way Ilhami had. Joy bit her lip.

"You like it?" Ink asked, evading the question like an expert.

"You kidding? It's a beauty." Joy's father circled the front and peered in, appreciatively. "Of course, an old guy like me couldn't get away with one of these. It's got *midlife crisis* written all over it." He looked at the tires. "Any reason you parked it out here on the grass?"

Joy laughed a little too loudly. "Hate to get it dinged," she said. "Ink's touchy about cars." She was very glad that he'd actually *touched* the Ferrari because then what she said wasn't *technically* a lie...

Mr. Malone crossed his arms over his chest. "Yeah, I can believe it," he said. "You two go ahead. I'll wave you out of the drive."

Joy's stomach splashed in a pit of cold acid. Ink glanced at her quizzically. She clutched the keys in her purse. She'd been hoping that her dad would head out, and then they could reengage the cloak and zip out unobserved. Joy's brain scrambled for some way to get them out of this.

"Joy?" Ink said. She looked up. "I think you have the keys."

"You want me to drive?" she asked hopefully.

"Are you kidding?" Mr. Malone said. "Mark, don't let her drive. You have no idea what happened to the last poor vehicle she drove. I don't think we salvaged so much as a cup holder from the wreck."

Joy spun around. "Dad!"

Her father smirked. "Do you deny it?"

There were so many reasons why she couldn't. Speechless, Joy fumed.

"Give him the keys," her dad said. "Let the man drive his car."

Joy glanced at Ink, who looked impossibly innocent; his eyes held an almost imperceptible shrug. Almost.

"Fine," Joy said and placed the keys in Ink's hand. She walked around to the passenger side and got in the car, slipping into the leather seat. She tucked her purse against her stomach, trying to smother the fluttering butterflies of doom.

Ink dropped into the driver's seat and closed the door, nodding to Mr. Malone through the window. Joy held her breath against the prickles crawling steadily up her spine. Nobody moved.

"Put your hands on the wheel," she muttered while pretending to glance at the side mirror.

Ink placed both hands on the wheel, thankfully at ten and two.

The keys fell on the floor.

Bending to pick them up, Ink rose slowly, avoiding banging his head on the steering wheel.

Joy lowered the sun visor and wiped at the eyeliner under her eyes.

"Put the keys in the ignition," she whispered behind her palm.

Ink flipped the keys in his hand. "Which one?"

"The one with the horse on it."

"Ah," Ink said, picking the right one. "Filly would like this one." He paused. Mr. Malone stared at them curiously through the driver's-side window. Ink studied the shape of the thing in his hand.

"Problem?" Joy squeaked.

"Where is the ignition?"

Joy couldn't help it—she started laughing. Ink joined her, his strong shoulders bouncing with suppressed glee. His eyes sparkled with two dimples, grinning.

"Here," Joy said and leaned over Ink to wave at her dad, tapping the ignition with her left finger. Ink slid the key in and turned it. Joy pressed down on his knee, pushing the pedal. The engine roared.

"Bye, Dad!" Joy called, waving out Ink's window. Her father waved back.

"Be back before one, okay?" he said. "We're leaving day after tomorrow, and I want to go over the plan in the morning."

"Okay," Joy said. Her heart was revving faster than the Ferrari. She'd hoped that her dad would start walking to his car, but it seemed he wanted to watch Ink take off. Joy slipped her hand over the button Ilhami had shown her. *Short range auto-drive. Cruise Control for Dummies.* Joy crossed her mental fingers and prayed.

Ink sounded positively chipper. "Have a good night, Mr. Malone."

Her father stepped back as the engine gave another testosterone roar.

Ink adjusted the mirror, hiding his mouth with his forearm. "Now what?"

"Now drive," Joy said and pushed the button. There was a tiny, high-pitched beeping sound like a baby bat on helium, and the car's video cameras snapped on, giving a full-color, split-screen view out the car, front and back. The stick shift moved with a heavy *ka-chunk*, and the car began backing out of the driveway. Fast. Joy gripped the car door handle as they reversed into the street, stopping sharply. She glanced back. *No traffic, thank God!* Ink calmly kept his hands on the wheel.

Ka-chunk-chunk.

The Ferrari 458 Italia growled and shot down the road. They waved as they drove off, Joy's hand flat against Ink's to keep at least one on the wheel. The car accelerated steadily as they turned off Wilkes onto Main, taking the corner with a sharp, g-force nudge. She could see their plotted course on the GPS. The Ferrari clearly had its own ideas about speed limits, and, knowing Enrique's driving habits, they were probably on manual override.

Ink was experimenting with the various pedals, wheels and dials as the car zoomed down the open lane on its own. "Acceleration, deceleration, direction, speed..." He flipped a dial. The stereo blasted. "Music!" he said, smiling.

Joy cringed, keeping a sharp eye out for the nearest stop sign before they hit the highway. This was too far, too fast and too reckless for her tastes, and neither of them could afford to get pulled over.

"Turn here!" she said and pulled on the wheel. Either Ink or the autopilot or her reflexes obeyed because they peeled neatly on to the side street, slick as a whip. There was a brown squirrel bouncing across the road. Joy screamed, *"Stop!"*

The car stopped on a dime, rumbling like a panther in place. Ink grinned, both dimples.

"I like this car," he said.

Joy turned the keys, killing the engine.

"Get out," she said, her voice tight and loud in her ears. "I'll drive."

Packed in a crowded club of strangers, Joy felt safer than she had all day. In the hot, sweet, sweaty dampness, she finally felt like she could *breathe*. Tucked close together, Ink, Monica, Gordon and Joy pushed their way into the familiar chaos of the Carousel on the Green—the hottest indoor/outdoor club scene in Glendale, not that there was much competition.

A wide aisle ran along the edge of the refurbished carousel, thick with people and thumping music. The circular floor rotated slowly, gold-painted columns reflecting the mirrored undercarriage and the spinning, glow-stick colors on the overhead fans. People writhed and bumped and twisted and sang beneath the huge canopy rimmed in twinkling carnival lights. Joy watched the brass ring pass—the last, original piece of the massive six-row carousel that once housed hand-painted horses and jewel-encrusted sleighs. That was where she'd been dancing when she'd first seen Ink across a crowded room—*this* crowded room—seeing what no human was meant to see.

Then again, she hadn't known that she wasn't fully human.

Monica stumbled as someone pushed past her bearing drinks. "What is *up*?" she said, miffed. "Is everybody in Glendale out dancing tonight?"

Joy looked around. It was unusually crowded for a weekday night at nine.

"Must be something in the air," Joy said. "Last fling of summer?"

Gordon lifted his head above the crowd and sniffed. "More like cigarettes and beer."

"There could be echoes of *il Palio*," Ink said in his crisp, clear voice. "The Glen was once considered a *contrade* on its own. It was a great honor to run the horses, but that was many years ago." Joy stared at him. Ink shrugged. "It means something very different now," he amended.

Gordon tapped a hand on his chest in time to the beat. "I have no idea what you're talking about," the buzzed-blond rugby player shouted happily over the noise. "But if we're going to go in, we'd better have an attack plan."

Luckily, Joy did.

"Follow me," she said and tugged Ink in front of her. When they got to the edge of the Carousel floor, she gestured to her boyfriend. "After you."

He shot her a mischievous grin, a sharp splice of white in the dark. "You are taking advantage of me, Joy Malone."

She grinned back. "Maybe later."

Ink smiled and put a foot on the shivering baseboards, pulling Joy up behind him, followed closely by their friends. The crowd parted, unconsciously making way for Ink as he walked unencumbered into the heart of the club. He raised a hand to one side as if parting curtains, making space for Monica and Gordon. Joy slid close against him as the crowd filtered back around them. She flung her arms over his shoulders and gave him a quick kiss.

"My hero," she said.

He cupped the edge of her ear with his fingers and slid them down her jaw. "You are easily impressed."

She took Ink's hands, moving to the rhythm, keeping him close. As much as Joy fought to keep her mind on her plan, she couldn't help getting swept away in the spinning energy of the Carousel. Through the glamour, she stared into his eyes, as dark as the night, sparkling with pink-and-purple stars. She felt herself falling like she had so long ago, but this time, his arms were there to catch her and press her against him. His skin was smooth under her fingers. His hair tickled her face. The silver chain links caught the club colors and *flash-flashed* them on the edge of her Sight.

Joy draped her hands against Ink's sides, leading with her body, letting Ink feel the way the music ebbed and flowed. Ink learned quickly and knew how Joy danced, mirroring her motions, complementing her moves. Rolling forward and back, his hand slid up her side, gently caressing the outside of her arm. He breathed near her ear, his legs twined in hers. Joy smiled as she inched back and back and back, forcing him backward until he slipped to one side, supporting her back bend over his arm. She unfolded upright slowly and gave him a spunky kiss on the nose.

He smiled. "Show-off."

"Show-off?" she said in mock offense. "Watch this."

Joy stepped wide and tapped her heels to the backbeat, splaying her fingers on her hips and catching Monica's eye. Her best friend grinned, white teeth purple under the black lights, a sharp, crescent moon in her midnight face. Monica and Joy synchronized their moves, step for step, Monica taking the lead as she pivoted and ground down into the soles of her shoes. They popped their shoulders and their hips in unison, inching in increments up from their knees, extending their hands above their heads and rotating their wrists to the melody. Slamming back and forth, back and forth, pumping rhythm with their palms and their chins, the two of them did not so much dance as *be*.

The music switched tracks, and they were right on top of it, in it, drilling deep, punching through it. Twining their fingers, they circled each other, laughing, to the appreciative hoots of lookers-on. Joy and Monica loved to dance and had danced together for years. It was the closest thing Joy had to being with her team back on the mats, synched and psyched in harmony with her sisters, and the feeling bubbled up inside her, a pounding high—like the bonfire revel without the pain of loss.

Thump-THUMP! Thump-THUMP!

Her pulse drummed thick in her ears, far too big and far too loud for it to be hers. It was a lion's heart, a dragon's heart—it drowned out all the noise in the room. Joy didn't know how no one else could hear it, how no one else was turning around and staring at her. It felt like... It looked like...

The funeral. Enrique. Fire. Color. Light.

Thump-THUMP! Thump-THUMP! Thump-THU—!

The hot flare, when it came, raced along her limbs. Joy gasped, the energy skittering like quicksilver up her nervous system, then slipping, fading, draining into the floor, leaving her twitchy and weak. She stared at the carousel floorboards, the scratchy surface dark with shadow and refracted light. She was afraid to look up. She couldn't see—she couldn't tell—had she changed? She stared at her hands, which looked normal under the flashing carousel lights.

"Joy?" Ink said. "Are you hurt?"

Joy touched her arms, her face, her stomach. She shook her head. It didn't hurt. It didn't...anything. But she'd felt it, remembered that feeling of deep, driving light. It didn't show. It hadn't changed her on the outside. *Not yet.*

A lightbulb flash went off inside her brain, and she suddenly realized that the last time she'd felt this way, they had been dancing in this spot Under the Hill—*this* hill—somewhere under the Carousel around the funeral pyres on the edge of the Wild. It had happened right here, deep underground.

What is happening? What am I becoming? How long before I'm no longer human?

Monica tapped her shoulder. Joy barely felt it.

"You okay?" she asked.

"Just dizzy," Joy said and hooked Ink's elbow. "I'm going to grab some water." She mimed drinking, and Monica nodded, going back to static-clinging Mr. Wide.

The whole episode was a splash reminder of why she was really here. Even as she felt the press of bodies grow bolder and the music thump wilder, Joy felt the entire Carousel recede into a low hum, a shadowy blur, unimportant and unfamiliar as the faces in the crowd.

Joy spun around, keeping an eye on the central pillar. Backlit and covered with band stickers, the hollowed-out DJ booth was a tangle of electronic equipment and old turntables. The DJ held court—an iPod silhouette, a dance avatar in reverse. The stacked speakers blasted out a deep, driving bass. She tried to get a good look at who manned the tables as they spun slowly past. It looked like a woman with her hand on the keys. *Damn.*

"He has to be here," Joy muttered, looking around. "He's got to be here..."

Ink tapped her hip. "Who?"

"The DJ," she said. Joy craned her neck, still moving as her mind and the floor continued turning. He was the only local Folk she knew on this side of the Twixt, guarding the Glen entrance Under the Hill, the one beneath the Carousel. She berated herself for not having called first to see if he'd be spinning the tables tonight, but what could she have said? She didn't even know his name, or his human alias, and doubted she could ask for the guy with the goat legs. Joy let herself rotate along with the rest of the world, distracted, off-kilter and confused.

That was when she saw the eyes.

They glowed or scintillated or had slits for pupils. Joy stared. There were Folk—dozens of Folk—dancing in the crowd, their secret identities revealed in her Sight: a mane of feathers, a sheen of silvery wings, a round-bottomed girl with a third, glowing eye. Joy kept turning, seeing more of them, as more of them saw her. The Folk stared back, beautiful and deadly, laughing and writhing alongside their clueless mortal partners, teeth and tails tucked under glamours or glyphs. Joy faltered as several faces looked up, several pairs of eyes locking on both her and the Scribe. Several lips grinned. Terror thickened her tongue. The whole scene went off, like bruised fruit.

Joy had a flash-moment panic that she'd somehow changed, sprouting horns or pointed ears or spots. A sudden wash of goose bumps skittered over her body like bees. She wanted to wipe them off, she wanted to scream—*run!*—but Ink's arms were around her, grounding her, rooting her here.

She took a long, shaky breath and tried to focus.

There were Folk dancing in the Carousel.

They'd started a trend.

The music slowed to a crawl, tinny and wrong, like broken music boxes thrown down the stairs. Joy shook her head, swallowing against the pressure in her ears, staring at them under the flash and stutter of lights. What were they doing here? The Folk *hated* humans! Feared them. Many, like the Tide, wanted her and her kind wiped out. She watched their *signaturae* flash in the black light, trying to make sense of it. Why would they risk being discovered, being ousted, hunted or shackled by their True Names? Wasn't that what the Scribes and *signaturae* were for—to shield them from humans? Act as a buffer between worlds? Yet here they were dancing with teenagers in the Carousel!

"Ink...?" she whispered, eyes locked on a reptilian figure whose scales sparkled under the fairy lights. His smile was serpentine-wide, and the girl in his arms ground against him, eyes closed. Nictitating membranes blinked as his pupils yawned wider. He slid the back of one hand down her body as if taking a long lick.

Ink's hand automatically went to his wallet, but Joy's hand closed over his, and she hooked her thumb in his pocket to hold him there.

"Wait," she said, trembling with déjà vu. Sharp objects and rave music had clashed in the Carousel once before, and Joy didn't want a repeat performance tonight. None of the Folk were closing in or looked more than curious. The humans looked obscenely young and fragile next to the Folk's alien immortality. The residents of the Twixt didn't look afraid—they looked defiant.

Joy's pulse jumped, thrumming double-time to the dance track hammering on her bones. It was as if each bark of laughter, each slit-eyed stare, each claw fondling a breast was aimed at her—an unspoken threat, a school of sharks swarming, circling at arm's length, threatening her and her people. She held on to Ink as his expression hardened, his shoulders becoming solid, face stony and grim.

"Come on," she urged. She moved past the crowd of human and not. "There!" Joy said, going up on her toes. She saw the DJs switching shifts, the woman handing a Post-it to a guy wearing massive earphones like a Viking helmet. Joy grabbed Ink by the hand and pointed. He stepped into the dancers, who shifted aside under his invisible hand.

They crossed the dance floor easily. Joy pushed up next to the central pillar and tapped on the wall. The DJ didn't even look up as he arranged the next set.

"You got a request? I can put it in queue."

"Yeah," Joy shouted. "How about something for my boyfriend, Ink?"

The DJ looked up, his fingers still on the screens. He glanced between Ink and Joy before he wagged his curly chin hairs at the woman disentangling herself from the nest of power cords on the floor.

"Hey, Sticks," he called out. "Mind spotting me for a sec?"

"Just got off," she said, discreetly lighting up a hand-rolled cigarette.

The DJ shot her a winning smile. "I'll help you with that, too, if you like," he leered. "But can you spin me for five? I gotta hit the cave."

The lady DJ smirked, tossed a box of matches back under the keyboard, pinching her cigarette, and took back the playlist. "Five. And you owe me."

"Big-time, just like me," he said, slipping past her and ducking under the cutaway. He snapped his wrist in the air. "Follow me."

He plunged into the thick of things outside the booth. Ink forged ahead, cleaving a line, allowing Joy and the DJ to walk in his wake. The guy acted not at all impressed, but grabbed a few fists and clapped shoulders with some of the regulars as he passed, a minor celebrity in his element, a kingdom of noise. Joy wondered how none of them realized he was a satyr—his only disguise was a thick head of hair and a pair of baggy jeans. His glamour barely covered his horns, for Pete's sake!

He took the lead as they crossed the aisle to the ticket booth at the Carousel's entryway. Behind it was an old trailer covered in pressboard, painted black. The DJ opened the door and pushed inside, flipping on a bare light. Sound was smothered dead as he closed the door behind them. The walls of the tiny office had been covered with squares of egg carton foam staple-gunned and duct taped into place, cheap soundproofing against the outside din. The satyr fell into a swivel chair by a secondhand desk buried in security screens and flipped his massive headphones to hang like a necklace on his chest. His tufted ears ruffled, and he stuck a pen in his mass of curls.

"Nice to spy you again," he said to Joy. "And with the eye candy. Very nice." He kicked a foot up on a plastic egg carton. Joy was surprised that he was wearing shoes. The DJ eyed Ink and Joy, his gaze lingering on their entwined hands. Joy hadn't realized that they threaded their fingers together automatically nowadays. The satyr withdrew the pen and pointed it at each of them. "I heard you two kissed and made up. Good to see love conquers all now and again," he said. "But I wish you hadn't put the bee in everyone's bonnet. You see the mess out there? It's like every pix and nix is trying to get in on some of that action."

Joy squeezed Ink's hand. "Some of us are just lucky, I guess."

The DJ stopped smirking. "Yeah. And then some." He curled the tip of his half beard over the pen. "So what can I do 'for' you as opposed to 'to' you?"

Joy took a deep breath. This was why she'd come. "I need your help."

"My help?" he said. "Really, now."

"Yes. With a spell."

"Whoa!" The satyr sat up and hit a few keys under the security monitors. A mute icon popped up on-screen. "Will you keep it down, natch? What do you want to come in here and say a thing like that for?" He cursed under his breath in some tangled language. "Do I look like a *segulah* to you?"

"The last *segulah* was an elder dryad bent on destroying

the human race," Ink said matter-of-factly. "I am not interested in meeting another."

"Yeah, well, you're barking up the wrong tree spirit." The DJ sniffed. "We might both be Forest Folk, but I can't help you out. Sorry." He swiveled in place, then stood up. "You want a slick mix, I'm your guy, but spells aren't my scene. Now if you'll excuse me, I got a set with my name on the clock."

"I don't need you to cast a spell," Joy said, blocking the door. "I need help figuring out how to track one down." She swallowed. "The Forest Folk are the guardians of the Glen, this part of the Twixt, right?"

The DJ stopped, his interest piqued. "Yeah?"

"And this is your post—the entrance Under the Hill?" Joy said. "If a spell had borders, it'd be here." She swallowed back some of her anxiety. "All spells have a trademark, a way to identify who designed them," she said. "I'm looking for a Class Ten spell, at least. I want to know if there's any way to trace a spell by following the trademark back to its origin."

Twisting his curly head like an owl's, the satyr stepped back, considering it. "Yeah," he said slowly. "You could do that. Why?"

"I need to find out who cast the spell." Joy twisted her finger into the hem of her shirt. This was where things got risky. "I think there's a blanket spell over the Twixt."

"Probably more than one," the DJ said, crossing his arms, legs splayed in baggy jeans. "Gotta shore up the borders, such as they are. It's a 24/7 hazard. You don't have to tell me twice."

"This is different," Joy said. She debated saying everything aloud—from the King and Queen and the princess and the coup to the Bailiwick and the hidden door somewhere inside; maybe he'd remember? Maybe the spell was weaker here? But Ink stood next to her, and she'd agreed that he'd learn all of this from Inq. She tried another tactic. "I think someone did something...bad. Really bad. It goes against all the Folk and the Council. And if I can find out who did it, I can stop it."

"Oh, really?" he said. "You gonna kill 'em?"

Joy felt Ink's eyes on her. "No," she said. "No killing." What she could do was infinitely worse. "And you know I'm not lying."

The satyr stroked his chin hairs and stared at the screen, gently bobbing to the muted beat outside. He glanced back at Joy and Ink, weighing something in his eyes. "What's it worth to you?"

Joy frowned. "Excuse me?"

"This is your post," Ink said. "If it has been compromised, it is within your rights and duty to act in order to protect the Glen."

"So says Miss Joy Malone?"

Joy flinched a little at the sound of her full name, although she knew that it hadn't the power to control her anymore. Filly was right—she'd been vulnerable—but Joy was now protected by her *signatura*. She felt it like an itch between her shoulder blades, the sigil of her True Name linking her to the Twixt.

"Yes," she said. "I say so. This is my world, too."

Joy looked into his cherry-brown eyes under his mop of curls—he was remembering something else, some*when* else, when he looked at her.

"Yeah, okay," he said. "I think I can help you out." He snatched a business card from an open envelope and clicked his pen. "But if I'm going to go out on a limb for you, I'm going to want something special in return."

Ink spoke first. "How much?"

"Oh, I don't need money," the DJ said while scribbling. "I'm not interested in material suffering." He leaned forward, the headphones swinging from his neck like a yoke, his grin almost feral. "You said a Class Ten? So you know your brother's a wizard, right? I want you to arrange a meeting for me," he said slowly. "I want a meeting with your brother, Stef."

"What?" Joy said. She remembered Stef guessing that this guy from the club was probably one of his old clients—freelancing wizardry being one of the things that had been forbidden to him since he'd become an apprentice to Mr. Vinh.

The satyr looked smug. "That's my price."

"I can't do that," Joy said. "Class Ten is way beyond him."

"I don't care," the DJ said. "Arrange a meeting for me, and I'll make things happen."

"I can arrange things all I want, but I can't *make* him show up," Joy said. "I can't *make* my brother do anything! I can't even get him to get out of bed in the morning!"

The DJ held up the business card and shook his head sadly. "Let's try this again," he said. "You are asking me to risk something for the chance to help you test out this shiny conspiracy theory of yours, and, in return, I am asking you to make Stefan Malone show up and talk to me." He shook his head as he wrote something down on the card. "You can stay with him the whole time if you'd like, you can hold his hand, you can lay down any condition you want, but I have one—and only one—request for my cooperative and complicit participation and that is—" he violently scribbled out whatever he'd written and turned to her, resolute "—your brother will *be* there. End sentence."

Joy was surprised as she looked at the card. She couldn't make out what the DJ had originally written, it was obliterated under pressure and ink, but he sounded desperate. She wondered if her brother had been like Ladybird, some kind of magic drug dealer, and this guy was now jonesing for a long-forgotten fix? Doubt rippled inside her. She thought about Inq and the princess and the hidden door, the King and Queen, the ever-present rules and the inevitable change percolating under her skin. She rubbed her arms, smoothing down the memory of that driving heat on the dance floor above the Wild. Her own heartbeat scared her. But she couldn't risk what he was asking—she couldn't risk Stef.

She handed the card back. "No," she said. "No deal."

The satyr growled in frustration. "I'm not going to *do* anything to him, Miss Paranoid," he said. "I just want to talk."

Ink frowned. "Just talk?"

The DJ scratched his fingernails against the surface of his jeans. "Yeah, 'just talk.'" He sounded defensive, uncomfortable without his swagger and smirk. "I want him to show up, and I want words to come out of his mouth and words to come out of my mouth and for there to be a mutual exchanging of words," he said. "Talk. And, in exchange, I'll get you what you need to track down a spell."

Joy twisted her fists. "And you're not going to hurt him," she said.

The satyr paused and scratched his beard. "I can't promise not to hurt him," he said. "Words can hurt, sometimes."

"But you won't touch him, or come anywhere near him," she said, wavering.

Ink touched her arm. "Joy..."

But she flung his hand off her arm and kept going, hardly believing she was even considering this. Something in the DJ's face begged her to listen, but she couldn't quite make out what he wasn't saying. It looked like *Please.*

"You won't do *anything* at all that could possibly be considered an attack or a threat or anything intending him harm—just talk. Hands where everyone can see them, no weapons or spells, at least ten feet between you two at all times. And you'll come unarmed and alone." Joy tried to think of any way that she could bind it tighter, any loophole she hadn't considered.

"Do you swear on rowan, yew and ash and be by ironwood bound?" Ink said.

The satyr turned pale. Ink's words meant something to him. Joy nodded. "You agree to that," she said. "And I'll see what I can do."

The satyr stared at her with wide eyes and scratched his scalp near the nubs of his horns. "Yeah," he said softly. "Yeah. I can do that. By rowan, yew and ash, I swear, and shall be by ironwood bound." He dug into his many pockets and pulled out a glow stick. Grabbing a marker from the coffee mug, he drew swirly symbols carefully over the curved plastic sheath. The black Sharpie glyphs reminded Joy of Aniseed and her cache of wax-sealed potions. She flinched.

"I thought you said you couldn't do spells," Joy said.

"This isn't a spell, it's a beacon," he said. "How do you think half the Folk get in here? Ask your boy—it makes a door from one spot to another. We have to stick 'em up all over the place—on the walls, the ceiling, the doors, the fans. Pops folks in at twice the cover price. Increases turnout up to thirty percent." He handed her the glow stick and tapped it lightly with the cap. "Snap that and we're copacetic. Somewhere secluded and near trees would make things easier." He snickered and shook his head of brown curls. "And wouldn't it be nice if someone would make things easier for a change?" he said. "You'll have to be the one to break it since he's not here—imprint's for one. If you can do that, I'll get you what you need."

"After I bring you what *you* need?" she tested.

His grin tugged at the corner of his lip. "Maybe," he said.

He snapped his headphones over his ears, slid the strap over his horns and reached for the door. Joy noticed his knees bent backward in his jeans. "Now get out," he said amicably. "I got a rave to brave, and you have things to bring." He yanked the door open, and the sound crashed over them, the reverb nearly blowing Joy backward. Ink barely blinked. The DJ shouted by her cheekbone, "I'm trusting you."

She shouted back, "Same here."

He hopped out the door, gave a double-gun salute and backed into the throng. Ink took Joy's hand and slipped into the outer aisle, swallowed back into strobe light and noise. Joy looked around for Monica and Gordon and quietly pocketed another unbroken glow stick that had been taped to the door. Ink watched her make a ring of the black electric tape and thread it through the top. Now she could tell the two sticks apart.

"You are becoming more and more like the Bailiwick," Ink said.

"Is that supposed to be a compliment?"

"In a way," he said. "You are both cunning and careful with your words." He looked up at the ceiling full of spinning highlighter swirls, black lights and mirrors. "And you are fast becoming adept at the art of trading favors in order to get what you want."

Joy took his hand. "There is only one thing I want right now."

He grinned and squeezed her fingers, eyes wide. "Show me."

They stumbled through the breach and up against her bedroom wall, Ink cupping her face and kissing her mouth, her cheeks, her chin. Joy bounced off the dresser and twisted, grabbing his sleeves to steady them or pull him closer—she couldn't quite decide.

Ink stopped them with a hand flat on the wall that quickly slid into her hair as he kissed her again and again, drunk on kisses. She melted and tightened against him in turns. *How had they gotten so good at this?* She giggled, remembering Ink's offhanded words, *Some things are eagerly taught.* Monica had grinned wickedly at them when they'd made their hasty goodbyes.

He pressed the length of his body against hers. She moaned and pulled him closer, openmouthed, wanting. He slid a leg between hers, gaining another precious inch. She gasped, splayed against him and the wall.

His words fought for space between breaths.

"Is your brother home?"

Joy laughed in his mouth. "I don't know," she said, still kissing him. "Why?"

She felt Ink's lips crease in a smile over hers as he lifted her up by the waist with the strength he'd had Under the Hill. She laughed in delight, cupping her palm over her mouth to smother the sound, aware that anyone could be home—they might not hear Ink, but they would easily hear her. Ink grinned mischievously as he spread her gently across her bed.

Joy arched into the pillows, hooking a heel behind his knee, pulling him along, urging him closer. Ink stretched forward, his chest hovering over hers, his eyes fathomless and full of stars. It made her smile, his being so happy just looking at her.

"You know," she said softly. "Usually guys ask whether a girl's *father* is home."

"Your father cannot see me," he said.

She grinned. "Good point."

He hovered, holding himself up on his arms, lowering just enough to kiss her—only their lips touched. Ink gently explored her mouth, planting soft kisses along her lips, tracing their outline as they parted to breathe. She gasped as he touched his tongue very gently between her lips, sealing them closed with a kiss. Joy stopped giggling, stilled in the moment. He broke away, trailing a long, warm breath down the side of her neck, tracing the line of her shirt and back up her throat, encircling her, memorizing her with the touch of his lips. Joy turned her head to one side and twisted her fingers in his shirt.

He moved closer, the exposed edge of his stomach brushing against hers, a contact high, hot and searing, electric and intense. She gripped his shirt and held fast. He resisted for only a moment before resting on his elbows, melting with a sigh against her, burying his face in her neck.

She turned and kissed him—his face, his neck, the crux of his jaw until she met his mouth, warm and soft in the dark. Joy forgot all her schemes, all her worries, her choices, her secrets, until there was nothing left but her senses and him. She swam the moment and held on to Ink.

Urgent sounds whispered under their breath, both of them eager to feel more, fumbling over fabric and catching on buttons. The cool hiss of the wallet chain slid over her belly. She gasped, and he drew back, eyes wonderous-wide.

"No." She almost laughed. Almost. "Come back."

But he knelt up on the bed, his knees sinking deep into the comforter as he looked down at her as if she were something otherworldly, his face a soft expression of awe. Joy lay sprawled beneath him, disheveled, awkward, hair damp at her neck, lips kiss-swollen—she waited like a question. She barely dared to breathe.

Ink touched two fingers to his heart and rubbed them there. He gazed at her, unblinking, and laid the palm against his chest.

"I feel you," he said. "Here."

He'd said it before, but it sounded different now. He tilted his head and let his eyes slip closed, long lashes drawing curtains over his all-black eyes. His hand pressed harder, and he smiled a little bit.

"I can feel my heart pounding," he said.

Joy blinked, some of the tangled muzziness and deep want clearing.

"Your heart?" she asked slowly. Her tongue felt thick.

Ink's eyes opened, bright with tiny flashes. "Yes," he said. "I made myself a heart," he admitted almost shyly. "To feel joy."

She sat up, drawn forward into his eyes. Joy slid a hand under his shirt, her fingers soft under his. He pressed her there, and she could feel it.

Thump-thump. Thump-thump. Thump-thump.

Joy smiled, and her eyes shone with sudden tears.

"I can feel it," she whispered. "I can feel your heart."

Holding her hand against him, his eyes enveloped her.

"I love you, Joy."

He pulled his shirt over his head, revealing Joy's hand resting on the fissure between his pecs. They had carved his body together with a figure-drawing book; she'd seen him bare-chested before—but not like this. Nothing like this. It was as if she didn't recognize her own hand, or his skin, or their bodies, together. She spread her fingers, and he let her explore, watching her watching. Her fingertips traced his muscles and ribs, his furrows and edges, returning to the center of him, a dance around the drum call of his heart.

Thump-thump. Thump-thump. Thump-thump.

Growing faster, louder, calling out to her from under his skin.

She looked up into his eyes as he whispered, "Now you."

Without a second thought, Joy peeled her shirt off over her head and flung it somewhere on the floor. She smiled. Ink smiled, his eyes riveted on her. She watched his midnight eyes follow the shadows, tracing her curves. He very tentatively reached up, fingers extended, as if afraid to touch a bird that might fly away. Joy waited in that moment, impossibly long and longing, so attuned to that first, delicate touch that she almost missed it—her senses rising to meet his.

His fingers touched—two, three, four—tracing the top of her clavicle to where it dipped at the base of her throat, following down over the swell of her breast. Ink watched his own fingers explore the curve, stroke slowly underneath, cupping the soft weight in his hand. Joy tried to breathe, letting him see, letting him feel—so present in that intensely magical moment like they'd shared when he'd first touched her ear. Curiosity was beguiling. Innocence was a drug. There was no rush getting here, there was just *here*. Now. This moment. This touch, like a surprise. Both of them so very, very here.

She watched him as he saw her skin tighten. She felt him understand what it meant. What she wanted. His eyes, mesmerized, widened.

He froze.

"I have to go," he said, rocking the mattress as he nearly leaped off the bed.

"What?" Joy said, her skin growing cold. Her words tripped to keep up. "Wh—Where are you going?"

Ink pulled his shirt on inside out and snapped his razor open, eyes averted, chain swinging wildly.

"I have to see Raina," he said and sliced open a door.

Joy sat up.

"What?" she shouted, but he was already gone.

EIGHT

JOY STORMED AROUND THE HOUSE IN THE MORNING, slamming down dishes and yanking drawers. Her father and Stef stayed ominously quiet and got out of her way wherever she went. They exchanged looks from across the kitchen and quietly holed up in the den as Joy mutilated a fresh box of cereal, managing to tear the bag sideways. Special K flakes flew everywhere.

"Everything okay, Joy?" her dad ventured.

Joy smashed in the box top, her voice louder than she intended. "Everything's—" she sputtered. She couldn't say *fine*. Grabbing the spoon in her fist, she said, "Everything's *d*— Everything's *peach*—" She licked her lips, tasting the words, and slammed down the bowl. "Everything is completely, utterly *p*—!"

But she couldn't say *perfect*, because it wasn't.

She ground her teeth and sat down at the table. Hard.

Stef kicked his foot up on the arm of the couch. "Well, *I'm* convinced."

Joy scraped the bowl and stared across the table, at the very seat where Ink had first explored her earlobe and filled her with querulous butterflies. She closed her eyes for a moment, got up and switched seats. She chewed as if she were pulverizing each awful thought before swallowing it.

She rubbed her eyes as she chewed. It had taken her several fitful hours to finally get some sleep. She'd had to scrub the memory of Ink's touch off her body with a loofah and peppermint soap, and yet his eyes stayed with her as if watching her still. Her body itched. Her fingers clenched. Her worries spiraled like a storm. *Raina?* followed quickly by *What went wrong?* chased the screaming tail of *Did I do something wrong?* only to loop back to *Raina?!* again.

Raina. The mysterious sophisticate with the exotic Pantene hair and the shimmering, gold-gloss lips; the one who'd shimmied out of Enrique's funeral with Ink just as smooth as you please, her arm hooked in his, leaving Joy and Inq behind. *THAT Raina?!*

Joy squeezed her head in her hands.

That mental merry-go-round had been enough to keep her up all night.

Her father pointed a finger at Stef, who held his hands up, the picture of blamelessness. Dad sighed and came over to the table but held back from actually touching her. He knew when Joy was all-over prickly.

"Anything I can do?" he asked.

Joy shook her head and crunched her breakfast, feeling sadder and more frustrated by the minute, as if having witnesses made it worse. She ignored the men silently calculating the date and swore to herself that if one of them offered her chocolate or used the word *period* except at the end of a sentence, she would completely lose it. Period.

"Okay, then," her father said, "I was going over the route with Stef and wanted your—"

"It's fine," Joy said.

"Right. Well. On the way to the site, I thought maybe we could—"

"Fine," Joy said and scooped the last spoonful of cereal into her mouth. "It's all fine. Whatever you've planned is one hundred percent fine by me. Just tell me when I'm driving and when we leave."

Mr. Malone tapped his finger against his lip.

"We leave early, 4:00 a.m. tomorrow morning," he said. "And we'll drive in shifts."

Joy stood up with the bowl and spoon in hand. The chair squeaked sharply across the floor.

"Fine," she said and went to the sink.

"Okay..." her father said, resigned. "Fine."

Joy rinsed and dropped her dishes in the rack. She wiped her hands on the towel and spied her brother's head peeking over the back of the couch.

"Get up," she said. "We're going out."

Stef frowned. "What?"

She threw the towel on the counter. "We're going out," she said. "Now. Grab your keys."

"Hey, I'm not your—"

"*Now.*"

Stef leaped off the couch and grabbed his keys out of the dish in the hall. He glanced at his father. "We're going out," he said needlessly.

"So I heard," her dad said, trying not to grin. "Nice talking to you both. Please, come back in one piece."

Joy held the door open as Stef flipped the keys in his hand. "You gave her the other X chromosome," he said. "I blame you."

She nearly slammed the door in her brother's face. Turning, she took the stairs two at a time, forcing him to follow.

"What's your problem?" Stef said, trailing after her. "Where are we going?"

Joy hit the pavement, both feet slap-slamming down. "Abbot's Field," she said automatically. It was where she went when she was feeling like this, but the truth was that it was exactly where they both needed to be. She needed answers, and she needed them *now*. It was the only thing keeping her from thinking about Ink.

"I'm not your off-mat trainer anymore," he said. "Or your chauffeur, by the way. You can get there on your own."

She turned around, grabbed his arm and pulled him bodily along. "We're both going," she said, head full of steam. "You said you're willing to help me? Fine. You're helping me get to Abbot's Field."

Stef marched up to his Nissan, looking annoyed.

"Joy..."

She glared at him. Whatever he saw made him stop. The alarm beeped off. The locks snapped open. She got in and sat down in a huff. Stef dropped into the driver's seat and keyed the ignition. Watching him turn the key made her think of Ink, which made her clench her fists under her armpits and cross her legs.

Stef backed out of the spot with a muttered, "Yes, Your Majesty."

They drove away in silence, both fuming in their separate seats. Stef squeezed the steering wheel until his knuckles were white. Joy distracted herself by texting her mother and Monica on her phone. Both messages were basically the same: Men suck! The scenery sped by in a whirr of tires and air-conditioning.

"The only reason I'm doing this is that it's the quickest way to get you off my back," Stef said.

Joy shrugged. "Whatever works." She flipped back to her contacts and scrolled through the names, knowing that Raina and Ink weren't among them. Her thumbs paused over one name. She tapped it and held the phone to her ear.

"This is Antony."

She could picture his face—Antony was very distinctive.

He'd once said his parents were a mix of African, Native American, Spanish, Japanese, English and Haitian. He looked like a model, ran triathlons and was an environmental architect. She could hear big machinery grinding in the background.

"Hi, it's Joy," she said, plugging one ear. "I have a quick question."

"As long as it's quick."

"Who's Raina?"

There was a loud beeping, and Antony moved away from it. "Raina? You met her at Enrique's funeral. Tall woman, fast talker, great hair."

"Yeah, I know that," Joy said uncomfortably. "I mean, who is she? How does she know...us?"

"Oh, that," Antony said. "She's one of us. One of Inq's."

Joy's mind flipped one-eighty. "She's a Cabana Girl?"

Even with the noise in the background, she could hear Antony snicker. "Yeah, well, I wouldn't call her that," he said jovially. "She's a woman—all woman—and she'll kick your ass if you forget it. Raina's the hen that rules us roosters. She's in a class all by herself."

Joy swallowed another pang of jealousy. "Then, what's she doing with Ink?"

"Ink?" Antony said, enunciating the hard *k* to make sure he'd heard the right twin. "Huh. Well, if there was ever any guy, it'd be him..."

Joy hung up, furious. A cold fist of realization squeezed her stomach into a ball. She'd never said anything to Ink about them being...exclusive—she hadn't thought she had to!—but with Inq and her torrid band of harem hotties as his only reference, Joy had been stupid not to think of it before. And therefore, it was stupid to feel angry or jealous or hurt, and even *more* stupid to feel betrayed, and *insanely* stupid to feel hot, seething anger curdling in the back of her brain—but she did. All of it. All at once. She bit the inside of her cheek and banged the phone against her forehead.

Stupid! Stupid! Stupid!

"Try hitting harder for me," Stef quipped. Joy slammed her head back against the headrest, blinking hard. Stef sighed and made a concerted effort to sound sincere. "What's up?"

"It's just...hard," she said. What she didn't add was *dating one of the Folk*, but her brother heard her anyway. Their family was really good at hearing things unsaid.

"Yeah," Stef said soberly. "I'll bet."

He pulled along the woody stretches surrounding Abbot's Field. Driving far from the scattered camp kids and Frisbee games, he wound down the gravel path to the old soccer field with its pristine, well-trimmed grass and its spongy, level ground. He didn't need to ask her where to pull over; she had practiced here for years, and Stef, as her home coach, would put her through her paces here at Abbot's Field. Once upon a time, Stef was her number-one fan. Now he looked like he was going to hit her with a brick.

And the worst was yet to come.

"Come on," she said, stepping out of the car. "Over there."

Stef got out and shut the door. "Am I supposed to have any idea what's going on?" he asked. "Or am I about to get Punk'd?"

Joy turned. "Look, I'm sorry," she said as she walked, welcoming the familiar feel of Abbot's Field under her feet. This was her place, her space to dare to go beyond her comfort zone, and if there was ever a time she really needed it, it was now. "I really need your help, and I agreed to meet up with someone in order to find some way of tracking whatever spell is on the Twixt."

Stef paused. "This isn't like last time, right?" he said. "Because I haven't quite recovered from watching a monster muskrat eat his own heart and you taking off through a tree."

"No," Joy said. "It's not like last time." She took out the satyr's glow stick and turned it in her fingers. She took a deep breath, smelling the grass and the dirt and the wind through the trees. "This guy just wanted to talk to you," she said. "That's all. Just talk."

Stef's eyes widened behind his rectangular lenses.

"What guy?" he asked.

She tried to act nonchalant as she snapped the glow stick and shook it. "Some satyr from the Carousel," she said.

Stef paled. "A *satyr*?"

There was something in his voice that pierced every wall, every protection she thought she might have managed to keep him safe, but by then it was too late.

A neon-colored globe of light lit up the grass, outlining individual blades and the fractal bark of trees. It expanded, enveloping both of them in a bubble, blurred at the edges, poking a neat hole in space. Joy could see Abbot's Field in the distance with its familiar fence posts and well-trodden grass, but her feet stood somewhere else—another field, another wood—thick and unfamiliar. It wasn't the meadow inside the Bailiwick or one of the conifer glades she'd been dragged through with Kestrel in pursuit of the Red Knight, but there was something about it that tugged at her memory. It was like she'd been here before.

Joy squeezed the plastic tube in her left hand and her scalpel in her right. She wasn't taking any more chances of something going wrong. And when she saw the DJ in the wild grass, she thought he looked familiar, too, but not because she'd seen him only yesterday—it was because the look on his face was exactly like Stef's.

Her brother spun around, arms hanging helpless and

loose like a question, like they didn't quite know where to belong. Joy forgot that he wasn't used to travel in the Twixt. That wasn't it—she knew that wasn't it—but she couldn't help trying to act like it was.

She stepped nearer to him. "Stef, this is—"

"Dmitri," Stef whispered.

Joy stopped. The satyr stared back, unblinking, his breath coming fast in his chest. Her brother put a hand over his mouth. The red bracelet on his wrist was knotted with iron beads, his last protection. "Oh my God, Dmitri," he spoke through his fingers. "Oh my God. Oh my God." He shook his head and leaned away until his foot shot back to keep his balance. He was rooted to the spot. "I can't—"

"Stef."

Stef froze as if the satyr's voice were a spell, his words of disbelief evaporating into nothing. Joy touched her brother's arm and kept her eyes on the DJ, who crossed and uncrossed his dark, curly arms, looking uncomfortable and shy.

"I've heard of you," Joy said. "When I was little—" she glanced at her brother "—you were one of his imaginary friends." Her voice got a little harder. "Not so imaginary, though, are you?"

Dmitri shook his head, a tiny waggle of his chin hairs. "No," he said quietly, not looking away from Stef. "This is real."

It looked as if Stef might speak, but the words were gone. His mouth trembled, frowning, opening and shutting with a million, billion unsaid things. It scared Joy to see Stefan like this. He was beyond upset—he looked trapped, terrified—and when his eyes began to shine with angry tears, she couldn't take it. She lifted her scalpel and pointed it at the satyr.

"Stop it!" she said at Dmitri. "Whatever you're doing, *stop it*!"

"I can't," Dmitri said, nervously bobbing on his strong goat legs. "And I won't."

"Yes, you will," Joy said. However the satyr might be twisting their deal, it ended now. "By rowan and ash and whatnot, you promised!"

"*You promised!*" Stef shouted. Joy spun around in surprise. Stef glared at Dmitri, nearly vibrating in anger. "You promised me that you would never, *ever* come looking for me again," he said. "By rowan, yew and ash and be by ironwood bound!"

Joy nodded. That was the phrase. But she had the feeling that they weren't talking about the same thing at all.

"I didn't come looking for you," Dmitri said softly. "I've always known where you were, where you'd gone, where you've been." He smoothed his cheeks down his jaw and curled his fingers around the end of his beard. "I just waited." He gestured vaguely at Joy. "I waited until you could come to me."

Stef turned on Joy, eyes blazing. She stumbled over a rock in the grass.

"*You* did this?" he hissed at her. "*Why?* Why would you do this?"

Her older brother had never asked her such a question; it was the sort of honesty that she'd wanted from him when their mother had left, realizing that he had known—or at least he'd suspected—about the affair and hadn't told her. All she knew was that, afterward, she'd been left out and left wondering *why*? That was how he sounded now, hurt and betrayed.

"I'm sorry," she said quickly. "I didn't know."

He quickly switched targets, stabbing two fingers at Dmitri, who stood unarmed and unarmored before the wizard's wrath.

"That summer," Stef said. "When it was over, they told me—" He stuttered and took a breath. "They told me that you were *sent*," he spat the word. "That you were sent there to lure me in, to bring me over."

Dmitri shook his head. "No."

Stef thundered. "Bait for the trap!"

"No."

"Those are the rules!"

"No!" Dmitri shouted. "It wasn't like that!"

The satyr's voice cracked like a branch in a canyon, echoes rebounding inside the bubble, ricocheting against her ears. Joy stared at the two of them. Stef towered in his rage. Dmitri was trembling, defiant. Joy wanted to pull a Winnie the Pooh blanket out of nowhere and hide. She felt five years old all over again with the grown-ups shouting, and she didn't understand; she was only scared and confused.

"Stef!" The satyr almost laughed. Almost. But he was too angry and too honest to care anymore. "Don't you get it? Didn't you hear? *They told me the same thing!*"

The words hung in the air and fell like dead birds, each one landing *smack* as they hit. The two men faced each other, the air between them crackling. Dmitri's tufted ears lay flat against his mop of brown curls.

"They told me the *same thing*," he said again slowly. "That you were going to trap me by my name and sell me to a zoo or to scientists or something equally horrifying. And even if you were innocent, they said that the adults were probably using you to tease me out of the forest and that they were ultimately after the Glen. The elders talked about humans ransoming me back or torturing me to find the graftlings. That they'd burn the First Forest down." His fingers shook, and the cords on his arms stood out in wiry tension. "Stef, they said *anything*—everything they could think of—to make me believe the worst, to believe them and not you. And I did." He wiped his hands on his shirt. "I did. And I'm sorry."

He shook his head, eyes full of apology and regret. "I kept my promise, *and* I waited because I needed you to hear it. I needed you to know. I needed you to know that I didn't—"

And his words snuffed out like a candlewick. Stef stood waiting for them, but there was only the plucked-string silence.

"You waited," Stef said, finally. "You waited for over a decade on the off chance you could trick my sister into setting up a meeting that I might never come to?"

Dmitri smiled as if he couldn't help it. "There was always a chance."

Stef stepped forward. Dmitri stepped back, surprised.

"What?" Stef said. "What is it?"

The DJ waved at Joy, who would have been just as happy to be forgotten completely at that moment. "I promised her I wouldn't threaten you or attack you or be within ten feet of you." He took a step to one side, pacing along the edge of his promise. The pact kept him back. "I promised that I wouldn't come near you. I wouldn't touch you..." His voice slowed as he looked at Stef, taking in the glyphed glasses and the red-iron bracelet and the inside-out/backward shirt—all the protections Stef wore to keep the Twixt at bay. "I promised that I would be alone—and I am," he said. "I am very alone." Dmitri's gaze crossed the distance like a physical touch. "And I promised that I wouldn't intend to do you harm." He crossed his arms protectively over his chest and bowed his chin. "Stef, I *never* intended to do you harm."

A great shuddering breath whistled through Stef's teeth. He stuck his hands deep in his pockets.

"Well," he said. "You did."

Dmitri nodded. "I know."

"A lot," Stef said.

"I know," Dmitri said. "I'm sorry."

Stef nodded, and something inside him shifted. Joy could see it melting his face, smoothing his posture, softening his eyes and changing his voice into something liquid, quick and rushing.

"Do you have any idea how long it took?" he said. "How long I hated myself for being duped? For being stupid? Hating the fact that I let myself be so easily used?" His voice gained heat. "I felt like an idiot for believing that anyone could—" his words skipped tracks "—let alone *believe* me—and not make me out to be some sort of *freak*." He kicked the dirt, his words growing softer. "Do you know how long I thought I'd been under some sort of spell and if I could just figure out how to break it, then I would be normal and not...*not*?" Stef pulled at his short sleeves as if he could cover his arms. "That's how I got into magic in the first place," he said. "That's how Vinh found me—trying to somehow bleed it out of my veins."

Joy felt a chill thread down her spine. Stef tugged on his bracelets and straightened, glaring intently at the young man from the Twixt. "I thought it was because you were one of them, an Other Than," he confessed. "I thought it was because I was human and you weren't and that you had manipulated me with magic and that if I was with someone human, I would feel different." Her brother stared at the satyr in rough blue jeans whose every look, every gesture wanted to deny it, his face crumbling, but he stayed silent, listening, although it clearly hurt. "But it never felt different, and I never felt the same." Stef took a deep breath and stressed every word. "It wasn't because you were Folk, Dmitri. It was because it was you."

Dmitri's arms dropped as he suddenly jerked backward and spun in place like he'd been struck. He coughed and slapped his legs helplessly, bending forward, half laughing, half crying, gasping as if the air had been punched from his lungs. He curled his stomach over his joined hands tucked in his gut and stamped the ground with one hoof.

"*O theé mou,*" he groaned. "I *hate* hasty promises!"

The oath worked, preventing him from taking even one step closer.

Stef shrugged shyly—there was nothing he could do.

"I release you," Joy said quickly, waving her hands from the sidelines. "I take it back. All bets are off!"

Dmitri laughed, staring imploringly at Stef. "Too bad it doesn't work like that," he said through a wide, silly grin. "Would that it did. But we agreed that for here, now, these are the rules. And the rules can't be broken." He fished out another glow stick with fumbling fingers tripping over themselves and held it out to Joy, eyes still on her brother. "But next time, things can be different," he said. "And this is for you, as promised." He handed her a short branch shaped like a Y, worn smooth with oil and age. He pressed it into her hand. "It's a dowsing rod. But instead of seeking water, it seeks *hana*—residual spell energy—straight to its source. You'll have to name the spell, but it can guide you from there." Joy nodded, her fingers slick on the wood. He looked at her then, brown eyes sparkling and fervent. "You will have to be the one to light the beacon again, but not for another twenty-four hours. Bring him back," Dmitri said quietly. "Bring him back to me. Please." He backed away from them, then, smiling, arms wide. Beaming, he pointed at Stef and laughed with a rolling, bouncing gait. "I can wait," he said like a promise. "I can wait."

He snapped his fingers over his head and the bubble popped.

They stood in Abbot's Field, the neon an afterimage on their eyes.

Stef stared around as if he couldn't quite believe it...or didn't want to believe it. His head turned slowly—wide-eyed, scanning, searching. Joy stayed very still as he took a shaky step toward the car. Then another. The crunch of stones grinding underfoot confirmed which reality was real.

Her brother opened the car door, watching his fingers lift the handle, and dropped heavily into the front seat. Joy hesitantly climbed into the passenger's side. They both clicked their safety belts and sat in the parking lot, staring out at the grass. There was a long moment of quiet.

Stef shifted gears and backed out of the lot. Flipping on the turn signal, he exited slowly onto the road. Joy tucked the glow stick and the scalpel into her purse. She squeezed her fists against the ball of suppressed sorry that she wanted to say, but couldn't quite find the words. She hadn't known. She hadn't realized. She felt Stef's every twitch like the edge of a ward, crackling.

They stopped at a red light. Joy looked at her brother. His hands hadn't moved from their death grip on the wheel, and his eyes didn't turn away from the road as he spoke.

"I don't know if I love you more or hate you more right now than I have in my entire life," he said. "Don't talk to me for a while, okay?"

Joy pressed her hands between her knees. "Okay."

"No," he said calmly, exasperated. "No talking. I mean it. Not one word."

Blinking back tears, Joy nodded. This was what happened when people weren't honest—when they kept things from one another, from the people they loved. They got hurt. She saw it in her brother's eyes. She'd heard it in Dmitri's voice. She should have told Stef right then how they were part of one another's worlds, that he was part-Twixt, too, but now she was too late. She wanted to respect his wishes and really didn't want to add another shock to what was already obviously tender and bruised. She didn't want to disrespect what he'd just heard, what he'd just said. She glanced at his wrist beneath his bracelet. There were old scars there. *I didn't know!*

She stared out the window, feeling invasive. Joy shouldn't have been there for that entire conversation, but because of their rules, she'd had to accompany him there, and she'd have to bring him back. Stef knew it, Dmitri knew it, and she was sure they all wished that she had chosen her conditions better. Some rules were *definitely* meant to be broken.

Joy pulled out her phone. There was another conversation that had to happen—if anything, this whole mess had convinced her that some secrets were too important to be kept between siblings.

Respecting Stef's silence, Joy typed a text to Luiz.
You there?

It was only a moment before she got an answer. Always for you. There was an ellipsis as he typed more. Antony called. Said you were on the warpath. Something about Raina?

She wiped moisture from her eyes. This wasn't about Raina. This was about secrets. She was sick of secrets. She typed with her thumbs. Tell Inq that "when" is now & I want to be there or I'm telling him first.

There was a slight pause before he answered. That sounds bad.

Joy typed back, Hopefully it gets better.

Stef parked the car and slammed the door behind him. He didn't look back as Joy exited her side and walked away from the condominium. The last thing she needed was to be locked inside a pressure cooker with her brother upset—she remembered the feeling all too well during the Year of Hell when everyone stewed in their own, private juices, the air fairly thick with loathing. She'd soaked up her dad's depression like a sponge and had made it her own. Whatever

Stef was feeling was too much for her right now. She took the sidewalk around the back and followed it east.

She typed a quick text to Monica as she walked.

I think I want a do-over starting from about midnight on.

Monica's reply came quickly. Rough morning?
Joy grimaced. It's going to be a loooooooong weekend.

Family vacay = CRAZY TIMES. *hugs* Call me later!

Joy shut off her phone and stopped on a park bench to write another sort of message. She dug a small pouch out of her purse and loosened the strings. Inside were tiny rolls of translucent paper, a mini pencil and a box of matches from Antoine's Café. Joy unrolled a piece of vellum that hadn't been there before. *Call Inq immediately*, it said. Joy remembered smelling burnt vellum back before Inq had appeared at the door. She'd never checked her messages or written back. Filly would be itching for news. Joy took out a fresh piece of paper and spread it out on the back of the matchbox. She wrote: *Got it. Thanks! Heard about my gala? GC is worried about SL's motives. Suspects there will be trouble.*

Her agreement to keep Filly informed as to the latest gossip was a tightrope walk over a pit of poisonous snakes on fire, but the young Valkyrie had been good to her word to be there for Joy in case of emergencies, and she'd also saved Joy's life more than once. If sending her a little bit of news kept Joy on her good side, it was a price she was willing to pay. Besides, the brash warrior woman had proven that she did not play into politics and respected Joy enough to try to keep her from being played. Neither Graus Claude nor Inq had told her that they had manipulated her by using her

True Name, forcing her to let go of her scalpel or Ink, and Ink himself hadn't a manipulative bone in his body. In fact, he didn't have bones.

But now he has a heart.

There was only one more match in the matchbox. She'd need to find more soon. Joy scraped the match to light and burned the vellum to ash. Filly would get the message in her matching pouch and would send a reply. It wasn't quite Verizon, but it worked.

Brushing the dust off her fingertips, she continued down the sidewalk, winding toward the C&P. She debated whether she could grab a Clif Bar without Hai or his father thinking she was there for some other reason, but then considered that she might actually have another reason. She hadn't actually *promised* Stef she wouldn't go. She removed the strange branch from her purse as she walked.

It looked new and felt old, like it was an antique that had been recently polished. The wood was faded, and the whorls looked almost like writing, the grain more like panels, the knots more like knobs. It reminded Joy of a wishbone, something superstitious that harnessed all the power of wishing. It felt strong in her hands, solid, sure. She held on to the handles and pointed the leg ahead of her, feeling nothing. She whispered the word "Glamour."

A quiver tickled her palms and buzzed up her arms. It swung to point at the C&P. *Figures*, she thought. *Wizard At Work.*

She let go with one hand and the feeling stopped. She could reset it with a word, but the glamour spell was the only one she knew by name. She stopped experimenting as she neared the convenience mart with its bright posters advertising cigarettes, lottery tickets or a Mega Gulp for only $1.99. Joy hid the Y-shaped stick back in her purse and caught a whiff of smoke. The tiny pouch coughed up a curl of gray. She tugged out the small piece of vellum that had appeared. It read *Promise?* She smirked at Filly's thirst for mayhem as she pushed her way into the convenience mart, passing through the door with its two-tone hello chime.

The C&P was empty save for Hai behind the counter flipping through a magazine, looking bored. He glanced up as she entered and nodded. "Good morning."

"Good morning," she said, checking the aisles. "Is Mr. Vinh available?"

"He's not here," Hai said. "Can I help you?"

"I don't know," Joy said. "I had a question for him."

"Animal, vegetable or mineral?"

"Um...neither," she said. "It's sort of Other."

"Ah," Hai said, understanding. "Have you asked your brother?"

Joy bit her tongue and grabbed a Carrot Cake bar, handing it over with a five-dollar bill. "We're not speaking right now," she said. "But he didn't know. I'm trying to find the name of a spell."

Hai counted her change. "What kind of spell?" he asked casually.

Joy hesitated. Hai was as close to the wizard as she could get; his father bragged that his son was the 3-D computer imaging genius behind the glamours that were his mainstay with members of the Twixt. She wasn't sure if Hai was an apprentice like Stef, but he knew the business.

"It's a type of blanket spell," she said. "One that would make everyone forget—and not just forget, but be unable to remember what had happened, no matter how much they're reminded about it afterward." Joy pocketed the change. "A Level Ten or better."

Hai frowned, drawing his every facial feature downward.

"You're not thinking of doing anything like that, are you?" he said. "That's seriously bad magic."

"No, no, no—not me!" Joy said, trying to make her innocence quite clear. "I think someone else has done something like it, and I want to figure out who."

He tapped his fingers on the counter. "You'll need a dowsing rod."

Joy lifted the stick out of her purse. "Like this?"

Hai's eyebrows shot up. "Yeah," he said. "Like that." He grabbed a notepad. "The only spell I know like that is called an Amanya. It's one of those spells that belong in the black zone." He tapped her purse with his pen. "You use that to pick up the spell resonance—every crafted spell has one, and it would have to have a looping signal that would refresh over distance to compensate for spell degradation over time." He drew a quick Y-shaped doodle on the page. "The rod can pick up the base code and follow the resonant emissions back to their origin point or person. It's like tracing the ripples back to the stone that hit the pond." The pen stilled and he glanced up. "You know that if someone went to all that trouble to be forgotten, they won't be eager to be found out."

"I know," she said. "But I think they got caught in the spell, too. I'm just planning on pointing it out and letting the Twixt have 'em."

Hai tapped his pen on the paper. "Harsh."

Joy said, "In this particular case, I'm not a big fan."

"You know the *tien* will rip them apart," Hai said, using his father's term for the Folk. "But if whoever cast the spell doesn't necessarily *know* they cast the spell, and no one else can remember, either, then how are you going to prove that it happened at all?"

Joy unwrapped her snack and took a bite. "I'm hoping that'll be someone else's problem."

Hai shook his head. "You have to be careful—blanket spells can easily cause a paradox, and in a paradox, the earlier spell wins. Spells are notoriously time- and variable-sensitive. Negate one condition, and the whole spell unravels—that's why memory spells are tricky and why we don't use them in our glamours." Hai leaned on the counter. "There's a better way to handle this, you know. All memory spells have a safeguard built into them, in case it hits the caster, too. Sounds like that's what happened. You can sever a spell at its origin, which releases the caster and, in this case, would restore that one person's memory. It won't lift a blanket spell, but you can prove what happened by forcing the one who cast the spell to remember that they did it, and, if they are *tien*, then they'd have to tell the truth. Even if the rest of the Council doesn't remember, they know that none of them can lie about a known truth." He rapped the pen against the pad again. "That is why memory spells have a safety attached— if you do not know what's true, then you can lie, which is a nasty violation of their laws."

"Breaking the rules," Joy said.

"Which are supposed to be inviolate," he said. "The *tien* like things black-and-white, all-or-nothing."

Joy tipped her head. "So how do you sever a memory spell at its source?"

"Now, that we can do," Hai said proudly. "My father can ensorcel something for you. He'll be back after lunch, but you're going to need to give him something with an edge that can cut."

"I have a scalpel," Joy said. She wasn't thrilled at the idea of having a spell placed on it even if she liked having a way to prove the traitor's guilt and get the Council to believe her as quickly as possible. She had no idea what would happen if she used the scalpel for something other than erasing marks, but remembered quite vividly the gaping, black wounds on Inq's body and Ink's throat as she sliced them closed, as well as the horrible moment when she'd erased the Red Knight. She didn't know if she could use it for severing a memory spell, but there were some things she wished that she could forget.

Hai shook his head. "Sorry, that won't work," he said. "It needs to be a ritual blade, bone or stone, preferably. Those work better than metal or glass, but no plastic or artificial composites—they'll melt under pressure." He tore off the note and handed it to her. "Fortunately, you can find anything on eBay."

Joy took the paper, mind whirling. "Thanks," she said. "But I think I got it. I'll be back a little later." She swiped her phone on as she backed out of the store, pushing her way out into the sunshine, warm on her back. The call connected after the very first ring.

"Feeling better?" Monica chirped.

"It's been a day," Joy said. "Listen, mind if I borrow your letter opener?"

Joy came home at five-fifteen with a large Fiji water and an ensorcelled bone blade. Monica had met her at Starbucks for iced coffees and a kind ear after she'd told her friend that Ink had left her bedroom with another girl's name on his lips. Monica had raged in sisterly sympathy and had handed over Aunt Meredith's gift with barely a raised eyebrow. Joy hadn't even bothered making up lame excuses and simply promised to give it back soon. It said a lot about their friendship. That was what best friends were for: a safe shoulder, a strong cup of coffee and random sharp, pointy objects.

Joy was taking a drink and fishing for her keys as she rounded the stairwell. Given her purse was full of magic, including a scalpel, a dowsing rod, a pouch full of vellum and an ox-bone letter opener, she shouldn't have been too surprised to find her boyfriend zipping through a hole in space outside her door, but it shocked her enough that she splashed bottled water down her front.

Her hips shot back and water dripped off her shirt onto the carpet. She swallowed enough air to choke, forcing funny, sneezing sounds through her nose. Ink looked apologetic and moved toward her.

"Joy," he said. "I am sorry."

She swallowed again, coughed twice more and shook excess moisture off her arm. "For this or for last night's disappearing act?" she asked.

Ink dropped his chin. "Raina said that I handled that poorly."

Joy glared at him. "*Raina* said that, huh?" She unlocked the front door and pushed it open with a shove. "Did she say anything else?"

Ink followed behind her, guileless and frank. "She said that I should apologize and not do it again," he said. "Leave you alone suddenly, that is, not get undressed in your room. She thought that showed promise."

Joy stopped and turned sharply, rendered temporarily mute. She gaped at him. He blinked innocently. Joy shook her head and dropped her things on the table.

"I seriously do not believe you," she said.

Ink frowned, confused. "You know I cannot lie."

"That's not what I meant!" Joy said and stopped, squeezing her eyes shut for a moment. When she opened them again, Ink was watching her, looking more and more bewildered.

"I should not have left," he said, hazarding a guess.

"No, you should not have left," Joy spat back. "But that isn't the point."

Ink cocked his head. "It isn't?"

Joy flung her hands up. "No, it *isn't!*" she shouted. "It's about *Raina!*"

"Raina?" Ink repeated. "What does Raina have to do with it?"

Joy put her hands on her hips. "You tell me!"

Ink's eyebrows moved, and his lips parted, trying on different expressions as he watched her pace the length of the kitchen. He slid his fingers along his wallet chain, jiggling the links between his fingers.

"I am uncertain what to say," Ink confessed. "You are upset and I wish I knew why so that I could help—" his voice faltered at the glare she gave him "—you stop looking at me like that."

Joy stopped and crossed her arms, steeling herself. "Just tell me this, so I know—so it's all out there, okay?" She licked her lips and steadied her breathing. "Are you sleeping with Raina?"

"What?" Ink said. "No."

It wasn't enough. Not knowing the slippery language of the Twixt. "I mean intercourse."

Ink stammered, thrown. "Inter—what?"

"Are you *having sex* with her?" Joy asked, point-blank.

There was a sudden silence. Then Ink smiled, one dimple. Joy could have hit him just for that, but he was all the way across the room. He shook his head very slightly, daring to look amused. "No."

"Are you—" she struggled to find another euphemism for not-quite-having-sex-but-doing-something-else "—*exploring* with Raina? Or anyone else, in any way...physical?" she said, trying to make her anger and worries and fears sound less stupid as she said them aloud, but she was quickly losing steam as he stepped closer, a second dimple appearing and his eyes growing deep. He stood within inches. Her head filled with the scent of rain.

"Well?" she said. "Are you?"

"No," he said softly. "The only *exploring* I wish to do is with you." His gaze lowered and lifted, both shy and delighted.

Joy felt her cheeks warm. She wobbled and backed against a chair. "Oh."

He smiled. "So," he said, head tilted just so. "While I would like to offer to make amends and convince you of my sincerity, Inq sent me with a request to bring you to the Bailiwick's office." His hand hovered, decidedly not-touching a curl of hair by her eye. She could almost feel him there. Almost. He looked at her with a smile still tugging his lips. "She said it was at your behest."

Joy tingled, her feelings flipping over. This was it! Inq would tell him everything and it would be out in the open. She'd have the dowsing rod, the name of the spell, and they could undo every bad thing that had happened, including her changing into some inhuman something-or-Other Than. She'd deal with this Raina thing later. Relief hit her like another cold shower.

Joy launched past Ink and grabbed her purse, tucking the curl behind her ear. "Yes," she said. "Right. I did. Let's go!"

Ink calmly stepped beside her as she bounced in place. She could hardly stand still. He didn't know it yet, but Joy had managed the impossible. Ink would finally know who he was, where he came from—he would even meet his mother!—and, together, they would set her and everyone else free.

Ink opened his hand to her, still smiling, still innocent, but growing bolder.

"Perhaps later?" he said.

Joy curled her hand into his.

"Perhaps."

Ink smiled, both dimples, and sliced them through space with a scent of limes.

NINE

JOY FELT BETTER STANDING OUTSIDE THE BROWN-stone, properly waiting to be let in. She bumped into the decorative bamboo as they waited for Kurt, excited and nervous, still reeling from her talk with Ink and the leftover angst about Raina. The secret was now bubbling inside her, giddy and impatient, ready to burst out.

The stone step reminded Joy of the damp stairway inside Graus Claude and the princess who was waiting for this reunion. Joy wondered how Inq was going to explain it to him. *Not my problem.* She gave Ink a quick kiss on the cheek.

"What was that for?" he said.

"For you," she said. "For luck."

Ink tucked his hand into his pocket. "What about the four-leaf clover?"

Joy smirked at him. "That's mine."

Kurt answered the door, and they filed inside.

The cream-colored foyer was empty. No one was waiting for an audience with the comptroller of the Twixt, so the three of them walked straight to the back office down the sconce-lit hall of antique oil portraits and gilded mirrors. Joy avoided looking at Kurt, but that was because he was avoiding looking at her and was better at it. She tried not to think too hard about the last time they'd been here together—that had been awkward, to say the least. She wondered how she was going to manage to look Graus Claude in the eye without thinking about what lay under his tongue.

And Kurt had had to do that every day.

She privately hoped that the Bailiwick would already be frozen, mouth open and eyes glassy, and Inq would be there, all brass and vinegar, waiting for them with a ready explanation, but Joy and Ink walked into the office to find Graus Claude grinning in his massive chair, a long velvet case spread across his desk.

"Splendid," he rumbled. "Do come in. I have something to show you."

Joy tried to catch Kurt's eye as he closed the door, but failed. She looked around the office, uncertain. She didn't see Inq anywhere.

Joy sat down on one of the chairs, and Ink took the one next to her, still smiling in anticipation. She was too distracted to keep up the pretense. Ink noticed. One dimple disappeared.

"Miss Malone," Graus Claude spoke, and her attention snapped to him. He smiled with sharks' teeth, his icy blue eyes alight. "These are for you." He slid the box toward her with great aplomb. Joy took it and slid her fingertips over the black velvet fuzz before opening it. Inside was an incredibly long string of pearls fastened with a sparkling clasp of yellow stones.

"They are stunning," Ink observed. He'd become adept at compliments while preparing for dinner with Joy's family. She dimly remembered that the word *stunning* was reserved for beautiful-things-for-women. They'd made a spreadsheet.

"Aren't they?" Graus Claude said, sounding pleased. "Well, go on, pick it up." Joy felt the smooth golden pearls slide over her fingers as she lifted the heavy necklace. "Each one is flawless, matched for color and luster, particularly fine specimens for our purposes, don't you agree?" The great toad puffed up his chest. "I pride myself on using only the best materials."

"I'm—" Joy shook her head, still trying to redirect her thoughts from Inq's absence to the fortune hanging heavy in her hands. "It's beautiful. You made this?"

"Indeed," he said, pushing to stand, two of his hands on the chair and two reaching out to thread the pearls between them. "I made it for you—for your gala affair," his voice purred in its deep-bellied bass. "Try it on."

Joy stood and bowed, feeling the necklace pass over her ponytail and drop cool and hard along the back of her neck. The pearls slid against her skin as she stood, almost instantly warming to the touch. The decorative pin let the pearls slide between the clasps, adjusting the length. Graus Claude snapped it delicately closed at her waist and lifted himself to his full height to admire the effect. His eyes glinted beneath his browridge.

"Let's try them out," he said. Joy touched the pearls, confused. The Bailiwick smiled wickedly. "If I were representing the *Hur Barruk*, how would you greet me?"

Joy's head filled with a cool, white fog, a whisper without words. "I'd stomp my right foot and hold my palms out flat," she said while demonstrating. The answer had appeared in her mind without warning. The great toad smiled, wide and flinty.

"Very good," he said. "And if one of the Hollow asks for your hand?"

Joy felt the pearls' wisdom. "I would say, 'Only if you lend me your breath.'" She glanced at Ink, who raised his eyebrows.

"Excellent." Graus Claude beamed. "I imagine that will help smooth things along nicely." He chuckled, a distant thunder in his chest. "I have imbued each pearl with a bit of knowledge. Strung together, they should provide an adequate conduit of information that can be transmitted by the *eelet* into your inner ear via bone conduction." He tapped one of his claws against the necklace and gave a self-congratulatory chuckle. "Pearls are a particular specialty of mine." He gently tugged the strand into place. "Unfortunately, I could not knot them properly, else it would interrupt the necessary conduit. Also, know that this can only advise you with introductions and not prolonged interactions, so it would be best if you kept your conversations brief. It is a temporary solution, at best, but one which could well save your skin." He pursed his lips, pinching them with one hand as the other three sat on his hips. "Your dress is another matter worth consideration. Gold is traditional. White is passé. Would you prefer a more modern design or a formal ball gown?" He scratched his olive brow. "While Sol Leander dismissed a masque for the evening, it might behoove you to have a thematic ensemble, as is tradition. I would think the more commonly accepted customs we invoke in our favor, the better."

Joy was still toying with the length of pearls in her hand, a fortune in semiprecious cheat sheets. "I have no idea," she said. "But I trust your sense of style."

"You flatter me, Miss Malone," he said. "Do you have any opinion regarding your attire? I am not familiar with current social dance fashions."

Joy shrugged. "I went to the Girl Scouts' Daddy-Daughter Dance when I was nine," she said. "Otherwise, I wear club gear."

Graus Claude paused. "You do not know how to dance?"

"I know how to dance!" Joy said defensively.

"The waltz? The contra? The pavane?"

Joy frowned. "I've *heard* of a waltz."

Graus Claude rolled his eyes heavenward. "By the Swells..." he sighed. "Perhaps a second strand is in order."

"And I?" Ink spoke up.

"You?" Graus Claude said, surprised. "What about you?"

"I should learn, as well," Ink said. "I will be her escort, after all."

The Bailiwick clapped his hands together in sets of twos. "Ah. Indeed. Another knot in the noose," he said. "No matter. Cuff links will suit admirably." One finger per hand pointed to each of them. "Black," he said at Ink. "Gold," he said at Joy. "Transformation, metamorphosis—damselfly, I should think. Hunter, sharp-edged—heron," he declared finally. Joy and Ink exchanged glances.

"Don't herons eat frogs?" Joy asked.

"Don't be impertinent," Graus Claude warned. "I will not be the one on the hunt, nor, I wager, will I be the prey. Not directly, in any case. In any event, you may leave the details in my capable hands—" he gestured magnanimously "—or, more specifically, my tailor's."

Joy kept her grin. "I hear you have an excellent tailor."

Graus Claude's browridge quirked. Ink blushed. Joy was surprised that it was a true blush, a shade of delicate pink. *How did he do that?*

"I do," the Bailiwick said firmly. "She is without peer."

Ink smoothed his hands down the front of his shirt and stood up. Joy removed the pearls and slid them into the velvet box, still waiting for Inq to appear. She arranged the strands into straight lines, stalling for time.

"Thank you, Bailiwick, for your generosity and attention to detail," Ink said. "We are both very grateful."

"Well, it is not the least I can do, but it is a pittance compared to maintaining appearances and my charge's good graces." He inclined his great head to her. "It will be my honor and privilege to welcome you both properly into our society and disappoint those colleagues who might underestimate us," he said. "Would that I could spare you from it longer, but a deservedly smug victory will have to suffice." The gargantuan amphibian looked positively delighted at the prospect. Joy was getting more nervous, her insides fluttering like the proposed damselflies. *Where is she?*

"Now," Graus Claude said, taking his seat once again, "if there is nothing else, I will bid you good day."

Ink moved to go, but Joy hesitated, still waiting for some sign of Inq. She glanced at Kurt opening the doors. He looked at her knowingly, daring her to...what? Put the pieces together? Ink said that Inq had asked him to bring her, but Inq wasn't here. They were alone with Graus Claude. No, the *Bailiwick*.

Joy stiffened.

Oh, no. She wouldn't... Joy thought. *She wouldn't dare!*

But Joy knew that Inq certainly would.

She'd typed it herself, that stupid ultimatum: *Tell Inq that "when" is now & I want to be there or I'm telling him first.*

Checkmate.

Joy spun around quickly, her voice cracking in panic. "I demand entrance to the Bailiwick!"

Graus Claude slowed, solidifying in place, his eyes misting over as his mouth opened wider, his tongue curling back upon itself and revealing the set of stone steps going down. Ink stared at the transformation with something like terror, one of his razors already in hand.

Joy came from around the desk, her footsteps unnaturally loud on the floor.

"It's okay," she said, taking Ink's hand. "I want to show you something."

* * *

Ink stepped into the grove, wide-eyed and alert. Joy trailed behind him, feeling a familiar mix of nervousness, excitement and dread. She wanted to tell him to put away his straight razor, but didn't—he'd find out soon enough that there was no reason to fear. Still, the butterflies in her stomach had turned into bees.

He stepped into the stillness of the unnatural forest, his eyes skipping over the bubbling brook, the knotted trees and the waving meadow grasses. Joy watched him puzzling out the details, trying to make them fit. She tried to be patient and not so nervous, but the place prickled her skin.

"What is this?" he breathed.

"It *is* the Bailiwick," Joy said. "A pocket universe inside of the Twixt." She moved to touch him but hesitated; his every move was as tense as a spooked cat.

"Why?" he asked.

"To keep secrets safe," a voice lilted from somewhere in the meadow. Both Joy and Ink turned, searching for the source. Ink's hand lowered, the blade drooping, all but forgotten.

"Joy," he whispered in his crisp, clean voice with something like a warning. "Who else is in here?"

She hesitated, still unsure of what to say—how to tell him. "Inq should be the one..."

He turned on her, eyes wide. "Wait," Ink said. "Wait—I know this place," he whispered. Suddenly, he spun around shouting, *"Inq!"*

"Ink?"

Joy hadn't said it.

The tall, elegant woman stood between the shadows of the trees, leaf patterns playing over her skin, merging with the indigo glyphs like watercolor paint. She smiled at him, both dimples. Joy wondered what he must be thinking, but she saw only his body in stillness, like a long-held breath.

The princess also seemed at a loss, her lips shaping themselves for words, but no sound came out. A smile painted her lips, and her eyes shone bright.

"I am so happy to see you," she said, "after all this time apart."

Ink said nothing.

She tipped her head to the side, just like Inq. Joy twisted her fingers.

"The last time," she said slowly, each word bringing her another step forward, out of the wood, "you were injured. Do you remember?"

Ink's face turned in sharp profile, his eyes following her as she circled closer like a shy doe.

"Inq brought you to me," she added softly. "She told me what had happened. I was very proud of you—of what you did." She shifted, and her curtain of hair fell into her face. Joy thought if she'd been like Inq, the dark marks would be flying over her skin. As it was, her voice was both tentative and strong. "I know that must sound strange, but it's true." She cupped her hands together, fingertips only just touching; it was the most peaceful gesture Joy had ever seen. "Do you remember what I said when you woke?"

Ink moved, only a very little, the tips of his hair shaking *no*.

The princess smiled. "I think you do," she whispered.

Joy bit the inside of her cheek. Ink could not lie.

The princess stood before Ink, smiling down on him; he was considerably shorter than her—but the resemblance was unmistakable. Joy knew that that had been on purpose. Inq had given him a hint, even if he didn't know it. They looked like her.

Ink sized her up with his fathomless eyes, searching for

something in her face. She matched him stare for stare, but hers was softer, like her voice as she spoke.

"I said, 'Look how they tried to break you—'"

"'—but you proved yourself stronger,'" Ink said, completing the sentence, almost without meaning to. Joy's breath hitched at the sound of his voice, like mist fogging the crisp, clean rain.

The princess nodded, a slow dip of her button chin. "And then I called you by your name and you woke."

A shiver passed over his body. It raised goose bumps on Joy's skin.

"That was my *name*?" he whispered. It carried a weight of heartache and years.

"Of course," the princess said through her smile. "A mother knows the name of her son."

It was as if her words struck him physically—he veered back, stung or stunned. Joy watched the flash-flurry of emotions, from awe to loss, hope to rage, and disbelief to something frightened and frightening. The princess endured it all without resistance. She waited. Joy waited. A breeze tousled the leaves and ignored them entirely.

"You—" he said and stopped. "You are...?"

"I am the last," she said quietly, although her voice carried some of the timbre of Ink's and Inq's that pierced through all other sounds. "And you were the second to be made by my hands. But, yes, you are and I am and here we are, together, as it was when I first held you like a dream brought to life. Do you remember that day?" The princess spoke gently, but with the strength of conviction. "You opened your eyes and looked at your sister and smiled."

Joy heard the tiniest crunch of grass and a smooth, mellow *shunk* as the razor sank point-first into the earth.

Ink collapsed to his knees.

The princess knelt in the ground and held him, petting his hair as he began half-sob-laughing. Joy pressed her hands to her lips, pushing her smile against her teeth. This was the moment she'd been waiting for—the one that he'd never known and had wanted all of his life. It ached beautifully.

It made Joy want to call her mother, but she doubted she'd get good reception down here.

Ink touched the princess's shoulders, holding them at arm's length. "Tell me," he said. "Tell me everything."

And she did.

Joy hid in the dappled shadows trying not to overhear the long, detailed history of what had happened to the princess and why she was here. Words like *King* and *Queen* and *traitor* and *coup* as well as *hidden door* floated over the make-believe brook. Joy rubbed her arms and tried to remain inconspicuous as she grew more uncomfortable the longer they stayed.

She squinted out over the meadow and into the wood. Where was Inq? Was she going to come down anytime soon? Was she afraid? Contrite? Pissed? Ashamed? Joy was all too familiar with Inq's protective wrath and wasn't eager to experience it again. From the shadows, Joy watched Ink listen to his mother's voice with an intensity she could all but feel on her skin. She remembered what it felt like to be under his scrutiny, to be so completely the object of his attention, for him to be totally absorbed. He looked as if he was storing up every word, every second of the time spent discovering this person, learning where he came from, who he was, where he belonged in the world.

"And that is why you are here? Trapped inside the Bailiwick?"

There was something in Ink's voice that caught Joy's attention.

"I came here for my safety," she said. "But I remained here to safeguard our hope for Return." She sat up a little straighter, the runes on her neck black as ink. "Your sister and I fashioned you both in our family image in the slight hope that someone might recognize you and remember... but even our closest allies could no longer recall their King and Queen and there was no hope of convincing them otherwise."

Ink considered this as he replaced each of his instruments into his trifold wallet and tucked it back into his pocket, sliding the chain through his first two fingers. "So either the Council must locate and open a door that they cannot remember, or the door will open when all the Council members are dead?" he said. "And then you will be free?"

The princess closed a hand over his. He stared at her hand, at her fingers, the same way he'd once watched Joy's hand take his—curiously and academically interested.

"I will be free when our people are reunited," she said. "When they can return to our world and I can greet my mother and father and introduce them to you and Inq. When all families will be whole once again." For the first time in what felt like hours, the princess looked directly at Joy. She felt pinned, caught under glass. The woman smiled. "We have a plan."

Ink looked at Joy.

"A plan?" he said. He didn't sound happy. "You have a plan?"

"It was Inq's plan," Joy said, rubbing her palms against her capris. "Remember Enrique's funeral? She said she needed a favor. She thinks I can find the traitor."

"And kill him," Ink said, his eyes flat as chits. "She wants you to kill a member of the Twixt."

It was more a statement than a question, and it put her

in dangerous territory—she could not deny it, and yet she wanted to refute it. The *way* he said it squashed any inclination she had of telling him about what had happened to the Red Knight. She'd already done much more than just kill someone in the Twixt.

"I said I wouldn't do it," Joy said.

Ink hardened—his skin, his muscles, the planes of his face, the tone of his voice. It was a frightening, instantaneous transformation. Joy shrank back.

"Good," Ink said and stood up. "You should not be the one to do it. And since we do not know who the traitor is, our priority is to open the door." He touched the wallet in his back pocket. "By any means."

"No—" Joy started, but he pushed past her, walking quickly and resolutely up the stairs. "Ink?" Joy said helplessly and glanced at the princess, who stood up slowly, solemnly. Her gaze locked with Joy's.

"Stop him."

Joy needed no other prompting and launched up the steps.

"Ink!" she screamed, not caring that her voice bounced back in the dark. She couldn't see him up ahead. She gasped for breath. "Ink!"

She exploded into the moist doorway of Graus Claude's open mouth ringed in teeth, blinking to clear her eyes just in time to see Ink stalk past Kurt and Inq by the door.

"I'd start with Maia," Inq called helpfully after her brother. He ignored her as he unsnapped his straight razor with a flick of his wrist.

"Ink! Stop!" Joy cried, tripping over the line of ruby-red fire. She stumbled out onto the carpet and fell to her knees.

But he didn't stop. Ink swiped a line in the air and strode through, leaving her behind without a second thought.

Joy blinked at the space that was no longer there. The moment held its breath. The stone fountains gurgled. Graus Claude squatted, eyes milky, mouth wide. The fibers in the carpet scratched Joy's skin. She felt tender and raw. Tears wet her face.

"Delicious," Inq preened with barely contained glee.

Joy pushed herself up. "Bring him back," she said.

Inq shrugged. "I can't."

"Then take me to him."

Inq clasped her hands primly. "No."

"He's off to kill everyone on the Council!" Joy said. "Do you know what that will *do* to him?!"

Inq's eyes glinted like gems. "Nothing I haven't endured," she said. "I'll say one thing for my brother, he gets straight to the point."

Joy stared at her. *She'd meant to have this happen all along!* Joy shook her head. This was wasting time! She grabbed her purse and Filly's pouch, but the matchbox was empty. The office was full of watery things, not a bit of fire in sight. She blinked around helplessly, taking stock. Inq was unwilling. Kurt was stoic. Enrique's car was back in Glendale. She was stuck. She *had* to get Ink. She had to stop him. *Now.*

"We all have to grow up sometime," Inq cooed. "Just remember, Joy, you started this."

"And I'm going to stop it," Joy shot back as she scrambled behind the desk and started opening drawers. Kurt moved swiftly to stop her, but she grabbed the top drawer and saw a glint of glass. She snatched up the familiar stained-glass box and fumbled with the latch, upending the pouch on the desktop and grabbing the chalky dice. The knucklebones felt soft in her sweaty palm. Kurt grabbed her wrist. She glared at him. She didn't know what else to do.

"Help me," she said. "Please."

The butler hesitated, then his mask came down, his not-so-human persona comfortable with being and doing uncomfortable things in the name of the Twixt. His hand squeezed her wrist. Joy winced and dropped the knucklebones. They hit the desk and rolled over once, inert. Inq smirked.

"She made me promise not to try," Inq said. "But she never asked him."

Kurt snorted in disgust and grabbed a piece of paper from the printer. He took a familiar-looking silver pen out of his jacket pocket and pressed it into Joy's hand. Her fingers curled around it—it was expensive and heavy. Inq took a step toward him, but Kurt gave the cap a twist and a concealed well appeared, filling with viscous black fluid shot through with neon light.

"Write and he will hear you," he said.

Joy took the pen and wrote the word *Stop* and then quickly added *Please*. Inq squinted at the words as if she were fighting a headache. Kurt touched the paper, eyes on his lover.

"It is written in blood," he said. "Their blood. That way, they can hear you inside their head...even without voice." He straightened and glanced at Joy, ignoring the Bailiwick yawning behind him. "Tell him that this is not the way." She dutifully scribbled those exact words, accidentally smearing the *w* with the side of her hand. She gave the pen back to Kurt and rubbed at the oily stain, feeling jittery and sick. He scooped up the old bones and pushed them into her palm.

"Stand there," he said, gesturing to the carpet. Joy moved aside as he typed a password into the computer.

Inq cocked her head as she approached the mahogany desk, arms crossed. "You told me you didn't know his password."

Kurt was busy typing in coordinates, his focus on the keys. "Sometimes you forget—I am human," he said in his gentle tenor. "I can lie." He clicked the mouse and nodded to Joy. "Now."

She tossed the yellowed bone dice on the floor, where they tumbled and rolled to a halt. Kurt clicked the mouse, and a laser level to the floor shot out, striking and rebounding off each of the knucklebones, creating a fractal pattern that hovered over the carpet. Joy stared at the Spirograph pattern as it grew more solid, more intense.

"Go quickly. You can catch him," Kurt said. "I will take care of the Bailiwick."

Joy nodded as she stepped into the light that seared her eyeballs and stung her nose. She opened her mouth to say something, but all the breath funneled out of her as she was yanked downward/outward/forward and forcibly spat out into a wall.

She bounced off a gleaming slab of birds' eye maple and laid a hand against it to steady herself, dimly realizing that it was warm to the touch. It was shaped like a door but had no handle or knob or keyhole—it was a single bumpy sheet of golden, polished wood. The light was dim and she felt moist, underground. Joy tried to figure out where she was while slowly coming to terms with her feet holding her up. Ink rounded a corner and stopped dead in front of her, his eyes burning hot as coals.

He stared at her warily, trying to pierce an illusion that wasn't there.

"Ink," she said, her voice scratchy. "Please, stop."

He moved slowly toward her, accepting the possibility that she could be real.

"Joy?" he said. She nodded. His grip fanned along the razor's handle. He touched a finger to his temple. "I heard you—"

"Yes," she said quietly. "Thanks to Kurt."

Ink's jaw tightened. "I hate that pen," he muttered. He tested the blade's weight in his hand. He focused on the door behind her. "You should not be here for this. You should go. Now."

"I can't," Joy said. "It was a one-way trip."

"To catch me," he said flatly. "To stop me."

Joy took a step forward, "Ink, please."

"Move."

The word was like a fist. Joy stumbled, realizing that she was physically barring his way. She was literally the last thing standing between him and his intended victim, the first Council member whose death could both free the princess and undo him completely, demolishing everything he believed in—the same thing he'd loathe in her if he knew the truth: that she hadn't merely killed the Red Knight, but obliterated him completely. It went against everything Ink was made to do, what he stood for, what he believed. *Murdering one of the Twixt.*

She licked her lips. "I can't let you do that."

"Move," he said, deadly calm. "Now."

Her fingernails bit into her fists. She stared at Ink, hot-pink fire roiling in his eyes. She had a horrible flash-thought of her scalpel—his scalpel—but couldn't imagine ever raising it against him. She would never, ever hurt him, and she knew he could never hurt her—but to be this close, blades drawn, seething, made a small part of her doubt. The rest of her stood her ground.

He was beautiful, terrible, his breath coming in heaves—she could see his heartbeat pulse in his throat—and somehow she stayed, feet planted as if she could hold him back with her bare hands.

"Ink," she said. "Please, stop. Listen to me."

He roared, *"No!"*

Ink swept his razor, and Joy flinched, but it wasn't aimed at her—or anywhere near her—and it tore a hole in the air near the doorway, gaping like a mouth in surprise. But there was only half a line; the slash that should have continued to pierce the golden doorway disappeared, repelling Ink's magic to slice through time and space. With a snarl, Ink attacked the walls in a mad fury, slicing the air into ribbons that gaped and bled scenes of several faraway places, but wherever the gouges scored the wood, they were neatly absorbed without so much as a peek into another place. Joy watched him throw himself into his furor, arms bulging, hands sweeping to slice again and again, his hair whipping across his eyes, the silver chain slapping against his leg. His breathing became desperate, the world around him shredded and torn. Ink finally flung himself at it blindly, but reeled back, deflected like the blade itself. He twisted in a miserable, tight-fisted rage.

"They *wasted* her," he cried, his eyes hot and furious. "She has wasted her life alone in a cell, choosing to remain behind to help the Twixt, and for what? For *them*?" He kicked the door. Joy was surprised it didn't break. His fingers spun the handle of his razor, shining bright and wild in the placid, golden light. "They threw her into the Bailiwick and they *forgot* about her! Such gratitude! Such *sacrifice*!" Indignity trembled in his throat and down his arms, shuddering in his chest. "They torture her still by forgetting *everything*! Betrayal hangs over her head *to this day*!" he seethed. "Traitors walk freely among the Council while she hides down in a hole!" He stamped his heel and slashed at the air, tearing another space into jagged ribbons, holes leaking moonlight and starlight and sand, windows to anywhere, so many lost places. His hands became fists. "It's not *fair*!" he shouted.

Joy edged closer, calm trembling in the air.

"That's not why you're angry," she said.

INSIDIOUS 173

"No," he said, watching the wounds in the world slowly zip themselves closed. "That is not why I am angry," he agreed. His eyes squeezed shut, curtained by the tips of his hair. "I am angry because Inq never told me about her, about where we came from—*who* we came from—and I never knew." His breathing was deep and lionlike. It rattled something primal and pained in her veins. "I am angry because my mother, my creator, never revealed herself to me, that I was not worth the risk. I was not given the honor—the *courtesy*—of the truth." Ink's handsome face slid into a petulant sneer. "And I am angry because you, whom I have known for a heartbeat, got to know her before me."

He swung a hand dismissively, shining and bright. "I *feel* now. To be more human, to love such as you, I learned to *feel*." His eyes narrowed, his tone bitter. Two fingers rubbed the spot over his heart. "This is jealousy, I think, and I know it now because of you. This is why you asked about Raina." He almost smiled, one dimple. Almost. But it looked like a cruel slash, like a scar. "How did that feel?"

Joy swallowed. She'd thought he'd be happy—happy with her; she hadn't considered how this might make him feel like he was the last to know. *That* was something Joy understood all too well, and had never meant to share with him. *Doubt. Jealousy. Pain. Betrayal.*

"I'm sorry," she said. "It hurts to be the last one in on the secret. It feels like everyone in the world knew the truth but you, and no one cared enough to tell you."

"It is worse than that, Joy," Ink said. He spun the blade in an idle gesture. "I was the last to know of those who *can* know. And no one else can possibly know of her while the door remains closed." He gripped the sharp instrument as if it underlined his words. "And I mean to change that. By any means."

Joy shook her head. "You don't mean that."

"Oh, but I do," Ink said. "I remember this feeling." His voice grew softer, salted with loathing but with less regret. He was a hand's breadth from her, and energy poured off him, malevolent and reckoning. "I have been patient—patiently waiting even before I knew that this was what I was waiting for." He seemed to tower over her, his righteous rage making him seem larger. "It was for *this*. For her. For the truth. *This*. After hundreds of years, I have found my place, my impossible answer, and it is trapped, hidden and cannot be forgotten—at least not by me. Because now I *know*." He punched his own chest with the meat of his fist. Joy jumped back. "I *feel* now. You gave me this—this heart, this need, this love—and now it is *mine*! And I will destroy anything and everything that threatens those I love." He pointed an accusatory finger at her. "What I would do for you, I would do a thousand times over for her." His voice simmered to something curious and cruel. "Does that bother you?"

Joy faltered. He sounded like a monster, inhuman.

He sounded Other Than.

"Yes!" Joy said hotly. "I mean, no—not like that. I'm not jealous that you love your mother or that you would do anything to save her." She tried to soften her voice with real effort. Ink was frightening her, and she felt they were walking on a very thin line with a very long way to fall. "I know what it means to have a mother who isn't there. I know what it means to you to protect the people you love, *and* I also know how important it is for you to protect the Folk from harm."

"I do not love them," he said dismissively. "They have used me and Inq, as if we are tools to be made or unmade at a whim. They threaten us with nonexistence when all the while our lives were never theirs to take—they were not the ones who created us, and we have the right to our own lives."

He swept his hand angrily. "All this while the Bailiwick had me believe that the Council had commissioned us, drawn us from the Twixt itself—but now I wonder if that was their forgetting or if it was a merely another ruse that they had intended all along." He looked disgusted. "The phrasing is not wholly a lie, but it is far-flung from the truth." Ink raised his straight razor. "However, I can show everyone the truth."

"So can I," Joy said and took out the dowsing rod. She held it up in both hands so that Ink could see it. "We can use this to track the spell back to the one who cast it." She saw her words momentarily pierce through his anger; the shocked look in his eyes made her bold. "We can find whoever did this and sever the spell at its source. We'll make them confess to the Council. Let them exact justice. Then they can find the door and open it, and this will all be over." She shook the rod for emphasis. "All you have to do is *don't do this*."

Joy's voice broke. She was having trouble breathing, he was so close. She licked her lips and fought the urge to run away or hug him. She still remembered the sting of alchemical fire on her skin—it felt like this, like she was losing him, watching him get hurt, watching him fall, collapsing on the warehouse floor.

"Ink, I love you," she said quietly. "Don't let me lose you."

He paused. His wild eyes looked afraid.

"We can do this," she pleaded. "We can save everyone."

His gaze flicked from her to the doorway and back to her. Seconds ticked by like the pulse in his throat.

"If we do things...your way," he said, the words grinding against stone. "If we follow the rules. The *Council's* rules."

"Yes," Joy said. "For now."

She dared to reach out and touch him, a soft hand over his heart. It startled her to feel it beating, a caged bird fighting flight, like a real living thing thrashing under his chest.

Thump-thump-Thump-thump-Thump-thump! Her eyes lifted to his.

Ink sighed as if all the breath were leaving him at once. His arms slackened. His face softened. He leaned forward into her palm. She bent a little at the elbow, bringing him closer. They slid together like puzzle pieces, familiar and worn and tired and glad. They held one another and said nothing for a while.

"I love you, Joy," he said, sounding serious, resigned and resolute. "Only you could ask me to do this. And I will do this." He pulled back gently and spoke in his crisp, clear whisper. "For now."

Joy felt the door swing open behind her. A cool breeze slapped her back.

"Well," a voice said. "After such a pretty speech, ye migh' as well come in."

TEN

JOY AND INK WALKED THROUGH THE GOLDEN THRESH-old into a wide room with a bowl-shaped ceiling and mossy, comfortable-looking chairs. Joy wasn't certain how much their hostess had overheard, but Ink had tucked his blade into his wallet, and so the threat of impending assassination had been delayed for a while at least.

The room was spacious and circular with pendulum lights and squashy cushions. Everything was rounded and hand-carved; every edge of a shelf, every table surface, every stick of furniture was patterned and whorled with designs. Joy felt as if she'd walked into a Hobbit hole in New Zealand.

"I've been wonderin' when I might be seeing you," the squat woman said as she waddled across the floor. Her soft, doughy face crinkled in a grandmotherly grin, and her long, dark hair trailed behind her like a cape. "And with yer handsome escort? Wise beyond your years, child—ye'll live longer that way." She gave a wink and patted the arm of one of the low, scooped chairs with elaborate claw feet. "I'm called Maia. 'Ave a seat."

Joy did and found herself smiling. The room had many modern-looking shapes scooped out of natural materials, low tables and high shelves full of statues, beautiful lockboxes and vases of fluted flowers. The esteemed Council member had a string of bright purple blooms tucked into her hair that made her look like an island native who had rarely seen the sun. She wore a simple brown dress trimmed in colorful beads. Her pudgy feet were bare, her hands chubby as a baby's.

"Tea?" she offered. "Or somethin' stronger?" She chortled as she waddled closer to one wall. "If'n ye came straight from the Bailiwick, ye may be wantin' something to wash it all down."

"How did you know...?" Joy began, but stopped; first, because it might be considered rude, and second, because the squat woman had reached up for a bellpull that was at least two feet above her head and had smoothly morphed like taffy into a taller, stretched-up version of herself, given the rope a quick tug and then puddled down into her normal, squat bubble-shape. Her dark eyes twinkled in mischievous glee.

"Ye smell of water weeds an' shoe polish and somethin' I can't quite remember," she said with a shrug. "Who else?"

Smiling, Joy settled into one of the chair cushions, soft and squishy and cool.

"We have been to the Bailiwick," Ink said from behind Joy's chair, evidently taking the role as her formal escort seriously. "He was assessing Joy's wardrobe for the gala and reviewing their lessons." Joy nodded. All of it was accurate, if not wholly the truth.

"Pssht," Maia muttered. "Stolen civilities from an Imperialist era. I suspect the Water Folk of baiting the lure." She tapped a row of orb-shaped planters on a high shelf; each emitted a different, mellow note up the scale. When she reached the end of the weird xylophone, her entire body flattened and oozed to the left, plinking the last, tiny bowl with her littlest finger. *Ting!* "Proper ceremony should echo earth, rock, rain an' fire." She nodded into her puffy double chin. "Even Inq's *lehman* knew that—ashes strewn proper.

Another ex-*lehman* as well, I s'ppose." She nodded at Joy and cackled at her own wit. "We all escape our bonds eventually. Jus' takes time."

A small trolley came in through a side door, pushed by a furry animal wearing a ruffled apron. Its eyes were bright as it nudged the wheeled tray forward and then dropped on all fours while Maia stroked its back. She plucked one of the flowers out of her hair and fed it to her pet. It munched happily, a soft purr burbling in its belly fuzz.

"Off ye go now," she said gently. Maia grinned at Joy. "Tea, then?"

"Please," Joy said, remembering her manners as the small mammal shuffled off behind the door.

"A simple blend, then, but one o' my favorites," Maia said, sprinkling pinches of dried things into a clay bowl. "Hibiscus, chicory, rose hips, vanilla." Maia proudly recited ingredients as she added them together, rapped a mortar to grind it and poured steaming water over the lot. "Let it steep," she said as she offered the cup to Joy. "The bitterness will sweeten, given time."

Joy blew over the surface of the water, watching the flakes of flowers dance. She could feel Ink's eyes behind her. If this was the mastermind behind her discredit at the gala, Joy was having trouble believing it, but respected Graus Claude enough to keep the possibility alive and wary.

"Are we still talking about the tea?" Joy asked.

Maia smiled while stirring. "As well as other things."

The mushroom woman mixed herself a cup and did not offer one to Ink. Joy wondered if she knew that Ink had no need to eat or drink or if there was some other casual bigotry. She didn't ask; it felt rude. The smell of flowers and vanilla did little to soothe her suspicions.

"Thank you for this, Councilex Maia," Joy said and held up the cup.

"Just Maia while at home," she said. "It's nice to feel welcome. And why not?" she said, taking the first sip. "Yer one o' the Folk, there's not a doubt—no matter what yap-waggling there might be—and yer mine, in a way, so I feel obliged to let ye be welcome here."

The cup stopped at the edge of Joy's lips. "Yours?" she said.

"Well, yea, certainly," Maia said with a lick of surprise. "Yer Earth-born. Did no one tell you?"

"No," Joy said, sipping the tea. It was bitter on the surface, but also floral and earthy-sweet. She could taste how the flavor would ripen near the bottom of the cup. "No one came forward to claim me, but it's been generations, so I figured they might have forgotten."

"Pah. No one *forgets* somethin' like that," Maia said from her little nest of pillows. Her body had pooled to fill the crevasses, and her mug sat on her belly, jiggling when she spoke. Joy might have imagined Ink twitching at the mention of things too important to forget. "Even under the stink o' mortality I can scent the salt of the earth on you—fair taste it in the air you breathe. 'Course, it could be whatever thing's stuck in yer ear." She sniffed and nodded her flowered head over her tea. "Oh ho ho, yes. Earth Folk, not a doubt. I thought that's why you came by." Maia took another long sip, the heat raising color to her doughy cheeks and the tip of her nose. Or perhaps her drink was a bit stronger than Joy's. Maia smacked her lips and set down her mug. "The role of Earth is that of life, which is a cycle of growth, persistence an' rebirth. But there are lots of types of Earth Folk, so I can't advise ye on ought else save to wait fer it, and the truth will win out 'fore long."

Joy thought back to Graus Claude's comment about wing

nubs and squashed her shoulders against the seat back, all too aware of Ink standing there. She felt obliged to keep talking to prevent him from doing anything else.

"Well, I doubt I'll learn anything more before the gala," Joy said.

"Huh. Well, certainly. Tha's more like a comeuppance birthed long before your time," Maia said darkly and drained her cup. "Between Water and Air, most like. Yer acceptin' a *signatura* provided a most convenient excuse for a tug-o'-war." She gave a little yawning stretch that lifted her head into a cone before it settled back down into her shoulders with a sigh. Maia scratched her belly button and wiggled her toes.

"Really?" Joy said, taking another, sweeter sip. "I thought that it might be Sol Leander's gripe with me. Or yours with Graus Claude."

Ink touched her shoulder with the barest tips of his fingers. Maia's lined eyes opened a fraction before her face broke into a grin, which was toothless and gummy as an infant's. She laughed, which jiggled her all over, pale and puddinglike.

"Oh, I wouldn'a mind watching that Fat Frog fall flat on his watertight bum, I don't mind tellin' ya that! An' ye be smart to keep a sharp eye on the Tide's man as he's got sharp eyes and sharp things pointed at you. Sol Leander's got a sore spot when it comes t' humans, and you in particular." She nodded once, a jostle of jowls. "But I have less than nothing to do wi' the likes of a gala an' politics if it can be helped. I'd much prefer to stay in my little nook with a cuppa tea and a good fire, but I'll be there in my resplendent best to honor yer welcome, as I should. I am the Earth Seat, after all."

Joy sat up. "Is there something I can do to honor the Earth Folk?" While Joy grasped that every subtlety would be closely monitored and analyzed like a red-carpet commentary, she wondered if Graus Claude would *really* tell her what she needed to do to show her loyalties beyond himself as her sponsor and comptroller of the Twixt. "The Bailiwick will present me," Joy said. "And since the gala is so soon, he asked to be in charge of my appearance, as well."

"He never!" Maia said, aghast.

"Idmona is his tailor," Ink said.

Maia's ire ebbed a bit. "Well, small thanks fer that," she said. "Ye won't be dreary-dressed, at least. Who better to craft tailcoats for a four-armed frog, eh? Still—wait 'ere."

Maia hopped out of her seat and waddled across the room, bending herself in bubblegum directions as she peered into drawers and top shelves and counted out boxes, her chubby baby feet plodding against the floor as she twisted in elastic circles. Her hands stretched upward and grabbed a wooden chest the size of a small shoe box.

"Here we are, then," she said as she toddled back to Joy. There was a stylized design carved into the lid, a teardrop shape that swirled around itself. It reminded Joy of her own box etched with Ink's ouroboros. Maia pressed a dimpled palm to it, and it shone briefly beneath her hand. There was a deep hum, and all the latches popped open. "Let's 'ave a look-see."

"Is that...?" Joy whispered and then shut her mouth. She noticed for the first time how often the swirling teardrop shape repeated itself throughout the room. Nearly everything had one: doorknobs and drawer pulls, wall panels and floor tiles. Two teardrops set together made a sort of yin-yang design. Maia tapped the top of the box knowingly as she continued to search its contents.

"My *signatura*? Aye," she said. "I like to lock things up good 'n' proper. Using my True Name means it can't be fiddled with by anyone 'cept me."

"You are not concerned that someone could learn it and

make use of it?" Ink asked idly, but Joy could hear his suspicion in the question. There was a long history of the Folk keeping their True Names secret, commissioning their use only to Graus Claude for use by the Scribes. It was the reason for his and Inq's existence. Aniseed's recent betrayal underscored the importance of keeping *signaturae* safe, yet the Councilex seemed to have used it liberally throughout her decor.

"Wi'out my willingness, it would do Folk little good," she said, peeking over the chest lid. "Or for you, for that matter." Their eyes met over the edge of wood, and Joy could see the Council member acknowledge Ink for what he was—not born of the Folk but made for grunt work—and Ink simultaneously acknowledge that he might have been prying. Joy tensed in her seat, suddenly feeling confined. However, both Ink and Maia seemed comfortable with their level playing field, the invisible politics of the Twixt balanced on a razor's edge. Ink averted his eyes first. Maia nodded, satisfied.

Joy let out a slow breath. If this was a sample of Twixt etiquette, the gala was going to eat her alive.

"Besides," the Councilex said, brushing off the momentary showdown. "What's the worst tha' could happen? I am not afraid of death. Quite the opposite, in fact—I am immortal an' I've served on the Council since the beginning. I've seen an' heard an' smelled overmuch, which is why I prefer my humble hearth over grander thrones." She stroked the edge of the wooden chest with her pudgy fingers. "We of Earth know death is part of life, resilient and impermanent." Her smile was ancient and wise. "An' when the cycle turns, we tend to grow back stronger!"

Joy heard the tiny jingle of Ink's fingers sliding over the chain at his hip.

"Now, then," Maia said, setting her cup aside. "I imagine

the Bailiwick's got ye wearing something traditional—white or gold?"

"Gold," Joy said, grateful for the new topic. "And pearls."

"Pearls?" Maia looked horrified. "Water pellets! Expelled irritants coated in spit an' nacre—how appropriate is that for a welcoming, might I ask? Mollusk puke!" She shook her head in disgust. The flowers wobbled, furry stamens wagging like tongues. Joy bit back a laugh. "Will you be masked?"

"Themed," Ink said. "Damselfly."

Joy pointed a thumb at Ink. "Heron."

"Bah!" Maia spat. "The frog's got no mind fer it, no mind a'tall! Subtle as a stick to the head!" She rummaged farther inside the box, deeper than the chest should have rightfully allowed, her arm disappearing up to the shoulder. "Unimaginative, narcissistic, ill-advised...'less he means to insult Sol Leander by getting a rise outta Avery, which—in tha' case—would be fairly well played, but it'll put the two o' you in an awkward position." She glanced between them, her jowls bunching. "Though I doubt ye care much for the Tide's high opinion."

Joy frowned, remembering Graus Claude's self-congratulatory glee. "Who's Avery?"

"Ye've seen him," Maia said, distractedly. "The dandy in the feather cloak? Sol Leander's boy. He's usually somewhere underfoot bein' all courtly and justified."

Joy flashed on a swallowtail coat and sea-colored eyes. *Avery?* Now she had a name but didn't know what to think of him. He'd last left her with a warning and a confession that he'd been assigned to spy on her. *Whose side is he on, really?*

"Not a bad sort," Maia said. "More the fault o' the comp'ny he keeps."

Ink frowned. "But why would he—?"

"Ach! Here we are," Maia said as she lifted something

from the depths of the chest, cradling it in her palm. It was a hair-comb set with crystals, dangles of sky blue, aquamarine, pale purple and yellow-gold. It winked as Maia held it up against Joy's hair. "That should suit," she said. "An' be no more objectionable than the Water Folk's pearls." She rolled her eyes. "*Pearls!* Hmph." Maia shut the box with the flat of her hand, and the latches slammed home. "Now, ye wear that an' Folks'll know that you've been t' see me and that Earth's acknowledged yer right to wear it and claims ye, as well." Her face slid side to side as she began to morph, holding the box. "Water Folk may school you, but we've got yer roots."

It was a lot more than Joy was asking for, deeper than she'd bargained, but it was another token in her political arsenal, and she wasn't about to pass it up. She took the comb gently in her hands.

"Thank you, Councilex—Maia," she said and paused before asking, "Does it *do* anything?"

Maia smiled slyly. "It looks pretty in yer hair."

That was all the answer she was likely to get. "It does," Joy nodded. "It will. Thank you again."

"Now let's wrap it up nice an' tidy," Maia said, pulling a handful of cotton batting out of one of the seat cushions and massaging it into a ball. "Wouldn't want t' break it *by accident*." She winked as she tucked the comb in its cotton cocoon, and Joy folded it in tissues from her purse for good measure. She tucked the bundle into her purse pocket along with the scalpel and pouch. She zipped the whole thing closed over the dowsing rod, wondering if she should buy a bigger purse.

"We should go," Joy said and levered herself out of the low chair. Ink lent her a hand, strong and smooth as glass.

"I'll see ye at the gala," Maia said good-naturedly as she toddled back to her wall, kicking her long hair out of the way and stretching her body to set the chest back in its place. She drew a wormy finger over the shelf's surface and tutted at the dust. She bobbed down, wobbling back into her original shape, jiggling a little as she licked her finger clean. "You an' yer feathered friend ought to have quite the night." She laughed as she bowed them out. "Can't wait t' see it!"

"Many thanks, Councilex," Ink said as he stood by the door.

"Mmm," Maia answered. Joy knew the Folk did not say "You're welcome," which could be taken literally. Her head bobbed gently as she ushered them out the door. "Good day, unless I lost track o' the time—else good night and fare well."

The bird's eye maple shut with a deep *thump* behind them.

Ink withdrew his straight razor, and Joy was relieved that he had kept it in his wallet the entire time. "That was nice," Joy said. "Now, aren't you glad you didn't try to kill her?"

"I likely would have failed," Ink admitted. "I did not consider that those on the Council might be particularly adept at maintaining their long lives. You are right, I must be patient," he said. "And try it your way."

"*Our* way," Joy said, taking his hand. Ink hesitated, fingers on the blade. He didn't draw a door. He barely moved. She felt a curl of fear. "Ink?"

"I do not want to see them."

Joy touched his forearm. "Who?"

"My mother, Graus Claude, Inq—all of them." The words squeezed from his chest. "I do not want to face them. I do not know what to feel." He ran a hand over his chest, his wallet chain swinging against his hip. "They *lied* to me, Joy," he said, almost marveling at the idea. "How can that be?"

And while they hadn't exactly *lied*, Joy understood what he meant.

"I'm sorry," Joy said. "I don't know why. But I'm certain it was done out of love." She took his hand and shook it slightly, loosening his fingers enough to tuck hers inside. They slowly threaded their hands together, and Ink looked like he might smile but was too tired, too tense. Not even one dimple creased his cheek. He looked defeated, unmoored; without his plan to kill the Council, he needed a plan B. Joy leaned closer and tapped her purse. "Do you want to find out who did this?"

Ink turned, eyes sparking like fireworks. His voice was almost hungry. "Yes."

He switched his grip on the straight razor, arcing it forward. Joy took out the dowsing rod and held it like handlebars, its base pointing forward. She felt like they were finally doing something, seeking answers, getting closer. She would help Ink make things right by finding out who was to blame. She squeezed the worn wood and whispered, "Amanya."

Nothing happened. Joy hesitated, worried that Hai might have given her the wrong spell. She turned in a slow circle, waving the end of the Y-shaped stick in each direction, repeating the word, desperate to have something to show Ink.

She felt a tiny tremor in her palms.

Wondering if she'd imagined it, Joy turned back counterclockwise, passing the same point in her circle; there was a baby bee buzz, growing stronger. Excitement bubbled in her chest.

"I think I've got something," she said as the buzz became a tickle and the tickle became an itch, an almost uncomfortable sensation crawling up her bones. She wiped her right hand on her back pocket, and the rod swung violently to the left, whipping her arm and popping her elbow. Ink blocked with his forearm. Joy grabbed hold again. This time, she held on tight. She could feel the shiver in her teeth.

"Let's go," Joy said as the force began dragging her elsewhere. "Now!"

Ink wrapped a hand over the center of the rod, somewhat stilling it, and concentrated on a point she could not see.

"I will have to cut a series in order to follow," he said. "We will be traveling blind. I will have to be quick, and you will have to be nimble. Do not stop. Do not let go. For anything." Joy nodded, and he sliced a door open just as they were yanked forward with a jolt that she felt in her shoulders. "Run!"

She tripped on the edge of the world as they were sucked through, Ink's arm flashing in swooping arcs, slicing a series of half doors through the length of the world, one after another after another flying by in a montage of light and sound and smell, the terrain churning and shifting under their feet. Joy held on, remembering her violent chase through foreign forests, yanked through pine trees leashed to Kestrel hot on the trail of the Red Knight. For a moment, she could almost believe Filly was beside them as the terrain changed from wood to grass to snow quicker than she could blink. They followed the insistent pull of the magic, racing to the source of the spell on her lips. Joy squinted against the torrent of light and blurring color and tried to wait it out, keep running, wondering when it would stop, imagining where they'd end up when it was all over.

What would they find? Who was the traitor? Would they remember? Would they confess? Would Ink try to kill them and lose himself, a price he was more than willing to pay, but one which Joy could not allow?

They halted violently, skidding into a set of steps—
—wide, stone steps—
—leading to a door with a brass knocker—
—flanked by Chinese urns filled with stalks of bamboo.
Ink and Joy stared up at the brownstone, mute.

ELEVEN

"THEY MUST BE INSIDE," JOY SAID, FEELING THE ROD pulling up the stairs. "Whoever it is might be in there. Right now. With Graus Claude—" Joy didn't finish, because if the great amphibian was still frozen in his office, who knew who might have gone down into the pocket universe and found...

Ink vaulted the stairs and sliced through the door, pulling Joy behind him in his stony grip. There was a shock of light and sound, and Ink threw up his arm, shifting his body to shield Joy as three shots rang out in quick succession. Joy screamed.

There was a neat hole in Ink's arm and two in his chest. Black stains spread and dripped slow, oily blood. Ink ignored them. Joy felt faint.

"The Bailiwick," he called crisply into the foyer. "Is he here?"

"He is in his office," Kurt said sharply. Joy peeked over Ink's forearm as Kurt holstered his gun. "You know better than to rush in unannounced," Kurt said unapologetically and glanced at Joy and the quivering thing in her hand. "Even emergencies knock."

"He's in danger," Joy said. "The traitor's here!"

Kurt didn't pause. He turned quickly and led the charge down the hall. Joy hurried after him, following the rod, with Ink at her side, dripping thin trails of neon black, his chiseled profile determined and grim. The large bodyguard grabbed one of the office door handles and slipped his gun easily into his other hand. It looked heavy and dangerous. Ink's razor was sharp and deadly. Joy gripped the rod, its quiver rattling her jaw. She wanted to be somewhere else. Anywhere else. This was too much, too soon! This couldn't be right. This couldn't be happening. She felt a trickle of heat spiraling up from inside her, familiar and flush. *Not now!* Kurt pushed the door open.

Graus Claude sat at his desk holding a Taser, a snub handgun and a remote-control detonator in three of his hands; the fourth rested gently on the wireless mouse. His eye ridge rose calmly over his ice-blue eyes. Joy glanced around the office. The Bailiwick was alone.

"I heard shots," he said mildly.

"Yes, sir," Kurt answered. "There was a frontal breach."

Joy looked at the curtains, the fountains, the floor. There was no one inside. No one else there. The rod pointed unerringly forward, trembling.

The Bailiwick's gaze slipped to Ink.

"Is that blood?" he asked.

Ink paused, his every move a question.

"A little," he admitted.

Graus Claude put down his various implements with a sigh and thumbed a key code into the remote, which stopped beeping. "Kurt, please, clean up our guests before they stain the carpet. Then I expect a full report after your rather abrupt and untimely departure without leave during our lesson, Miss Malone." A growl crept into his erudite lecture. "We are here to learn *decorum* and *etiquette*, and I dare say you are off to an abysmal start. This will be corrected immediately. Is that understood?"

Joy's mouth moved, but no sound came out. The dowsing rod yanked in her arms. Ink's grip tightened on the razor's handle. Kurt, noting both reactions, swiftly pushed both of them back into the hallway, bowing to the Bailiwick and shutting the doors with a deferential click.

Joy dropped the rod. It shivered against the floor with a rattle, then stopped, still pointing at the office doors. She shook out her fingers. She felt sick. "Graus Claude—?"

Stone-faced, Kurt ushered them down the hallway. Joy grabbed the inert rod and stumbled before Kurt's insistent grip. Ink allowed himself to be led, pressing his thumb into the bullet hole and massaging the skin back into place. He spread his flesh with strong, even strokes like a sculptor with living clay. The three of them stopped before a familiar archway with its overlapping, dragon-scale slats.

"Are we going to the back rooms?" Joy said just to irk him. Kurt knew that she'd been there with Mademoiselle Lacombe, the French Canadian water sprite who had sought to escape her sadistic lover by removing his mark. She'd petitioned the Bailiwick, the keeper of secrets and tugger of strings, and Joy had removed the *signatura* at the cost of exposing her power to Graus Claude.

The wall opened under Kurt's hand, revealing the brass-and-velvet elevator. He marched them inside. "We are going upstairs," he said as he shut the door, cranking the lever at his left with a twist.

Joy touched the mirrored glass, which was its own hidden door, wondering how many secrets were buried in the walls. She felt the lift shudder under her feet and squeezed the rod in one hand. How loyal was Kurt? How trustworthy, Graus Claude? How much did they know about the princess and the door? Did anyone else know what was happening here?

"To Graus Claude's private apartments?" she guessed. She hoped that Ink heard her warning, but he stared at the holes in his shirt and pressed his stained fingers inside, fishing for bullets. It made a gruesome reflection in the mirrors.

"No," Kurt said as the elevator shushed to a halt. "Mine."

The door opened. Ink wiped his black-stained hand on his pants. Joy kept a hold on the rod but wanted her scalpel. She was feeling less comfortable by the minute; Kurt's tight-lipped silence was different than when he was in butler mode, different than when he'd been mute, mutilated to save him from Aniseed's deadly curse. The stark scar above his mandarin collar seemed a violent and foreboding reminder of what this man had survived, what he was willing to do and what he was capable of doing.

Joy stumbled through the doorway under his no-nonsense coaxing, stepping onto the edge of an enormous patterned rug. Red, shuttered windows cast complicated jigsaw patterns of sunlight on the hardwood floor, and the dark walls were interrupted here and there with silk embroidered paintings, exposed brick and artful triptychs of carved abalone and inlaid wood. There were racks of weapons in one corner along with a set of weights, a punching bag suspended from a chain, a pair of thick, spongy mats, a gun cabinet and rolls of tied grass stacked like firewood against the wall. Sleek black leather couches formed a neat square by a set of bookshelves, and where a coffee table would be squatted a circular cast-iron fire pit. Ultramodern suspension lights hung tangled with colored ropes of various widths attached to shining pulley chains and various cranks set in the wall. Kurt's apartment looked like a cross between a dojo, a private study and a professional training gym. Joy took a step beyond his reach and adjusted the purse strap on her shoulder, hooking her finger there to anchor her hands. She felt fidgety and anxious, suddenly unsure of her company. Who was Kurt loyal to?

Three doors led from the main room to other rooms beyond. Kurt evidently lived on the entire third floor. Joy glanced at the door they'd come through—there seemed to be only one exit, and Kurt stood grimly before it.

There was the splash of water from behind one of the doors, and the gentle squeak of a tap made everyone turn.

"Hello, Lover," Inq chirped as she entered the apartment, wiping her hands on a towel. She stared at Joy and Ink, her lips curving into a grin. Her smile was all teeth. "Excellent!" she said, glancing at Ink. "Who'd you kill?"

"No one," Joy said quickly. "He didn't kill anyone."

Inq tipped her head. "Then whose blood is that?"

Ink frowned. "Yours."

Inq rolled her eyes. "Oh, don't be so dramatic," she said, crossing the thick, hand-knotted rug. "You are my brother. What's mine is yours."

Joy flashed on a memory of Ink feeding himself to Inq, his fingers sliced off and brimming like a grisly champagne flute.

"You mean like our mother?" Ink said. "The one you kept secret from me? The child of royalty trapped in a forgotten cell inside the belly of the Bailiwick?"

"Yes. And now you've met her," Inq said. "Isn't it wonderful?"

"It is *not*—!" Ink seemed to realize that he was being baited. He inhaled slowly, his anger cooling to a simmer instead of a boil. "Why?" he asked. "Why did you not tell me?"

"*Why?*" Her demeanor changed instantly like storm clouds gone black. "Because you didn't *care*," she said. "About her, about me, about *anything*—and then you did." Her gaze snapped sharply to Joy, who quailed from her glare like a lick of a whip. "You *learned* to care," she amended. "So I'm telling you now."

Ink growled. "Now is too late."

"Time means nothing to us," Inq mocked. "Don't speak to me of time. It was *you* who refused to remember—unlike the rest of the world, who conveniently forgot. You left me alone to deal with everything all this time. You, who were more a thing than a person, that I helped nurture for centuries until you could awaken. I didn't tell you to keep you *safe!*" she spat. "I was the one who couldn't depend on *you!*" She swept her arm angrily, and a buzzing ripple cascaded through the air. Joy took an involuntary step back, recalling Inq's attackers exploding into a pink mist of atomized blood.

"I have been carrying this secret around like a poison snowflake on my tongue, trying to quietly discover whoever led the coup, disguising a long and arduous hunt in outrageous antics and elaborate charades to keep the focus off of *you* and off of *her* and on *me*," Inq sneered. "I've had to plot in the spotlight, deflecting suspicions and staying silent because I *had* to survive in order to be her eyes and ears." She stabbed a finger at herself. "I am her only conduit to the world outside the Bailiwick, the only immortal keeper of the secret, and *what have you been doing all this time*?"

Her voice shattered like mirrors reflecting Ink's dumbfounded expression. Inq stabbed an accusatory finger at him as she stalked closer, eyes flaring like firestorms. "I have been waiting for the day when I could unburden half of this responsibility on to you—you who have flitted through the years like a child's windup toy, leaving such matters as knowledge and politics and responsibility to the grown-ups while all along I've been waiting for you to *grow up!*" Her gaze sharpened like a knife. "But I couldn't risk her faith in me, and I wouldn't risk handing her fate over to *you* when you hadn't yet learned to value your own life, let alone someone else's." She stopped inches from her brother, trembling in fury. "You cannot *judge* me!" she said. "If I kept her heart to myself, I deserved that love for all my hard work and sacrifice." Inq's lips quirked in a sneer. "Didn't you ever wonder how I got to be the one to feel first? Did you ever ask me when I first felt love?" She splayed her sparkling fingers wider, fanning them like a magician's trick. "It was her! It was always her. I learned to love and be loved ages ago, but you were always too blind to see it!" She cocked her head slyly to one side, spying Joy. "Until you found the Sight."

Joy shook her head, not wanting to be part of this. Inq turned back to Ink, patting him twice on the top of his head.

"Well, Ink, welcome to the world!" she said. "It's time to grow up now that you're a Real Boy."

Ink stood still, a statue of marble smeared in oily blood—a Gothic angel without mercy. Joy could barely breathe.

"I am sorry," he said.

Inq goggled at him, off balance and confused. "What?"

"I am sorry," he said again, pocketing his razor and slipping the wallet chain through his fingers. "You were correct—I did not understand. And I think you were also correct that I could not have understood," he said slowly. "Until recently." He glanced at his sister through shaded lashes, looking like a small boy and an old man all at once. "Now I do."

Inq took his hands, shaking the right free of the shining silver chain. She squeezed their arms together and rested her forehead against his. Both of their eyes slipped closed, and they stood still for a long moment. Joy watched Inq's eyes flutter open as she whispered with paper-cut clarity, "We are not enemies, Ink, and I love you dearly." She chucked his chin with her fist. "And together we can hunt down the traitor to the Twixt."

"He's here," Joy said, the words popping out of her mouth.

Inq dropped Ink's hands. "Who's here?"

Joy shook the dowsing rod in her hand. "The one who cast the spell of forgetting, the blanket spell over the Twixt," she said. "We tracked it here."

"Here?" Inq stepped away, her words heavy with scorn. "No. You cannot be suggesting Graus Claude?" She almost laughed. Almost. "The toad doesn't cast spells. He can't even move while anyone is inside the Bailiwick." Inq shook her head. "He conspired with me to keep her safe."

"Or conveniently out of the way," Ink said.

Joy rounded on Kurt. "Is anyone else here? In the gallery? The archives? The back suite? Anywhere?"

"No," Kurt said plainly.

Inq's voice rose to a dangerous pitch. "Then who else could it be?"

"It could be you," Ink said logically. "Or you." He nodded at Kurt.

Kurt shrugged. "It could be any one of us."

"No," Ink said. "The rod tracked the spell here before we arrived. And it would have been cast long before either of you were born."

"I thought the coup happened shortly after the King and Queen left," Joy said. "How long have you been alive, Kurt?"

"Too long," he said quietly and glanced at Inq, who looked stricken. "And yet not long enough," he amended. She gave a tight smile.

"I still don't believe it," Inq said. "It's too sloppy to be Graus Claude."

"There was no one else in the office," Ink said. "No one else in the building."

"The Folk are, at their core, true to their Names," Kurt said, his voice as smooth as an oiled sword slipped into its sheath. "They are who they are, a fixed point of their auspice, and no amount of forgetting can erase that fact. They remain true to themselves because they have no other choice." The muscles of his arms bulged at his sleeves. "Aniseed could not change who she was despite her many false fronts, and that is what made it possible to defeat her, exposing her by her True Name. The Red Knight may have had many incarnations, but all adopted the same base True Name in order to share the auspice of the unstoppable mercenary. Hasp remains chained to his crimes by his True Name, which is why he'd been seeking to alter it." He glanced at Joy. "Your power over Briarhook is much the same, holding his heart in your hands." Joy didn't like the way he said it, as if that were something evil, something wrong. She pressed her purse against her stomach like a shield between them. "Therefore, I do not believe it could be the Bailiwick," he said. "Who is many things, but nothing if not loyal to the Twixt."

Inq nodded. Ink hesitated, tense and uncertain.

"What about *inside* the Bailiwick?" Joy asked. There was a long pause where no one said anything, unwilling to voice the next logical thought, but she had to ask. "What if it was her? What if *she's* the traitor?"

Ink and Inq were quick to pounce.

"That's ridiculous!"

"That makes no sense."

"How could she—?"

"Why would—?"

"No," Ink said with a swift, slicing hand. "I could invent a hundred theories, but the truth is that spells cannot penetrate into the Bailiwick, else she would have forgotten like the rest of them under the Amanya. The rod cannot trace anything or anyone beyond the confines of the Twixt," he said to Joy. "The Bailiwick was designed to be the safe space between worlds, a place to hide the door until the Imminent Return." His eyes hardened like marbles. "It cannot be her."

"I think we are pursuing the wrong question," Kurt said. "What we should be asking is, who can cast an Amanya spell?"

"My brother says that human magic and Folk magic aren't

the same thing—Folk work with glyph magic, not spell magic, unless they are druids or something, and a blanket spell like this one is *dangerous*. Even the Wizard Vinh's son didn't want to talk to me about it."

Inq cocked her head. "Why not?"

"Because I'm not a wizard," Joy said. "Or a witch or whatever. Mortals pass down their knowledge from generation to generation as a closely guarded secret that can be traced back through lineage. Each wizard has its trademark," she said. "Like a True Name, that marks the spell as theirs. The Amanya's like that. If we can find the originator of the spell, we can *prove* what happened. We can find the traitor and get answers." She felt the weight of the collective stares on her. She felt weak and frayed thin. She hadn't eaten in far too long. She felt dizzy, halfway between a headache and floating on air. *What time is it?* she wondered. *What day is it?* She took a deep breath through her nose and unwrapped her fingers from the purse strap.

"So it's a wizard," Inq said. "Or a druid."

"Or a *segulah*," Ink added.

Kurt crossed his arms. "She's dead."

Inq tossed her arms wildly. "Well, if it was a human or Aniseed, they would be long dead, and then the spell can *never* be broken!" She spun on her brother. "If we cannot break the spell, we cannot find the door. And without the traitor, we cannot force anyone to reveal its location, let alone open it." Inq's crystal-crisp voice was zinging. "If that option is closed to us, then there is only one option left—"

"*No!*" Joy snapped. "No killing! Not if we can help it, remember?" She was sick of this. They were so close and Graus Claude was *right downstairs*. She could all but feel his icy blue gaze through the floorboards. "The dowsing rod can follow the spell to its source," she said calmly in even-measured words, like counting out change. "We have to be absolutely sure."

"And what will you do when you find it?" Inq asked, deadly curious.

"It depends," Joy hedged.

"You say this because Graus Claude is your friend," Inq said. "Would you feel the same way if he'd plotted to kill *your* mother?"

The idea so stunned her, Joy was unable to speak.

"Give it to me," Inq said, opening her hand for the rod. "I'll do it."

"No," Joy squeezed the dowsing rod. She'd paid a heavy price for it, and she was going to see this through. "It's mine. I started this. I'll do it."

"I will go with her," Ink said, staring down Inq. "I know what must be done." He said it with a dark weight, a challenge all but spoken. "We will find the source and regroup here." Inq opened her mouth to protest, but he turned to Kurt. "You must stay here. If we fail, all hope of the King and Queen's return will fall to you. This is your task even in defiance of your debt to the Bailiwick. Are we agreed?"

Kurt's lips tightened, but he nodded. "Agreed."

Joy took the rod and Ink's hand with a certainty she didn't feel.

"If it's Graus Claude, he'll kill you," Inq said. "He'll have no choice."

Joy wanted to say *He wouldn't!* as well as *He didn't do it!* but since she didn't know if either of these things were true, all she could say was "We'll see."

Kurt, ever the butler, opened the elevator door, allowing Ink and Joy to step inside. He entered the conveyance himself to man the controls. Joy's last look of Inq was of her deep, thoughtful scowl.

"Good luck," she said softly.

Joy remembered Ink's warning that one could never win against Graus Claude's luck; he was Fortune's favorite.

The door closed, and they slid downward, the dowsing rod hanging loosely in her grip.

The elevator opened into the sconce-lit hall. Ink stepped out first, razor in hand, while Joy held on tightly to the dowsing rod. It was slippery in her sweaty hands. She glanced back at Kurt, almost pleading. He spoke quietly under the hum of the lift.

"Trust that they are who they are," he said. "No spell can change that."

"I know," she said.

He nodded as the elevator door slipped closed.

Joy and Ink exchanged glances before she pointed the Y-shaped stick down the hall and whispered over its crux, "Amanya." The low bee buzzing drew her forward, down the hall, passing the old gilt mirrors and oil paintings with growing dread. The spell shivered up her bones, rippling along her insides, pulling her inexorably toward the office doors. Joy hoped that there was a secret visitor, an assassin behind the curtains or another hidden waiting room tucked behind the walls. Anyone—anything—could be the source of the spell, but doubt chewed inside her. She couldn't help but wonder. *What if it is Graus Claude?* she thought. *What then?* Her steps slowed as she considered the letter opener in her purse. If Stef was right and the spell was like a wizard's, did she trust that Mr. Vinh had placed the right spell on the blade? Had his son, Hai, given her the right name of the spell or merely the one to implicate the Bailiwick? Was she doing the right thing, or was she an instrument—like the Scribes—forged to do someone else's bidding? Mr. Vinh made it no secret what he thought of the *tien*, and yet he coveted their power. Suspicion curdled like milk. Who did she trust? She glanced at Ink beside her. How many things hadn't she told him? How could she claim to trust him when she hadn't trusted him with her secrets?

Twelve tears paid to Wizard Vinh. Three drops of blood for Ladybird. Filly's pouch. Inq's secret sigils. The Red Knight's death.

"Ink," she whispered past the chattering hum in her teeth. "I have to tell you—"

"You may as well enter," Graus Claude's booming voice came through the ironwood doors. "I can hear you there."

Joy swallowed her confession as well as a thick lump of fear. The Bailiwick's deep bass rumble joined the tremor in her chest. Ink tucked the open blade into his back pocket but not into its wallet; he was keeping the weapon in easy reach. Her stomach lurched as he opened the doors.

The Bailiwick sat at his desk, all evidence of his armaments gone. He looked slightly puzzled as he removed his gold-rimmed spectacles and placed them in their case with a snap.

"Where is Kurt?" he said as he pressed the call button. "And where have you been?" he asked with equal gravity as he steepled two hands. "I was informed that you had been called elsewhere, which accounted for your rather abrupt departure, but not the why of it." He looked at the rod shaking in Joy's hands, dragging her almost bodily into the room. His eye ridge rose. "Care to explain?" he asked. She was no longer sure if he meant her absence or the jerking thing in her hands pointed unerringly at his chest.

Joy shook her head. *No. No. No.*

"We apologize," Ink said smoothly. Joy watched his hand slide toward the shining razor blade. "But recent circumstances required our attention—"

Graus Claude stood up, looking slightly alarmed.

"Is that a *dowsing rod*?" he demanded.

"Yes," Joy said quickly, trying to still it. "No, Ink! Don't—"

But Ink was already drawing the razor at the same moment two of Graus Claude's arms lifted a broadsword and a heavy shotgun out from under the desk. The giant frog smoothly brought both weapons to bear with expert reach, the massive desk yawning between them like a fortress. Two hands curled around the wide, wooden throne, flipping it around to act as his shield.

It happened too fast for Joy to believe it.

Ink sprang onto the desk, slicing a line of time and jagged light. A ward sparked and died. A reverberation shook the room, rattling the books on their shelves.

"Yield!" Ink barked with a rage Joy had never heard before.

Graus Claude lowered his head, his many rows of sharks' teeth bared. "I think not," he said. His mouth opened wide. Joy knew his tongue could strike out and yank prey back into his crushing maw. She opened her mouth to scream, but the Bailiwick's battle cry cut her off with a thunderous roar. The sound slammed Joy back, the dowsing rod jerked to follow the Bailiwick's every move.

Ink spun, folding on a knife-edge, and winked out of sight.

Ink. Joy mouthed the word. Graus Claude's eyes shifted minutely as his four arms took up a defensive cone around the chair. When the world shuddered open, the old toad was ready. Sweeping the broadsword level, he cut Ink's pounce short. The black-eyed Scribe shifted against gravity, turning his midsection, evading the blade, feet dancing spryly along the wall. Grabbing the curtains, Ink flung himself forward, using the heavy material as handholds, cloaking his movements, slashing bits of fabric free to toss like soaring birds into the air. They fell in ragged patches, obscuring vision, wrapping weapons, blurring his escape. Joy turned her head, trying to follow, but Ink slid behind the edge of the fountain, out of the line of sight.

Graus Claude's shotgun followed Ink's progress as the broadsword circled behind, two hands still gripping the throne back, covering himself a full three hundred and-sixty degrees. Another flicker peeled away from nothing, and Ink rolled out, narrowly dodging the barrel of the gun. With a sweeping arc, Ink severed the end of the shotgun as he slipped swiftly into another neat sliver of light. Hollow metal tubes clanged off the floor.

"I imagine that there is something you wish to discuss," Graus Claude said. Joy could not tell if he spoke with humor or malice. He trained his sawed-off gun along the edge of the desk, changing hands as he circled. Joy was being pulled inexorably closer, dragged across the Persian rug, her arms vibrating in her shoulder sockets. She wanted to let go, but her fingers wouldn't obey. She wanted everything to stop, she wanted to explain, but she couldn't speak through her chattering teeth and neither Ink nor the Bailiwick seemed inclined to notice.

Joy was nearly at the desk, the grip of the spell dragging her into the line of fire. She had to let go! She had to get out! Her mind was a jumble of panic. Her hands weren't her own. Her whole body shook. *This isn't happening! This can't be true!*

There was a rip and a flash as Ink dropped from the ceiling. The Bailiwick shifted his grip and swung the broadsword, forcing Ink back, gaining a few inches. Ink quickly recovered and wove his blade in a furious motion. A ward glistened in place. Graus Claude's hand shot out from behind the throne and slapped upward, under the desk. There was the decisive sound of breaking glass. The new ward winked out.

"Now, then—" the Bailiwick said reasonably.

Ink charged. Leaping high into the air—a diving falcon, talons raised—but Graus Claude calmly lifted his massive throne above his head, slamming the solid wood between them. The straight razor *shinged*, scything six inches into the hardwood, biting deep, but the giant amphibian snapped the chair sideways, momentum throwing Ink along the rest of the curve. He landed crouched behind the podium, black eyes hard and intent. Graus Claude lowered the chair. The cleft was barely an inch from his hand. There was a moment of wary quiet.

"Master Ink," Graus Claude rumbled, his sword en garde. The ruined shotgun swiveled to point at Joy. The Bailiwick inclined his head courteously. "Miss Malone, my apologies."

Joy's world shrank to two dark, silver-rimmed holes.

She stopped breathing.

"No!"

Ink sprang, blade gleaming, aiming for the Bailiwick's throat.

The broadsword came up as the chair flipped down. Graus Claude didn't even turn his head as he spun the shotgun in one smooth motion, slamming the butt of the grip into the space between Ink's shoulder and left breast.

Ink dropped like a puppet sans strings.

Joy screamed and wrenched herself sideways, fearing the hot punch of bullets. Her legs collapsed as the dowsing rod shot out of her grip, bounced off the toad's breast pocket and clattered to the floor, inert.

Everything stopped.

The Bailiwick inspected Ink dispassionately as he replaced his chair in its customary spot. "Now that that's all in order," he said, laying the weapons on his desk and wiping dust from his lapels. He cocked an eye at Joy sprawled on the rug. She held her breath, her lungs shuddering with leftover adrenaline. He loomed over the desk. "What is this all about?"

Fumbling against the floor, Joy tried to think. Graus

Claude didn't seem to be gloating or defensive, he didn't even seem to be very surprised—if anything, he was acting mildly interested, his curiosity piqued. Her synapses lit up like fireworks, screaming questions with no answers. She could see Ink's limp arm from around the side of the fountain, its calm burble oddly distant in her ears. She reached for him.

"Ink?" she managed and grabbed his hand. Joy was relieved to feel his new pulse beating in his wrist.

"He's fine." Graus Claude's eye ridge rose, and he sounded quite pleased. "A safety precaution I felt would be a prudent addition to their design, a condition of my employment, which was approved by the rest of the Council." He nudged Ink's body with his size thirty Oxfords. "You can hardly blame me, given this recent demonstration."

Joy was confused, dismayed, disgusted. "You made an *off button*?"

Graus Claude had the grace to look chagrined. "More like a snooze button," he said. "Normally, in the case of malfunction or malcontent, the Scribes would be decommissioned if they failed to adhere to their prescribed duties, which, as I understand, might include attacking their employer." His icy gaze slid to Joy. "To err is human," he said as he sniffed through thin nostrils. "But to forgive is divine, quoth Alexander Pope." He straightened his suit jacket while two hands adjusted the knot of his tie. "And while I required the Scribes be fitted with appropriate safeguards if they were to be under my charge, I have never once employed them. I confess that I find the results to be both abhorrent and demeaning." His gaze darkened under his browridge. "So. I am wont to believe that there are extenuating circumstances that do not necessitate informing anyone of this incident beyond the confines of this room."

"You won't—" Joy struggled with the words. "You won't kill him?"

"Of course not," Graus Claude scoffed. "Obsolescence is an outdated mandate fit for tools and base machinery, and we both know that the Scribes have become much more than that. I consider Master Ink and Mistress Inq proper allies, even friends, recent affairs notwithstanding." The Bailiwick sat back in his chair, which groaned heavily under his weight, and clicked his claws on the desktop. "He will be unconscious for several hours, maybe more. This is the first time I have had cause to use the fail-safe, but it seems quite effective." He settled against the wounded chair back and checked his timepiece. "Hmm. Ingenious of me, perhaps, but ill-suited for our schedule. Still, better than a close shave to the jugular, I suppose." He leaned toward the intercom, one claw hovering delicately over the call button. "Would you care for some tea?"

Joy draped Ink's hand over his chest and struggled to her feet. "Tea?"

"Yes," Graus Claude said, gently crunching some shattered glass under his shoes. "I find that I would like some tea. And, given that I expect you to explain your actions in a lengthy and no doubt fascinating tale, I imagine that you may grow quite parched and might appreciate a hot, soothing beverage." He pressed the button. "Tea, please, and a light repast," he said clearly. "And ready the guest suite for Master Ink."

"But—?" She pointed at the gun. "You almost shot me!"

Graus Claude frowned. "Don't be ridiculous, Miss Malone," he said. "I had no intention of firing the weapon—I needed the reach, nothing more. Scattershot in close quarters? In my own office?" He harrumphed. "Really! I keep a collection of rare antiquities here. Not to mention the powder burns—it is simply out of the question." He waved a hand at her. "Only by placing you in danger could I hope to goad Master Ink into rash action...and the resultant inaction." He glanced down, his low head giving a palsy shake. "The ruse worked quite well, as you can see, and I *did* apologize in advance."

Joy dropped into the proffered chair, arms and legs crossed protectively around her. She kept stealing glances at Ink's body rather than at Graus Claude, wanting to go to him, wanting to wake him up. The giant frog was a presence greater than an elephant in the room. Joy had too many questions and not enough answers, and nothing matched what she believed. The Bailiwick settled himself in his customary chair, his seat of power, unshaken. She couldn't even look at him.

"So he's okay?" she whispered into her shoulder.

"He is...o-kay," Graus Claude's lip curled around the slang as if he'd swallowed something sour. "I assure you, he is simply resting under duress. He will wake when the inset panel disengages—it is more mechanical than magical."

Joy shifted uncomfortably, still unconvinced, still uncertain of her loyalties and too aware of Ink on the floor. Kurt and Inq were somewhere upstairs, and she was here, alone, before the Bailiwick. *Is he a friend or enemy? Mentor or traitor? Did the rod work? And if so, does he even know what he's done? Why would he do it? Is he guilty or not?* She looked up at the great, hunchbacked, four-armed toad in his old-fashioned three-piece suit and silk tie. Joy didn't know what to believe. *They are who they are*, Kurt had said. *They are true to themselves—no spell can change that.*

Graus Claude was still Graus Claude. And she would respect him. Always.

"Okay," she said, relaxing something inside with an effort.

"Very well," Graus Claude rumbled as he leaned forward slightly. One hand disappeared under the desk and passed the dowsing rod to a second hand and a third before holding it up to Joy. "You were tracking something with this, and you found it," he said with a low rumble. "Care to tell me what you were looking for?"

Joy swallowed the taste of moist air on her tongue. A lily pad spun lazily in the ripples of the fountain. "That," she said, "is a dowsing rod that I got from a satyr guarding the Glen. It was set to find the origin of a spell affecting all of the Twixt."

"Resourceful," Graus Claude said, sounding impressed. "And absurd." He placed the weapons dismissively to one side of the desk. "What spell?"

"An Amanya."

Graus Claude still looked suspicious, but unaffected by the revelation. "Not being a spell-caster myself, you will forgive the cliché when I say I've never heard of it." He straightened his cuffs. "I could look it up, of course, but if I am to be considered your suspect, I would highly recommend you not grant me access to my vast network of available resources." His bass voice grated. "It is still my job to teach you to think like one of the Twixt."

Joy sat up a little straighter, a little bolder. "I know what an Amanya spell is," she said. "It's a blanket spell that covers a set area and affects everyone within those borders." She wet her lips. "It's a forget spell."

"How convenient," Graus Claude said, unimpressed. "And we are to surmise that I have forgotten that I cast it?"

Joy bit her tongue. It sounded stupid when he said it aloud, but also true. And he hadn't denied it. She considered his words carefully. *The Folk cannot tell a lie.* As crazy as it was, the theory was proving itself out time and time again. Her silence gave him the answer that she'd left unsaid.

"I see." The Bailiwick held up a patient hand. "Might I ask what it is that I have forcibly forgotten?"

Joy hung her head. *So much for No Stupid.* "I could tell you," she said weakly. "But you'd just forget again—or never remember being told in the first place. I'm not sure how it works."

"Ah, of course. How silly of me," Graus Claude said drily. "This begs the question that if *I* cannot remember, then why are you unaffected?"

"Because I'm human."

"No," he said. "You are not."

Joy rolled her eyes. "Okay, technically I was born human, and I wasn't part of the Twixt when this spell went off, and so I wasn't affected the same way the Red Knight wasn't affected each time he resurrected after the initial Edict was announced. The spell doesn't account for a new addition to the Twixt." She couldn't talk about the princess or the royal family or the door. Her voice grew from smallish to stern. "Look, it's a *loophole*. Yet another convenient loophole in your precious rules that, for once, seems to be in our favor, so can we agree that I'm human enough to remember and Folk enough to be telling the truth?"

That took him aback. The frog sat up, his hunch receding as he straightened his spine, his long jowls wobbling as he rose to an impressive height. "Indeed," he said. "You do well to remind me that you have earned my trust. Well said and well played." He dropped his head to a more comfortable crouch. "There is hope for you yet." He threaded two of his hands together as numbers three and four cupped the chair arms. "So, let us establish a sense of scale. What are the purported boundaries of the spell?"

"The Twixt," Joy said. "The entire Twixt."

Graus Claude's eyes widened in alarm, his mouth hung slightly open, his four hands stilled. "That would be—" he began and stalled, exhaling a moment of silence. "That would be a heinous treason as well as an incredibly subtle coup de grâce. Should I be inclined to undo our world, that would be an effective strategy. I should be flattered by the implication of my abilities if not utterly scandalized by the accusation." For once, it seemed as if the Bailiwick did not know what to do with his many hands. His head wobbled in distress. "Do you understand the gravity of what you are saying, Miss Malone?"

Her words were stronger, older somehow than her. "Someone cast a spell over all of the Folk, making everyone forget something important," she said. "Something *very* important. And that person did it in order to take power, to usurp the Twixt without any memory or regret, knowing full well what they were doing. I can't believe it was an accident." Joy nodded to her mentor. "You once told me that there are no accidents, but you forget that I was born human. I had choices. I had free will. The Amanya spell is *brainwashing*. It's mental rape. It is forcefully, knowingly killing free will." Her fingers formed into fists. The enormity of it hit her all at once—this was what Ink had fought to keep for her, this was what she'd given up by joining the Twixt. It wasn't about wings or gills or heat in her hands, it was about being bound to something, now and forever. But she didn't have forever. She was still mortal and had known what it was to have a choice. Someone, somewhere, had stolen all of the Folk's choices, as well as their leaders' and their families' and everyone else's. "Yes," she said, understanding all too well. "I know what I'm saying."

The Bailiwick's eyes slid over the dowsing rod, his palms resting on either side of the Y-shaped stick. "And you believe that I could have done this thing." It was a statement aching to be a question. To be refuted outright.

But she couldn't.

"Is there any way it could be wrong?" she asked. "The rod tampered with? The wrong spell? A false positive?"

The Bailiwick paused. Never one to shirk a puzzle, even one pointed at him, he considered the variables, his head easing into its familiar palsy shake. He ran a dozen fingers over the dowsing rod's runes.

"As I said, I am no spell-caster," he said. "Anything is possible."

"So it could be wrong," Joy said hopefully.

Graus Claude gave a wan smile. "And it could be right," he said. "But thank you for having faith in the possibility of my innocence." He let his hands drift back to his lap. "Do we have the means to cleave theory from fact?"

Joy felt her face warm as she unwound her fingers. "I can prove it, once and for all," she said. "I can sever the spell at its source, freeing the caster from the forget spell, although it won't affect anyone else." Joy gazed at him. "But I won't do it without your permission."

The Bailiwick leaned on his two elbows and crossed the other two arms over his middle. The tension was thinner but still hung in the air like perfume. Joy's nerves felt like the shattered glass underfoot.

"I should welcome the opportunity to prove myself after such a vigorous introduction to the topic," he said softly. "But I find I cannot work up the necessary enthusiasm as your doubts feed my own." He shrugged two sets of shoulders. "How am I to convince you what to do, Miss Malone, when I cannot know myself what I have done except to know that I would not do such a thing?" Joy had no answer, feeling both angry and ashamed for what she could say to him and more for what she could not. She wanted to tell him that she knew he was innocent, and yet she didn't. She couldn't. *Is it true? Do I believe it or not? What does that say about me, about what I truly believe? Or is it the fact that I am no longer human, that I am becoming more of the Twixt?*

Was she being honest or afraid?

Joy drew the purse strap across her body and slid the zippered compartment to rest on her stomach. She paused before standing before the giant toad on his severed throne. She pointed to her open purse. "May I?"

He gestured with two of his hands. "Of course."

Joy gently lifted the first thing from its pocket. "This is a beacon I got from one of the satyrs." She held up one of the glow sticks. "He's the one who gave me the dowsing rod, which I needed to track down the spell." She placed it gently on the desk, next to the rod itself. "And this pouch belongs to Filly. She gave it to me so that I can communicate with her without ringing any bells, my backup in case of emergencies." She placed that down, too. Graus Claude continued to look intrigued but still nonplussed. "And this..." She lifted up the bone blade. "This has been ensorcelled by the Wizard Vinh to help me sever the Amanya spell at its source. If the caster was caught in its effects and failed to remember, it will free that one person from the spell in order to confess." She held it up but kept a firm grip on it, knowing that while the Bailiwick's hands might be out of reach, his tongue could cross the desk in a blink. "I'm telling you this because I want it all out there. Now you know what I have, what I've done and what I'm willing to do for everyone in the Twixt because I am trying to do what's right." Joy shifted her grip on the blade, still matching his gaze eye to eye. "You have always stood by me, even though you had little reason to trust me, a human with the Sight."

The Bailiwick's eyes were impassive. Her voice shook just a little, a slight tremble on her lips. "Now, I don't know if I got the name of the right spell, and I don't know if this blade will do what it's supposed to do..." She circled the desk, sliding by the stone basin, coming closer by degrees. Graus Claude watched her quietly, letting her come. "But I have to trust someone," she said. "I trust Ink. And I'll trust the Vinhs. And I trust you." She stopped within two feet of the giant amphibian, who, even seated, towered over her with his hunchback shoulders and cold, icy glare. She didn't blink. "Will you trust me?"

Graus Claude pushed himself slowly to stand, rising to fill her vision as he unbuttoned his jacket, removing it in a dance of limbs and draping it gently over the back of his chair. He straightened his cuff links and let all four arms rest by his wide sides. His head lowered like a wrecking ball, and his voice unfurled from deep in his chest. His gaze pierced through the back of her skull.

"I trust you, Joy Malone."

She nodded, held her breath and stabbed him in the meaty part of his arm.

Joy was knocked backward by a burst of light that slammed her into the stone fountain, cold water and soggy tendrils sloshing over the edge. Her back smacked against the lip of the basin, her feet skittering over broken glass, but true to his word, Graus Claude kept all four hands at his sides, eyes clenched and body bent over the blade sticking out of his arm. His face was splotched, his mouth a tight grimace, his blood—red and runny—streamed down his sleeve. All Joy could think through the sharp fog of pain was how she'd just ruined his shirt.

The letter opener bobbed with each beat of his heart, but he made no move to remove it. It wasn't a mortal wound, but it looked painful, and Joy wished that he'd take it out. A sort of shimmer danced in front of her eyes. She thought, at first, that she'd hit her head, the sight of his blood and her own hypoglycemia probably taking its toll, but the strange light rippled through the air from every direction, coalescing down into a smudgy, static haze, pressed like a tight bubble over the four-armed frog before it burst, a sonic punch that whipped Joy's hair back from her eyes and dropped Graus Claude to his knees.

The floor shook.

"Bailiwick!" Joy called out, but she wasn't certain whether it was out of concern or fear. Kurt appeared, weapon drawn, and used one hand to support the massive bulk of his otherworldly employer. Joy turned her head and moved her fingers and toes, methodically squeezing her muscles, checking her limbs as she'd been taught back in gymnastics safety training after a spill on the mats. Her back ached, but it felt more like a scrape than a bruise. There was a long, slow moment as Graus Claude pushed himself up on one knee. She saw that he wore argyle socks. Joy felt terrible that she suspected someone who wore argyle socks.

"My apologies," he hissed through pointy teeth as he stood, yanking out the blade and dropping it contemptuously on the desk. One hand squeezed the wound as he reached out an arm to Joy. "It has been a while since I have been in close proximity of physical threat without my armor, and I had forgotten about the Ricochet."

Kurt pocketed his weapon as Joy accepted the frog's clawed hand. He lifted her gingerly with little effort. She was sore, but nothing was broken.

"Did it work?" she asked, rubbing her back.

The Bailiwick paused in his ministrations. His eyes glazed over, and his face slackened like melting candle wax—but it wasn't the spell. Realization dawned, painting his face gray with angst. He placed a single hand against his heart and pressed it there, crumpling.

"Yes," he whispered hollowly. "I remember." He sat down with a great groan. Kurt moved swiftly aside. Joy felt something loosen inside her, shaking like the dowsing rod.

"It *was* you?" she said in disbelief. "You're the traitor?"

"No," he said quickly, tight with insult. "And yes. But certainly..." He sighed and unknotted his tie with two hands. "It was I who cast the spell."

The admission stung, stapled in the air like a Wanted poster, undeniable and condemning. Joy could barely think beyond the roaring in her ears.

"But it was not for me," Graus Claude added softly. "And I did not realize what I had done."

He tied the length of silk over his arm, staunching the wound. It bled through, quickly turning the blue tie a vivid red. He sighed as he fumbled with the knot. Kurt moved to assist, and the Bailiwick relented. He squeezed his arm and blood trickled down. Finishing his ministrations, Kurt silently set the tea service on the desk and lifted Ink's limp body from the floor. Joy stood up to join him, but Kurt glared. She sat down. He left the room carrying the one thing that made sense in his arms. A piece of her went with him.

"I have failed my Lady," the Bailiwick said to no one. "Utterly and completely."

"I don't understand," Joy said, turning back to face him. The admission still lingered, tense as a pulled string, a crossbow waiting to loose. "You cast a blanket forget spell, and forgot about it, but you didn't *mean* to do it?"

"Oh, no, I did," Graus Claude said, easing himself into his seat and tucking the gun and the sword back wherever they'd come from as he poured the tea. His hand trembled and the spout rattled against the cup. "As I recall, I cast the spell—but it was not meant to affect me or anyone in the Twixt besides one, and that had nothing to do with...with our King and

Queen." He sighed and pursed his wide lips together. "How strange it feels to say those words again." His gaze slipped lower in shame. "And to know that I have robbed our people of them for all these years...unthinkable."

"Please," Joy said, trying to follow, "tell me."

Graus Claude looked older under the shadow of his brow. "An explanation is long overdue," he agreed. He glanced at the intercom and hesitated. "Ah, I see now—Kurt," the Bailiwick sighed and then sat back. "Of course. He is human—he remembers. As do you, Miss Malone. Humans live outside the borders of the Twixt. And the Scribes—" He nodded. "'Made not born.' Yes. It all comes together, then. Very wise, I think, for my manservant to be indisposed elsewhere at this time. I shall not fault him for his suspicions." He rubbed at his throat. "Nor any of you, for that matter. In fact, I should thank you when the time has come, but at this moment I find that I am not yet so inclined." He rubbed a kerchief over his face, which had blossomed a sheen of yellowish sweat. Joy had never seen the Bailiwick so shaken and out of sorts. He seemed to deflate in his throne like a mottled green balloon.

"Where to start?" Graus Claude murmured to himself as he poured water from his carafe and drank it like a bolt of scotch. He ignored the tea. "As you have no doubt discovered, the role of Bailiwick is more than title. It is a sacred duty—to be the physical gateway between one world and the next. It is our 'loophole' as you describe it—a space inside, yet outside of the Twixt where we could safely place a door. My office is manifold, but this one condition was sacrosanct—someone had to personally accept the gateway into their keeping, and I did so with honor and gravity. It is a solemn act and responsibility which I ascribed to my every effort on the Council." He glanced at her furtively, but with a smoldering passion. "I would have you believe that."

Joy wrung her fingers in her purse strap. "Of course I do," she said.

"Indeed," Graus Claude sighed, unconvinced. "In any case, this placed me in a seniority, although I was not the first to hold the post—at death, the title of Bailiwick must be claimed by another in accordance to the rules." Joy's hackles rose, bringing a fresh wave of pain over the bruise on her back. *It always comes back to the rules!* "The same is true of the Council Head, and for one other role—a secret post—the courier to the King and Queen."

"But if—?" Joy started, then stopped at Graus Claude's raised hand.

"Tut-tut, Miss Malone," he said. "You asked for an explanation, and you deserve one in full, but I request the courtesy of an uninterrupted narrative." He smiled a little to himself and shook a manicured claw. "Etiquette and decorum," he said. "I am obliged to remind you that, no matter the circumstances, there are standards we must uphold." He poured and drank another glass. And another. And a third. He paused at the fourth glass before continuing. "So I became the Bailiwick and assumed the Water Folk seat. There are only four original members of the Council from when—well, from when the King and Queen assembled them, I suppose. The rest of us have had to assume the mantle of those who came before without the benefit of their instruction." His gaze darted around the room, settling everywhere but on her. "When Ironshod died during the Old War Insurgence, I elected to have the newest Council member placed under my charge, much as I was sponsored by Bùxiǔ de Zhēnzhū himself, and much the same way as I volunteered to be your sponsor." Graus Claude hissed ruefully as he adjusted the makeshift bandage on his arm. "Both decisions I came to question quite shortly after the fact." Joy tried to not feel guilty, but it didn't quite work. "In any case, that is how Aniseed came under my charge."

"Aniseed?" Joy nearly shrieked. "But she—"

"Stop." Graus Claude sounded patiently irked. "You must learn to *listen*, Miss Malone, which is a function of your ears and not your tongue, if you please." He pushed the carafe aside with one hand as still another fussed with the tie bandage. "Young Aniseed was my charge when she assumed her role on the Council, the Forest Seat—one which, at the time, was not so unlike my own as to cause unrest. Quite the contrary, we once shared a similar mind as to how the Twixt was progressing in the absence of our rightful rulers and what might be done to hasten the reuniting of our people."

"The Imminent Return," Joy said.

The Bailiwick looked pained. "Please, Miss Malone," he said wearily. "Must I resort to physical restraints?"

Joy grimaced. "Sorry."

"Just as well," he rumbled in agreement. "The 'Imminent Return.' Interesting how the phrase itself escaped the confines of the spell—would that it had never worked at all!" He sighed heavily. "But I digress. As you might imagine, the destruction of large swaths of forest threatened the bulk of Aniseed's kin, still bound to their trees. Theirs was a strain of Forest Folk deeply tied to their phylum, dependent on *twaining* to reproduce—the graftlings could not be moved until their cleaving, and the elders refused to leave their young unguarded. It went against their grain." He looked introspectively at his banker's lamp, which outlined his profile in a warm green glow. "They thought to defend their territory based on old knowledge, pre-Industrialite knowledge. It was a slaughter." The Bailiwick raised his chins to deliver his next words. "This by no means excuses or accounts for what follows—I include these details only to provide proper context, you understand." Two of his hands thread together and squeezed, their knuckles gone pale. "Full disclosure," he added, nodding to himself and to her. "I trust you'll listen well."

Joy, saying nothing, barely nodded.

"Aniseed was my protégé, but she visited often with many questions, ever eager to learn more." He cast a weary glance at Joy. "She was an apt pupil. Driven. Passionate." He coughed and fussed with the things on his desk. "One evening, Aniseed came to me saying that she felt she could no longer continue to serve the Council with the loss of her people clouding her mind. She was, politically and by auspice, a proponent of balance, responsible for holding the peace until the King and Queen could return by Council consent. But after the decimation of her people, she confessed that she harbored a deep resentment of humans and a dark desire for revenge that was eating her heartwood like maggots. I remember those words, 'like maggots.'" He raised his hands helplessly and shook his head. "She came to me in confidence, begging for answers, for some sort of peace. I devised every way that I could conjure and some that were, in hindsight, well intended but ill wrought. Yet, I feared for her—for her sanity as well as her life. She was the last of her kind and one of our youngest Council members. She was ardent, well-spoken, intelligent and fair. She had become a symbol of the uncertain future of the Twixt, one with few offspring that had dwindled to none, and someone the Folk were watching closely. I believe that is when she gained power—she was a light in the darkness, a candle in the night, the youthful, determined face of our dwindling hope. I will admit that I was desperate to keep that flame alive."

The Bailiwick's bulk shifted, his jowls quivering as he touched the ruined tie. "After she had exhausted all efforts, she came to me, hollow and destitute of spirit, with one last request—an ancient spell of forgetting. At the time, it seemed an elegant solution." One of his claws traced a line in the rich mahogany grain. "As I've said, I am no spell-caster, but, as *segulah*, Aniseed was without peer—able to manipulate the few, latent magics that remained in our shared world. It was her vision and creativity that made her eligible for the Council, and she spearheaded the adaptation of *signaturae*, replacing our True Names with symbols that could not be spoken, which saved our people in the dark times." He grew quiet as he remembered who sat before him. "But you know all of this," he said, "far better than most."

His claws tapped an irritated pattern as he took a deep breath. "In any event, the spell required a number of difficult conditions which made it quite impossible to be both caster and recipient, clearly a built-in safeguard of the spell, and so she asked that I be the one to perform the spell, following her instructions." Graus Claude's voice hinted steel. "She claimed that she wished to forget the loss of her people, which might allow her to carry on as a member of the Council and—by her own admission—make her immortal life bearable." His hands became fists. "You must remember that, to the best of our knowledge, Aniseed was the very last of her kind. Without such comfort, she feared that she would eventually cause her own people's extinction by taking her own life and complete the eradication that the humans had begun, which was a fate she considered inexcusable. She had no desire to *ever* let the enemy win! But, in order to survive, she had to continue living despite her suffering. She had to forget what humanity had done to her if she could not forgive. Surrender was something she did not know how to do." He wiped a single palm over his face as he shifted in his chair. His voice, when he spoke, was strangled and strange. "She could not bear it any longer—I could see that in her eyes, I could hear it in her voice," he said. "It was killing her...and that was killing me."

Realization hit Joy like a fist. She bit her lips and her tongue, but Graus Claude saw it and nodded.

"Yes," he said. "I loved her once." His hands rested together like a stack of books. "We were lovers for nearly three hundred years."

He leaned back as if to put distance between himself and his confession. "But, of course, afterward, I'd forgotten about the spell, forgotten about everything but the fact that she had been sad, and after we last spoke, she was able to go on." He gave a wan smile, remembering. "I believe I enjoyed taking credit for that accomplishment, knowing that I had done well both as her mentor and her friend, even if I could not pinpoint what it was, exactly, that I had done. Even now, having memory thrust upon me, I remember that my first thoughts were that the spell had not worked, or that, perhaps, she had forgotten, but could not forgive. I had wanted to believe that it was still possible for her to have been other than what she was." His face fell. "How telling that is. How foolish the heart."

Graus Claude lifted one delicate teacup and took a sip. "In any case, as the years continued, Aniseed's disquiet became more pronounced, her official stance on the Council became more extremist, our political positions became diametrically opposed, and our desires wandered into other beds, which is often the way of the immortal heart and the price of longevity." He shrugged and winced as the wound gave a small gush of blood. He pressed his pocket kerchief against his sleeve. "I did not overburden myself with the parting. I thought, perhaps, that not even my best efforts were enough to heal one so wounded or that her pain ran deeper than the roots of her lost kin. We privately went our separate ways and publicly clashed evermore." Joy shook her head, and the Bailiwick stopped sipping. "Do you have comment, Miss Malone?"

Her mouth barely shaped the words. "You *loved* her?" she said, her voice hitched in disbelief. "How could you say you *loved* her? I heard how you talked about her, the witch, the betrayer. I watched you flip out when you figured out what she'd done with the *signaturae*—piggybacking hers on to everyone else's in order to spread her antihuman plague. I saw you leading an army, demanding that she surrender or die!" Confusion grappled with anger and scratched in her throat. "You raised her killer in your own home, extending his life for the chance to murder her—*which he did*—and you...?" But Joy stopped, remembering how the Bailiwick had prayed over the dead, his hands of benediction outstretched across the warehouse floor. *Who had he been mourning?* She whispered, still confused, "How could you have *loved* her?"

Graus Claude looked at her pityingly, his voice once again a fatherly burr. "Ah, Miss Malone, you are new to Cupid's game," he said. "Know that the greater the love, the greater the risk of its reverse—love and hate are two halves of the same coin, flipped. There is no greater pain than that which is caused by a loved one, and no greater fury than that which was once fanned by love's flame." His head shook gently. "It is a deeply destructive game we play with one another's hearts, and I would not wish it on anyone nor trade it for the world."

With that, the Bailiwick hauled himself upright and, with great dignity, came out from behind the desk, draped his suit jacket over one of his arms, proud and noble, and walked toward his double doors. Joy watched him pass her, uncertain whether to stay seated or run.

"You should take your belongings before you go," he said. "And be sure to include the velvet box next to the printer—it has your pearls as well as Master Ink's cuff links. Don't forget the clasp. And do remember to go for your fitting—the calling card is in the box and has my tailor's complete information." He patted his pockets as if searching for lost keys. "I must apologize for not continuing your tutelage as is my duty as your sponsor, but, circumstances being what they are, I find that I have pressing obligations elsewhere." He lifted a walking stick from a stand by the bookshelves, his wounded arm tucked close to his chest. "I regret to say that I doubt I shall be able to attend the gala, after all. I can only offer my profound and sincerest apologies for the unforgivable lapse and beg your leave not to take it as a personal slight," he said with a sparkle of a smile. "On the contrary, I am quite proud of your achievements, and I am certain that yours will be an event to remember."

Joy leaped to her feet. "Where are you going?" she asked.

"I am going," he said grandly, "to turn myself in."

"*What?*"

He'd reached the coatrack and busied himself by draping a cloak over his wounded arm, buttoning it at the collar to hide the bloody stain. "I am going to the Council to confess my crimes and submit myself to their justice," he said, picking lint from the shoulder. "I could hope for leniency, but, given the extent of the transgression, it is an unlikely outcome."

"But—!" Joy sputtered, trying to include the words *you can't!* because, obviously, he could and would and was.

Kurt appeared in the double doors looking professionally grim. Without a word, he adjusted the Bailiwick's travel cloak and ran a lint roller briskly down the front and sides. Graus Claude submitted to his butler's ministrations with quiet dignity.

"And how are our Scribes?" the frog said while loosening his collar.

"Master Ink is resting and Mistress Inq watches over him," Kurt said crisply, but spared Joy a glance. "Both are well, considering." He tugged the shoulders straight and lifted his chin, flashing the long, serrated scar. "They accept your confession and will abide by your decision."

"Very well," the Bailiwick said. "Thank you, Kurt. You have your orders."

"Yes, sir."

The aristocratic amphibian cut an impressive figure as he trudged into the hallway with a dignified air. Joy stood next to Kurt by the ironwood doors, close enough to smell the starch on his shirt. She felt helpless, hopeless and horribly to blame.

"They won't remember, Graus Claude," Kurt said.

The Bailiwick paused. Joy had never heard Kurt use his employer's proper name before. "More than that," the butler continued, "they *cannot* remember. They will not understand your crime because they are unable to recall that there ever was a King and Queen or that the rest of their kin are locked away behind a door," he continued. "They cannot be reminded or remember even after you tell them—the spell is well forged and can only be broken by the one who cast it," he said. "Or when the door is opened."

Graus Claude didn't turn back, but his voice filled the hall. "I cannot open the door because I do not know where it is," he said patiently. "I know only that I hold it inside me, in the Bailiwick, as well as our lost princess." His voice lifted. "The courier would know—but I do not know who that is, either." He sighed with a great swell of his back. "They could be dead, they could be lost, I do not know—but the courier most certainly cannot remember their post, let alone their charge," he said. "I only know that that person is not me." He faced the door once more. "I am sorry that I cannot help you."

Kurt's voice was hard as stone. "You must break the spell before you can ask for forgiveness."

Joy stared at him in disbelief.

The Bailiwick lingered on the threshold, his hunched shoulders drooping even further under his cloak. "I cannot," he said, lifting one finger from his cane. "Not that I fear the repercussions, mind, but because I do not know the true nature of the spell." His voice slithered to a whisper. "Only its maker could untie such a knot."

"Aniseed," Joy said.

Kurt raised his chin. "Aniseed is dead."

Graus Claude said nothing—Kurt spoke the truth, keen and sharp as any Folk. He might have been mortal, but he wasn't quite human, having lived and worked among them for so long. Joy knew Kurt was many things, but she hadn't realized that he could be cruel.

"But you aren't to blame," Joy said desperately. "Aniseed tricked you! She must have tampered with the spell—she *had* to have known what she was doing! She could have been planning this all along, having you cast the spell instead of her—it fits! If the spell was discovered, all evidence would lead back to you and not her." Joy crossed the long hall and placed a hand on his cloak. "You said the Folk can't disobey the rules—the rules were made by the King and Queen, who wanted humans and Folk to live together. Your loyalty, *everyone's* loyalty, must be absolute. You can't act against the King and Queen—it's unthinkable! How could there have been a coup?" Joy tugged at the light wool of his cloak. "The only way to disobey them would be *to forget that they ever existed.* You can't be loyal to someone you don't remember. Loyalty is a *choice.*" Joy's thoughts were tripping over themselves in their hurry to make him understand. "Don't you see? It's a loophole! The *ultimate* loophole! With the King and Queen out of the way, Aniseed could go against their wishes and bring about her crazy Golden Age!" Joy's voice was shaking. "*She's* the one who did this! *She's* the traitor!"

"*Yes*," the Bailiwick said sharply. The word banged like a gavel. "But she is dead, Miss Malone, and the secret to the spell's undoing died with her."

Shame colored his words black with scorn, and he continued his exit. Joy dropped her hold on him. Her fingers wrapped themselves in knots.

"But...then there is no reason for you to turn yourself in," Joy said, her face wet and hot. *This is wrong! This isn't happening!* "Graus Claude, please, it wasn't your fault!" Her voice pitched high in alarm. "They'll kill you!"

"Nonsense," he said with false gaiety. "The Council do not sentence one another to death." He tugged on his lapel. "Trust me, it creates far too much paperwork. Although, for a crime of this magnitude—it *is* quite an exceptional offense." He paused, resting his claw on the handle of the front door. "And I have never been known to be anything other than exceptional." He lumbered sideways and gifted Joy with a rare smile. "Even if they kill me, they will name another Bailiwick, and the young Majesty will remain safe inside, never fear. As for me," he said, straightening his back. "My Lady Fortune oft smiles upon the brave. But when you see the princess, please, tell her—" He paused again, his gaze lost and faraway. "Tell her that I am truly sorry, and I leave her in the most trusted and capable hands I have known."

He threw the doors open. The Bentley idled at the curb.

"Your confession will be meaningless," Kurt called after him.

The Bailiwick glanced back, both proud and sad.

"It will not be meaningless to me."

TWELVE

KURT SHUT THE DOOR AND LOCKED IT. PRESSING A SEries of buttons behind a gilt frame, he hit Enter. A ward shimmered into place.

"We have to go after him," Joy said.

Kurt marched down the hall, eyes forward, face grim.

"I have my instructions."

Joy ran to keep up as Kurt summoned the elevator. "I know, but we can't let him go to the Council. That won't work—" She stumbled after him. "They won't believe him because they *can't*! They can't remember anything!"

Kurt stepped into the small brass space, and Joy hurried in next to him. He clicked the lever to the second notch, and the doors slipped closed.

"What do you think will happen to him?" she said.

Kurt kept his expression impassive. "I don't know."

"Guess."

Kurt sighed, his eyes inspecting the mirrors. "I imagine that they will either dismiss him, convict him or condemn him."

Joy gaped. "We can't let that happen!"

The elevator door slid open, and Kurt entered a long hallway with striped wallpaper. Joy followed close behind.

"The Bailiwick is honorable and wishes to seek justice in the company of his peers," Kurt said. "There are few opportunities for the Folk to exercise their free will, far be it for me to deny him his as he denied me mine."

Kurt walked into the next room, swiftly crossing the rose-colored carpet to a four-poster bed by the window. The bedroom was tall and airy with a tapestry loom, a painted screen and a large, marble hearth. Inq sat in a Queen Anne's chaise with a book on her lap. Ink lay pillowed in the bed, eyes closed. Kurt plucked another chair from beside the fireplace and set it next to the nightstand. Joy sat down.

"Should they sentence Graus Claude to be stripped of his title or life, it will be his choice whether to abide by their decision or refute his Name, as Hasp did," Kurt said as he checked the window's ward. "In any case, my service to the Bailiwick will have ended." He paused, hand loose on the curtain pull. "Then I will be free."

Inq glared at him with hooded eyes.

Joy turned to Ink. His eyes were gently closed, his chest rising and falling in a slow, even rhythm. She brushed his long bangs away from his face, which looked even more boyish and innocent in sleep. She'd never seen Ink asleep—he claimed he never slept—and Graus Claude claimed that he'd never shut Ink off before. The Bailiwick's betrayal left a hot lump of guilt and anger and confusion roiling in her gut, but it was hard to think about it while watching Ink's eyelashes twitch.

How long would he be like this? Would he be okay? Was he dreaming? Did the Folk dream? Did Ink? Joy stroked his cheek and brushed the side of his neck, laying a hand against his chest—the spot on his left breast felt as solid as ever, hiding the Bailiwick's secret fail-safe somewhere beneath her fingers. Joy could feel the dull beat of his heart through the comforter. *Thump-thump. Thump-thump.* She tugged the blankets a little higher and wished he'd wake up. Soon. Now.

She badly needed a number sixteen.

Inq was reading her book with all the signs of barely contained fury. Her face was a calm mask, serene as porcelain, yet she turned the pages with a sharp *snap!* She straightened in her seat, calm and aloof, deliberately not looking at Joy. *Great.*

Joy knew, intellectually, that Ink would be all right and that the princess would be safe inside the Bailiwick, no matter who the Bailiwick might be. She knew that it would be easiest to sit here quietly, to stay and wait for Ink to wake. She wanted to be here for him. She wanted to see him open his eyes. She wanted to tell him everything and ask him what to do.

But she needed to save Graus Claude.

Soon. Now.

Joy pressed a kiss to Ink's forehead. Kurt adjusted a baroque clock on the mantel. Inq turned another page in her book. *Snap!*

"Will you take me to the Bailiwick?" Joy asked.

Inq closed the book. "Where did he go?"

"He went to turn himself in to the Council," Joy said. "I think he's gone to the Council Hall."

Inq chuckled under her breath. "May he have better luck than most when begging them for mercy."

"Luck is his auspice," Kurt said.

Inq nodded. "True. That's probably the only way he managed to beat Ink in close combat," she said, glancing at her brother. "I swear I taught him better than that." She opened her book again. "Fortunately, it doesn't matter to me who is the Bailiwick as long as I can access the gate. If Graus Claude is stripped of his title or executed, that makes things simple. It's only a problem if he is incarcerated while maintaining his status. Then things get tricky," she said, glaring conspiratorially at Joy. "But we can always deal with that."

Kill Graus Claude? Joy balked. *Never!*

"But he didn't—" Joy hesitated. *Inq doesn't know!* She didn't know what had happened in Graus Claude's office. The Bailiwick didn't beat Ink, he *shut him off*. Inq didn't know about the snooze button, the secret fail-safe, the safety switch. It was a secret Joy had over her. "He...didn't stand a chance," Joy said, switching gears. "I mean, how long has Graus Claude been on the Council? He's probably had assassins attacking him for years. Why else have a butler bodyguard?"

Inq and Kurt exchanged a wordless glance, like an old married couple.

"Ink will be all right, won't he?" Joy asked.

Kurt examined Ink again, pressing firmly on his wrist, checking his new pulse. "He's unconscious," he said. "But otherwise unharmed. I am not sure how he managed it since I did not think the Scribes had anything to concuss, but Ink has evidently been shaping himself to emulate humans far more than we'd realized."

Inq pursed her lips at Joy. "I blame you."

"Fine," Joy said. "Blame me. Blame me all you want. But we need Graus Claude. We can't let him get arrested or banished because of something Aniseed did." Joy tried appealing to Kurt. "She *wanted* him to take the blame. She *wanted* the spell to get traced back to him. She tricked him into casting the wrong spell, and we can't let her get away with it! Then she's won!"

Inq hissed under her breath, curling her lip. "Manipulative snake."

Joy leaned forward. "So, will you take me to Graus Claude?"

Inq licked her thumb and turned a page.

"Nope."

Joy gave a wordless snarl and launched out of her chair, stalking across the room in mute frustration. Ink might be fine in a couple of hours, but she didn't know if Graus Claude *had* a couple of hours. How long before the Council would be called together in session? What would happen when he tried to confess? What would the Council understand other than he was guilty of casting a blanket spell upon the entire Twixt? That was obviously a major crime. The Folk had invented the entire system of *signaturae* to avoid being manipulated and turned into slaves. Joy remembered the chaos in the Council Hall when she'd accepted her True Name, the wave of outrage, threats and noise. What would happen to Graus Claude?

She turned in tighter circles, her distress hemmed in by the fireplace and the loom. How could she get there? What good would it do? She wouldn't be able to convince them of anything, especially not those like Sol Leander. He'd love the excuse to have her dismissed, thrown out of the Hall, discredited before the gala. *The gala!* She'd never survive it without Graus Claude. He was her sponsor. And her friend. He was the Bailiwick, keeper of the door between worlds and the last, loyal subject to the missing royal family. She couldn't let it happen! Ink had never bothered with Folk politics, and Joy had only the vaguest idea from Graus Claude's notes—there was so much that she didn't know, that she didn't have to work with: status, influence, contacts, magic...

Joy stopped. She squeezed her purse strap. She had *a lot* of magic.

And she knew how to get Under the Hill.

Fishing out the glow stick with the black electric tape, Joy snapped it in half and shook it quickly. Both Inq and Kurt looked up at the growing neon-colored globe, yawning open, engulfing her in purple light. The bubble expanded, blurring at the edges, outlining the furniture and the side of Ink's face. Kurt moved deftly between her and Inq. Inq stood up, frowning.

"You are being foolish, Joy," she said. "You cannot save him from his fate."

Joy's hair billowed out in static waves.

"I can try."

And she stepped onto the packed-dirt floor under a ring of dark fairy lights.

Joy glanced around the Carousel club, trying to get her bearings. She wasn't used to the place being empty—it was eerie without the music and noise. It was like an entirely different place, an old museum or an abandoned theme park. The black walls and dull mirrors made the Carousel feel spooky and surreal. She walked around the perimeter of the massive merry-go-round, her every motion reflected in the mirrored panels, mocking her, chasing her, slipping along the undercarriage and bouncing off walls, leaving her wondering if she was alone or not.

She half ran to the office trailer and tried the doorknob. Locked. She knocked on the hollow wood. No answer. Joy crossed the aisle and hopped onto the circular floor. It tipped ever so slightly and gave a tired, rusty groan. The sound skittered up her spine. How had she never noticed that while dancing? The music must have drowned it out. The crowd must hold the dance floor steady. She walked toward the center pillar, her footsteps creaking off the fun-house mirrors and clanking against the metal mounts where the poles used to be. As she moved, her shifting weight pressed uneasy moans out of the gears. Joy ducked into the hollow DJ booth and poked around the tables, feeling around the walls, her fingers sliding over the edges of bumper stickers and band posters and buried staples. There had to be a way in!

"Hello?" she called out. "Anyone here?" As hard as it was to imagine the Carousel silent and empty, it was impossible to imagine the Folk abandoning their post. This was the Glen's entrance Under the Hill. Joy knew it was guarded against encroachment by humans—the very thing she was here to do—and she hadn't much time. Shouldn't someone be here to arrest her already? Joy knocked her knuckles against the table. "Dmitri?" she tried. "You here?"

Silence. Nothing but dust and the faint smell of beer.

Joy slid her hands under the table and over the console. She found a baggie taped to the underside full of rolling papers and dried leaves. Joy remembered the lady DJ and lifted the keyboard, finding her discarded matchbox. She rattled the matches inside and tucked it into her pouch. If she couldn't find her own way in, maybe Filly could bring her? She wanted to get to the Council Hall as quickly and with as little noise as possible, and while the blond warrior might be able to help with the former, she'd be abysmal at the latter.

Inq had escorted her to the Hall from here. Joy *knew* there was a way inside.

Quickly crossing the carousel, the creaks and moans chasing her footsteps like ghosts, Joy dropped to the ground and got down on her hands and knees, peering under the rotating floor at the exposed machinery. If there were any doors or wards or glyphs, she couldn't see them with her Sight. She sat up and wiped the dirt off her hands and then stared at the ground. She flipped over one of the sticky black indoor-outdoor mats, exposing the bare packed earth. She banged the flat of her hand against the ground.

"Hey!" she shouted near the surface of dirt. "Let me in!" She knocked and dug at the ground, trying to feel her way to a trapdoor or marked stone, but there was nothing. She slapped her hand against the soil and pushed herself standing, brushing her palms against her capris. She kicked the mat flap over and walked out the nearest exit, looking for a break in the security fence that surrounded the club.

The entry gate was chained and padlocked. The old town green stretched past the chain link and down the hill. Joy remembered approaching the Carousel with Stef when she'd gone to meet Inq to stand trial. Maybe the entrance was farther downhill? Joy looked up at the fence. Was it easier to go over or under? She took the scalpel out of her purse pocket and picked up the padlock, then poked the blade into the keyhole and drew it slowly around, feeling the tumblers click and clunk into place. The padlock popped open.

Easier to go *through*.

Joy slid past the door and relocked the padlock through the chain link, letting it fall heavily back into place. She let gravity pull her down the incline, pacing the circumference of the hill, trying to use her Sight. She kept a hold of her scalpel and, curious, kicked off her shoes, wondering if she could feel anything through the soles of her feet. The grass was thick and cool, the earth pebbly and warm—the two sensations made her feel like a little kid again, running through the backyard and doing cartwheels in Abbot's Field, but it did nothing to indicate an entrance Under the Hill.

Joy sighed, disappointed, and wondered what she was going to do now.

Now call Filly, she figured and opened her purse.

There was a tremor under her toes.

At first, she thought it might be something rumbling in the distance, but she realized it was something trembling under her skin. It rippled up her arches, electricity zinging along the fine hairs on her skin. She was hyperaware of her body. Her skin crackled, her nose twitched. She fought back a sneeze. Her lungs felt like they were filling up with light. Her eyes widened. Her ears popped. A rising feeling, like panic, tickled like the early stages of hypoglycemia or heatstroke. Joy stood, light-headed, heavy-lidded, drunk on something like Inq's armored glyphs. Everything was yawning, spinning, reeling.

Where's it coming from? What's happening?

The prickling feeling slid up her limbs, percolating just below her ribs. She swiped at her arms, feeling the tickle of legs and wings, a thousand imaginary butterflies or bees, but there was nothing there; just the growing feeling that something was happening, something was *wrong*—or, not wrong—*different*. Joy pressed a clenched fist to her stomach, swallowing against the threat that she might throw up or faint or explode.

It was happening again. The building-pressure-light, power leaking through the cracks, the almost-pleasure-pain...

Too much. Too much!

She bent forward. The wash of feeling built quickly and broke, erupting in her chest, through her limbs, down her arms, out her toes, diving underground, deep into the dirt. It flowed into the earth, disappearing, absorbed by the bottomless world.

She felt a sudden emptiness, a punched-gut moment.

She coughed, her mouth dry, and looked up.

No door.

She glanced at her body.

No fins. No scales. No spots.

But she stood in the center of a thin crater, a layer of grass and topsoil blown away, leaving a smooth, perfect circle like a trowel through the mud. A fading line of red fire licked along its edge.

A slow, ominous shudder passed over her. Sweat trickled down her neck. She stared at the deep, dark wells of her footsteps, ringed in hairline cracks—she was the middle of it. She'd been the source. It had been *her*. Joy blinked to clear her eyes. The red fire winked out like a trick of the light. Slowly she pulled up one foot, caked in mud, and stepped on the smooth, moist surface, pulling her other foot free. Her toes sank slightly in the soft, wet clay. Her shoes had been blown somewhere downhill.

She backed carefully out of the circle, leaving a trail of bare footprints. She stopped on the torn edge of the lawn and wiped her feet in the grass. The perfect hole seemed impossible, surreal, like a crop circle with no crops. Joy's brain struggled to make sense of it, debating whether it could be real, what it meant, what she should do now.

She had no idea. She stomped her foot in frustration, eyes teary and tired.

There was an answering *thump*. She felt it kick under her feet.

Beneath the hill, Joy could feel something approaching—many somethings—like heavy feet running along the underside of the earth. There was a *pip-pip-pip* sound behind her, loud enough to make her turn. Tiny gaseous bubbles were rising out of the smooth surface of the mud, simmering and popping like rain in reverse. As she watched, the bubbles grew larger, pushing fat dollops of mud into the air, spitting brown water and caving in gaping holes as the earth continued to churn.

Her body shut down. Her limbs went slack. Joy watched the ground boil like a thick soup, chunks of earth swelling and breaking through the thin smear of soil. Dim lights appeared in pairs, glowing an angry, ruby red.

"Ink," Joy whispered without moving her lips.

Cracks formed in the upturned earth. Dribbles of water ran down like drool. The glowing orbs slid sideways and upright, mounds breaking off and lurching forward, shedding clumps of grass and clay. Buried roots became bones, twigs coiled into ribs, thick, heavy limbs hauled up grubby midriffs, stony knees, muddy hands, rocky feet. There was a rough glyph gouged into each dirty forehead, and their inhuman eyes burned like coals.

Joy stood stock-still in front of a mob of mudmen.

The squat creatures glared at her, slammed their fists together and screamed.

THIRTEEN

JOY HAD NEVER REALIZED THAT IT WAS POSSIBLE TO run upward.

She launched vertically, clawing at the chain-link fence, not registering the futility of it until she felt gravity's hand yank her down. Hard.

The clay men clambered after her, eyes burning, mouths gaping, surrounding her with slow, deliberate steps. Their feet sank into the ground, sucking and drinking the earth up their bodies in great gulps of sludge, adding mass and muscle, growing larger as they came.

She gave a wordless shriek and flipped the scalpel over in her hand as the creatures drew closer. She held it up in front of her.

"Stop!" Joy shouted. "Stop! *Duei nis da Counsallierai—*" she gasped "*—en dictie uellaris emonim oun!*" The Old Tongue passcode evaporated in her mouth. Nothing registered. These things didn't think. Their eyes were empty of everything except a clear, single-minded purpose: their hands outstretched, coming for Joy.

She was an interloper, uninvited, human enough. These were automatons, animated sentries. They wouldn't—or couldn't—recognize Joy.

"Crap."

She hooked her toes between the chain links, climbing

higher, faster. Clamping the scalpel in her teeth, she tasted metal and dirt. Threading her fingers through the wire, she grabbed desperate handholds, scrambling up and over the top. Joy wrenched herself sideways, dropped and landed softly on the other side, knees absorbing the impact. She glanced back at the horde.

The mud creatures pressed themselves against the fence, pushing their faces through the square chain link, their glyphs and eyes and limbs slowly passing through the open spaces, their clay flesh yielding and re-forming around the wires as they continued to advance. Joy didn't stick around to watch; she ran inside the Carousel, looking for the beacon door.

It was dark. There was nothing. No purple light. No portal out. The bubble had faded somehow, disappeared.

Mudmen filled the exit, pressing forward into the club.

Joy jumped on to the rotating floor with a loud creak and scrambled up the decorative supports, hooking her fingers on the bases of lightbulbs that framed the outer hull. Grabbing the metal crossbeams on the undercarriage, Joy curled herself with a gymnast's control, up and onto the roof. She braced her feet against the scalloped edging and steadied herself between the slats. Legs split wide over the painted panel, she grabbed her scalpel and wrapped her purse across her back.

Something solid hit the carousel. The entire thing shuddered. Joy flattened herself along the circus tent topside and tucked her legs under her body. There was another jarring thud! This would be the perfect time for a rescue. This was not the perfect time to be trapped on the roof of a refurbished six-row carousel surrounded by rampaging mud golems. Joy tried to think as another heavy slam rattled her teeth.

The old machinery buckled, its parts splintering on impact. Once. Twice. Joy clenched her teeth and her knees. She heard mirrors shatter. Glass bulbs popped against the ground. Wooden beams broke with a bone-jarring snap. Needing both hands to hold on, she spat the scalpel into her purse and looked down. The clay creatures slammed themselves into the sides of the Carousel, one after another, trying to knock her down.

Joy held her breath as she stretched one foot forward, crawling higher up the peaked roof, timing her movements in between assaults. She corkscrewed her body around the metal flag mount and pressed herself against the cap, farthest from the sides, likely directly over the hollowed-out central pillar where the calliope used to be. The painted wood scratched her stomach and scraped her chin. She willed herself tighter as another blow struck.

The creatures hadn't attempted to climb after her, but they'd shrunk, becoming stouter, larger, heavier, like solid blocks on legs. Three of them were slamming into the carousel in turns while two more leveraged themselves on one side, pushing down against the floor with each jarring *thud*. The old metal gears whined and broke, panging and clanging in loud fits and bursts. It was as if the mud golems were trying to capsize the carousel. Joy was pretty sure that it was mounted into a concrete base. If that was their strategy, then maybe she had time to escape.

Joy uncurled from the top and scanned the catwalks and the ceiling fans, calculating whether she could safely jump onto the office trailer or the bar. Then what? As she looked for likely exits, she saw that the rest of the muddy mob had crouched together like a halftime football huddle by the door. She watched four creatures stuff themselves into a bunch, pressing tightly together, melding into a massive, shifting mound of clay flesh and broken limbs, their coal-bright eyes swimming aimlessly through the malformed body, rolling slowly toward a broad, flat head that split lengthwise, forming a wide, fractured mouth.

The hulking glom-monster took a drunken, lopsided step. The whole club shook.

"Oh God..." Joy breathed and clenched tighter around the flag mount, dearly wishing she had something like the Red Knight's flaming ax instead of a blade the size of a thumbnail.

A small, squat head peered over the edge, red eyes burning.

Joy screamed, opened her palm, exposing Inq's sigil and *pushed*. The creature's head spattered like wet clay under a hair dryer. It grunted, and she gave it another full blast in the face, obliterating the glyph in its forehead and punching one of its eyes deep into its socket. The gaping mouth hissed a thin, airy wail, and its remaining eye winked out. The body collapsed backward and disappeared over the edge of the roof. There was a heavy, wet *thump*.

Joy coughed a quick exhale. *Their glyphs keep them alive.*

There wasn't time to savor her victory as the resounding *thuds* below came faster, pushed along with heaving *cracks*, splintering something deep inside the building that Joy could feel under her stomach. The peak tipped dangerously as the roof began to tilt. The semiautomatic *snap-snap-snap* of pylons breaking joined a deep, grinding groan, the last sigh of defeat. She had to jump!

Something reckless and wild flared inside her, bringing a flush of heat to her surface, like sunburn from the inside. Joy bunched her knees, cracked her toes and pounced.

The rooftop tumbled, smashing on impact, thundering behind her as she landed on two of her foes, their muddy bodies absorbing the impact. Joy felt the buried branches snap. Knee-deep in ruined torsos, she drove her hands into their foreheads, grabbing fistfuls of sticky earth and raking gouges between their eyes, obliterating the glyphs, watching the red orbs dim and die. Joy sank, settling deeper as their skeletons went slack, stick figures collapsing under her weight and loose earth.

It fed something inside her, like fuel, like fire.

A golem slammed into her back, a sudden weight that threw her forward, but she shot back an elbow and buried her arm deep into the soft and yielding flesh. Another creature charged, mouth opened in a scream. She lifted her palm and *pushed*, but its mouth clamped over her hand up to the elbow, and she screamed as shattered branches pierced her skin like teeth. Pain and outrage condensed into a white-hot stab, feeding the flame. Joy stopped pulling and drove forward instead, drawing strength out of the clay corpses, from the earth, up her shins and into her pelvis, lighting her spine and spraying out her arms like cannon fire.

The head around her forearm exploded. The golem gripping her shoulder blasted in half. She stood clean and clear; the surrounding mudmen spattered against the black-painted walls in a ring. Joy gasped, hunched over, heaving for breath, her arms scratched and bleeding, still unspeakably *angry*, surging with a burning, driving need to fight, to destroy.

It was as if, alone in the chaos, she had permission to let go.

There was a hollow howl, and Joy turned, arms outthrust, slicing through another pair of mouths and arms, raking her fingers through their faces and blasting great gouts of air through her palm. She waded forward, pushing through the mud that dried, baked and cracked against her skin, pressing through the line of golems, clawing her way out. Toward the exit. Toward the light. Joy gritted her teeth, grunting with effort, breathing through her nose. Her eyes watered as she squinted into the mirrored shadows, sharp-edged and broken, swarming with fiery eyes and lipless mouths. She punched weakly through another block of heavy, animate clay and ripped out a handful of solid forehead, then dropped it in the dirt. Eyes blackened and fell, lifeless. Joy stumbled onward. Her arms were growing tired. Inq's push was growing weaker. Her adrenaline surge was starting to flag.

She'd forgotten about the glom-monster.

The fused-golem creature screamed as it lurched toward her, mandibles dripping, multiple eyes burning, its crablike arms raised to hammer her flat. Joy crouched low, digging her arms into the earth, feeling broken splinters spike under her fingernails and buried rocks scrape against her wrists. The heat was boiling up inside her again—the anger, the rage. She could feel it. She pushed deeper into the mud, instinctively seeking coolness, seeking heat, seeking escape, seeking vengeance—she didn't know which. The grotesque mass stalked forward on its thick, stomping legs. Glass shook. Part of the ceiling collapsed. She glared up at it, face full of dirt, body half buried in clay. She couldn't let go. She couldn't call for help. She couldn't lift her arms. She was too tired, too heavy. There wasn't enough.

Darkness dropped over her shoulder and rose like a cape, shielding her unprotected head as the thing's arms smashed down. There was an *oof* as two bodies sank deeper into the inanimate muck. Joy's arms were trapped in the dense soil up to her shoulders, the sizzling energy skittered hot quicksilver along her limbs. She didn't know who was there. She couldn't see—couldn't think clearly.

"Filly?" she whispered, but it wasn't. Her heart leaped. "Ink?"

There was a grunt as the next barrage *slam-slam-slammed!*

down, beating loudly against the shield. There was a resigned sigh near her ear.

"No."

Before she could react, the glom-monster shrieked and swept its arm sideways, knocking whomever it was prone. Exposed, Joy blinked up at the shifting, globular thing as it advanced; her arms were stuck like steel girders sunk deep into the earth. She should be panicking. She should be screaming. Instead, she felt something building beneath her, drawing closer, light squeezing sound, tense and pressed, feeling both heavy and huge.

"What are you doing?" The voice behind her was familiar even if the anger wasn't. Joy couldn't turn to see who it was.

"I don't know," Joy shouted.

"Stay down!" There was a flip and flicker of movement, a quick series of spins behind her head that Joy could barely see, the broken mirrors playing tricks. There was a bellow of rage, crashing wood and the crackle of glass. Something heavy spun past and smashed into the ticket booth. Joy tried to turn to see what it was, but couldn't move. Her arms trembled. Steam eked out of the muddy cracks.

There was another sharp sound that crumbled into a shower of heavy dust. Something that felt like fur whipped across her back. She could feel the dead eyes of the ex-golems swimming through the earth, the coarse clay, the cool sandstone, the fissures forming far below...or was it something else, something inside her? Something cracking, breaking, trying to get out? She shuddered with more than fear. Her *signatura* burned between her shoulders. Her hands felt like they were spreading, pushing wider, her bones elastic, her fingers thin. Her elbows bucked, vibrating madly; her arms locked.

Joy didn't know where she was or who she was or what she was anymore—she only knew one thing:

"Get off of the ground!" she shouted. "Get up! Get clear!"

The diving, driving energy between her fingers squeezed into her chest, shot through the earth, fanning out like a deep sea net and...

The ground erupted, fountaining in great gushes of earth. The gouts flowered open, thick fingers punching through the ceiling, clawing against gravity, slow-motion plumes, then—after a still-motion moment—wilting, collapsing, swallowing the monster beneath a tide of dirt. A sinkhole opened. The geyser crashed. A belch of earth thrust upward and broke in the sudden, gasping silence.

Great clods of dirt rolled down the sloppy volcano-shaped mound and bounced quietly off the bar stools.

Joy fell onto her back, her body singing, white-hot ash wisping off her limbs; the mud on her skin had baked into dust. She kicked her feet blindly against the rocklike clay. The turbulent dirt had hardened instantly, transformed into a solid, misshapen mass, a great geologic scab that scored the earth. She stumbled to her feet and backed up against the bar. It was solid and real.

"Nice work" came the voice overhead. Joy looked up and saw a great owl perched above the curtained-off shelves. Only when the sun shone through the veil of dust did Joy make out the crown of white hair among the feathers.

"Avery," Joy said, both disappointed and confused. She stumbled over what looked like a stumpy leg, hardened at an angle, crooked and crude. "What are you doing here?" Her head ached, and her arms felt like overcooked noodles. Her stomach growled. How could she be hungry at a time like this?

"I told you. I've been following you, which is no easy task," he said, dropping from the great height and twirling his cloak into place. "And you keep such interesting company—" He stepped closer, his boot heels scraping against baked clay. His eyes reflected the broken mirrors like a cat's. "Who *are* you, Joy Malone?"

She swallowed, still trying to get her bearings and collect her scattered thoughts as she stumbled through the wreck, not quite seeing where she was going, not quite knowing what to think. She wiped her fingers uselessly against her shirt. "I've been asking myself the same thing."

Avery kicked at the solid mound in the middle of the Carousel, testing it with his foot. A few cracks leaked wisps of steam. "Interesting," he said. "Any reason these homunculi were after you?"

Another surge of heat, weak and spent, frayed her nerves. It might have been fear if she'd been smart, but it felt more like satisfaction. Whatever they were, she'd beaten them. "I'm guessing the Folk don't like humans knocking on their back door."

The Tide's aide paused, his eyes silver as the moon. "You're not human."

"I am," Joy said, and it twinged something inside that made her wince. "And I'm not," she admitted. "I'm different. I'm both."

Avery lifted his chin. "You can't be both."

"And yet, I am."

"No, you are one of the Twixt," he said. "I saw it just now."

Joy swallowed back fear and some spit. *What had he seen? What did she look like? Had she changed?* She examined her hands, touched her face—they were dirty, but normal. She tried to act nonchalant with her nerves sparking haywire.

"I don't know what you saw," she said. "But believe me when I say that you can't trust your eyes. Especially here."

This was where it all had started—the first time she'd seen Ink, the first time she'd fallen into his fathomless eyes, the first time she'd used her Sight. She looked around the wreckage. The Carousel was ruined, shattered. It broke something inside her.

"I have to go." Her words were becoming slurred with post-adrenaline crash. She felt a shiver up her spine although it was still August-moist-hot. She kicked over a coal-black stone, a sightless eye, and felt sick. They had been the same ruby red as the fire behind the Bailiwick's teeth. What did that mean? Was it coincidence? *Twice is coincidence, thrice is suspect.* Joy felt a fresh wash of paranoia. She took a few more steps, then turned—the exit door was half buried behind a wall of earth. She felt trapped. Lost. She didn't want to be here talking to Avery—she didn't want him asking questions. They were standing in the Carousel on the Green in her hometown in the middle of the day, and everything was falling apart. The world felt dark and dangerous.

"I have to go," she said again. " I have to find—" *Graus Claude? Filly? The courier? The door?* Joy shook her head and swallowed. Dust motes coated her tongue. "I have to get back to Ink."

"Why?"

He said it honestly, cautious, curious. Joy frowned and stepped farther away from the feather-cloaked man.

"Because he's my *boyfriend*," she said with an unspoken *duh*.

"Ah, yes, your protector and paramour," Avery said. They both turned at the distant wail of sirens. Joy's first thought was *Police!* Her second thought was *Dad!* Avery smiled at her alarm. "Perhaps you should leave here first?" he suggested.

"Right." Joy prayed that the security cameras in the trailer had been utterly destroyed, otherwise this would be her second difficult-to-explain battle on tape. She climbed over to the smashed ticket booth by the trailer and eased herself past the crumpled frame and broken glass. Arching her body, she was able to twist herself between the buckled walls and slip out onto the grass. She checked the slope of the hillside, not wanting anyone to witness her leaving the site of the crime. What she saw made her smile—her shoes! She hurried down the incline and scooped them up in one hand. Dashing across the edge of the Green, she cut through the line of shrubs and crossed the street, then doubled back, circling the corner and jogging behind the tiny strip mall where Dumpsters lined the alley. She sat down on an egg crate to check her feet, thankful she hadn't stepped on any glass during the fight.

"You should keep moving."

Joy jumped. Avery stepped out from behind a lamppost, looking smug.

"Why do you keep following me?" Joy demanded.

"I told you, it's my assignment," he said. "And fortunate for you. I can't very well report on anything if you are dead or detained."

He'd been the one to save her. The Tide's lackey. It galled her to admit it.

"Thank you," she said gruffly.

Avery bowed at the waist of his swallowtail coat. She marched past him, past the Dumpsters. He flipped the edge of the feathered cloak over his right shoulder and followed. Joy picked up the pace, wanting to put more distance between herself and the Carousel and Avery.

"Go away," Joy said over her shoulder. "I don't need an escort." She didn't dare go for her scalpel or her pouch to call Filly. She didn't need Avery knowing any more of her secrets than he already did.

"I'm not here for you," Avery said flatly. She remembered how he'd glared at her when he'd figured out who she was—

the rogue human girl with the Sight. No, he certainly wasn't doing this for her. "Besides, it's not as if anyone else can see me."

Joy bit her lip. "You sound like Ink."

"Ah, yes. Your *boyfriend*," he said.

"What about him?"

Avery sighed. "You really shouldn't lie," he said. "It's a bad mortal habit."

"Excuse me?" Joy snapped. Her voice cut like glass.

Avery stepped past her, ignoring her ire. "You obviously no longer need protection or a claimant," he said. "You've been accepted by the Council, so you do not need to pretend that you are bound to the Scribe." He held the edges of his cloak close to his body as they passed an overflowing trash bin. "Lies come easily to humans, but eventually the mis-said will cause you pain—and can ultimately kill you—so it's best to avoid such unpleasantness before your change is complete."

Joy's stomach flipped. He knew about the change. Had he seen something happen? Was it already too late? What if it happened before she found the King and Queen? Joy felt hot and hollow and altogether exhausted. It took too much energy to worry about that now. She'd failed to break into the chambers Under the Hill. Graus Claude could be anywhere, and the Tide was spying on her every move. She had to get back to Ink. *Soon. Now!*

"You don't know what you're talking about," she said, which was nothing but truth.

Avery gave another small bow, too brief for Joy to be sure whether it was mocking or not. "It was a ruse—and a clever one—I'll grant you that, but it is a ploy that is no longer necessary." They stopped at a hinged gate. He gestured with his wrist, *After you*. She flicked the latch and pushed past him, keeping an eye out for black-and-whites and ruby-red eyes as he continued chatting conversationally. "Binding yourself to one who is not actually Folk and oversees no real auspice was genius, calling it 'love' was almost poetic, something emotionally elusive that cannot be proven before the Council—it gave the Bailiwick the weapon he's so badly needed and gave you time and protection that would have never been granted under any other circumstances. You managed to revise the Council's opinions about those with the Sight, neatly eliminating many who would or could oppose you." Avery nodded, his admiration muffled under his cloak as he followed her across the street. "It was masterfully played, and that, more than anything, qualified you to join the Twixt. Your charade has earned you high marks and high praise, but I'd be wary how far you can push."

Joy stepped gingerly around a puddle of oil by the side of the gas station, choosing her words like her footfalls, treading around what was true and what was—at least originally—a lie. She and Ink *had* pretended to be lovers in order to cover up his mistake, marking her eye instead of blinding her outright, but their lie had grown into truth somewhere between dropping a milk jug and Briarhook branding her arm.

"I don't know where you get your information," she said, cutting through a line of pine trees. "But you should know that, once I accepted my *signatura*, I became bound to the rules of the Twixt. I cannot lie." She turned to match her guide, eye to eye. "I love Indelible Ink."

She let go of the branch. It smacked Avery in the chest.

The shadows caught the curl of his lip. "Then one of us is a fool."

Joy shrugged. "You said it, not me."

Avery shook his head, bemused or aghast. "You honestly believe that you *love* the Scribe?"

She stepped onto the sidewalk, praying she didn't look

too bad. Would people notice that she looked suspiciously grimy? She rubbed at her arms and retwisted her hair into its ponytail. Well, better dirty than wings or a tail!

"Why is that so hard to believe?" she asked.

"Come now," he said. "That's like saying you're in love with a chair."

Joy poked him with a finger. It caught him unawares. "Ink is *not* a chair."

Avery slapped away the offending hand. "Listen to yourself!" he said. "The Scribes aren't *people*. They're barely alive. They have a shape, like dolls or mannequins, like the homunculi—nothing more. It was a good story, very well played, but don't make the mistake of believing your own fairy tale." He gazed at her with contempt. "Only humans would be so gullible as to think a real heart beats inside a wooden boy."

Joy sneered. "He has a heart."

"So does a valentine."

Joy shoved Avery out of her way. It ruffled his feathers, but he held himself back.

"Shouldn't you be reporting back to Sol Leander?" she snapped.

He fell into step beside her. "I will," he said. "Shortly. And, for everyone's sake, pray that I am permitted to heavily edit." Avery sighed and calmed his voice. "You are now one of the Folk, shortly to be formally presented to the Twixt—you cannot afford to be foolish," he said. "You're going to get yourself killed."

Joy almost laughed. Almost. Death threats were becoming commonplace. What did *that* say about her lifestyle choice?

"Don't worry about me," she said. "I live by a sacred motto— No Stupid." Of course, if Monica could see her leaving the ruined Carousel before the police showed up with her worst enemy's sidekick in tow, she would *definitely* say that this qualified as stupid. This was one of those moments that she really wanted her best friend beside her and not some annoying, self-righteous prat.

"You will not be bringing it to the gala, I presume?" Avery said as a matter of fact.

Joy frowned, having lost the topic. "Bringing what?"

"Indelible Ink."

Joy growled. "He's not an 'it,' he's a 'he,'" she snapped. "And yes, I'm bringing him!" Joy scraped her shoe free of some gunk. "He's my date."

"That would be a grave insult," Avery warned. "The Folk will not permit it. They do not acknowledge...*him*...as a valid escort, which would be considered an auspicious honor that you may bestow on any that night. It is one of the best ways that you can indicate your strength in alliances." He shook his downy hair. "Your sponsor should have explained all of this. He is charged with teaching you proper etiquette to save you from embarrassment, or worse. There are many who are more than willing to make even the slightest offense their advantage." Avery adjusted his cloak over his left shoulder. "I wonder if the Bailiwick intends your failure? Your disgrace might suit his purposes..."

Joy didn't want to talk about Graus Claude. That felt more dangerous than golem monsters or getting arrested.

"What do you care, anyway?" she said, picking dried mud out of her hair. "I thought Sol Leander wanted me to fail."

"He does," the young courtier said. "But even he knows that, as one of the Folk, you have an obligation, a place in the Twixt, which outweighs anything else. You can survive humiliation, but you would not survive disgrace, being ostracized by your own people to live on the fringes without protections. We are all that's left. None of us can afford to be wasted—there are far too few of us as is." He glanced sideways at her, inviting comment, but she didn't say anything. She knew that the lack of births in the Twixt was a sensitive subject, and the fact that there were tons of Folk forgotten somewhere behind a lost door was a moot point. He nodded, misunderstanding the unsaid. "It is our mandate to preserve the magic of this world. Every one of us is precious in that respect."

Joy hesitated. If only he knew...if only any of them could remember that there were so many more of them living somewhere just outside this world, then they could be fighting for the same thing—they could be working together, with her, rather than against her, to find the traitor and open the door. Graus Claude would be cleared. None of this had to go on.

She dared a test.

"What if I told you that there are thousands of Folk hidden behind a lost door somewhere inside the Bailiwick?" Avery walked alongside her and said nothing. She waited a tense moment. "Well?"

He looked up at her curiously. "Did you say something?"

No luck. Joy stopped on the sidewalk and tried something smaller. "Do you remember the King and Queen?"

Avery paused midstep. His face registered something, but then it was gone. He blinked once, then dropped his gaze to her feet.

"Do you intend to keep moving?"

Joy sighed and started walking. She knew some group memory, some small details, still remained beneath the spell, but the direct route wasn't working—maybe she could get around it?

"So, according to the Folk, each of us preserves some of the magic in this world," she said carefully. "Until the Imminent Return?"

Her words were like lightning. Avery smiled. His eyes lit

up. "Yes," he said. "You see? You *do* understand!" He laughed in relief. "Each of us has a duty and obligation to maintain what power still exists until the Golden Age dawns, and we can use it to once again rule this world!"

Joy's smile fell.

"No. You're wrong." Her gaze was like needles, her body gooseflesh. "We share this world—Folk and human. It belongs to *both* of us. I may be learning what it means to be one of the Twixt, but I *know* what it means to be human," she said. "And I haven't forgotten what's important."

Not like you. I'm not like any *of you!*

He wouldn't—couldn't—remember, and that made him a worthless zealot.

Joy pushed forward angrily. Avery quickened his pace. The feathers of his cloak betrayed his furious breathing. She broke into a jog, then a run. She could hear him following. She stumbled onto the footpath. *Wrong shoes.* He was almost upon her. She put on another burst of speed.

"Wait!" he said.

She didn't.

"Joy!"

She spun around, full of fire and fury. *"What?"*

He stopped, his feathered cloak flapping in the breeze. "I was once human, too," he said strangely. "Do not make the mistakes I did."

Joy hesitated, anger fizzling into curious confusion. She didn't know what to say. She turned around, half surprised to find herself home. She touched the keypad by the gate with the prickly feeling of déjà vu.

"I cannot follow you here," he said. He was right—Ink's sigils were still in place. She punched the key code behind her back, blocking the pad with her body, keeping her eyes on his blue-green gaze, so like the sea. His face betrayed everything—she could see memories and unspoken regrets.

"That's right," she said, stepping backward through the gate. "You can't."

She shut the gate, crossed the courtyard and vaulted the stairs, not slowing until she'd slammed the front door behind her and thrown the bolt for good measure.

She slid down the wall and crossed her arms over her knees. Whatever else happened, she would wait for it behind warded walls. This was one place where she belonged—*Home.*

When Ink awoke, he would look for her here.

She was safe, here.

For now.

FOURTEEN

SHE WOKE UP IN THE BACKSEAT OF THE SEDAN; THE car's sharp incline pushed her face against her pillow. Joy had a vague memory of getting up before sunrise, stumbling into her clothes, grabbing her gear and climbing into the car while her father and brother chided her from the front seat. Her eyes were crusty, and her skin itched. Sleep had been a good escape, but guilt crashed down as yesterday's events hit with awful clarity.

Graus Claude had cast the blanket spell. Aniseed, his lover, had tricked him into doing it. Aniseed was dead. The spell could not be undone. The door was still lost, the courier, unknown, and the Bailiwick had turned himself in to the Council as a traitor to that to which he was most loyal—in fact, he had been more loyal than any other member of the Twixt would or could remember, and he would be condemned for it. Ink was still out of action. Inq was unhelpfully vicious. Kurt had closed the brownstone. She'd been attacked by red-eyed mud monsters, rescued by Avery, the Tide's spy, and had destroyed her favorite dance club, which also happened to be the Glen's hidden entrance Under the Hill. She'd even gotten a text from Monica with the news link and sad faces. It made her sick to think about it.

It was all Joy's fault.

Another jolt bounced her head against the glass. Joy

groaned, remembering that she had gone to bed with just enough brain power left to shove the velvet box into her knapsack before falling on her face. The gala wasn't until after the weekend, but she didn't want to risk having her fortune of CliffsNotes and the crystal gift from the Councilex out of her sight. She'd fallen asleep, her mind a jumble of flashing thoughts. Her alarm had been set for three thirty. Stef had splashed her face with ice water at three ten.

Joy turned in her seat and blinked out the window. It was morning on Lake James.

"Good morning," her father called from the front seat. "You slept like a rock on Xanax."

"And missed your turn at the wheel," Stef added. "You're driving a double shift home."

Joy stretched and rubbed her eyes, squashing her feet against the sleeping bags stuffed under the seats. "Sorry," she mumbled. "Late night."

Her father frowned. "I thought Stef said you went to bed at nine thirty."

"I meant I didn't get much sleep," she said. Yesterday she'd...what? Gone out with Stef, brought him to Dmitri, gotten the rod and a beacon, met Monica for coffee, ensorcelled a letter opener, introduced Ink to his mother, stopped him from killing Maia, failed to stop him from attacking Graus Claude, found the source of the spell but not the true traitor, destroyed her favorite dance club, fought off mudmen and Avery and woken up still not knowing if Ink was all right. Hours and days had lost all meaning. Travel in the Twixt completely scrambled her internal clock.

And her brother had covered for her. Again.

The car trundled into the parking lot. Stef lowered the window, welcoming all the scents of forest, lake water and pine. They were soothing smells reminiscent of childhood summers and outdoor memories, now layered with flashes of red armor, Filly's blood in the snow, Kestrel's feral screaming and the mothlike *zing* of Inq's touch, leaving behind a Grimson's mark. Joy reflexively touched her shoulder and felt a slight chill that had nothing to do with the wind.

"Everybody out," her father said, and three Malones opened their car doors. Joy was surprised to find that she missed Mom's fourth slam. She wondered if Mom and Doug ever went camping in California. As far as Carolina camping, the last time had been a disaster.

Her father seemed to hear her thoughts as they traded a look across the roof of the car. "Now, remember," he said. "No fancy knots this time."

"Dad—"

He raised his hands in defense. "I'm just sayin'."

Joy yanked her pack out of the back. "That wasn't my fault!"

"Clearly," her father said as he shouldered the tent bag. "It was a diabolical plot by mischievous bears."

Joy slung the supply bag over her shoulder. *"Dad—"*

"They never did get over the Goldilocks incident," he said. "Turned them on to a life of petty crime." He shook his head sadly. "Such a waste of wildlife."

Stef laughed as they trudged across the hilltop field to the foot trail, his Adam's apple bobbing above the collar of his backward, inside-out tee. "I can't wait to hear about this one."

Dad smirked as he led the way. "You're one to talk, Mr. Butterfingers."

"Ugh! That was *fifteen years ago!*" Stef groaned. "Enough already!"

Mr. Malone smiled. "Now, there's our spot. It's got a great view." He pointed across the lake as they walked under the locust trees. "The lakeshore's down the bluff, and you can see Shortoff and Table Rock from here. There'll be plenty of time to fish and swim and hike, but no s'mores. Shelley'd kill me." He dropped their gear on the picnic table and stretched. Joy thought her dad looked like a younger version of himself, which was weird since she felt older. Of course, in the past year he'd started dating, and she'd become half-human. It was enough to change anyone.

Mr. Malone slapped his chest and grinned. "Let's set up the tents and get in a quick hike before lunch. I think they said we can see the Pisgah from up there."

Stef glanced at the park's brochure. "The Fox Den Trail's only two-point-two miles," he said. "I thought you said we'd be *hiking*."

"We'll do a more serious hike tomorrow, okay?" his father said. "I want to take it easy and branch out from here. Consider this base camp. We'll explore some more options later tonight. I just want us to enjoy some time together as a family. Talk about ourselves and our plans for the future."

Joy got the hint. She'd been occupied with a lot of things besides family, and the only future she could think of was the gala Sunday night. She had to focus—this was their last family gathering until Thanksgiving. And Dad was serious about next year—would she be going to college? What would she do? Her life had once been all about Olympic training, and now it was all about the Twixt. She wanted the freedom to choose, but didn't know *what* to choose. *What do I want to do? Where do I fit in?*

She tugged on her tent bag, which was half under Stef's butt.

"Get off," she said, yanking harder. "C'mon! I want to pitch my tent."

Stef ignored her as he double-tied his boots. "You mean pitch a fit?"

"Stef," she whined. "Move your keister!"

"Keep your shirt on."

"Dork!"

"Dweeb!"

"Dad!" they chorused.

"I'm sorry, what was that?" Mr. Malone placed a hand theatrically by his ear. "I can't hear you over all the loving family bonding time we're having." He tossed the stakes in the dirt and glared at each of them. "You, stand up," he commanded. "And, you, grow up. Now let's get this camp in order before I send you both to your tents without supper."

Stef and Joy jumped. With Dad on a diet, this was no idle threat.

"Yes, Dad," they said.

Mr. Malone went back to pitching his tent and unpacking essentials like aluminum foil and DEET. Joy glanced at her brother staring out at the pines. She could see the longing on his face as plainly as the glyphs on his glasses. She rattled her pack's buckles and caught his eye. Joy mouthed, *Sorry.* He nodded and unclipped the bungees with a shrug. She snuck her hand into the pack's pocket and showed her brother Dmitri's glow stick. "Soon," she said and winked.

Stef's ears turned pink.

Mr. Malone kicked some rocks out of the nettles. "Hey, you two make up yet?"

"Yeah," Stef said, picking up a handful of stakes.

Joy nodded. "Yeah. We're good."

"Wonderful," Dad said. "Glad to hear it. Now, would you mind coming over here and helping me get this thing upright? I don't want the nylon lying in the damp grass."

Stef and Joy took their familiar positions on either side of the deflated tent, quickly threading the rods through the flaps and lining up the loops without saying a word, working together like a well-oiled machine. When they were little, everyone had shared a tent, cuddled in separate sleeping bags, sharing one lantern and damp, sleepy air; but the family had split into smaller tents sometime around Joy's first training bra. Joy secretly missed the family tent—including Mom and her unladylike snoring. They'd felt together then, a family, even if it wasn't all roses and song. She still remembered hitting Stef with a pillow every time he farted in her direction on purpose.

They zipped up the tents and tossed their valuables into the car, then filled their water bottles at the spigots and strapped on light packs. Dad had his naturalist guide, and Stef packed extra gorp. Joy took her essentials, which now included her water bottle, cell phone, emergency soy butter, Burt's Bees lip balm, a pouch of vellum notes and two magic blades. Joy paused to consider what this said about her life as she locked the Pearls of Wisdom in the glove compartment and double-tied her hiking boots.

Dad led the way from the fishing pier south along the lake into the woods along the orange-blaze trail, pointing out tulip trees and hemlock, shelf mushrooms and Indian pipe, their boots crunching on the cleared forest floor as he and Stef chatted about life at U Penn. Joy snapped a pic and sent it to Monica with the text Gorgeous morning! The sloping treetops were a dozen shades of green cradling Lake James, full of silver-gold ripples, the shining water an unbelievable blue. The pic almost looked Photoshopped. She laughed when she got a text back, a pic of Gordon waving Monica's teddy bear at the camera. Monica's text read Gordon-ocious morning! Joy typed back You win! and tucked the phone back into her pack.

She wished she could text Ink.

Her dad's voice cut across the trail. "So, Joy, if you're not into U Penn, are you interested in Raleigh or Chapel Hill?"

Joy kicked a stone off the trail. It was hard for her to imagine being so close to home when her original plan had been to train in Australia. She tugged the straps on her pack and took a deep breath of clean air.

"It would depend on my major, I guess."

Stef chimed in. "What do you want to major in?"

She'd given it some thought. Logically, she could go into phys ed, teaching or coaching, or something in physical therapy or sports medicine if her grades were good enough, but the truth was that she wasn't really interested in any of these—and she could only tell the truth. The truth was that she didn't see herself doing anything but traveling the world, watching black tattoos burst and re-form on people's skin alongside Indelible Ink. How stupid was that? She knew that she had had her own dreams once, but those were gone. So, what did she want for herself now? What was her future? If she could do anything, what would she like to do?

If she stepped with both feet into the Twixt, she wouldn't have to worry about things like money or a career. She would be with Ink, and her job would be keeping magic and herself alive.

Was that all she wanted?

"I thought about a lot of things—phys ed and sports therapy—but those were part of my old life," she said, scraping her boots in the grass. "I'm trying to think about making a new life, and I'm still figuring out what that looks like."

Her dad smiled. "I'm glad you're thinking about it seriously, and I don't mind if you want to take a year to figure it out, but trust me—time has a way of sneaking up on you. It's good to have a plan, but it's also good to be with other kids your age who are figuring it out, too." He looked around the skyline, contemplating the clouds. "And even if things don't work out the way you planned, you'll be closer to something better than where you started." He smiled. "You grow."

"I *had* a plan," she said. But so had her dad. So had Stef. Life sometimes had different ideas. Plans changed, and you had to change with them, whether you wanted to or not. But Joy was afraid that she was changing in more ways than one.

She glanced at her father and brother—what would happen if she changed completely? What if she all of a sudden *disappeared*? Stef would still have the Sight, but what if he, too, began to change? And what if he didn't? What if she never saw her mother again? Joy still had Inq's elixir, the last drops that Aniseed had made for Inq to give the Cabana Boys the Sight. But would she do that to her parents? What if the sight of her drove them mad like Great-Grandmother Caroline? Joy shook her head with a shudder. She couldn't let that happen.

"I had dreams of winning the gold," she said. "I had dreams of sponsorship and endorsements and going on the circuit." Athletes didn't earn much money until they were a "face" that could be marketed beyond medal bonuses and into coaching or philanthropy careers. She'd had her eye on a few leads, included subtle product shots in her online profiles and promo pics. She and her mother had mapped out her next steps according to a plan. And then everything had changed. *Mom changed. I changed.* "Now I'm not sure what else I'm good at." Joy hiked her pack higher and shrugged. "I don't want to be folding sweaters forever."

"It's a job," Dad said. "But you want to think about a career."

"I've never dreamed of being anything other than an Olympian." It was weird to say it out loud after burying it for so long. It didn't hurt the way she'd thought it would, but it left a blank silence afterward.

"It's good to have dreams," Stef said. "But maybe it's time to make some new ones."

She knew he meant *college*, but she heard *Dmitri*.

That brought her back to her life in the Twixt. She didn't want to wonder if Avery was in the shadows or when Ink would wake up or what the Tide might come up with next. She didn't want to think about sprouting wings or fins or horns when she'd be wearing her cap and gown. And she didn't want to think about the surrounding pine trees sprouting unkillable knights...but such was her life. *Is it paranoia if everyone really* is *out to get you?* Her insides twisted as she adjusted her pack, imagining the scalpel tucked in its pocket. She wanted to talk to Kurt. She wanted advice from Graus Claude. She wanted Ink by her side.

How could she think about *college* when she was to be formally presented to another world in two days?

Joy kicked a rock to the side of the trail, debating what would happen if she skipped the gala altogether. She suspected that it would be a bad idea, given Graus Claude's reaction, but it was tempting. She'd been offered the chance to walk away from the Twixt, to never be part of that world again, and instead she'd accepted her place among them, as well as her *signatura*. She'd taken a True Name. She'd made her choice. It wasn't possible to back out now.

Or was it?

What she needed to do was talk to Ink, clear Graus Claude and free the princess. While Graus Claude *had* cast the Amanya spell, it had been altered by Aniseed, and with her being dead, Joy couldn't break the spell by forcing a confession out of her. So the only thing left to do was to find the mysterious door and open it. Bringing the King and Queen back would negate the Amanya spell. *In a paradox, the earlier spell wins out.* If the King and Queen returned, then they would be remembered, canceling out the spell of forgetting. They could return to this world and bring the rest of the Folk back with them. Then everything would go back to normal, and she could ask them to stop the changes happening inside her.

Find the door. Open it. Break the spell. Change the rules.

Joy had a plan.

Stef marched down the trail with extra skips and hops, fairly bursting with energy as he dived off trail, then returned with a smile while picking burrs off his clothes and brushing cobwebs from his hair. Joy wondered if he was feeling the surge that came from being outside, the excitement of anticipating his next meeting with Dmitri, or if his extra energy was because the mountain somehow called to him as part–Earth Folk. She felt it, but the sensation was dulled, tethered by worry and blunted by thick rubber soles between her and the ground. Stef's obvious glow made him smile more, laugh more, there was a lightness to him that she envied. *He didn't know.* A gray, guilty feeling wormed inside her as she wondered when and how she'd ever tell him the truth.

"Okay, enough puttering," Stef announced as they rounded the next bend. "I'm going to run the rest of the loop." He slapped Joy's arm. "You coming?"

"I was going to help Dad with lunch," Joy said. Lunch sounded good. She'd finished her gorp. Now she wanted her soy butter. And possibly a pizza.

"Awww," her brother teased. "Are we still a widdle sweepy?" He tossed a pebble at her playfully. It bounced off her head.

"Hey," Joy said with an edge under the laugh.

Stef back-jogged, kicking up his heels. "Dad's old," he said. "What's your excuse?"

"You leave me out of this," Dad protested. He turned to Joy. "It's okay, honey, you go on ahead." He walked past her, muttering loud enough to hear, "Do me a favor and leave his smug mug in the dust."

Joy grinned. "Okay, Daddy," she quipped and gave him a quick kiss on the cheek.

"Suck-up!" Stef called through cupped hands.

"Suck this!" Joy shouted and took off. Stef whooped, turned tail and ran.

Joy pounded after him, gratefully losing herself to the run, but her brother had a good lead, booking a straight line through the woods flanked by controlled-burn regrowth and trail-marker signs. Only a few straggler branches reached into the path like outstretched arms. Joy bent forward and put on a small burst of speed, feeling the quick-time pounding of her feet against the ground, something oddly removed and buffered, as if she were running on a spring floor—a slight give, a detached feeling, removed from reality, breathing canned air. Joy tried to ignore the weird sensations as she watched her brother's easy pace; she recognized his stride— he'd kept up running while at college. Wasn't he supposed to be staying up late partying and getting fat?

Joy took the next turn at a clip, leaning into the curve, pumping her elbows tight against her sides and chugging her way up the incline. She passed two strolling hikers and a couple of kids, but she was too busy concentrating on catching up to Stef. Chin down, shoulders tucked forward, she angled her spine and sprinted.

She burst into the next stretch and checked the trail, right and left—she'd lost sight of him. Joy spun around, still jogging. There was no way he'd gotten *that* far ahead. Joy wondered if he was hiding in the woods, planning to spring out at her. The trail snaked up ahead, the path interrupted by mossy boulders and a steep, rocky slope. The ground felt harder; the air crisper, cleaner. Joy didn't have enough breath to spare calling his name, but her mind begged the question, *Where's Stef?*

Alone on the trail, her calves started to burn, and her breathing began to change—the gooseflesh on her arms had nothing to do with running but rather the vague, eerie sense that something was wrong. The worry began to bloom in her brain, a premonition, a certainty that something was off. Her thoughts leaped to the scalpel. The one thing she wouldn't tolerate was the Twixt putting her friends and family in danger. Monica's scar was one close call too many, and the guilt was something that she lived with every day.

No, she silently swore. *Not again.*

Joy flung herself around the next bend, hoping to see her brother safe and smug up the trail, but before she could call out, his voice reached out to her. She sagged in relief until she heard the shape of his words.

"Joy! Look out!"

She staggered to a stop. She punched the clip at her breast and swung her pack off one shoulder, grabbing the scalpel just in time to see the first homunculi clear the turn.

They boiled out of the woods, ruby-red eyes and mouths gaping wide. Her body froze, fighting the incline and the fear, before she started backing away, almost sliding in her hurry to retreat. The horde charged, glomming together as they came, merging seamlessly into pairs and triads, their bodies smashing together, eyes bouncing like billiard balls against one another as multiple limbs matched pace in a grotesque pursuit until only three long bodies snaked their way over the mountain trail, fiery eyes lining their sides, a sinuous caterpillar wave. Triangular heads rose, glowering down like baleful dragons. Joy balked as her body smacked hard against a rock.

The monsters leaped into the air and dived into the ground.

The earth churned and exploded as they resurfaced, arcing through the air, swimming through the mountain like an ocean. The land re-formed behind them, swallowing itself closed. The golem-serpents dived closer. The earth buckled. Joy screamed.

The ground below her feet erupted. Three massive underbellies spun upward, twining around her—beneath her, beside her, surrounding her as they coiled, circling closer, beady red eyes zipping past like highway lights, cutting off the sunlight, encasing her like a fist. She twisted in place—there was nowhere to run. The bodies slid together, a gritty friction, squeezing shut.

The cage closed. The lights died. The air cut off.

Joy was completely entombed in stone.

FIFTEEN

JOY SLAMMED HER HAND AGAINST THE WALL. THE muddy creatures had solidified around her, rock-hard and unyielding. The sound in her ears was cottony, the darkness, absolute. She could feel her breath echo back at her, animalistic and afraid. There was barely six inches between her and her egg-shaped tomb. She scraped the scalpel against the rock. Nothing happened. Not even a spark.

Graus Claude's warnings whispered to her: *Just because you cannot be killed does not mean that you cannot die.*

"Stef!" she screamed, but her voice was thick, muffled in her own ears. She kicked at the wall and felt it in her toes. It was unyielding and immovable. There was no getting out.

"I'm under the Edict," she gasped aloud, slapping the stone with her palm. Her tongue felt hot and dry. She blinked against the darkness. It made no difference; it was black on black. She turned in a tight circle. She felt dizzy, light-headed. "I'm one of the Twixt!" She beat her fist against the rock. "Let me out!" Her legs felt shaky. Her eyes stung. She needed more room. She needed more air. It was too small. Too tight. Her pack scraped the wall behind her. *"Let me out!"*

She blasted the wall with her Inq-glyphed *push*. Air whipped her hair back and smothered her face. There was no change to the rock, but she could breathe a little better.

She blasted again, twice more, just to be sure that she could. Joy took deep lungfuls of air and tried to think clearly.

Okay. I'm not going to asphyxiate. I just have to get out.

Unzipping a pocket, Joy fumbled for her phone. Stef had his, and he was right outside. He'd seen what was coming. He'd tried to warn her. She was sure he'd be right there. She pulled her phone out with shaky fingers, fumbled and dropped it. Cursing, she sank to her knees only to find she couldn't quite bend them all the way—her bones bumped against the baked clay stone. She tried stretching her arms past her hips, but her shoulders were crammed against the walls, her pack wedging under her back.

She swept her feet to kick the phone closer and blasted air from her palm into her face. Was it weaker this time? Panic scrabbled in the back of her throat.

She closed her eyes in order to concentrate and untied her hiking boots blind, kicking them off and rolling her socks into tiny, tight balls. She searched the ground barefoot, drawing her feet through the gravel and grass, scooping the flat phone against her arch and grabbing the corner between her toes. She tensed her midriff, curling, easing her leg upward like a stork, keeping her balance, arms low. She grabbed the phone in her right hand and swept it live.

No bars. The walls were too thick, but the light was a relief.

The image fuzzed. Her eyelids felt heavy, as if she were being tucked into bed standing up. Joy shook her head and blasted herself in the face again. It was little more than a breeze.

I'm fading.

Flipping the phone over, she squinted to see if Ink had placed a glyph there, pressing her thumbs all around the case just to be sure. Nothing. She wished that she had his *signatura*, or the carved ouroboros box in her room; without them, there was no way she could signal him, even if he'd recovered from the Bailiwick's blow. Panic began to ebb into something sinister and sleepy.

She shook her head again, bouncing it against the stone wall. She was missing something obvious. She could feel it. Something important. But she couldn't quite think of what it might be. Why couldn't she think? She needed more air. More light. She needed to get *out*.

Air. Light. Fire!

Joy felt around for her pouch and slipped the ties loose. Snatching the matchbook, she lit one in the dark. The gritty scrape produced a tiny star that tattooed her eyes with winking lights. It died quickly. She dropped the dead match in the dirt.

Joy swiped her phone live again and dug inside the pouch then unrolled a tiny curl of vellum. Grabbing her Frisbee golf pencil, she wrote: *Trapped in rock Lake James, NC*. She scribbled the return sigil, blasted more air, lit a second match and watched the vellum's corner burn...then go out. A third match barely lit. Joy sobbed, the note still in her fingers, the message unsent save for half the last words. She was using up oxygen. She was going to pass out. She stamped her bare feet against the ground. *What could she do?*

She used the screen to examine her cell, desperate to find any chink or crack. If there were any mouths or eyes, she couldn't see them. The ground that she stood on was undisturbed, but digging a toe along the edge revealed that the wall sank underground. The cage closed overhead in a sloping peak and she could only guess that underground was the same—like a giant egg. She was encased in solid, seamless stone. She cupped her hand to her face and let trickles of fresh air wash over her nose and eyes. Her ears popped.

There was only so much room in here, and she was building pressure with the added air.

She placed a hand against the cell wall as if she could push through to the outside. Was Stef out there? Did he know where she was? Could he find her, or did she look like any other boulder along the trail? Would he guess what had happened? Would Filly? Would Ink? Would anyone? Or would she...

No!

Joy swiped her phone again to keep the black at bay. Shadows crept over the crags of rock, tracing ripples in the stone. A shadow caught the edge of a paper-thin loop. Joy bent closer and saw the barest hint of a glyph. She traced its hairline curve with her fingertip.

A baleful eye rolled open, bathing her in firelight. She shrieked, dropping her phone, and the eye closed lazily, cloaking her once again in darkness.

Joy held her breath and shied away from the wall. Then, imagining more eyes/hands/mouths behind her, she stood rigid, touching nothing, mind screaming, tensed for an attack.

None came.

They didn't need to attack her. They had only to wait for her to die.

Joy struggled again to grab her phone with her toes and swept the screen alight. The air tasted thinner. The tomb felt tighter. She felt like she was sinking. Joy squeezed the familiar weight of the scalpel in her hand. The lightness in her head gave her a floaty courage. She was getting used to being threatened by the Folk.

I can do this.

A cool calm washed over her. She was trapped. Okay. Graus Claude had called this an art, a subtle game the Folk played to while away their immortality. There was a trick to it, one that her enemies knew well, using rules that she was just learning—but they'd forgotten something, something very important:

Joy was the most dangerous human in the world.

Focusing on the glyph, Joy traced its shape with her scalpel, watching the sparks of undoing like a welding torch in reverse; little black-hole fireworks that sucked the surface clean. She ignored the red eyes that opened, glaring, the mouth tearing wide as if wailing in protest. Undeterred, she curved her blade up the last jagged swirl.

There was a hollow cry as the eyes winked out and died. The rock cracked and loosened as the entire side of the stone cell shifted, as a section disappeared into dust, crumbling under its own sudden weight. With one of the golems undone, the stone shattered along the fault.

The cell tilted and Joy with it, pitching sideways, vomiting gravel and loose earth before the wall itself tensed like a muscle, snapping shut around the wound. Joy swayed, now forced into a half crouch at an angle. There was an angry shudder, and the cell wrung itself tighter, slithering like coiled serpents, squeezing the barest space around Joy as if in retribution.

Joy gasped, blinking hard. There was barely any room for air, let alone movement. Fine threads of pain squeezed up her limbs, puckering, twisting, like she was being wrung dry. Her elbows scraped against her sides. Her center of balance hovered over one hip. She bit the inside of one cheek. Her toes curled in the dirt, feeling cool, almost blissful, half buried in the ground. She wondered if she could somehow curl up and keep curling. Like the vellum. Tucked into flame. Turn to ash. Blow away...

There was a great crash. She felt a shiver where her knees touched the stone, shaking her awake. It came again. She pressed an ear against the rough surface, trying to feel what was happening, straining to hear a muffled voice. Instead, she felt the reverb of another impact along her jaw. Joy closed her eyes and welcomed the slight buzzing; it kept away the malevolent quiet in her head. She squeezed her eyes against a rain of dust. Cold sweat spread over her skin. Her head was heavy. Her bowels were loose. It was becoming very hard to breathe.

She tapped her scalpel on the rock, making a grating, scraping sound—her last attempt to keep herself awake, to save herself. Someone was outside, trying to get at her. Someone was here to help. *I wonder who?* Her vision swam. Her fingers went all pins and needles. She bumped her head and barely felt it. She heard the tickle of another impact from far away, somewhere about a mile behind her head and six feet underground. She imagined being underground, buried in the earth and the rich, dark soil. It didn't sound so bad, really. She was of Earth, after all.

My toes aren't suffocating, she thought with odd logic.

A foggy part of her brain argued that that made no sense, but her body was instinctively pushing down and splaying her toes wide. The last of the air in her lungs had a taste, but it was different under her feet. It was like a sixth sense, a sort of out-of-body feeling. The ground had something like a smell, like a flavor—it tasted like cool metal and the sea and old, old ice.

She wiggled her toes.

They felt longer.

She drove them deeper, digging down down down into darkness and quiet and something quite familiar.

Some part of her touched it.

A hot knife of power sliced through her calluses and broken toes, up the arches of her feet, through her tendons and veins; a network of white wiry threads shot up her legs, into her hips, curling a tight twist in the pit of her stomach. It trembled there, gathering, building, breathing, then burst— erupting out her mouth in a scream. Joy tilted her head back, jaw open, and pressed her hands against the walls, unable to contain the overwhelming need to *Get Out*.

GET OUT! *NOW!*

Her eyes rolled back. She saw white light. She gasped without air. Her elbows bent, her spine stiffened, and she *pushed*.

The stone glowed before it shattered in all directions, shooting rubble into the sky and spraying the trees with fine hail. Sunlight slammed down like a hammer. Joy collapsed, breathing hard, tasting sweet forest pollen, old leaves and dirt-peppered salt. Outside the ragged circle of debris, Stef dropped the golden shimmer of his ward.

"Joy?" he said, rushing forward. "Joy!"

Stef grabbed her by her elbow. She pushed against the mountain, pulling her feet from the ground, half expecting to see a knotty tangle of roots, but they were only her toes, dark and dirty with chipped Mango polish. Although her two old, broken toes were straight, perfectly healed. Her head spun with oxygen and light.

"Hey," she said hoarsely, coughing on fine rock dust. "Did you see that?"

"Which part?" he said, brushing off her legs. "The part where a horde of fire-eyed golems crawled out of the ground or the part where a Norse goddess blew you out of a rock?"

Joy was about to correct Stef, but the second part of the sentence caught her up to her head. She blinked into the light. "Filly? Where?" she said and winced. "Ow."

"It is good to see you, too, Joy Malone!"

Filly wiped her hands over her vambraces in the middle of the trail; a breeze tugged at the blond hairs that had slipped from her nest of braids and rustled her short cape of bones. She flicked her horse head pendant into place and looked smug.

"Hey," Joy said with a grateful grin. "How did you find me?"

The warrior woman raised her eyebrows, stretching the long lines of blue tattoos. "I received your bit of message and arrived to find a young wizard blasting at a menhir," she said. "It wasn't difficult."

Joy hugged her brother to her chest, squeezing hard enough to make it real. He hugged her back. Joy could feel that his arms were shaking. Or maybe it was her.

"Thank you," she said as Stef smoothed her hair. She blinked back at Filly. "And thank you, too." She didn't want either of them to guess what had really happened—that she had rescued herself, tapping into something deep within the earth. She was changing, even if she couldn't see it. She could feel it. She could *taste* it under the rocky soil—it scared her and called to her.

"Your life is rarely dull," Filly said with a smile. "And it is good to keep alert should the EverBattle come." She plunked her fists on her hips and propped her foot on one of the larger chunks of rock. "Your brother is a fine ally, but very stubborn—a good trait in a lover, but very bad in a soldier. We would have had you out sooner if he had listened to me." She chucked her chin at him. "You should learn to take orders like your sister without complaint."

Joy stumbled. "I only complain when you throw me off a cliff."

"True." Filly grinned. "But you agreed to it first. In fact," she said, "you should have thanked me for my help then, too! I was the one who guessed that there was a riddle to be solved—and the riddle was *you*!"

Stef's mouth was a thin, hard line.

Joy hastily tried to fend off Filly saying more in front of her brother, who was looking shell-shocked and murderous. "Yes. Thank you."

"*Þat var ekki.*" Filly waved her off, but smiled over the blue spot beneath her lip. "So, tell me, who is trying to kill you now?"

Stef's hands tightened on Joy's shoulders. She tried to sound reassuring. "No one should be," Joy said, scanning the rubble for any glowing red eyes. "I won't be formally presented until Sunday night. Maybe someone's trying to keep that from happening?"

Filly picked up a chunk of stone, examined it and tossed it aside. "Your friends from the Tide?" she guessed.

"Sol Leander?" Joy said. "Believe it or not, I don't think so." Joy rubbed her arms, smoothing down goose bumps, and tried to ignore Stef's radiating disapproval. "He's the one who moved the date up, so that I could fall on my face and humiliate Graus Claude in public. I don't think he'd want to miss out on the chance that I'd do myself in." Considering what Avery had said, Joy didn't believe Sol Leander wanted to kill her any longer—he wanted her to suffer humiliation and exile. Like Avery said, she couldn't do that if she were dead.

Filly pushed another chunk of rock off the road with her foot. "Where's Ink?"

The question hit her like a shock of cold water. Joy twisted her fingers in her shirt. *Where* was *Ink?* If he wasn't here, he was probably still unconscious, but it had been far longer than a few hours. *How long did Scribes snooze?* "He's...not available right now."

"Wait. Isn't Ink bound to protect you or something?" Stef asked.

Filly tossed her head and snorted. "She's not his *lehman* anymore, boy."

"Whoa!" Stef held his hands up in a T. "Time-out. *Lehman?*" He glared at Joy. "You were his...?" His face did a dance of disgust and outrage. "Joy!"

"No, no, no," Joy said quickly. "It was a mistake. Sort of." It didn't matter anymore—everything was different now. *Everything.* "Anyway, I'm not anymore."

Stef shook his head as if to clear it. "But that night—at the Carousel—you were going Under the Hill to formally accept his *signatura* so the Council couldn't oust you, right? So you could keep yourself protected under the Edict," Stef asked and glanced between her and Filly, putting two and two together. "That's not what happened, is it?"

Joy didn't want to try to explain. She pushed the scalpel into her pocket. "No."

"But you have a mark," Stef said slowly. "I saw it."

"Yes," Joy said quietly. "I have a *signatura.*"

She watched her brother as the information played across his face—from anger and confusion to disbelief and fear, the possibilities flickered over his features like a flip book, but none of them were right. None of them made sense yet. She had to *say* something. Joy glanced at Filly, who was witnessing it all—the young Valkyrie looked like she'd stumbled into Christmas morning, the moment when all the secrets came out. Joy took a deep breath. This was it.

"Stef—"

"No." Stef cut her off. "No. Don't say it. I don't—" He looked panicked, a danger zone way beyond scared. He shook his head, angry or sad or disappointed—it was hard to be sure. He wouldn't look at her. "I don't want to know."

It was like a punch to the gut, cutting her off, shutting her down.

"Stef, *please*—"

"No!" he barked and glanced a warning at Filly in case she'd opened her mouth. The blonde woman arched an eyebrow. "I want to talk with Dmitri," he said. "I want to ask him—" He steadied himself and focused. "You're okay, though? Nothing hurts?"

"I'm okay," Joy whispered. She looked at Filly, who touched the ground. "Any more of them coming?"

The warrior shook her head. "There are no more tremors," she said. "The magic's spent. It's over."

"Okay," Stef said, backing up through the rubble, glaring at the surrounding trees as if daring them to spit out any more monsters. "Let's hurry up and go, then."

Joy lifted her boots up by their laces and shook out the dust. Filly caught Joy's eye and shrugged, rattling her cape of bones. She kept her voice low as Joy yanked on her socks and wound her laces through hooks.

"If you don't know who sent the homunculi, it is possible that they were preset."

Joy tried to imagine that as she tied her laces. "Like a ward?"

Filly shrugged. "Like a trip wire. A trap. Most likely an old one—using golems is outdated, too easily noticed in your world at this time." She watched Stef scan the trees. "Your brother said that their eyes were red."

"Fiery red," Joy said. "Like coals."

"Then they were set for humans," Filly said. "Most likely, they were guarding something you'd discovered—they were clearly hunting *you*." She ground her foot purposefully. "I wonder what you've uncovered lately that sent them after humans."

Joy tried not to look as guilty as she felt. "Why do you think that?"

Filly snickered. "There is a color to the craft—blue for wizardry or witchcraft, gold for protection, green for Folk, red for human." She kicked at the debris. "These were clay golems, guardians of Forest and Earth, set against humans. Know why?"

Joy swallowed, thinking of Maia behind her bird's-eye door. She hadn't thought she'd upset the Earth Council seat—Maia had even given Joy a gift. The hair comb was in her box of pearls in the car. Could it have been a trick, a way to track her here? Or had she heard enough to know that Ink had tried to kill her? Or did it have something to do with the zip of fire behind the Bailiwick's teeth? Blue for Inq, red for her. She was human enough, she guessed, but then what did that have to do with Earth golems? Had they followed her from the Carousel, the entrance Under the Hill? But then, why here? Why now? It didn't fit. The fiery eyes reminded her more of another Council seat—the flame-eyed figure of black rock and crystal with fissures of lava glowing like veins. She struggled to remember the faces of the other Council members, the names of all the different Houses, Courts and Clans that Graus Claude had made her memorize. Which one would want her eliminated? Of course, it could be any of them. She hadn't endeared herself to the Council by forcing their hand. Who else?

"Could it have been one of the dryads?" Joy whispered.

"Easily," Filly said. "Forest is technically under the Court of Earth."

"Huh," Joy said, swallowing another ripple of fear. But if the spell made everyone forget, why would the Forest Council seat have anything against Joy?

"What about Sol Leander?" Joy asked while double-tying her bow. "What House is he?"

"Air," Filly said. "Sky seat. Along with the Council Head, Zhēnzhū."

Joy shook her head. "It doesn't make sense."

"Have you gone anywhere lately where you oughtn't?" Filly almost smirked, but the warrior was serious, and her tone was as grave as her eyes. Joy thought about all the places she'd been, tramping all over the world and beyond, and there were many places she probably "oughtn't" have gone, but only one stood out in her mind: the Bailiwick. Joy let out a long, slow breath.

"Joy," Stef called like a command. "Let's go."

"Well fought, young ones!" Filly raised her fist to the sun. "Victory, Joy Malone!"

"Victory!" Joy said and stepped back as Filly lifted her chin, the air suddenly pregnant with ionic charge, which incandesced with a boom like thunder. Joy blinked reflexively. Filly was gone. The roar in her ears took a moment to fade.

"Nice friend you've got there," Stef said sarcastically.

Joy shouldered her pack. "She's come through for me before."

"I prefer you hang out with Monica and Gordon What's-his-hoffer," he said. "They have to save your life less often. Come on."

Joy joined him on the downward path. Their crunching footsteps sounded too loud in her ears. Her brother laid a protective hand on her back, almost at the place where her *signatura* burned. What was he thinking? Did he understand what she'd been about to say to him? She wondered if he had figured it out and just didn't want to say it aloud?

Joy stumbled, feeling the fine granules in her shoes. She'd been nearly smothered to death, and all she could think about was that she'd have to change her socks. And why was she thinking about socks when someone was trying to kill her *again*?

But it wasn't that simple—this wasn't within the rules. Her enemies thought to trick her or trap her, force her to die a mortal death as a side effect rather than a frontal assault. She'd gone against Aniseed and the Red Knight and the Council and now this. But she was different now—she wasn't just a mortal girl with the Sight; she was powerful and had powerful friends in the Twixt. She was one of them. And not. Joy had tapped into Earth and shattered her cage. She'd become something else, something more, all on her own. Something new now breathed inside her. The thought made her feel taller, stronger. She almost smiled. Almost.

They thought they could destroy her? Well, Joy was going to beat them at their own game, and she was going to *win*.

She flashed one of her Olympic-class smiles.

She wasn't going to just bend the rules; she was going to break them apart.

SIXTEEN

FOR THE REST OF THE DAY, JOY TRIED TO LIVE IN THE moment. This moment. Now.

She traded the gritty rock dust for sand between her toes. It felt good to be on the shoreline, calm and clean and cool. The danger had passed, and now Joy's job was to let it go. She had to be here—Joy Malone—now.

Spreading out towels and rolling up shirts, the Malone family stretched out with books and tablets angled against the late-afternoon sunshine, getting crappy reception and drinking sun-warmed tea. Joy texted Monica about "roughing it" on the lake and Stef plotted his route back to campus, stealing glances at Joy, neither of them fully distracted by whatever they pretended to be doing. With one eye on the forest and the other on Dad, they hadn't any eyes left for the things in their hands.

Hello?

Joy jumped at the buzz in her palm. Sorry, she texted. 2 bars max.

Excuses, excuses, Monica typed. Maybe we should write letters? Very retro. U have a letter opener = official equipment!

HA! Back Sunday. Would beat the stamp home! she typed. Her father made a loud, fake "ahem" and coughed into his hand. Joy smirked and kept typing. Dad wants a Scrabble rematch. Miss you muchly! Xoxoxox.

Joy tucked her phone into her back pocket, grabbed her flip-flops and towel and trudged back up the beach. Stef jumped to his feet, flanking her like a sentry. She glanced at him sideways. He pointed to the woods. In the higher branches, leaves buckled and danced as a couple of squirrels raced from tree to tree...if squirrels were dark orange, wore capes and carried spears. Joy sighed and let her brother escort her back to camp. Just because they were safe, didn't mean they were stupid. Joy and Monica swore No Stupid. *Ha!*

Scrabble was the family game. Joy and Stef could both remember the glorious day when they'd each managed to beat their dad—it was a Malone rite of passage. Joy had been twelve when she'd placed *xenon* on a triple-word score. Dad was always up for a rematch.

Sitting around the picnic table with a bag of chips and hot salsa, Joy tried to forget that anything was out of the ordinary. She watched the treetop Forest Folk leap across the branches, capes and tails flickering, and scamper on. The Folk lived here in the woods—they always had—she just hadn't known it before. They went about their lives, and she went about hers. That was what it meant to have a shared world; they were sharing their forest home with her, not the other way around.

She took a deep breath and let it out slowly. The wind carried nothing more than the sound of the woods and the smell of neighboring campfires. The view stretched to the horizon, balmy and blue. Joy arranged her letters as Stef discreetly carved a protective sigil in the picnic bench. Chuckling, Dad set down his tiles. Stef's phone was already set to Dictionary.com.

"'*Faqir*—a Muslim Sufi ascetic who rejects worldly possessions,'" Stef recited. "Damn. I thought it was spelled with a *k*."

"It's an alternate spelling," Dad said, grabbing the pen.

"Tsk, tsk. What are they teaching you at that fancy school of yours?" he teased as he added up his total score. Stef ignored him and started rearranging his letters. Joy could barely sit still; she couldn't wait to put down *qadis* and blow Dad away.

"I think I need to update this app," Stef grumbled.

"You're just sore you didn't think of it first," Dad said.

Stef stared at his letters with a scowl. "Can you guess what word I'm of thinking now?"

Dad laughed. "Go wash your mind with soap, young man."

Stef changed *ousted* to *jousted* by putting down *ajar*. He hadn't used any key spots, but it conveniently blocked her move. Stef tallied his meager points.

Joy hunched her shoulders. *Jousted* reminded her of the blood-colored Red Knight. She hadn't known what she was capable of then and still suspected that Inq had tricked her into erasing the deadly assassin, exposing the fact that she'd *somehow* defeated the undefeatable Red Knight. Even if they'd managed to blame it on the scalpel and not her own intrinsic magic, Stef's warning haunted her: *Secrets don't stay secret forever.* If the antihuman factions of the Twixt hadn't already hated and feared her before, they surely would once it was known her power could erase Folk out of existence! It was yet another reminder that she had to do something to free Graus Claude and the King and Queen soon, if not to prevent any changes happening now, then to protect her from things that she'd already done.

"Joy?"

"Hmm?"

Her dad tapped the table. "Your turn."

Joy squared her shoulders and flipped her vowel tiles. She had to get her head in the game. She didn't even gloat over her score; she was too distracted.

"How about kinesiology?" her dad asked.

Joy blinked at her letters. "I don't have enough tiles."

"No," her father said. "I meant as a major. It's the study of human movement."

Joy arranged her new tiles. "You just looked that up."

He shrugged. "Maybe I did."

"Are we going to talk about this now? I can't concentrate!" Stef snapped.

"Sorry," Dad said. "Some of us can do both at once."

Joy stuck out her tongue. Stef grumbled into his fist.

Dad studied the board. She caught a whiff of pine on the wind, electric and spiky, tickling her nose. It called to her, welcoming her. Joy discreetly slipped off her shoes, resting her bare feet on the ground. She tried to picture what had happened in the stone cage, how it had started—her feet in the grass, touching the earth. She pictured herself, feeling the grit and crackle of old leaves, dusty bark and rich soil beneath her toes. There was a sort of shimmer in her mind's eye, darting like a fish just out of reach. It was as if she stood on the surface of a bubble and the slightest give, just a little push, and she could tap into that distant energy and let it flow over her again—but she wasn't certain what would happen if she did.

She'd blasted herself out of the rock and still—no gills!

Joy widened the space between her toes, playing along the edge of the sleeping power, testing the shape of it, the taste of it, in the back of her mind. Digging her toes into the ground, she pushed down, imagining herself delving deeper, seeking out the strange flavor of dirt and metal, the sea, the salt and old, old ice. She could picture glaciers carving out the mountains. She could imagine layers of rock pushed up and forced down, grinding against each other, heating and cooling, the surface of the earth growing and dying and growing again. She experimented with a feather touch, the lightest tickle, and felt what sounded like an echo in her head, like a whisper from the *eelet* in a language she didn't know, but could almost recognize. Almost... Almost there...

"Joy?"

Joy pulled her feet up. "Hmm?"

Dad frowned. "Your turn."

"Sorry," she said. "Spaced out for a minute." She checked the board. Stef had used the *r* she needed. *Crap.*

"Thinking of Mark?" Dad said, picking fresh tiles. It took her a second to mentally switch *Mark* with *Ink*. Hearing his name was an unexpected jolt. She wondered where he was. How he was doing? Was he awake yet? She tucked her hair behind her ear, and her fingers lingered there. She cupped her hands, remembering his. She tried to form words, suddenly conscious of her lips—she missed him in every part of her.

"Well I am *now*," she said, flustered. And now all she could think of was Ink's boneless arm behind Graus Claude's desk. His face pillowed in the giant four-poster bed. The nightmare memory of cutting his torn throat closed... And here she was playing Scrabble? Her two worlds couldn't get any farther apart.

"Why don't you give him a call when we're done?" her father said, tapping the table. "In the meantime, eyes on the board. No throwing the game."

"C'mon, Dad, you know me," Joy said, snapping all seven letters on the board, spelling *acoustic*, and snagging a triple-letter score. Both Dad and Stef groaned. Joy smiled.

"I play to win."

Joy wandered out of the bathhouse with her toiletry bag, bath towel and a stomach full of butterflies, hot dogs and baked apples. The fact that there had been no further incidents at Lake James hadn't made her feel much better; in fact, the waiting made it worse, like a storm approaching, anticipating another giant foot about to fall. Between the golems and the gala and the talk of college majors and not knowing what was happening with Ink, Joy was twitchy and unsettled, caught somewhere between feeling hopeless and mad.

She opened the door and nearly ran into Stef.

"Hey." Stef tried to keep his voice casual, but it sounded impatient and strained. "Ready to go?" He didn't need to say where and didn't need to say *please*—every move, every look, said it for him. His eyes were bright behind his glasses.

Joy gave an easy smile. "Isn't it a bit early?"

"No," he said. "Trust me, this is *long* overdue."

Stef grabbed her hand and tugged. Joy laughed and started walking. Her brother's excitement was infectious. "Aren't you worried that it's not safe?"

His smile faltered. "Should I be?"

"No." Joy was willing to believe Filly that there'd be no more golems, that she'd tripped something by accident, even though Joy believed that there were no such things as accidents. A part of her felt wild, a part of her felt wary. She could imagine Monica whispering a warning: *No Stupid.*

Stef's eyes widened cartoonishly. "So...?"

Joy gave in with a laugh. "Okay, fine. What'll we tell Dad?"

Her brother tapped her toiletry bag. "Female problems," he said. "We have to go into town for supplies."

Joy rolled her eyes. "You can't blame *everything* on women's hygiene."

"What? Why not?" he said. "You do all the time."

Joy pushed his shoulder. "Do not!"

"Do, too," he said. "And don't deny it—I used to count the number of excuses per month. You fibbed at least thirty percent of the time. Science doesn't lie."

"Stef," Joy said seriously. "I can't lie anymore."

Stefan slowed, his smile fading, replaced by something dangerous behind his eyes. Did he understand what she'd said—what it meant? She wanted to tell him, but until the words actually left her lips, it would still qualify as being unsaid. As a fallback plan, Joy was pretty good with unsaid. She was no longer quite as ready as she was before. Selfishly, she needed *something* in her life to stay the same.

He forced a smile. "Leave it to me," he said, jogging ahead. Joy watched him go, wondering how long they could play at being normal, how long she could go on keeping a secret that wasn't her secret any longer.

Stef ran back before she even made it around the bend. He grabbed her shoulders and spun her around, pushing her toward the parking lot. "Dad says he doesn't want to know," Stef said triumphantly. "We'll go to the car, drive around the loop, park somewhere and snap the beacon. You have it on you, don't you?"

She did, in fact. Now she didn't go anywhere without the beacon, the pouch and the scalpel in reach, but she was tempted not to tell him that. She wasn't quite ready for a road trip. She was wearing pajamas and flip-flops. "Yeah, but—"

"Excellent," Stef said, unlocking the car door with his key fob. "Get in."

Joy sighed and dropped into the passenger's seat. "Pushy much?"

"You're so hormonal," Stef teased. "And we have an appointment to keep."

"Appointment?" Joy said. *"Crap!"* She dropped her bag on the floor and opened the glove compartment, hurriedly flipping open the long velvet box.

"Holy—" He stared at the fortune of pearls. "Please, tell me those aren't stolen."

"They're not stolen," Joy said dutifully. "Only bears turn to a life of crime." She moved the comb aside and pulled a white business card out from under the black elastic bands. It was an embossed linen card with a starburst logo and two blank lines for Appointment Date and Time. No number. No email. No web address. Joy turned it over, trying to use her Sight. Graus Claude hadn't said how to use it. *Great.* She was mortally sure she didn't want to miss her tailoring appointment and piss off someone else in the Twixt. She took a pen from the glove compartment and wrote *August 17th, 5 a.m. EST.* Both Stef and Joy watched as the words disappeared, replaced almost immediately with the words *Appointment received. This card serves as your confirmation. Tear to transport.* Joy sighed in relief, slipped it back into the box and snapped it shut.

"You made an appointment for tomorrow morning," Stef said, pulling out of the space and driving onto the road.

"I know," Joy said, shoving the box back into the glove compartment. "You'll have to keep Dad busy, and I'll be back before you know it."

"Are you out of your mind?" Stef said, turning the wheel. "I'm not going to let you go anywhere alone!"

"It'll only take a moment," Joy said, unzipping her bag. "And, besides, you want to see Dmitri, don't you?" She lifted up the glow stick and waggled it in front of his face.

Stef opened his mouth, closed it and scowled. "You're living dangerously."

"Not me! Remember? No Stupid," Joy said, only half joking. "I promise I won't go alone."

He raked his hand through his hair. "How long did you say Ink was unavailable?"

"I don't know." She wished that she knew, but speaking wishes would be a lie.

"Then who's going with you?"

"I'll find someone," Joy said, pulling out her phone and swiping it on. She hoped Ink would show up by then, but just in case, she'd better have a contingency plan. She was sure Graus Claude wouldn't be happy if she insulted his tailor by missing her appointment. Even if he were pleading his case behind bars, Joy suspected that this was one of those things that was considered an unpardonable offense. *Etiquette and decorum*, she thought as she quick-typed a message with her thumbs.

Can anyone come with me to GC's tailor, 5am EST? Have an appt I can't miss. Camping at Lake James State Park, site 11. Help?

Hitting Send to the Cabana Boys was like a group shout-out. Joy was confident that one of them would be able to come, or maybe get a message to Inq. Whatever Invisible Inq might feel about her right now, Joy was her best chance at getting her mother out of the Bailiwick and bringing the King and Queen home. At least, she hoped that was still the case. Joy dropped her phone into her bag.

"Got a ride?" Stef asked.

"A sweet one," Joy said, thinking of Enrique's invisible Ferrari. Unfortunately, it didn't have an auto-retrieval option. Maybe she could install an upgrade? She checked herself in the mirror as they took another corner. "I should be getting a callback soon."

"Good enough for me," he said, pulling over by a copse of trees. Joy doubted that Stef would be so easily appeased if he hadn't been so distracted. He snagged the keys and popped the doors. "Get out."

Joy frowned. "Manners?"

"Get out, *please*," Stef said and shut the door. Glancing around, he checked the road. He'd doubled-backed and turned around, making sure there was no one on the trail. Satisfied, Stef pushed into the brambles, climbing up the hillside with eager, steady strides. Joy grabbed her things and followed, remembering their instructions were to go deep into the trees. Unfortunately, she was still wearing her flip-flops. She wasn't eager to go bushwhacking uphill.

"Stef?" she called out.

"I found a clearing," he said through the maze of trunks and leaves. He waved for her to follow. "Come on up."

She put a foot on the slippery incline. "Now who's living dangerously?" she muttered.

"Hurry up!"

Grumbling, Joy grabbed a thin sapling and hauled herself upward, picking her way up the slope in foam footgear. She stubbed her toes, scratched her arm and got rocks in her flip-flops. She was close to swearing as she crested the rise, muddy and scuffed, feeling none of the energy she should have while slogging through the earth—all she really felt was pestered and damp. Stef held out a hand to her, which she took, and he yanked her onto even footing. There was a downed tree with mushrooms growing beneath it and mosses eating the bark to crumbly rot. It smelled rich and ripe—death and life together. Joy sat down and inspected her toenail. Stef stood impatiently over her.

"You're fine."

"Give me a minute," Joy said, holding the glow stick in her palm. The fluid sloshed around inside its hard, plastic shell as she dug a chunk of wood out from under her nail. Her brother looked anxiously out in the green. He took off his glasses and wiped them clean. His smile was gone. The corner of his mouth twitched.

"What is it?" Joy said, looking around. She knew that there were Folk here in the preserves, where their magic remained untouched. Kestrel lived in a place like this. And the not-so-squirrels. And things like Briarhook. She wondered if Stef had seen something. She wasn't used to being around others who had the Sight.

"It's nothing," Stef said.

"Stef—"

He shook his head. "Just do it."

What went unsaid was *Please!*

Joy snapped the glow stick, shook it and watched blue light fill the runes. The glow in her palm grew stronger, pushing beyond the confines of the clearing—tracing every cord of bark, every vein on every leaf, every broken twig in sharp neon light. The beacon's orb enveloped them, a wide globe stamped through space, welcoming them back to that distant forest in the heart of the Grove.

Stef stepped forward as if mesmerized. Joy hurried next to him in case the spell needed her to go first. She didn't want anything going wrong. *Not with Stef. Not this time.* She squeezed the scalpel in one hand, fighting another bout of déjà vu.

Her ears popped as they entered the Grove, and she blinked back blue sparkles. Little sounds sprang to the surface: the crunch of Stef's boot changing from bramble to meadow, the rhythm of his walk as he took one step, then two, and a strange coughing sound as he turned toward the forest. In the distance, there was movement—a crashing, leaping shadow darting toward them, coming fast between the trees.

Stef's arm held her back, hand open. A sigil had been drawn on his palm—a wizard's mark. He'd come prepared. Joy went cold. What had he seen that she hadn't? Was it a monster? A trap? She switched hands, palming the beacon and flipping the scalpel sideways as the shadow gained shape, bounding through the deep wood, gaining speed.

Stef bolted toward it.

"St—!" Joy caught herself before she said his True Name. Her brother wasn't safe here—he didn't have a *signatura* to protect him. She cursed herself for being so stupid! His name could control him. It was her fault for not telling him! She squeezed her fists and bit her tongue. She couldn't call his name, and she couldn't catch him in time.

The grass parted as he ran. A crackle of twigs answered. Joy saw the shadow resolve into the curly-haired satyr, bare arms swinging, shoving branches aside, fighting his way through the wood. He broke through the tree line at a gallop, leaping into the grassland, arms pumping, legs bounding, a thin braid trailing behind him like a kite string.

Stef ran straight for him, full-out.

The sound punched from their bodies on impact. They wrapped their arms around each other and held on tight. Joy didn't know what to say as Dmitri grabbed fistfuls of Stef's shirt. She didn't know what to think when Stef pulled back, holding Dmitri's curly-haired head in his hands, pressing their foreheads together, gasping for breath, and kissed him full on the lips. They turned, spinning, almost wrestling to hang on; drinking in one another like they were drowning in the meadow, waves of grass undulating like the sea around their legs.

Joy didn't know what to do. She'd never seen her brother so happy.

Tearing up, she smiled.

Overly conscious of being the third wheel, Joy wondered if there was a discreet way to make her exit and what excuse she could give her father for bringing the car back to camp alone. Lies were tricky business and half-truths even more so. Her father would want an explanation. She heard carefree male laughter behind her and started picking up the pace. She would just wait in the car. Time did funny things—it might only be a moment. She could still see the mushroom-covered tree outside the beacon's glow. She concentrated on her footsteps as she flattened the meadow grass underfoot, tiptoeing toward the edge of the bubble and a quick trip home.

There was the creak of heavy wicker baskets.

Joy froze, ears straining for the sound that haunted her nightmares. She shook her head in disbelief. Her brain was playing tricks. It was probably the sound of the trees in the distance. But standing on the edge of the Grove, her body refused to move, every hair on her skin rising in a prickle of prescient fear.

The low creak of wood came again, tracing a sharp finger up her spine.

Joy spun, scalpel out, arm forward, now sure. She crept along the clearing, circling toward the woods, where the sound hid in shadow. Joy crept forward, ignoring everything but the low creak on the edge of her hearing, expecting to see a flash of orange foxtails in the corner of her Sight. She pushed into the forest, following a thin deer trail pocked with scat and rocks, winding her way deeper into the wilderness cloaked in dappled shadows and dark thoughts.

It can't be...

The eerie echo came again, this time accompanied by a light scraping of feet. Joy crouched down. There was a flicker of movement to her right, maybe a bird or squirrel or something worse. Her fingers went cold. Her burn scars itched. She eased out of her flip-flops, trading the thin layer of plastic for the pressed-grass ground. She didn't know what it could do for her, but she wanted every advantage, even the unfamiliar ones. Fear bubbled below her surface like the distant roar under the earth.

Joy followed the trail.

Five satyrs were walking down rough rows of saplings, laughing and joking. They had leather bags slung across their chests and cloth bands tied over their foreheads, dark with sweat. There were wheelbarrows of earth and giant barrels of water. One rust-colored faun, covered in dirt up to his elbows, wiped the back of a hand across his brow, leaving a muddy smear. A chestnut fellow splashed him with a small bucket, flattening his curly fur. He shook himself out like a giant dog. The others erupted in jeers.

It would be a magical sight if not for the creak that had shivered Joy's spine. She turned aside, hunting it like a scent on the wind, moving south along the tree line. Joy dug her toes into the ground, feeling the undercurrent of old rock like a taste in her mouth, letting it fuel her feet forward when every other impulse was screaming at her to run. *Run away! Go now!* But she had to know if her ears were lying. *They have to be lying.* Joy had seen Aniseed's death with her own eyes—but she knew that eyes lied. *It has to be a mistake.* But there were no mistakes; she knew that fact better than most. *There must be some other explanation*—there were always exceptions to the rules: the Red Knight had beat the Edict, the Tide had tried to kill her, there had been poison in *signaturae*, Ink had been emptied, Kurt had been brought back to life, even Briarhook had fought on the battlefield after his heart had been ripped out. Joy never knew what to believe. In the Twixt, anything was possible.

She crept forward.

There was a wide, circular clearing up ahead, dotted with enormous stumps like ruined Roman columns cut at different heights. Each broken tree was the center of its own tended circle of upturned earth surrounded by white stones. Each stone had a single glyph, which together made a long sentence—a spell—creating a protective shield out of the granite and quartz. Each stump sported a sprout or burl or crust of new green. A glimmer of pollenated sunlight reflected gently off one of the shields, an invisible dome like a terrarium membrane protecting the delicate plants within. Rich, loamy earth had been raked along the bases and watered enough to produce a smell of deep spring. A breeze tickled the clearing, ruffling the tiny, sprouting leaves and red baby buds. Air could pass through the shields, and sunlight, and water. It had the soothing, cuddled quiet of a nursery's afternoon nap.

But the sound came again, and this time, Joy saw it—something on the farthest stump *moved*.

She was walking before she realized it, the energy under her heels channeling her forward. Joy circled the clearing, exposing more stumps as she walked around the glen. As she stared at the knobby growths, the patterns in the bark formed impressions of tiny mouths, tiny eyes, curled fingers, bald heads, but her eyes fixed on one lengthy, adult-size limb that hooked around the base of the farthest tree, creaking with stiffness and age. Joy stopped. Her gaze followed the bulb of the ankle up the bow of the shin, the knob of the knee, the swell of the thigh to where the bark bristled and blistered with swollen bores, melding the thigh to a wedge carved deep into the stump, leaking sap and bandaged in moss—and from the split grew a small figure with thin, weak limbs, a swollen belly and a dark, bulbous head. Sunlight slid off its skin like oil. Its wide eyes, riddled with dark veins, rolled in their sockets, looking faintly Eurasian, tilted up at the tips.

Joy screamed.

The Grove exploded into motion. Satyrs charged out of the woods, carrying bags and wicked staves as Joy stumbled back, smacking into a thick tree trunk and falling to the ground. A cobweb of woody vines squeezed together, smothering sunlight as a shimmering ward appeared, slamming down with enough force to kick up a puff of leaves and dirt. Joy kicked feebly away from the fetal thing wearing Aniseed's eyes, Aniseed's face, growing out of Aniseed's severed leg.

Joy swung her scalpel, and the ward lit with sparks. She pointed the tip with the edge of her finger and attempted to pierce it like an illusion, praying it *was* an illusion, hoping it would pop. There was a hot, searing buzz that trembled angrily up her wrist, seeping up her arm and quivering in her chest. The ward shuddered, flared and threw her back. Joy crashed into a swath of ferns and tumbled through the leaves.

Hands in the earth. Belly in the earth. Her fingers clawed the ground. She reached for something wild and roiling. Old and powerful, mountainous, *crushing*—she burned with rage and fire in her throat. Her eyes filmed over. Her mind honed sharp. She would rise up, destroy this abomination and BURY HER ENEMIES FOREVER!

Her head rang with fury as spearheads pointed at her throat. The satyrs shouted an Italianate garble, angry and insistent, but she couldn't understand and didn't much care—the keening in her head rose to a high whine as she saw a dark hand crawl out from beneath the stump, pushing the raked soil aside. A flat head rose to the surface and glared at Joy with fiery eyes, its mouth opening in a howl.

The golem pulled itself from its grave and squatted like a watchdog at the feet of its mistress.

She could hear Stef's voice from far away, "Joy!" and Dmitri's rough, babbling cry ended with a sudden English "Don't!"

Joy heaved slowly, belly pressed against roots, body smeared in the earth, ears buzzing with something nameless that called to her, lighting a fire where there was emptiness, clanging loudly in her silent chest. She wanted power.

She wanted it to fill her. She wanted to crush everything around her. But a small part of her, a human part of her, held back. *What's happening?* She trembled with need and fear and vengeance.

"Joy?" Stef appeared, filling her vision, forcing her eyes to his as his shoulder blocked the golem's ruby-red-hot glare. "Joy, listen to me. Drop the weapon." He looked disheveled, confused, sweaty and afraid. "Drop it, Joy. These are guardians of the Glen. No human can be here. We have to—"

There was a bark of noise and a shove. Stef pitched forward but caught himself on one hand, the other shot up, exposing the wizard's mark, gaining fast attention. Dmitri waved his arms and spoke in fast, husky assurances. Joy let the pounding feeling recede until her fingers were her own, no longer an extension of the ground, and opened her fist slowly. The scalpel rolled into the earth. She stared up at her brother.

"It's—it's Aniseed," she said, hardly believing the words. To say it aloud was to admit that it was true. *"Aniseed!* That! Over there! We have to—" Her fingers reached for the scalpel again. Stef's hand came down hard, pressing hers flat. Joy shed tears of fury and fear. "No," she pleaded, tugging. "You don't understand—!"

"It's not her," Dmitri said in English. His troop of satyrs stood behind him. A few had been dispatched to check the other stumps, concern clear on their faces. None of them looked twice at the golem. One of the satyrs with gray in his curls and scars on his chest lifted his weapon to neutral position and glared down at Joy.

"It is not Aniseed," the old satyr said. "Not yet."

"Not *yet*?" Joy cried, horrified.

"Not even when she's grown and cleaved from the tree," he said. "She is a graftling, a cutting grown from the parent limb."

Joy's insides tumbled over. She tasted sick in the back of her throat. "That's Aniseed's *leg*," she said. "You cut off her leg?"

"In order to *twain*, dryads must donate a significant portion of their body mass," the old satyr said. "We mold substitute limbs out of willow to promote quick healing and regeneration. For some, it is the only way."

Joy imagined the *segulah* when they'd last met—Aniseed strutting slowly around the glowing warehouse floor like an old woman too proud for a cane. She could picture her stroking her fox-fur collar with long, precise fingers, flicking drops of burning alchemical fire and tearing Ink's throat with her teeth. And when she walked in her long, trailing dress, she hobbled with the sound of creaking wicker baskets.

Willow baskets. A willow leg.

She'd planned this all along.

"That's...Aniseed's *baby*?"

"More like Aniseed's clone." Dmitri said. He nodded to his friends, who cleared the wood but for the elder and two armed guards. Many exchanged staves and spears for shovels and rakes, but the black looks remained. One of the satyrs spoke to a handful of squirrels in elaborate saddles carrying tiny brown mounts. Dismissed, they scattered up the trees in winding spirals. The fingernail skitters ran prickles up over Joy's skin. Dmitri caught her stare. "The graftlings share a genetic makeup, and even some memories, with their parent, but the bud will grow up to be her own separate entity. She will not be Aniseed."

"No," Joy said. "You *can't*—!"

"You may not threaten the graftlings in any way," the elder satyr warned. "We will not permit it."

Stef helped Joy to sit up, but she shoved his arm away. "She'll still be Aniseed inside!" Joy shook her head and clawed her hands. "She tried to kill *millions of people* by spreading a magical poison through *signaturae*," she snapped. "She tried to lead a coup against the Council! She was sentenced to *death*! I was there—I saw her die!"

"The one responsible for those acts has been held accountable for her crimes," the old satyr said calmly. "Her sentence was carried out. Indeed, she died. The rules have been preserved. By our own laws, a graftling cannot be held responsible for the actions of its parent."

Joy cupped her head in her hands and squeezed, wishing that Ink or Kurt were here. This was Aniseed before the battle on the warehouse floor, Aniseed before she fell, Aniseed now protected by the laws that she wished to break. *How neat*, Joy fumed. *How perfectly played*. Her mind reeled with revulsion, forced to admire the witch's last loophole. *How like Aniseed! Graus Claude would be impressed*.

Joy's eyes snapped open. Her head shot up.

"It has Aniseed's memories?" Joy asked.

Dmitri stood warily near Stef. "Possibly some," he admitted. "Lineage, language, things to help accli—"

"Can it tell me about the Amanya?" she gasped.

Stef frowned. "What are you talking about?"

"The Amanya! It's a spell. Aniseed changed it before it was cast, and she's the only one who knew how. That thing might know—it might remember. Look!" She pointed at the homunculus at the foot of the stump. "She sent those after me! She *knows* that I know! She *knows* that I can stop her!"

"Impossible," the elder satyr said.

"No," Stef said. "I saw those things attack my sister this afternoon."

"It is a guardian golem left by the parent to our keeping, which predates the graftling's life—and yours—by decades, if not more." The old satyr scratched his scarred chest. "Aniseed bequeathed it as additional insurance for her young, suspecting that it might be threatened—" His tired eyes glared down at Joy. "A wise precaution, it seems." He poked the ground with the butt of his spear. "This troop is defined by its neutrality within the Twixt. Our first and foremost authority is to care for those living in the Glen and to protect all who grow here. It is not unusual for parents to leave gifts for their heirs, and this golem is tethered to the graftling's roots." The battle-scarred satyr sounded weary and wise. "I can assure you that it has never left this spot."

"But the other golems—they're *hers*," Joy cried. "Aniseed's! Her clone could be controlling them—"

"Her offspring has barely gained sentience," the elder said patiently. "She is too young even to speak."

There was a high, thin gurgling, too tiny for a squeak. It was unmistakably laughter.

The satyrs turned. Stef hissed in shock. Joy glared at the half-formed thing, unsurprised, and pushed past her brother. The spears came to bear. Joy stopped and glared at the mahogany eyes spinning in their oversize sockets. Fear crawled a carpet of spider's legs down her back.

The graftling was laughing at her.

"Tell me how to break the Amanya," Joy said.

The baby Aniseed's bulbous face blinked; its mouth formed a moue.

Joy's hands balled into fists. She wanted her scalpel, but to go for it would be suicide—she'd be skewered in an instant. She wanted Inq's wood-chipper hands. She wanted Kurt's gun. She wanted Ink's razor. She was so close that she could reach out and break it apart with her bare hands if not for the ward.

"Tell me how to open the door!" Joy shouted.

Aniseed's graftling gave a small shake of its head, unmistakably impudent; its hands clutched the air, its spine curled and stretched. The chuckle came again along with the slow, wicker creak. The shapely leg coyly stretched and relaxed. The graftling almost smiled. Almost.

Joy stood as close as she dared, the ward humming like heat against the soft down of her face. Her eyes watered.

"Where is the door?" she screamed at it. *"Tell me!"*

The small mouth 'o'ed, the frail hands opening and closing, the fat head wobbling as Aniseed's immature clone laughed and laughed and laughed. The whirling eyes locked on Joy as if focusing on her for the first time. It squirmed, leaning forward.

"Bah-lee-*wick*," the graftling whispered with mocking glee.

Joy stumbled back into Stef's arms, her mouth echoing the word.

"Bailiwick?"

The little Aniseed twitched its twiggy arms against its chest, wheezing thin laughter. "Go." It laughed. "Bah-lee-wick. In Bah-lee-wick. Go!"

"I know it's inside the Bailiwick!" Joy whispered hotly. "But *where*?" She struggled in her brother's arms. "How do I open it? How do I bring them back?"

"What are you talking about?" Dmitri asked.

Aniseed's clone laughed again. "Locked. In. Bah-lee-wick!"

Joy stopped struggling.

"This conversation is inadmissible as evidence of any wrongdoing!" the elder satyr shouted, waving his arms. "As has been decreed by the Council of the Twixt!" He crossed his spears and brought them down sharply, scattering the guards with a burst of authoritative garble. He pointed at Dmitri and snapped his fingers. Dmitri grabbed Stef's arm.

"We must go," Dmitri said.

"Joy," Stef urged and pulled her back.

Joy felt herself being pushed, stumbling and numb, away

from the sparkling clearing; she had no words or strength to resist. The forest receded into blurry shapes, the satyrs disappearing, the shadows thinning, growing light—but the whole of her was focused with horror on the twisted brown thing curling out of the stump, perched atop Aniseed's leg like a trophy, with the fiery-eyed golem squatting at its heel and the nail-slate scratch of the graftling's mocking, cackling laughter.

She knew. She remembered.

Aniseed was the courier.

She was behind it all.

And now she was protected by the Twixt.

SEVENTEEN

JOY CRASHED THROUGH THE UNDERGROWTH, HER FEET slipping on mushrooms and decay. The blue neon light flashed behind her eyes as she ran past Stef through the beacon's doorway, groping blindly at the felled tree, her bare feet surfing through the soft mulch before lurching to a halt.

Aniseed! She was still alive—somehow, though not quite. Growing, getting stronger, protected under Twixt law.

Graus Claude! The door was locked inside the Bailiwick—along with the princess—hiding the King and Queen and most of their people inside a pocket universe, lost to everyone but the courier who'd betrayed them all.

Aniseed! She'd visited the Bailiwick frequently, Graus Claude's student/lover/friend. She could go to him at any time, crawl inside him, access the door and lock her opponents away by making everyone else forget. Aniseed was the courier, the traitor, the spell-caster, the key, the missing link. Aniseed had carved herself a loophole at the cost of her limb; a small price to pay for ultimate power, as well as a fresh, clean slate. Was that what she'd promised to do for Hasp? Could she have grafted other Folk, giving them the freedom of a new life, a new body, beyond the Council's decree?

A hand closed over her wrist, and she gasped, half expecting Stef, and not at all expecting the thing that grinned at her with rotted teeth and piggy black eyes.

Briarhook!

"Lost you?" Briarhook grinned. His claws squeezed harder and his hedgehog bristles shook. "Lost in my wood?" His breath stank of fetid meat. Joy gagged as he leaned closer. "I lost, too, you," he sneered and thumped the metal plate in his chest. "Lost my heart!" He hissed and slapped the plate again, harder. He lifted her by the arm and shook her violently. *"Want my heart!"*

Her head swam, and her shoulder socket screamed. She blasted him with Inq's air glyph, but it only rattled the black-brown quills, blowing bits of leaf and rags from his back. Briarhook snarled, and his fat rat's tail whipped against the ground. He smacked her against a tree, and she grabbed hold of a branch, eyes tearing, ears ringing, gasping in panic.

"You'll never get it if you hurt me," she said hoarsely. *"Never!"*

He let go in an instant, his eyes scrunching to slits. Joy tensed, wondering what could come next. She remembered the feel of Briarhook's white-hot quill as he'd branded his *signatura* into her arm—a *signatura* that was no longer there. She'd erased it, breaking the rules.

Blue neon hissed behind him. A figure dropped from the trees.

"Is there some quarrel, Wood Guardian?" Avery said as he straightened, the feather cloak settling in the leaves like wings. It might have been a question, but the words held steel. Joy didn't know what to think of it. She could barely think at all.

Briarhook grunted warily. "Lost, she," he said. "In woods."

Avery nodded. "Fortunate, then, that I have found her."

The hulking hedgehog crouched, eyes lidded as he quailed before the Tide's man. In his bid for freedom, Briarhook had changed sides during the battle against Aniseed. He knew the power that the Tide held on the Council.

"My heart," he muttered.

Avery turned his sea-blue eyes to Joy. "She does seem to have that effect on Folk," he said. "Poor fools. Such women are heartless, I'm told. Pay them no mind."

Briarhook snarled and opened his paw, which grew red in the center, bleeding to white. The heat was palpable, like waves off summer asphalt, curling some of Avery's feathery edges. Avery twitched his cloak aside. Joy stood firm and held her breath.

Briarhook dropped his hand slowly. The fire died. He sneezed, a burst of sound. He pointed a single claw at her, its point barely above her chest, and laughed a grating, sawing laughter as sick and black as tar. Briarhook shook with glee and lurched back one step, then two.

"Lost." He laughed merrily. "Yes, you. My heart—know you!" Briarhook chortled. "Yes, know you now. Heartless. *Ha!* Good, yes. *Good*."

Briarhook backed his way into the woods, opening up his arms, embracing the forest, fading away, laughing, into the bramble dark.

Joy sucked air into her lungs, unwilling or unable to move until the tingling seeped slowly back into her limbs. She mashed her dry tongue against the roof of her mouth. Avery swept his cloak back into place and eyed the neon-blue globe.

"A beacon," he observed. "You are full of surprises, Joy Malone."

"*You!*" Her nerves snapped as she spat. "You *knew!*" Joy shook with rage and shock and disgust. "I bet the Tide's known all along!"

Avery rested his long hand on the hilt of his sword; the scabbard flicked the swallowtails of his cloud-colored coat.

"Perhaps if I had more information, I could admit or deny it. As it is, however, I have no idea what you are talking about."

Joy blinked furiously against tears. "Aniseed!"

Avery frowned, the name of his martyr spoiled on her lips. "What of her?" he asked.

"She—" Joy said, slowly registering the look on his face, a mix of annoyance, confusion and, oddly, of hope. *He didn't know!* She switched gears. "Sh-She started all of this—Briarhook, the Tide, the Red Knight, *everything*." She pushed real fear into her words to cover her near slip. "She tried to kill me!"

"You and a great many others," Avery said. "A crime for which she was declared a traitor, dismissed by the Council, stripped of her honors and publicly executed." His voice hardened, spiky and grim. "You were there."

"Yes," she said, gulping for composure. "I was."

Joy imagined herself as one of the witnesses who could have sworn that they'd seen Aniseed fall, giving her graftling time to grow stronger in secret, but the Tide didn't know that; or perhaps it was only Avery who didn't. She couldn't risk telling him more and having it get back to Sol Leander. She swallowed, forcing calm, desperate to throw him off. *He mustn't know! He mustn't find out!* She wracked her rattled brain to find something to throw him off. "Did you know that before they were enemies, Graus Claude and Aniseed were lovers?"

Avery shrugged. "What of it?" he said. "Immortality has a way of making lovers out of enemies and enemies out of friends. Such scandals belong to humanity, not us...with the possible exception of your favorite chair." Joy deliberately ignored the insult as she struggled to stand on her own two feet. Avery offered her a hand. She ignored that, too. He sighed, sounding exasperated, cross.

"Well, then," he said, "if there's nothing else—"

"Of course there is," Joy muttered. "There's more. Much more."

Avery stepped closer, almost daring to touch her shoulder. "Tell me, then."

She wondered how long before Stef would appear and gave him the truth: "I can't."

Avery shook his head, a dry chuckle on his lips. "Stubborn to the last," he said. "I fail to see how I can be of any help, then."

"I'm not asking for your help!"

"Indeed," he said. "You should."

Something in his tone hinted a warning; something in his gaze tried to tell her that there were words he could not speak aloud. Being part of the Twixt made her realize there was a great advantage to having grown up with things going unsaid. If you cannot tell a lie, always look for what's unsaid—therein lies the loophole. Aniseed had found one. So could Joy.

"Okay," Joy said. "Help me, then. Bring a message to Inq."

"A message?" he said. He didn't say *Why?* which was surprising. His next words were "What is it?"

"Say—" Joy stopped and chose her words carefully, knowing that anything said would get back to his master. "Say that Aniseed was the courier."

Avery frowned, his curiosity piqued. She could see it—like a cat's gleam in his eyes. "What does that mean?" he asked.

Joy paused. Did the Amanya erase even that? "Say it back to me."

"'Aniseed was the courier.'"

He could remember that much because it was meaningless. The members of the Tide might know the name of their martyr, but none of them—not even Sol Leander—would recognize her post since they'd forgotten its purpose. If the Amanya spell didn't do the trick, the secrecy surrounding the courier's identity would. Fortunately, both Inq and Kurt would understand her message, and she could tell them the rest when they came for her. Watching his face, Joy wondered if Avery might half remember, a fleeting thought pushed aside, déjà vu dismissed. Could she somehow jog his memory? Could a human do what the Folk could not?

"Does that...mean anything to you?" she asked.

The question hung in the air, sprinkled with neon light.

"No," he said, finally. "Should it?"

"Yes, it should," Joy said, disappointed. "It definitely should. But it doesn't."

Avery stepped aside, the beacon's blue light reflecting off his pale hair and blue-green eyes. "I will do as you ask, if only to prove my point."

"Your point?"

"*I* am not your enemy, Joy Malone."

She considered that. *He cannot tell a lie.* "All right," Joy said slowly. "Prove it. Last I knew, Inq was at Graus Claude's."

Avery futzed with his cloak. "The Bailiwick's domicile is closed."

"Yes, I know," Joy said. "He's gone to speak with the Council."

"Yes... I know," Avery said.

Joy's hopes sank. She heard what was unsaid—her mentor had already confessed, the Council had convened and Sol Leander had heard the Bailiwick's crimes if it was already known to his aide. She wanted to ask more but thought better of it. Stef would come through soon, and Graus Claude was currently beyond her reach. She'd find a way to help him, but right now, she had more immediate threats to worry about.

"I see," she said slowly. "Thank you."

He almost smiled. Almost. "I will deliver your message," he said as he raised one edge of his cloak and a single white eyebrow. "Try not to die before the gala tomorrow—it would be considered crass." He let the cloak fall, and the weight of it wiped him out of the world with a sweep of feathers, gone. In a wink, there was nothing but the woods and the beacon's fading light.

Joy blinked. She took one breath, then two, shuddering on the exhale.

Too close. Much too close. She made a small sound in the back of her throat as she tore down the incline, sliding and scraping until she hit the gritty roadside, stumbling on gravel as she raced toward the car.

She jumped into the passenger seat and locked the doors. Breathing deeply, she smashed the meat of her palms into her eye sockets as if she could smudge the terrible images from the back of her brain. She ground her teeth. She kicked the floor. Clenching her jaw, she screamed, loud and long. Trembling, she wiped at the feeling of claws on her skin, but couldn't scrape the look of Aniseed's fetal clone from the back of her eyes.

They were *screwed*! Graus Claude had turned himself over to the Council and was more than likely behind bars or worse. He could be anywhere in the world, anywhere in the Twixt. Even if she could make Aniseed tell her how to open the door, she couldn't get to him now, couldn't get to the door...

But the Scribes could.

Yes! She needed Ink. She wanted Ink. *Here. Now!*

Joy dumped out her toiletry bag and sifted through its contents. She was clawing through her things as Stef keyed the locks, climbed in and shut the door.

"You dropped this," Stef said and handed her the scalpel.

She snatched it, stuck it in her bag and continued her panicked searching. She wiped tears and snot from her face. She had Filly's pouch and Kurt's number. Her fingers stumbled to choose. She had to tell them! She had to get a message out!

"You're welcome," Stef said.

"Just drive," Joy snapped.

"O-kay," Stef said, rotating the wheel for a three-point turn. "Don't have a heart attack."

A heart attack? Ha! She could tell him about what had just happened, but the words wouldn't come. She couldn't stop to think about it. She had to concentrate on making her fingers work. She tried scribbling a note on a scrap of vellum pressed against the window. The pencil needed to be sharpened. The vellum tore. "Damn!" She bit the end with her teeth, tasting graphite. "I need to tell someone who can remember!"

"Are you going to tell *me* what's going on?"

Joy dropped her pencil. "Yes," she said.

And she did.

She summed up everything she could from the King and Queen to the traitor and the spell and the lost, secret door and what Aniseed's betrayal meant to the Council, as well as to the Folk. She talked until she ran out of words, Stef's face hardening with each passing moment. Her voice grew scratchy, her eyes puffy and sore. It was good to say it aloud—good to get it out there, good to have it be Stef.

"Right," Stef said and flicked the headlights as a warning as he rounded the curve. He checked his mirrors and shifted gears. "Hang on."

He floored it. The car's wheels spun on the road as he peeled out at a speed not recommended by the legal limit. Joy hung on to the door handle as they raced around the bend. She had a crazy thought of jumping out of the car while it was still moving, but held her place and her breath as she clung on, arms locked. She had to send a text. She had to tell the others. If she could tell the Council about Aniseed's clone, they might listen. If Aniseed was alive, Joy was as good as dead.

This changes everything.

Grimacing, Stef spun the wheel and slammed the car into Park, killing the engine and popping the locks in one quick sweep. He barked orders as he moved. "You get in your tent. I'll get Dad. Stay in your tent until we pack up and leave."

"What?" Joy said, halfway out the door. "Why?"

"Because I warded it," he shouted over his shoulder as he ran down the road.

She was already sprinting for her pack, barefoot, as Stef waved to their father taking pictures of the dying sun. Joy saw the thick ring of salt ringing her tent as she dived inside. She flipped over, quick-dialing Kurt. She nabbed her flashlight and a pen as it rang. Testing the Sharpie on the back of her hand, she started scribbling a note to Filly. *Aniseed made the golems & a graftling of herself. Find out where Graus Claude is STAT!* She messed up the return sigil and had to draw it a second time. Her fingers shook as she lit the match, one of them flaring too close to her fingers. She yelped, dropped it and burned a hole in the floor. Nylon melted and blackened. She stamped it dead with her shoe.

Kurt's message machine was a simple beep, no introduction. Of course, he'd been mute for years.

"Kurt, it's me, Joy. I just saw—" She swallowed bile. *Aniseed. Briarhook. A graftling clone.* "Tell Ink and Inq—it's Aniseed. Aniseed's the courier. And Aniseed's alive." She stopped writing because her words were growing more jumbled, her thoughts a flurry of panic. The tent felt suddenly smaller. Dense. "Not alive, okay? But not dead. She grafted her leg and somehow made a new mini-me and the satyrs said they're sworn to protect it and it's outside jurisdiction, but it knew about the door. It told me—"

There was a snap outside the camp, and Joy's words froze in her throat. *What am I doing?!* She couldn't leave a *message*! Anyone could find it. Anyone could overhear. Her fingers quivered. Her voice wrung to a tight, whispery squeak.

"Call me," she said and hung up.

Joy held her breath, tucked the flashlight behind her knee and opened the zipper of her toiletry bag, tooth by tooth. Had she been followed from the Grove? Was the ward active, or did it still need a drop of blood? Did it have to be Stef's or could she do it? Had he preset the spell, or was it up and running? She'd never tried wizard magic but knew that human wizards guarded their spells ruthlessly, which was why Stef hadn't told her how to do it. Joy wasn't crazy about crossing Mr. Vinh, but if it was a choice between a wizard's wrath or Aniseed's, she was willing to take the risk.

Shadows slid across the nylon wall oozing unfamiliar shapes. She tried to find her scalpel without taking her eyes off the tent. Every rattle of her toothbrush roared in her ears, blotting out the smaller sounds outside. Was a shadow coming nearer? Or was her paranoia on overdrive? The tent flap shuddered in the wind. A branch fell.

"Joy!"

There was a sparkle of light, and she hiccuped in surprise. She snapped on the flashlight and tore open the flap.

Ink stood across the way, a lithe silver-black shape on the edge of the campsite. His face was half in shadow. His wallet chain caught the moonlight.

"Ink!" Her voice amplified in the dark. She held her breath as he crossed the campsite and knelt before the ward, crackling static and sparks.

"I am here," he said quickly. "I am sorry, and I am here."

Joy scraped her heel through the salt circle, breaking it, and grabbed his arms, pulling him into the tent, wrapping around him and squeezing hard. "Are you okay?" she asked, hardly daring to believe it. He was here. Now. With her. Now. "Are you all right?"

"I am," he said into her hair, his voice softening with relief, his arms curled where they belonged. "And I am much better now."

She spoke past his ear, unwilling to let go. "Graus Claude—!"

"I know."

"Aniseed—!"

"I know," he said again, breathing deep, his chest rising and falling against hers. The rhythm of his breathing calmed her, even if his words had to keep up.

"You know?"

"Yes," he said. His crisp, clean voice cut like the flashlight through the dark. "I came as soon as Avery told me where you were."

"Avery?" Joy shook her head. "I told him to tell Inq. I didn't know if you were—" She didn't know how to finish the sentence. Ink didn't seem to mind.

"Likely he did not hear the difference. You pronounce our names much the same. But he was most insistent," he said. "He left with Kurt, Inq and Filly to vouch for Graus Claude."

"Really?" Joy pulled away enough to look him in the face. "Ink, I saw her—Aniseed—in the satyr's Grove. She knew about the door inside the Bailiwick!"

"And now we know that she has *twained* herself," Ink said, pushing some hair out of her face, clearing Joy's eyes. "She is very clever. Very resourceful."

"It was horrible," she said.

"Her secret or her offspring?"

"Both." Joy shuddered. "It was horrible squared."

Ink crawled nearer. He cast no shadow next to hers. "Did she hurt you?" he whispered.

Joy shook her head. "No. It's...barely grown. But it had a golem guardian, like the ones that attacked me, and it *laughed* at me, Ink—it *remembers*," she said. "The satyrs said it has some of Aniseed's memories, maybe even those before the Amanya spell—if reincarnating acts like it did with the Red Knight, then being reborn outside the confines of the original spell makes you immune. She remembered where the door is hidden and that it's locked, so she must know how to open it!"

Joy saw understanding register on his face. "Graus Claude." She touched the soft space by his left shoulder, thinking about what he had done to Ink, shutting him off like a switch, making Ink seem less than a person, less than alive. It was *dehumanizing*, although the word didn't fit. Ink stared at his hands. "I thought he had betrayed us," Ink said. "I thought he would hurt you."

"I know. I'm sorry. It's my fault," she said. "I found the origin of the spell, but not the traitor, just the treason. Aniseed tricked everyone and used Graus Claude and the satyrs to do it. I accused Graus Claude, I tripped the trap—I made a terrible mistake, and now we're stuck."

Ink sat back, the light playing off his boyish face. "I recall someone once saying that there are no mistakes," he said. "Without you, we might never have known the extent of Aniseed's treachery. And now we are closer to reuniting the Folk than anyone has managed in over a thousand years." His fingers softly traced the side of her face, the curve of her ear. "If this is your mistake, then it is a mistake worth making."

Joy rested her cheek against the palm of his hand, tired and grateful. "We have to get to Graus Claude," she said. "The only way we can save your mother and access the door is to get inside the Bailiwick."

"That will be difficult," Ink said. "Graus Claude has thrown himself on the mercy of the Council for the crime of High Treason—quite the sentence given that they have no recollection of having a King and Queen. They have secured him in a holding cell until a formal trial, which will take place after the gala." He cast her a sidelong glance. "I believe they plan for the affair to overshadow any social unpleasantness that would normally arise when convicting the High Water Seat."

"Lovely," Joy muttered. Now Sol Leander's circus was a convenient cover-up for the Bailiwick's condemnation to be quietly swept under the rug. She rubbed her fists into her eyes, the empty roaring in her ears heralding an oncoming headache. "Ink, we can't just let them—"

There was a crashing and crunching of gravel and leaves as Stef's voice drifted toward them. "...mood swings," Stef said. "But, whatever. I live in a coed dorm. If I wasn't used to it before, I'm used to it now. It's called 'mandatory sensitivity training.'"

"Well, whatever it is, we're *not* going home early," Dad said. "I planned this camping weekend, and therefore we're going to be *camping* for the *weekend*. Got it?"

Stef sighed. "Got it."

"Good," Mr. Malone said and added after a pause, "Shelley thinks I should be more assertive. How was that?"

"Very impressive."

Joy slipped into her sleeping bag with a zip of denim-on-nylon, unfolding it width-wise like a blanket.

Get down! she mouthed. Ink crouched on his belly and slid toward the tent flap, liquid smooth. Joy shook her head, her lips an *o* of *No!* She didn't want him to leave and knew her brother would see him leaving her tent even if her father couldn't, which would be both dangerous and embarrassing. Ink glanced over his shoulder and smiled just a little—mischievous and clever. He drew the homicidal fairy wand out of his back-pocket sheath. His body flowed gracefully under the light. His face shone briefly in the flashlight glare, boyish and smooth. He reached a hand under the edge of the tent flap and eased the zipper wider with his fingers and thumb. He drew the wand through the salt, connecting the edges with a looping glyph. The ward sprang back to life, this time sparkling gold rather than blue. He withdrew his hand and slowly slid backward, lying next to Joy, slipping inside her body's shadow. She threw the sleeping bag over them both as she pretended to roll over.

"Joy? You still up?" Dad asked.

She pulled the sleeping bag higher to muffle her mouth. "Mmm?"

"Are you coming out?"

Joy glanced at Ink. His eyes crinkled in question. They were trapped inside her tent, under a sleeping bag, with her father and brother just outside. She turned away from him and called out over the zipper.

"No," she said.

"I think she's done for the night," Stef said. "And that's not a bad idea. We're getting up early with the fishes, right? I need my beauty sleep." He exaggerated a stretch and a yawn that she could see like shadow puppets against the screen of her tent. "I'm not used to getting up before noon."

"Remind me why I'm paying for college?" her father chided and called over his shoulder. "You're sure you don't want to come fishing, honey? The sunrise over Lake James is a sight."

"Mmph," Joy muttered, not trusting her voice. She'd had enough of the Sight for one day and as much as it irked her to play the menstrual card, she didn't trust herself to speak. She was in a pretty tenuous position with Ink pressed against her, and all of her attention focused on that fact. She shrugged herself lower, feeling his breath by her ear, his belly pressed into her back, his legs bent, fitting perfectly into the crooks of hers.

"All right, we'll skip the campfire tonight," her father said with fake gaiety. "We'll try not to wake you in the morning, honey, but I hope you can haul yourself out of bed for breakfast."

"Okay," Joy said, her voice smothered under goose down. "Sorry, Dad."

"Don't be sorry," he said as she heard the unzipping of tents, the shuffling of bags and the zip of shoes against fabric. "Just feel better."

"Mmm-hmm," Joy said, feeling a lot of things, but *better* wasn't the word that popped to mind. Ink's hand rested on the side of her waist, and his fingers followed the curve of her rib. She pressed her hand over Ink's to keep it still. He threaded his fingers through hers.

"'Night, Joy," her brother called.

"'Night, Stef."

The unsaid said, *He knows.*

Of course he knows! He can see the color of the ward. He knows Ink is in here.

And he's covering for me.

"Thanks," Joy added, gratefully contrite.

There was a long pause before her brother said, "You're welcome."

She tried not to think that he spoke to them, plural.

Joy held perfectly still as the Malone men continued shuffling, zipping, adding the crumple of papers and clothes, the soft thump of boots, the sharp click of buttons and lights switching off and on as she lay tense in illicit closeness, her boyfriend's body cupping hers.

Her brain was on overload; adrenaline made her quiver in

place. She tried to still the tremors so that Ink wouldn't notice, but how could he not? She didn't know what to do. She couldn't say anything aloud, and with her head turned away, she couldn't see his face—couldn't read his eyes. She had no idea what he was thinking. She was lying blind, dressed in her pajamas and hyperaware of the taste of her breath. She wanted to brush her teeth. She wanted to be in her own bed. She wanted to let go of his hand and see what happened next, but this was *not* the time, and this was *not* the place; her father and brother were nearby, and a gritty coating of dirt now peppered her tent, making the floor itchy and uncomfortable. This was hardly romantic.

Rubbing her arches together, Joy tried to scrape off some of the embedded bits of stone from her feet, but ended up moving against his hips. *Bad idea!* Joy froze. Ink moved an inch or two to make room, and she eased herself sideways, pressing one leg against the inside of his knee, and, misreading her, Ink followed in kind, slipping his leg between hers. They were now tangled together, a knot of consensual limbs. She pressed her tongue against the roof of her mouth and bunched her pillow under her head. They'd have to wait until Stef and Dad were asleep. Then they could slip out of the ward and go. There was so much happening and so little time—even with time standing still—and Joy was desperate to act on her new information. She knew the others were out there, waiting for them. She had to stop Aniseed! She had to find Graus Claude! She had to convince someone—the Council or the princess—to find the door and unlock it and bring about the Imminent Return! She and Ink shouldn't be lying under a sleeping bag when they had to—

"Turn off your light, Joy," her father said. "You're wasting batteries."

Joy let go of Ink's hand long enough to stretch forward and

grab the flashlight—aware that his hand now lay flat against her stomach, two of his fingers touching the skin where her shirt rose up as she reached across the tent and switched off the light. She returned to her prone position with not enough room to turn over; Ink's left elbow pillowed her head, his right forearm resting in the dip at her waist. She could feel the seams of his jeans on the back of her legs; the arches of their feet nested together like spoons. Joy pressed her ear against his arm and rested her hand against his elbow and waited quietly in the dark, her every muscle taut. She was so aware of him, she could picture where every part of his body touched hers in the dark. She smelled his scent like rain on her skin.

She was too nervous to enjoy it. Much.

Time crept by on tortoise legs. Joy had no idea how much or how little. Her ears strained for the sound of deep breathing, light snoring, carried off by the winds that had picked up during the night. Her eyes grew itchy, exhaustion nipped at her edges, but sleep was impossible. Ink was here. Ink was *everywhere.*

He lay very still, but she could feel him—he was reading her as intently as the first time he'd inspected her ear. She could almost feel the slow tracing of his fingers as he explored the whorls and shapes of cartilage and skin, how his touch had wandered over her face, her eyebrows, the tips of her lashes and lips, discovering her in awe, reading her like Braille. She sighed at the memory—she couldn't help it—and felt her breath bounce back, touching her cheek. His hand twitched and she squeezed his palm. His thumb stroked hers. She felt it in her stomach and down her back, resting along the line of his chest, curving in the ladle of his hips.

She moved her leg a fraction. He moved, too. Closer. He was misunderstanding her, and she couldn't correct him—

or, perhaps, he wasn't misunderstanding at all. She wanted to turn and look at him. She wanted to pretend she hadn't noticed how warm he was. She wanted to feel his lips. She wanted him to kiss her. She wanted to kiss him. But he couldn't read her face with her face turned away, so it was her secret—a secret her body was whispering even as Joy tried to hush it, to keep very still. It wasn't working.

She pressed his fingers against her lips as a signal to quiet them. He stroked a soft line over her bottom lip, making her salivate. *Damn.*

Someone turned over in their tent, and she stopped, midmotion. She pressed her tongue against the back of her teeth and clamped her knees tight. Ink held himself preternaturally still. As the sounds settled, the silence stretching, she started to breathe again. Her breath tickled his wrist. He responded by breathing into her ear.

Warmth coursed through her, reminding her of beaches, warm and inviting. She squeezed his fingers. He touched his chin against her shoulder and kissed the spot. She felt the touch of his lips all the way down her calves. Joy squirmed, tensing, one foot hooking behind his ankle. He moved his hand to the edge of her waistband and kissed the nape of her neck. She rolled her head to the side, pressing into the pillow, his right hand splayed over her belly between her shirt and her shorts, his two middle fingers just touching, flesh on flesh; she could feel them there, politely, perfectly still.

Joy closed her eyes and willed them to move.

Curling her head forward exposed the back of her neck. The scrape of his chin and his breathing tangled in the roots of her hair. She arched into him. He stayed grounded like a rock. She turned slightly, his hand brushing her rib. She tried to turn enough to kiss him, but it only rolled her under his touch—his palm slid across her waist, his fingers hot against her stomach. She twisted. He kissed her temple, her earlobe, her cheekbone, her throat; his hands stayed, fixed points of warmth—one cupping her head, the other just touching her belly button.

Belly button, singular. *Important things, belly buttons.* She stroked the back of his hand. She could feel where they'd traced bumps of veins and knuckles and skin ridges and tapped hardened nails. She knew these hands. She trusted these hands. These hands knew *her*.

"Joy?" he whispered a question.

"Yes."

Those hands *moved*.

Joy leaned into the pillow and clenched a fistful of down. The sound in her head was so loud, she was certain everyone could hear the blood rushing through her ears. Her thoughts whirling, gaining speed, crashing behind her eyes—all words ripped away. Her insides wrung taut. She held her breath as her legs curled around his. Heat zinged up her spine, a froth of champagne bubbles tickling on the surface of her skin. She let go of his hand and rolled to face him; his arm around her waist, his fingers in her hair, their legs wound together—his, hers—together, theirs. Always. *Always like this.*

She opened her eyes, opened her mouth and kissed him.

He groaned. She nearly whimpered for him to keep quiet, but it was as if he could taste the words on her tongue. He drank her lips like he was speaking into her. She covered his mouth with hers, pulling them closer, bodies tight, knees bent, tongues touching, but quiet—so quiet—that they could hide their breathing beneath the crackle of trees, the distant wind and the shush of leaves.

Joy melted. Her head was floating, filled with white sparks. His hands kept her grounded, holding her close. Her breath fed his, echoing in his mouth, and he gave it back, willingly, gratefully, awed. Slowly they separated into two people kissing; two pairs of lips, four pairs of limbs, two bodies under one blanket, stifling with sweat. Joy's clothes were damp, her bangs wet and her lips buzzed, soft and swollen, but Ink was pristine—his face unguarded, his eyes wide as waxing moons.

"Joy—?"

"Shh," she whispered and placed a finger on his lips. They were pliant and smooth. She traced the shape of them, muzzily entranced. His eyes slipped closed as he followed her touch. She knew his senses were awake, alive.

Remember, Inq's chirpy voice was like a half dream, *he will be learning everything, watching you.*

Smiling, Joy drew her hand away and rested it on his chest, feeling the pulse of his heart under the puddle of silvery silk. She nestled her head in the crook of his shoulder, curling one knee above his, shrugging the sleeping bag aside as her skin breathed in the night. She pressed her ear against him, listening to the gentle, liquid rush of him washing against the shore—or maybe it was the *eelet* singing, lulling her to sleep. She didn't care. She had this moment. *This. Now. Ink.*

Thump-thump. Thump-thump. Thump-thump.

His heartbeat slowed as sleep blurred the corners. Something about it nagged her—something she was forgetting, something *important*—but before she could shape it into words, it slipped away into dream.

EIGHTEEN

JOY WOKE UP WITH A START—IT WAS DARK, AND THE ward had flared in a warning shower of sparks, the fading post-fireflies still playing catch-can before her eyes. Ink was beside her, half crouched, razor open, leveled against the looming shadow of whoever was standing outside.

"Get up," Stef whispered and kicked the ward again. It rippled with a crackle of energy. "It's almost four."

Joy froze with her scalpel in hand. "Stef?"

"Come on out, Ink," Stef said. "Time to go home."

Ink glanced at Joy and then unzipped the tent flap, dissolving the ward with a flick of his wrist. He stepped out of the tent. Joy heard his feet crunch through the salt barrier as she scrambled to untangle herself from the bag. She crawled out of the tent in time to see her brother and boyfriend exchange a long look before Ink stepped past him, slicing a line of nothing and folding it quietly behind him, escaping to somewhere far beyond.

Stef kept his eyes on the gleaming rift until it zipped closed. Standing next to him, Joy crossed her arms over her chest and shivered. She almost said, *Nothing happened*, but that was a lie. It wasn't *nothing*, it just wasn't *everything*. Her brother wiped his glasses on his shirt.

"Remind me to kick his ass," Stef said.

"Stef..."

Her brother turned and gave her a brief once-over. "And remind me to kick *your* ass," he added with a yawn. "But later. After breakfast."

He crept around his tent, and she followed, circling the fire pit slowly in the dark. Joy stared at her brother's tent, seeing the shape of a sleeping body and hearing the low hush of his steady snoring. She stopped dead, goose bumps skittering to join the cold.

"Who's that?" she whispered. Stef grinned.

"That's me," he said. "Or, at least, a phantom of me." He tilted his head. "I slept somewhere else."

Joy didn't ask, although she could guess. "What is it?"

"It's a Level Three *doppelganger*, simpler than a glamour." Stef unzipped his tent and showed her his sleeping twin on the bed. Her Sight made it look slightly transparent, but it was an eerie likeness. "I had to film myself with the webcam sleeping for seven nights straight to get all the angles, and all it does is snore and sleep, but it works like a charm." He waggled his fingers in front of her eyes. "Wizard, remember?"

She squinted at it, impressed. "Is it enough to fool Dad?"

He smirked. "It's been enough to fool you," he said. "I haven't been home until about noon most of the summer. You were just lucky I was home to get an earful of ice cube that morning or you would have been in for quite a shock." She gaped at him. He tsked at her, and she pulled her shirt lower. "Some of us don't like having Dad within earshot."

"It isn't like that," she whispered. "We didn't—"

"La la la la. Don't want to know." Stef mimed covering his ears. "Plausible deniability." He jerked his thumb over his shoulder. It had a Band-Aid wrapped around it. "Go back to your tent. Get some sleep. I've got Dad, and you've got an appointment."

That was right—she did. *But Ink—?* Joy missed him already

in the cold early-morning-after. She sighed. There was nothing she could do about that right now. She picked her way back to her tent, grabbed her flashlight and keys and stuck her scalpel in her pocket.

Stef frowned. "Where are you going?" he whispered.

"I left some stuff in the car."

Stef rolled his eyes and followed. The glyph in his hand glowed very slightly. She noticed that his red bracelet was gone.

"I'm coming with you."

"Then hurry up."

"Dork."

"Dweeb."

The chill hurried her steps—it was dark and shadowy on her way to the car; the parking lot felt lonely, vulnerable and exposed. Late moonlight streamed over everything, washing it bright blue. Unlocking the car sounded like a gunshot. Joy popped the glove compartment, grabbed the velvet box and shut the door, holding on to the handle so it would click shut instead of slam. Stef kept his head up, watching the woods. Joy worried that any twinkles of light between the trees were unfriendly eyes, watching, waiting. She pressed her key fob, locking the doors. They ran back to the site—every crunch of their footfalls like a B-movie scream. She tightened her grip on the scalpel and ran faster.

Crawling into her tent, she felt childishly better, like pulling the blankets over her head to protect herself against the monsters under her bed. Except now she knew: monsters were real, and blankets wouldn't stop them. She took out her scalpel and held it between her finger and thumb.

"Now go to sleep," her brother said as he reset the ward.

She zipped the tent closed as he peeled back his Band-Aid and squeezed out a small bead of blood. Checking the contents of the velvet box and confirming the time, she turned the card over in her hand. The idea of being fitted for a dress seemed more impossibly ludicrous than snapping a glow stick so her brother could rendezvous with his imaginary friend. Of course, she'd just spent the night curled up with her invisible boyfriend, so who was she to judge? She touched the floor of the tent beside her, but not a hint of Ink's warmth remained. It made it hard to believe that it had happened at all.

But it had. It did. Joy lay back against the pillow. She could smell Ink there. *That was real.* She smiled to herself. *That was very, very real.*

Placing her scalpel next to her jewelry box, the business card and her phone, she tucked herself back into her sleeping bag and zipped it demurely into shape. She stroked her hand over his side of the pillow and switched off the flashlight. She dozed, listening to the zip of tents, the shuffle of shoes and the low whisper of male voices as they gathered their things—the click-clack of poles, the rattle of the tackle box and the crunch of receding footsteps as they made their way down to the shore. These were familiar sounds, family sounds, comforting and well-worn as slippers, and yet all she could think about was escaping to her other life full of danger and obligations. She was clearly insane.

Joy touched the burnt spot in her tent, the tiny hole the match had melted, no bigger than the tip of her finger. She felt the dry dirt, the small speck of earth, and closed her eyes. There it was again—the cool surface, the gritty texture she could almost feel on her tongue, the taste of salt and iron and old, old ice. That vein of thought and feeling blossomed, growing cavernous and awesome, widening into depths that shrugged off the rocky chill, pushing deeper, tighter, building pressure she could feel inside her body, filling up the empty spaces where she'd become cold and hollow after...after...

She sat up. Her breathing stuttered.

"Hello?"

Joy grabbed her scalpel and blinked back a jolt of panic. She'd fallen asleep. She'd just woken up. It was just a nightmare. She wasn't—

"Knock knock," a woman's voice said outside Joy's tent. "The boys asked me to take you to your appointment. I hope I'm not too early."

Joy stumbled forward and unzipped the tent, squinting past the ward.

"Raina?" she gasped.

The Pantene-haired beauty smiled. "Come on, Cinderella. Time to get dressed."

"Lift your arms—there we go. A little tighter in the bust, I think," Raina said with authority. "Take a deep breath. Now let it out? Fine." She pinched a half an inch. "That will keep you trim and show off your profile."

A giant black spider stabbed a silver pin expertly through the fold and swiveled around Joy, making similar adjustments with a dance of many legs. Joy tried to keep her eyes straight ahead, staring at her own reflection in the trifold mirror as Raina continued to prattle suggestions nonstop. Rather than being annoyed, Joy was profoundly grateful—Raina's constant chatter was staving off Joy's imminent freak-out. After Joy had torn the business card in half, they'd arrived in a sunny solarium draped in diaphanous fabric sporting a stunning golden dress, several polished mirrors and a five-foot-tall spider who'd politely asked her to strip.

Joy stayed very still, feeling the pins graze her skin.

"*Tuuuurn,*" the spider woman purred, and Joy obeyed, willing her skin to stop crawling. She'd hugged a giant frog, been dragged through a forest by Kestrel and been kissed by Invisible Inq. This shouldn't be a big deal.

The tickle of legs wriggled along the edge of her Sight. Joy squirmed.

The black spider logo—not a starburst—should have been her first clue. Still, it might have been something good to know before she'd nearly swallowed her tongue. Given Graus Claude had half as many limbs, Joy shouldn't have been surprised by his choice of tailor, but it was still a shock...almost as shocking as the naked torso protruding from the bulbous spider body covered in a fine sheen of gray fur, growing coarser and longer as it spread down her spine, across her abdomen and down each of her legs, which were black at the feet, fringed in long, silky white hairs. She'd introduced herself as Idmona, pronounced with long, drawling vowels that turned Joy's stomach to water. She wore only long loops of measuring tape around her neck and several strands of clunky beads. Idmona never stopped smiling—it was as if she was used to shocking people and secretly enjoyed it. Her full lips framed furry mandibles, and her teeth were fanged and sharp. She bit through the thread neatly as she sewed.

"*Gooood*," Idmona said approvingly and went back to adding crystals to the trim. Raina and she had discussed adding more color—"a little more sparkle, just a touch"—to the already impossible gown. Joy was swathed in layers of aquamarine organza and buttery gold silk, rich and delicate with thousands of crystals spilling down her latticed bodice, flaring out into scintillating "wings" that trailed along either side of the skirt, brushing the floor in a small train, gathered into waterfall layers in the back. Her sleeves were tight-fitting and laced with ribbons, like fingerless gloves attached by thin gold chains. Joy had shown them the jewelry box, which necessitated the last-minute adjustments. Both Raina and Idmona had admired the pieces in the velvet sheath.

"A seeeecond strand?" Idmona observed casually, draping the enormously long double string of pearls between three of her legs. A fourth brought Maia's hair comb up to the light. *"Aaaaaaand this?"*

"For my hair," Joy said. The tailor turned it over gently between two of her footpads as if spinning a cocoon. The spider woman smiled, her mandibles spreading.

"Of couuuuuuurse."

Joy turned her back to the large mirrors, the one in front of her having been moved to make room for the large rack of trims, crystals and beads that Idmona had wheeled in from one of the many other doors. There were eight doors from the solarium, each leading in different directions—other showrooms, other clients, closets, storerooms; a virtual hive of activity hummed behind the walls. Joy was a little vague about where, exactly, they were, but Raina explained that the card had been specifically linked to this room at five o'clock, Eastern Standard Time.

One was never late for an appointment with Idmona.

Joy tried to squeeze herself smaller. The lady spider was constantly moving, mandibles, arms and legs skittering with virtuoso skill, transforming the piece of clothing into a wearable work of art. But Joy kept staring at the many mirror reflections that made it seem as if she were surrounded by an army of hairy, wriggling things. It was excellent motivation for standing still.

"We ought to fashion a matching boutonniere or pocket kerchief for Ink," Raina said, ignoring the blinking Bluetooth in her ear. "Appearances are everything."

Idmona scuttled around the edges of the dress and conversation. *"Not quiiiiiiite everyyyyyyyyything,"* she said with a knowing twitch of her lips.

Joy fingered the pearls nervously, remembering Graus Claude's advice, but Graus Claude was in jail, awaiting trial for a crime he hadn't really committed, and she hadn't heard back from the others yet. At the gala, she would be a symbol of his patronage and carry a piece of his good name. Joy had to make a good impression. She had to keep up appearances—for the sake of his reputation, as well as hers. The Council might be swayed by her performance if she did well. Immortals had long memories, and Graus Claude had given her every advantage. She *had* to go through with this now—it might be her only leverage. This ridiculous charade was stealing precious time and giving it to Aniseed, but Joy would not fail the Bailiwick. The Folk needed her to succeed.

Raina tugged the damselfly wings into place. "These will complement Ink's tailcoat nicely."

"You've seen Ink's costume?" Joy asked tightly. She pretended it was the bodice's fault.

"I was there for his fitting."

"Really?" Joy said. *Was he naked?* Had she seen more than Joy?

Raina grinned. "He wanted my opinion," she said simply.

Joy lifted her chin, trying to stretch out the sudden tightness in her throat. Her neck prickled. Her palms felt hot. She teetered on the raised dais in her matching satin shoes. She knew a telling blush had crept up her neck and pinked her cheeks, which, being reflected a hundred times in the mirrors, made it virtually impossible to ignore. Joy knew that she had a visible tell, and her gymnastic coaches had all warned her not to get upset during a performance. This was a difficult performance.

"He asks you about quite a lot of things," Joy managed to say.

Raina paused her inspection of ribbon trims and burst out laughing, a delightful laugh that was as frustrating as it was genuine. It fanned Joy's jealousy even more.

"Oh, Joy, honey—it's nothing like that," she said in delicious glee. "You have nothing to fear from me! In fact, you should consider me your very best friend."

Joy huffed. "I already *have* a best friend."

"Yes, well, let's just say that I'm the friend who managed to save Ink from getting too many wrong ideas," she said, placing a string of glass droplets back on the rack. "I love them all, truly, but they're such *boys*." Raina gave the word an extra dig; the eye roll was implied. "And they're absolutely hopeless when it comes to women."

"Who? The Cabana Boys?" Joy said, twisting her fingers in her sleeves. Idmona's foot tapped her wrist sharply.

"Wriiiiiiinkles," the tailor chided with professional pride.

"Is that what you call them?" Raina said with a shrug. "More like the Lost Boys! And Ink is the most lost boy of all." Her voice sounded tender as she walked around the room.

"Does that make you Wendy?" Joy asked.

Raina smirked. "Please."

"Then what are you—?" Joy swallowed, feeling very much the little girl to Raina's woman. "Why would he—?"

"We've been talking," Raina said. "That's all. Talking frankly and honestly. He asks questions, and I try to answer them." She shrugged. "He knew you wouldn't want him talking to Inq, so he went to Tuan and Nikolai first. But when Luiz found out, it was like a stag party—you should have heard the bunch of them!" She reconsidered Joy's blush. "Then again, maybe it's best that you didn't." She checked her flawless makeup in one of the mirrors. "In any case, I dragged Ink away and offered to be someone he could talk to." Her reflection smiled knowingly back at Joy. "Someone who knows a little more about the subject."

"About me?" Joy asked.

"About women," Raina said. "And what women like." She smiled at Joy. "I like women. I like the way they sound, I like the way they smell, I like the way they think—and I've loved Inq for many years. And I also happen to *be* a woman. So who better?" She said it matter-of-factly, although Joy suspected that she was not-so-secretly pleased with herself. Raina turned back to the mirror. "He is curious and considerate. Given the questions he's been asking, you're a very lucky girl."

Idmona gave the dress a final drape and let it flutter to the floor in a sparkling cloud. Joy bit the side of her cheek and looked at herself in the mirror. She didn't recognize herself. Used to stretchy leotards with Swarovski crystals, Joy understood showmanship and costuming, but this was a ball gown fit for Disneyland. *Out of a fairy tale*, she thought. *How fitting.*

"Exquisite," Raina said. Idmona silently beamed, crossing four of her legs and winding her tape around her waist. Raina circled around Joy, inspecting the entire ensemble. "Now—your half-mask is almost finished and it has the advantage of being mounted. The stick will be sharpened and can buy you, oh, four or five inches, if necessary. There's even a needle stiletto in the base. You'll have to bring your own poison." She picked up a book full of looping curls of hair in various colors. She flipped to the browns. "We'll have to be sure your hairpiece can accommodate the scalpel." She flipped the page. "What other weapons do you have?"

Joy crossed her arms. Idmona's foot spanked her knuckles.

"Wriiiiiiiinkles!"

"Ow," Joy muttered, but dropped her arms. "I thought there were no weapons allowed?"

Raina looked at her as if she were being stupid on purpose. "No *obvious* weapons."

"Are you serious?"

"Of course," Raina said, taking out her lipstick. "You're heading into the heart of Twixt society in the middle of the Grand Ballroom Under the Hill. Everyone without fangs will be armed to the teeth. You don't want to be considered defenseless, do you? Aren't you supposed to be the most dangerous human alive?"

Joy felt her stomach lurch. "Please, tell me you're kidding."

Raina frowned. "Please, tell me you're not."

Joy's knees wobbled, loose in the foreign shoes. "No," she said flatly. "No. This is supposed to be an *introduction*—a formal party welcoming me into the Twixt!" She nearly pitched forward under her heavy dress. "I'm one of *them* now. The Folk don't kill one another."

Idmona laughed, quickly stopped, coughed politely and scuttled off, rolling the display rack through one of the doors.

"Who told you that?" Raina asked skeptically.

"Avery," Joy said. "Sol Leander, Graus Claude."

"Oh. *Idealists*," Raina said with sudden understanding. "Well, that's certainly the party line, but are you willing to stake your life on a bit of propaganda?" she asked. "I grew up surrounded by idealists. They called themselves 'freedom fighters.' America called them 'guerillas.' I called them 'family,' but I knew them for what they were. I wasn't naive. I consider myself a realist." She lifted her skirt to show Joy a snub gun tucked into a thigh holster. "My family is dead. I am alive. I learned that there is a time for idealists and a time for realists." She palmed the gun and snapped the chamber. "Realists tend to live longer."

"Right," Joy said, smoothing down her sleeves. If she kept wiping her palms over the silk, she might stain it with sweat, and then Idmona would *really* be angry, but she couldn't seem to stop. The dress was suddenly too heavy, too enormous, too tight. Her fingers were clumsy, and she forced them down at her sides. She tossed her head, flicking her bangs out of her eyes. Her hair caught on the chains. Her shoes pinched. She winced. She was out of her mind. What was she doing, going into battle wearing a fairy princess dress? This was crazy! *I have to get out of here. I have to save Graus Claude! I have to find the door! I have to rescue the King and Queen and stop whatever is happening from happening.*

She pressed a hand to her stomach to quell the vomit moths. She could only imagine how Idmona would react if Joy puked all over her dress. She watched her own reflection pale, the hollows under her eyes growing dark. She inhaled and saw the tendons in her neck flicker, sharp against shadow. She took a deep breath and let it out slowly.

One conniption fit at a time. Don't have a heart attack.

Joy blinked. *A heart attack.*

Heartless.

She expected to hear her heart beating double-time in her ears, but there was only an empty silence. Panic swelled. *Something missing... Missing something...*

And then she knew.

Joy's hand flew to her chest. She gasped, pressing her fingers deep into her breast, into the side of her throat, the flesh of her wrist. *Nothing.* Joy slammed her fist against her chest, hollow as a drum. *Nothing.* She inhaled, eyes wide, knowing with a deep, human certainty that her heart should be pounding—*slamming! thudding! thumping!*—but there was nothing. No sound. No pulse.

No heartbeat.

Ergo, no heart.

Joy slipped from the dais and tripped on her dress, falling with a dull rattle of crystal beads and petticoats. Raina moved, tapping the Bluetooth in her ear.

"Darling," Joy heard her say. "We have a problem."

Raina caught Joy's arm and supported her shoulders as she continued to hyperventilate. The room spun, winking spots and tilting, a high-pitched mental scream splitting her head from the inside, but not one beat betrayed her fear—her body was empty, silent, dead. *No!* It made no sense. *It made no sense!* She was *alive!* She *had* to be. She was here. She was now. She would *know* if she were dead!

Wouldn't she?

Fear lit a flame—a familiar, building pressure, a flush of heat that peppered her limbs. Joy crouched, squeezing her eyes shut, her breaths coming faster in rapid gasps. *No no no...* Red-gold energy winked behind her eyes. Joy panicked, scrambling blindly, trying to hold it in, tamp it down, stop whatever it was that was killing her from the inside—burning away the human parts, making her into something *Other Than*, making her *change*. But she couldn't stop. She felt herself reaching down and out, through her skin, beyond her body, seeking for the comfort of salt and earth and old, old ice...but she was too high, too far, too lost.

WHERE IS IT? WHERE?

Heat rippled through her nerves. She clenched her teeth, legs scrabbling, trying to escape whatever was coming for her. Raina's arms were strong—but not strong enough.

Joy lifted her eyes, growling, focused on Raina, and—

A snap of ammonia exploded, bringing a shock of sudden tears.

Idmona held Joy's head as she reeled back, the smell forcing Joy to her senses. She twisted away from the painful fumes and the coarse, hairy legs. The world swam and reordered, her mind windblown, off balance. Joy collapsed, shaken and completely derailed. Her fury had blown into mist.

Raina took a white capsule from Idmona's curled toe.

"*Smehhhhhhling salts,*" the spider woman said. "*It haaaaappens sometiiiimes. Some arrrrrrre eeeeeeeasily overwhelmmmmmed. Reeeeeeemove the dress, pleeeeeeease.*"

Raina helped Joy out of the petticoats. Her limbs moved, but there was no feeling in them, only a precarious numbness. *Like a doll. Like a mannequin.* The spider woman deftly lifted the gown over her head in several stages, all the while clucking about delicate fabrics and wrinkles, gentle nonsense like a lullaby, soothing and calm. Joy's head swam as if she might fall back into nightmares. Tears leaked from the corners of her eyes, although she did not blink. She stared sightlessly at the ceiling, feeling nothing.

The wall rippled with concentric circles, distorting the room like a pebble in a pond. Inq walked into the solarium and lifted Joy up with inhuman ease.

"Joy?" Her voice was a mix of stern concern and odd compassion. Joy turned her head and focused on the tight pout of her lips. "Earth to Joy?"

"*I'm not dead!*"

Joy startled herself with the force of her scream, beating her chest with the flat of her hand as if she could restart her heart with sheer force. Inq grabbed her forearm as Raina grabbed their things. Joy's face was a rictus of pain, reflected back at her in a hundred mirror images. *What am I?* A whimpering moan eked out of her throat.

"Ladies," Inq said, politely gesturing to the warped vortex. Raina hooked Inq's arm, and Joy clung to the Scribe. Idmona bore the weight of the dress.

"*Piiiiiiick up, twooooooo hours,*" she said primly and scuttled off.

Inq stepped forward and out.

A shift of light joined the smell of dusty roses as they funneled into Graus Claude's foyer, almost knocking over a chair that was blocking the hall. Kurt and Avery sat together. Filly jumped to her feet, rattling her cape of bones. Ink crossed the room, arms out, and folded Joy against his chest. She trembled, her thoughts scattered like bits of litter, numb to the fact that she was standing in the brownstone in her underwear.

She ground her forehead into Ink's shoulder. He held her tighter.

Thump-thump. Thump-thump.

She could hear his heartbeat. But not hers.

"Please, tell me I'm not dead," she whispered. She felt him tense in alarm.

"Of course not," said Filly brashly. "There's obviously not a scratch on you!"

"Hsst!" Inq hissed at her. Avery politely averted his eyes.

"Go clean up," Raina said, gently guiding Ink and Joy past the chairs and tucking Joy's clothes under his arm.

Kurt stood up.

"Wait," Inq said, raising a hand to stop him. "First, this."

Ink steered Joy into the pink-and-cream bathroom with the settee couch and the claw-foot tub, closing the door on the others down the hall. She stared at the striped wallpaper, the matching ottoman and the porcelain sink where Ink had once washed his arms up to the elbows, scrubbing them in soap and blood. He'd cut out Briarhook's heart. Briarhook still lived with a gaping hole in his chest and a thirst for revenge. She touched her breastbone, feeling for that hollow place inside herself, that empty, gaping, missing hole...

She sat down. Ink draped her clothes in her lap. Joy crossed her arms over her chest as he knelt before her on the tile floor.

"What happened?" he whispered, dipping his head to catch her gaze. "Joy?"

It took a while for the words to sink in, floating past her

ears like dandelion fluff. She looked at him. His eyes were ink and razors—cold and sharp and ready to murder.

"My heart," Joy said, her lip trembling. "Where is my heart?"

Ink shook his head, only the spiky tips of his hair moved. "I do not understand."

"My *heart*," Joy repeated a little louder, growing more certain of her fear. She slammed her chest with both hands. *"Where. Is. My. Heart?"*

"Your heart?" he said weakly. Ink stared at the unbroken skin of her chest.

"Please—" Joy leaned forward and grabbed his arms, her broken voice panging off the tile. "The Folk can live without a heart, but I *can't*! I'm not one of them," she panted, crying, desperate. "I'm human—I am *human*—I *need* my heart!"

Ink touched her gently. "You lost your heart?"

"I—" She shook her head violently. "I didn't *lose* it," she said, horrified. "It's still—it's still *there*, isn't it?" Joy felt crazily unsure, her fingers scrabbling against her skin, leaving long pink scratches. "I would've known if... I mean, I would have seen if someone...took it." There would be blood, like Briarhook—she would have noticed it if someone had cut out her heart! The idea of someone else taking it, having it, holding it, made her unspeakably ill. She felt violated, undone.

Ink leaned forward and took her wrist, turning it over, his eyes boiling.

"Briarhook?"

"He didn't—" Joy stammered. *Did he? Could he?* She heard his mocking laughter in the back of her brain. Joy wanted to throw up. "But I would know, right? There would be *something*—some hole? Some mark?" she said, her eyes spilling over. "There should be *something*," Joy insisted, tearing at her skin. "But there's *nothing*!"

Ink touched her gently, stilling her hands. "You are right," he said. "There is no mark. You are unmarred, so your heart must still be there." He rested his palm between the swell of her breasts. She felt it there, on the surface, but she felt nothing underneath. She pressed his hand harder against her. *Nothing.* She looked into his eyes.

"Am I dead?"

Ink's face was carefully neutral. "You are not dead," he said.

What he didn't say was *You are not human*, which, at that moment, felt like the same thing. Joy stared at her chest and their hands—his, hers, theirs—pressed over nothing. A roar in her head brought that strange, floaty feeling of being outside her body, looking down in disbelief.

"How can I not be dead?" she murmured. "Without my heart, how can I be alive? How can I breathe? How can I feel anything?" Her voice was fragile. "I can't love you without my heart." She reached out and touched Ink's chest, felt its quiet rhythm, *thump-thump, thump-thump*. It brought tears to her puffy, tired eyes. "I want to love you. Always."

Ink pressed her hand against his chest, a strange reversal. "I would give you my heart if I could."

Joy froze at his words. It wasn't just a saying, a throwaway phrase. She knew it was true—he could not lie. He would give her his heart if he could.

Frightened, she dropped her hands and stared at her knees. She pulled her shirt on over her head for something to do. The extra layer helped.

Ink went to the sink and leaned against the porcelain, the gilt mirror ignoring his reflection.

"Graus Claude said that things might change once you claimed your *signatura*, so let us assume that this is part of it," he said carefully. Joy, pulling on her shorts and shoes, nodded but didn't meet his gaze. "Have you noticed anything else unusual?"

She thought about energy popping under her heels, the fury bubbling just under her surface, the taste of salt and old, old ice, blasting open the stone cell, erasing the Red Knight—how much of it was the scalpel and how much of it was *her*? She'd been born with the Sight. Had she been born with other powers? Was this part of the change, becoming something no longer human?

She simply nodded as he settled himself at her feet. His voice was earnest.

"Think, then. It does not make you less Joy," he said. "You are still you."

Joy hugged herself. She felt cold. "What am I?"

He tucked long brown bangs behind her ear. "The girl with the Sight," he said. "The one I marked because I could not obey the decree. I could not bear the thought of taking your eyes, and in that last moment, I wavered. I questioned. I failed for the first time—and I was right." His words draped around her like a blanket. "You are Joy Malone. You are the one who has made me who I am. You are the one who made me see—and I couldn't look away."

Joy sniffled, tears flowing freely. "You 'couldn't'?"

"No," he said, cupping her hands in his. "I can't."

Joy lifted her eyes at the present tense. She wanted to say it, too, but she couldn't because she *could* look away, she *could* fail and be wrong, and she was the one who had made the choices that were remaking her into whatever she was becoming. Once she'd taken her True Name, she was bound to the rules of the Twixt.

For now.

She closed her eyes and took a deep breath. Breaking away from his touch, she went to the sink and cranked the hot water, letting the heat crawl up her fingers and the steam brush her face. She held her hands under until they hurt. Then she turned off the taps and dried her hands, rubbing them hot white and pink. An old feeling flared—the one that tingled under her palms, an echo of clapping chalk. Some called it a "competitive streak," but those who lived on the mats called it "the winning edge." Joy had been training for competition since she was five. Now that the stakes were higher, there was no way she was going to let Aniseed win.

"If we can get to Graus Claude, we can find the door," she said calmly. "We can stop Aniseed, and we can bring back the King and Queen." Her eyes were clearer now, focused, intent. "Your mother can return. Graus Claude will be cleared. And the Council will have to *listen*, because they must obey their King and Queen, and..." Her voice faltered, suddenly off track and unsure. "They can change the rules," Joy said, her hopes bared. "Do you think they could change me back, if I asked?"

Ink stood up in a single, sweeping motion, proud and tall in his silvery shirt and black jeans, the wallet chain swaying at his hip. "The King and Queen spoke the Twixt into being out of the elemental chaos of the world," he said gravely. "I imagine that they can do anything they wish."

"Except come home," Joy said, wiping her face.

"Yes," Ink said carefully. "Except that."

"Well." Joy swallowed, drying the last of her tears on a towel. She tossed it into the sink with a slap. "Not for long."

NINETEEN

JOY AND INK RETURNED TO THE GROUP HUDDLED around a low table in the foyer, maps and schematics spread out over laps and floor. Trusted with the knowledge of secrets he could keep, Kurt had gathered intel from the far corners of his employer's impressive vaults hidden somewhere inside the brownstone. Filly's eyes devoured every scrap in naked delight, and Avery pored over thick volumes with studious interest. Inq and Kurt argued tactics. Joy sat close to Ink, overwhelmed by more than just the sheer mass of information, concentrating on breathing evenly and slow. She understood that Graus Claude was being held under some sort of house arrest, having yet to be formally charged, yet stowed suspiciously close to where her formal presentation was about to take place. She sensed a trap.

"The Folk are nothing if not dramatic," Inq said. "And they do love to gloat." She pointed to the set of hallways and stairs that led to Graus Claude's holding chamber. "I wouldn't be surprised if Sol Leander had specifically placed the Bailiwick within earshot of the gala in order that he might overhear your every stroke of social suicide." She glanced across the table. "No offense."

Both Joy and Avery said, "None taken." They exchanged a quick glance and went silent.

Joy glared at Sol Leander's assistant, who busied himself

consulting a roll of papers. He had been both politic and apologetic, offering insight and advice, but she wasn't sure how she felt about his being there. Had he earned his place among them or was it simply too convenient for a spy of the Tide? She kept flicking glances at him as if she could catch him in the act of sabotage, oddly disappointed when she still couldn't pinpoint his tell. Being deceptive was not the same as lying. Joy knew that better than most.

Filly and Inq outlined strategies while Ink reviewed the gala itinerary—he had no mind or interest in politics and was the least prepared to master them, but he was determined to keep Joy safe within the gala's complex system of Court rules and etiquette. He rolled the pearl cuff links between his fingers, listening to the wise whispers the Bailiwick had wrought. Avery glanced at them curiously as he switched books. Joy frowned. She felt as if she was the only one with the Sight, the only one who could truly see things for what they were and the only one who noticed that Avery was still there.

"Are you sure you want to be in on this?" she asked aloud. Avery stopped examining a labyrinthine map to glance at Joy. She smiled without warmth. "I mean, call me crazy, but I'm not entirely certain we're fighting on the same team, here."

His smile was more relaxed, more genuine, looking much as he had when he'd met her while awaiting her trial Under the Hill. Of course, he'd had no idea who she was back then. It was odd to see him acting friendly now.

"Well, I am certain my master would agree," he said easily. "I am supposed to follow you and report back to him, and I imagine this is exactly the sort of information that he would most prize if he were able to remember any of it." Avery tugged at his collar. "But I believe I understand what is at stake, even if I cannot retain the particulars, so, yes, I believe I can be helpful to you." He tapped the map with his finger. "You may not believe that we are on the same side, Joy Malone, but we are both trying to protect those in the Twixt—which has always been my highest priority—so in this, we are aligned." He glanced at Inq. "If you do not take my word for it, consider it a favor due a friend."

Joy remembered Avery solemnly watching a molten star climb toward the ceiling full of memories. *Enrique.* She frowned, uncertain whether he was being honest or coy. *Could one make friends out of enemies instead of enemies out of friends?*

"All right," she said. "But how can we trust you if you can't remember any of this?"

Avery rubbed a finger over his brow. "You keep explaining it to me, but the story evaporates as soon as it's told," he said. "Still, I know something about memory spells, and therefore, these symptoms make sense. And I know that whatever is said by one of the Folk must—to the best of their knowledge—be true." He shared a glance with Kurt, another expert on saying things without words. "Although I cannot retain the details, I know that you are working to correct a great injustice and undo the harm that has been done. Therefore, I am with you."

"Be sure that you are," Ink said. His voice sliced through silence.

Avery paused, perhaps surprised that "the chair" could speak. He nodded in acknowledgment and went back to his maps.

Joy leaned closer to Ink, who gestured at a painting of the Grand Ballroom from an ancient portfolio. Kurt had said it was by "an old artist in residence."

"You are scheduled to arrive and enter here, at the East entrance." He pointed to a wide entryway down a very long path to a central bower that looked like an amphitheater. "You will stand before the Council, who will formally acknowledge you, and then you will be introduced to the whole of the Folk gathered here, in the Grand Ballroom." He touched the back of her hand in a gesture that was almost human. "I will then be permitted to join you as your escort." Joy glared at Avery, who said nothing. His voice pinched at the admission of their need to be apart. Ink didn't put much stake in propriety and liked it even less when Joy's safety was concerned. Joy tried to think about Graus Claude's hard-taught lessons about the importance of maintaining etiquette and decorum, but it just made her want to punch something. She would have made a terrible debutante.

"And that's when the fun begins," Inq chirped with glee.

"Why wait?" Joy asked. "Why not go in guns blazing? Why hang around waiting for trouble to come to me?" The more she thought about it, the more the whole gala seemed like a bad setup—walking into a gilded trap in a heavy, many-layered gown. "What if I *don't* get presented to the Twixt? What if I just skip it?"

Everyone shot her dark looks, which surprised her.

"Be grateful that we have such an opportunity," Filly said. "They would not normally admit you Under the Hill, let alone so close to your target."

"I've been Under the Hill before," Joy said.

Inq folded a map into thirds. "Yes, but then, somebody died."

Joy twisted her fingers into her shirt and shut up.

"Besides," Avery said, "the last thing you want to do is offend the Folk and make the Council look foolish." His simple words carried a weight of warning.

Kurt unconsciously checked his weapon in its holster. The simple motion spoke more than words.

"It's a mockery, anyway," Inq murmured. "Folk used to

be formally presented to the King and Queen. Now it's just the Council."

Joy held her breath and glanced around—she could almost imagine the tickle of magic as the Amanya spell wiped Filly and Avery's slate clean. Neither of them showed any reaction to Inq's statement whatsoever. It was a chilling reminder of what they were up against.

Ink silently took her hand. Joy squeezed it. Hard.

"The Bailiwick is on the Council," Avery said as if the conversation hadn't strayed. "Imagine how he would react to such a slight." Joy balked at the thought of those ice-blue eyes boring down on her, stern and severe.

Kurt noted her expression. "Now multiply that by six."

"Seven," Avery said, a reminder that the Tide now held a Council seat. Joy could imagine Sol Leander's cold, righteous smirk and how very much she'd like to wipe it off his face. The winning edge came back with a vengeance.

"Fine," Joy said. "I get it. I'm going. So, what do we do?"

"We—" Ink enunciated the word "—will remain in the ballroom and play politics with nods and curtseys and small talk and pearls." He squeezed the cuff links in his hand. "The others will use the advantage of our being the focus of attention in order to make their way to Graus Claude, remove him to a place of safety, then enter the Bailiwick and locate the door. Once that is done, then..." He paused. Avery attempted to find a page in a book, pretending not to overhear. "It is no longer our concern. Our goal is to survive the evening with your reputation intact. Filly and I will intervene on your behalf should it become necessary."

"That's the plan?" Joy said.

Inq nodded. "That's the plan."

Joy glanced around, feeling helpless. "I hate this plan."

"What's the complaint?" Inq asked. "You will play Princess

Tea Party with all the high-and-mightys and we'll spring the old frog and run backup in case there's trouble. You have nothing to worry about—you won't even spoil your pretty dress."

Filly snorted. "You have a pretty dress?"

Inq waved a hand airily. "It is vitally important that she makes a killer first impression."

Joy ignored the underlying threat/pun. "I may need *more* than backup. I thought you said everyone in the Twixt would be at this thing," she said. "Without Graus Claude, I could immortally offend everyone!"

"That's right," Filly said, eyes gleaming. "It ought to be glorious fun!"

Of course Filly's brand of "fun" tended toward mayhem and carnage.

"Do not concern yourself with the Bailiwick," Kurt said. "We will free him."

"You can't."

Everyone stared at Avery. He kept his eyes on the pages in front of him, his snowy-white hair shading his face as if embarrassed.

"Is that a fact?" Filly snapped with a smile plastered across her teeth.

"Yes," Avery said, closing the book with a *snap*. "It's a fact."

"Really?" Inq said. "I'd like to see what can stop us." Her fingers took on a slight blur.

Avery leaned forward. "You won't get past the door."

Joy wasn't confident about this plan, but she was confident in her friends. "Walls and doors mean nothing to them," she said. "They will rescue the Bailiwick."

The young gentleman turned to Joy, and his look of disappointment reminded her of Graus Claude. "You are thinking like a human," he said. "But remember—these are the chambers Under the Hill, the heart of the Twixt. Doors are not ordinary doors, and walls are not made of wood and stone. Your mentor's cage is a magical one. The spell holding him extends down the hall," he said, dragging his finger down the long corridor to the base of the stairs. "It is intended for specific prisoners—those who threaten the Accords, political assassins, suspects of treason—those whom the Council wish to make certain that no one would grant quarter, mercy or aid." He tapped the book cover meaningfully. "None who are his friend may enter the stairwell. That's why even the Council members cannot fetch him—they have been his friends and colleagues for too long. Guards must be changed daily in order to prevent friendliness forming." Avery sat back in his chair. "Despair is his door, and the walls guard themselves. The ward is merely window dressing for propriety's sake."

There was a long pause. Joy broke it.

"Is that exactly how it's phrased?" she said. "'None who are his friend?'"

"Why? What of it?" Avery glanced around the assembled crew. "If any of you wish him success, you will not succeed, by definition."

"That's not what I asked," Joy said. "I may not know much about the Twixt, but I've learned a thing or two about loopholes. No friend of his can break him out? Fine. We can work with that." Now it was the young gentleman's turn to frown.

"I am not his friend," Avery said carefully. "But I am not interested in defying the Council, whose tenets I respect. If Councilex Claude is innocent, as you claim, then you can trust in the law to prove it and not look for ways around it." He knocked on the arm of his chair. "The law is the law. Rules are rules."

Joy flashed her Olympic-class smile. "Some rules are meant to be broken," she said. "Kurt?"

The muscleman bodyguard didn't pretend not to know what she was asking.

Ink hesitated. "Joy—"

"It's mine, right? My call?" Her voice had tightened to a squeak. She was afraid, but worse, she knew that she was responsible for this. *This is my fault. I can fix this.* "He's not a friend, and he wishes us nothing but harm." Joy unclenched her fingers with effort. "And that's *exactly* what we need. We have what he wants, and he will do what we ask." She twisted her hands together. "It's perfect. It fits."

Avery blinked. "Who?"

"Briarhook," Kurt said.

"Briarhook?" Avery echoed. "The Wood Guardian?"

"Ah!" Filly grinned and slapped her thigh. "An excellent plan! Let the hog fetch the frog. Well planned and well played!"

Joy glanced at Ink, his boyish face hardened to tight lines and sharp planes. His fingers worked at his own nails as if picking at crusts of half-remembered blood.

"Well," she said. "It's a plan, anyway." She looked across the table at the mess of papers and plans. "Kurt, can you do the exchange? I have no idea what time it is, but I have to get back. My brother can't keep Dad fishing forever." Kurt nodded once, no words needed. They'd done this before. Joy sighed nervously. "Start at a fifth, you can go to a fourth. A third is too much." She was flirting with death. Briarhook would be eager to bargain, but when he got his whole heart back, he would kill her. She understood that a little better now.

Her fingers traced the single exit from Graus Claude's chamber to the public hallways branching out from Under the Hill, including the route she'd taken to the Council Hall that first time. She recognized the spiral stair and the archway where she'd waited in the wings. She frowned at the schematic. There were too many halls, too many doors and far too many things that could go wrong.

"We need more help," she said. "Kurt, do you still have my work files?"

Inq frowned. "Your *work* files?"

"Yes," Joy said. "Happy clients, all. I know the Bailiwick must have kept records, and I think there might be one or two who might be willing to help us out."

Kurt glared at Joy. Filly snickered and tossed her head in approval.

"If, like me, they cannot remember, then they do not know what is at stake." Avery said. "Do you believe that they will join your cause for the love of you, Joy Malone?"

Ink shot him a look, open and pure. "Yes."

Avery looked unconvinced.

"Either that or use blackmail," Filly said. "That's likely what the Bailiwick was keeping their records for, anyway." Kurt gathered up papers, neither admitting nor denying the claim. Knowledge was influence, influence was power and the Bailiwick was a powerful force in the Twixt. Filly tossed a book down, smug.

"You won't have to do either," Inq said. "You don't realize what this gala means—none of the others would have told you." Her black eyes sparkled. "This celebration is all about *you*, Joy. This is *your* presentation, *your* gala, and in the world of the Folk, this is one of the only times where they are free to make *choices*—do you understand what that means?" She gestured grandly, her black lacquered nails winking in the low light. "Everyone attending is bound to obey—it's not magic, but it *is* part of the rules. Whoever presides over the gala is sacrosanct. That is why the Folk work so hard to protect themselves behind proper etiquette and codes of conduct; otherwise, it could be an orgy or a slaughter! Your word reigns supreme for this one night," she said. "It is a delicate balance, and your skill at manipulating the line between timid caution and reckless abuse is what everyone's eager to see." Inq flung up her hands in excitement. "You can throw somebody out a window or invite people to kiss your feet. You get to bestow favors or slight advances, make friends and enemies, humiliate your rivals or your suitors or yourself. Every choice you make will have consequences, of course, but that's half the fun! The Folk will be watching your every move, following your lead, worried what you might do to them and be very thankful when you do it to someone else. This is where you, as one of the Twixt, will be tested among your people, establishing your True Name and what it means—either praised, whispered in terror or shouted with contempt. But, remember, Joy—this is *your* party. This is where the butterfly first beats its wings," she said with a wink. "It will be up to you to bring on the storm."

Joy stared at Invisible Inq, struck by how much Inq herself would have wanted this—to lord over those who had threatened her, dismissed her, knowing that she knew something important that all the Folk were too blind to see, fighting to keep safe those who so casually risked her life for theirs. Inq *wanted* this. She was jealous for something that Joy had never asked for, never craved, never dreamed. That seemed to be their pattern—two planets caught in opposing orbits.

"Nevertheless," Ink said, "it would be good to contact those who already find favor with Joy." He glanced at Kurt. "It is tactically sound."

Kurt rolled the maps into a tight tube. "I will be busy conducting the preliminaries."

"I'll do it," Filly volunteered. Joy knew the young warrior wished to keep her own name from showing up on Joy's client list since she'd asked to have a mark erased without payment, but the blonde warrior would also no doubt welcome the chance to get her hands on exclusive information. Joy hoped the Valkyrie would be discreet. Kurt nodded. Filly whooped. Joy winced. *Fat chance.*

"I will accompany Briarhook," Kurt said. "If the worst happens, best that they think that we are a revolution of one." Joy wondered if he was quoting Aniseed on purpose. "Inq will meet us at the crux and direct us out. She will then enter the Bailiwick and, with luck, locate the door. If she succeeds, then the results should be obvious—the blanket spell will be negated once we have achieved the Imminent Return." Avery could not help but look up in surprise, even if the knowledge was erased a moment later. "If not, then I will be the most likely suspect and will invite pursuit, which should allow you your freedoms and a future attempt." He addressed Filly. "Keep an eye on Ink and Joy during the gala. You are their second line of defense." Kurt considered Avery. "Given our positions, I would not ask you to act against your master, but perhaps you might direct his attentions elsewhere, should it become necessary," he said. "For his safety, of course."

Avery said nothing, his face furtive. Then he took a deep breath and addressed the largest map spread across the table. "The entire place is warded against entry and exit except by designated doors." He pointed to the obvious entries, which would be just as obviously watched. "You'll have to take the long way around if you want to get him out." Avery traced a pathway through a myriad of stairwells and floors. It was dizzying to watch, impossible to follow, labyrinthine and riddled with possible ambush sites. He was not apologetic. "It is the more prudent option."

"You misunderstand. We don't have to get him *out*," Inq said, turning her impish eyes to Avery. "We have to get *in him*." She waved a hand impatiently as the moment of comprehension was lost under the spell and Avery's look of curious alarm changed quickly to veiled boredom. Inq huffed in annoyance. "In any case, if I can find the door, I can open it," Inq said. "If the Council locked the door, they had to have sealed it with glyphs. Ink and I were made with the base ingredients of *signaturae*. Either one of us can slip through as long as we leave our bodies behind."

"What?" Joy said, horrified.

Inq flicked her wrist. "Don't be so squeamish. These are just shells," she said. "Beautiful, I admit, but shells, nonetheless. Our bodies, like yours, are merely containers," she said, gesturing to Joy. "It's what's *inside* that counts. Luckily, we always have a backup store, as you know." When Ink had fed himself into his sister, slashing his fingers open like fruit, and later when Ink gushed across the warehouse floor, he'd returned to her—just as Inq promised—whole and restored, but older, wiser, both more careful and more precious with the life he'd been given. That had been a gift from his sister and, unknown to him, his mother. *The princess, locked inside the Bailiwick, waiting to be rescued.*

"Okay," said Joy. "So you can get past the locks once you find the door, but how are you going to find it?"

"If Aniseed was the courier, I can find it," she said. "I'm a Scribe—I've been drawing her sigil for centuries. She'll have left her mark." Her gaze bounced from her brother to her lover to Joy. "Once I get inside, I'll find it."

From Inq, it sounded less like a promise then a threat.

Joy would accept either one gladly. "Done!"

Joy stepped onto the trail with Ink at her side, her shoes crunching on the gravel in the predawn dark. She planned to jog around the corner as if returning from a run. She took a deep breath of morning air and let it out slowly, loosening the pit of snakes in her stomach.

"Joy?" Ink asked.

"I'm nervous."

Ink squeezed her hand, offering what comfort he could. He was learning to understand and be understanding, to be more human, more like her, which meant that some things went unsaid. She looked at their entwined hands. *He even has a heart*, she thought. *Now he's more human than I am.*

"We'll be packing up and leaving before sunset," she said as if it was already happening—as if the world wasn't changing between this morning and the next. "We should be home by six or seven."

"I will come for you after dark," he said. "Raina said that you would need time to prepare."

"Raina said?" Joy mocked. Ink ducked his eyes and withdrew his hand.

"Yes," he said. "She has offered to help you, if you need her, while the others take their places. She cannot accompany you inside the gala since humans are not allowed, but she has extended this small kindness." Ink stared at Joy. "She is a friend, Joy, nothing more. I did not intend her candor to be inappropriate."

Joy touched his shoulder. "No. It's okay. I get why you felt you could talk to her. Better than the Hormone Boys, I guess! She's—very easy to talk to." *And mature. And gorgeous. And worldly. And Inq's. But Inq says* nothing *is off-limits...* Joy felt herself growing jealous again. *Crap.*

"It was in confidence," he said, catching her fingers. "But I did not ask all the questions I want answered." He straightened his arm, bringing them flush together, and his breath brushed her face as if tasting her lips. "There are some things I want to learn from you."

How did he have this way of speaking that reached inside her and squeezed? Joy touched her lips to his and felt the kiss through her whole body, filling her up slowly like a glow in the wan light. His tongue tasted hers, making her moan. He tightened his grip on her waist and let go. A flush colored his high cheeks.

"I am learning," he said.

There was a catch in her breath. "No kidding."

"Until tonight, then," he said with a bow.

"It's a date," she said as he whipped his razor sideways and stepped through the breach.

Joy blew out a long breath and bounced on her feet to get her blood moving—how could it move without a heart? *Was it magic? Did it matter?* It would all change back when she asked the King and Queen for a boon. She jogged in place, knees high, pumping her arms, forcing a sweat. When she got a steady rhythm, she took off down the trail, using an easy, lazy pace as she approached their camp.

Her dad waved from the fire, where two gutted trout were frying in a pan, spitting in a bed of greens, garlic and chives. "Hey, there, sunshine," he called out. "Feeling better?"

"A bit," she said, checking the words to see if they were true, like worrying a loose tooth with her tongue.

"Where were you?" Dad asked.

"Just coming back from a run," she said, which was true, albeit a very short run. "I needed to clear my head." She sniffed the campfire smoke. "Smells good. What's for breakfast?"

"A lean meal, I'm afraid," her father admitted. "I think our reputation preceded us. The fish weren't biting." He shrugged and jiggled the pan handle. "But Shelley will be happy. My weigh-in is going to look great."

Joy sat down. Stef offered her an open cereal box. "Kix?" he said through a mouthful. "Kid-tested, brother-approved."

Joy accepted a giant fistful of cereal. They crunched the hard, toasty-flavored nuggets as the tiny trout sizzled. Dad flinched as he flipped the fish, spraying droplets of oil. The fire crackled and spat. The sky wakened in stages. The woods twittered with life. *A new day. A last day.* Joy felt the moment, the nearness of her brother and father, bittersweet.

The fire spewed a few bright embers. Muttering under his breath, Dad stamped out a patch of smoking grass.

"Stop eating that junk," he warned. "And get me a towel."

Stef rummaged through the supply bag, covering his mouth with his arm. "Where were you really?" he asked. Joy crunched on more cereal, blocking out his question and keeping her eyes on the fire. The dawn was yellow, green and pink, turning the undersides of clouds a dusty purple. It was pretty.

"I heard there's going to be quite a party later this evening," he said. Joy choked on her cereal. Stef folded the towel in half. "Want to tell me about it?"

The last thing she needed was Stef knowing about the gala. She had enough to worry about. She shrugged and ate more cereal. "Humans aren't invited."

Stef loomed over her, his body split half in firelight, half in shadow.

"I know."

"Stef?" their father called. "Towel!"

Stepping around the fire pit, her brother squatted down to help salvage the fish. Joy hung her head. *He knows.* What did he know? *He knows about me. About him? About halflings? About the Sight?* She should have told him before, as soon as she knew—she was guilty of everything she'd once blamed him of doing: keeping secrets, half-truths, especially those things they should have shared. He was angry, hurt, and she understood, but worse, she deserved it. She was a hypocrite. She felt his unsaid words weighing her down with guilt. This time, it was her fault for keeping secrets.

But I can fix it. I know I can.

Joy watched the pale white moon fade into the sun-painted sky.

* * *

They spent their last vacation day hiking—real hiking—and that meant good shoes, thick socks, lots of water and a good map. They drove to Mount Mitchell in South Toe, where the trails were rough and steep, and the walk was more of a climb. Stef was thrilled. Joy was ambivalent, her mind full of plots and pearls. Mr. Malone folded up the topo map, shouldered his pack and grabbed twin walking sticks out of the trunk.

"What do you think?" Stef said, all boundless energy and giddy grin.

Dad looked up at the peak. "If I die, I want a Viking funeral."

Stef laughed and clapped his father on the back.

The sky stretched above them like wide-open arms embracing clouds and jutting peaks, green valleys and dots of faraway lakes that sparkled like jewels in reflected sunlight. They broke through higher altitudes where the wind was brisk and the treetops trembled far below, but Joy was distracted, feeling too much of the earth as she trekked the steep angles, inhaling the taste of mountain soil. She could feel the Earth on her tongue.

The burn in her legs and her lungs was too real in a world that had become completely surreal. She didn't want to think about the countdown of hours; she tried to savor the minutes, one at a time, following her father and brother and the sun. The day passed in a rhythm of one foot, then the other, step by step, up the mountainside, her steady footsteps mimicking the absent *thump-thump-thump* of her missing heart.

She felt sweat bead on her lip as they peaked a rise, checking her wrist and the soft part of her neck out of habit. *Nothing.* What did that mean, having no heart? What did that make her? *Inhuman? Undead? Other Than...what?* The Folk were like fairies out of fairy tales with magic and True Names; they were like vampires, having no reflections, and they were like ancient gods, powerful and petty. But what *were* they, really? What was she, if she was becoming one of them? And why did she keep seeking out that foreign feeling of salt and soil and old, old ice?

Joy wiped her forehead and picked up the pace, trying to outdistance her traitorous body and thoughts.

Her dad was in the lead, stabbing each walking stick in a rhythm, setting the pace with a *chunk-thunk* punctuating each step. Stef glanced back at her around the bulk of his pack, setting the aluminum water bottles swinging.

"You good?" he asked.

I'm good died on her lips. It was lie. She nodded and breathed openmouthed to keep from talking. But Stef waited, one boot propped up on a rock.

"Say it," he said.

Joy licked her lips. "What?"

"Say that you're good," he said again. Joy was too preoccupied to pretend she didn't understand. He was testing her. His demand caught her off guard. *He's guessing. He knows. He suspects.* Stef frowned, his eyes hard, his voice anxious. "Say it."

It only took a second, if that. While Ink had become more human, she'd become more like the Folk, and despite what Avery said, she no longer thought like a human. She might not be feeling "good," she might not be "healthy" per se, but if she thought about it another way, she wasn't *bad*, she wasn't *evil*, and she was working to make things right. Therefore—

"I'm good," she said.

His shoulders relaxed, the grip on the straps loosened. Joy tried to look innocent, or at least exhausted, as she trudged past him up the rocky trail. Stef watched her, suspicious. She felt his eyes boring into her back where her *signatura* burned. He knew—or at least suspected—that Joy wasn't simply marked, wasn't simply in love with one of the Folk. Had he already guessed? Why would he press her to see if she could speak the truth? Joy jogged up a root-lined path. Maybe she was overthinking things. Maybe she was being paranoid. And maybe she was quietly hoping to be let off the hook from having to tell Stef that he was one of the "Other Thans" that he'd hated all of his life. Great-Grandma Caroline had taught him to fear them, the Folk who had left her blind and betrayed and insane. *But now he has Dmitri—doesn't that make it better? Didn't that make everything okay?* She didn't know. She couldn't be sure. She knew she should tell him, but the wind washed away her words before they could make it to her lips. She had too much on her plate. She was too distracted. There was too much at stake.

The truth was, she was a coward.

"Only one more rise and we'll hit the top," her father called down. He leaned on the two walking sticks looped around his wrists. "C'mon, slowpokes!" he gasped. "Or do I have to carry you?"

"Now *there's* a picture," Stef said and poked Joy in the butt. "Move it, slacker."

She growled, tempted to squirt him with her water bottle. Ribbing, teasing, getting annoyed at her brother—*this* was normal, but it felt weird, choked by things left unsaid. She had to remind herself that this was the real world with her family, together, for maybe the last time until winter break. It was the one thing that her father had requested they do as a family since Mom left—she owed it to her father to pay attention, to be fully *here*. She mustn't *ruin* it. Joy glared at the sun, ticking like clockwork across the sky. She wanted to hold on to this day, hit Pause and have the world stop. But she couldn't—she could barely hold on to a moment before it slipped through her fingers like the dry dust underfoot. It was funny how she'd gotten used to time standing still.

Tonight she'd have to play her part, but right now she had to be Joy Malone.

Whoever that is.

She hadn't noticed that they'd made it to the top until she realized her feet had nowhere else to go. Dad wiped his face with a red bandana and smiled. Stef dropped the pack and twisted, making popping sounds with his spine. Joy stood between them and leaned slowly side to side, feeling her ribs bend, her lungs fill, savoring a muscle-deep awareness that stretched through her like a yawn. It felt good. It felt *alive*.

"This is it," her father said. "This is what it's all about."

They stood there, three Malones on top of the world.

"I'm really proud of you two," her father said, still squinting out into the view. "Who you are, who you've been, who you've become." He took a deep breath. "Who you're still becoming." It sounded like he might say more, but he'd never said this much, not stuff like this, anyway. It reminded Joy, uncomfortably, of their first real talk since the Year of Hell. He sounded lighter, somehow, and yet stronger.

"Are you dying?" Stef asked with typical Stef-ness.

Mr. Malone laughed. "No," he said. "Well, not any more than the normal day-to-day life passing. But I'm not planning on going anywhere anytime soon." He glanced over at his two kids. "Of course, I won't be around forever, so you two better take care of one another. When you're not fighting, you can be really good friends." He pointed at them the way he had for countless years, scolding them for roughhousing, being obnoxious or unkind—but this time, it was different. His finger might have shaken. Or it might have been his voice. "If there's one thing this crazy life's taught me, it's that family is what counts." He glanced back at the vista, and Joy had the strange feeling her father was about to jump, step off into the wind and fly out into the sky, but he just smiled and hooked his thumbs in his pockets, his chest rising and falling above his almost-gone beer belly. Crinkles cut deeper into the corners of his eyes, his skin was looser, his smile softer. *When did he get so old?* Joy stared at him, this man, her father, and barely recognized him. His voice was soft and sure. "Trust me, kids," he said. *"This* is what counts."

Joy stood quietly, feeling her father's words inside her. Stef stepped forward next to their dad and leaned into the wind. Bright sunlight bathed them both in a golden glow, father and son.

"Are there waffles?" Stef asked. "Because I wouldn't want to have all of this if I can't have waffles."

Joy smacked him in the stomach. Her brother doubled over, laughing. Her father grabbed the back of his son's head and smeared his hair in all directions.

"I love you," he said roughly. "But you can be a real prick."

Stef swiped Dad's hat and tossed it to Joy. Joy plunked it on her head and scooted backward as her father lunged after her. They played Keep Away briefly before Dad pulled out the big guns, squeezing his water bottle at them like a hose. Stef swore. Joy squealed. The three of them ended up soaked and muddy and laughing, and everything serious went back to being unsaid, but it was a quiet, comfortable, happy unsaid.

The most important things had just been said.

Joy drove all the way home with her foot on the gas and her mind somewhere else entirely. She was sad to have the weekend come to an end, but grateful to get away from the creatures smiling down from the trees and the lingering glow of the memory of fiery eyes. She nestled in her family's closeness even as Stef snored in the back.

They came home in a tumble of travel bags, shucking off packs and shoes like dropping fruit, stumbling into bedrooms and clicking on TVs and laptops, scattering like projectiles heading in opposite directions. Joy went to the fridge. Stef slumped on the couch. Dad opened and closed dresser drawers. Joy made a discreet circuit, checking the wards. At least they were safe in the house. Dad called from the hall.

"I promised to call Shelley as soon as we got back," he said. "I'm taking a shower and heading over."

Panic squeaked Joy's voice. "You just got home!"

Dad's head popped into the hall with a smile. "Home is where the heart is."

She went cold. *I don't have a heart. Do I have a home?* Joy glanced anxiously around the kitchen, twisting her fingers in her shirt. It struck her that this would be home for another year or so and then...not. She would be eighteen and leaving, like Stef. What then?

The shower splashed on.

"What about you?" she asked the back of Stef's head.

"I'll toss my stuff in the car when I feel like moving, and then I'm headed out."

"What? Already?"

"Yeah." He turned and looked at her. "Is there somewhere else I need to be?"

Here it was. *Say it. Say it! Tell him!*

Right now he was blissful, giddy, perfectly content. But he was leaving—leaving this all behind, leaving *her* behind. He'd reunited with Dmitri, and maybe it wouldn't be so horrible an idea to be part of their world. Joy thought about the past year, what she had endured; she wished she could shield him from the bad parts and let him enjoy the good. Did he really have to know right now? Couldn't she let him enjoy this not-knowing for a little while longer? Maybe he'd done the same for her, once, writing *Keep strong!* on a photograph instead of telling her about their mother's affair. Maybe she understood his motives better now—he'd been trying to protect her. He was her brother, and he loved her. She was his sister, and she loved him.

"No," Joy said. "I guess not."

Stef turned back to the TV and clicked the remote, flipping channels. "Don't worry, I'll be back to harass you soon enough. Just don't mope around here all day. It's depressing." He switched to the Weather Channel. "Why don't you call Monica?"

"Monica?"

"Yeah, remember her? Your best friend?" he said. "Don't you have things to do?"

Joy thought about it. Stef was right—she had things to do, things she couldn't put off any longer.

"Yep," she said. "You're right."

"As always."

She leaned over the back of the couch and kissed him on top of his head. "Bye, Stef. I love you. Have a safe trip."

Her brother turned around, the television light reflecting off his glasses and the etched metal glyphs. His eyes were full of unsaid things.

"You, too," he said and turned back to the TV. "See you later."

Joy gathered what she needed from her room and grabbed her purse as the shower squeaked off, stopping to scribble a note to Dad. *Going out* hardly covered things, but *I love you* did. What else could she say? She pocketed her keys and paused at the door. This was it. This was when everything changed.

"Dork!" Stef called from the couch.

Joy laughed. "Dweeb!"

She closed the door behind her, thinking that wasn't the worst send-off in the world.

Monica approached Joy in polka-dot pumps, her eyebrows crinkled in that way that said you better not be messing with her because she was *so* not in the mood. Joy pushed the caramel latte across the table as a peace offering. She couldn't help but smile, even though her insides were knotted up tight.

"Aren't you supposed to be sending Stef off right now?" Monica said. "Not that I'm complaining, but I thought you were calling to check in, not bug out."

"I just got here," Joy said truthfully. "I needed to see you."

Monica took a delicate slurp of syrup and foam. "So you said."

"Yes, well, first of all—here." Joy handed the letter opener back to Monica. She'd tried to clean every fleck of Graus Claude's blood off of it, because wouldn't *that* be something fun to explain? "This is yours. Thanks for letting me borrow it."

Monica took her knife back, her expression a question. "Sure," she said slowly and tucked it into her purse.

"Okay, second," Joy said, holding her iced coffee in both hands, "I wanted to apologize for not telling you everything when you asked me to the first time. You're the person I trust more than anyone and I didn't—" Joy stumbled, and the sentence sat longer on her tongue than it should until Joy realized how true it was just like that. "I didn't."

Looking chilly, Monica sat up straighter. "Okay."

"No," Joy said. "Not okay. Not okay at all." This was harder than she'd thought. All the planned lines she'd been practicing in her head snuffed out like smoke. She sipped cold caffeine through her straw. "Look, you are my best friend and I've been acting stupid and afraid and it's not worth it—it's not worth risking your trust, your friendship. For anything." That sounded scary. It *was* scary. Joy rattled the ice in her cup. "Anyway, I came back to tell you."

"Now?"

"Yes," Joy said. "Everything. Starting now."

Monica blew gently across the coffee's surface She took a sip and set the cup down on the table with a papery clunk.

"Well," she said finally. "It's better than IM-ing."

Joy frowned. "What is?"

"This is," Monica said. "Are you gay?"

Joy's brain stalled. "What?" she stammered. "No. Uh. *What?*"

Now Monica looked embarrassed. "You're not gay?"

Joy shook her head. "No." She paused, confused. "Are you?"

Monica snorted. "No."

The two girls looked at each other for a long moment and burst out laughing, cackling in a bizarre mix of snark and silliness, love and humor, and above all...friendship. It was what Joy needed most, and even though she had doubts, it was undoubtedly there. This was *Monica*, after all. What was she thinking? Joy wiped at her eyes with a napkin and tried to compose herself.

"Then what's with all the drama?" Monica asked, relieved. "Jeez, you had me wondering about it all the way here. I kept thinking—is she pregnant? Is she coming out? Has she been abducted by aliens from outer space?"

"No," Joy said. "None of those." She handed Monica a plastic to-go top. "C'mon. Let's take these on the road."

Outside was warm and sunny with a nice breeze that tossed Joy's hair and barely moved Monica's, combed straight and curled inward like chocolate shavings on a cake. Walking helped bleed off some of Joy's nervous energy, but Monica was still with her—that was a good sign.

"So you know about my Great-Grandma Caroline," Joy said.

"Is this a Personal History lesson?" Monica asked.

"No," Joy said, taking another sip. "But I told you how much she freaked me out, right? Not her, but what happened to her." Joy watched her own feet on the concrete. It was strange to feel how normal it was, but how unlike the touch of her toes in the earth. *Is that why it took me so long to notice? Shoes?* "I thought that I could end up locked away—like maybe crazy was in my genes."

Monica shrugged. "Is it?"

"Sort of," Joy said, wondering why the words hadn't hurt—it wasn't a lie, exactly, but she was scared to discover how close it must be to the truth. "There is something that she and I have in common, but it's—" *unbelievable, difficult, scary, insane, true* "—weird. I know how you feel about your aunt Meredith, and I don't want you feeling that way about me." She dropped the dregs of iced coffee into a trash can and continued walking up a quiet side street. "So, can you just listen and not say anything until I'm done?" Joy felt herself tearing up; her precious Sight-filled tears. She'd paid off Vinh with only twelve drops—what would a total breakdown be worth? Joy checked to make sure Monica was still with her. "I *really* need you to believe me."

Monica drank her hot coffee, licked her lips and nodded. "Okay, shoot."

Joy let go. She let it all go.

"—and tonight, I'll be formally presented to the Council," Joy said through a parched and scratchy throat. She'd started talking about that night at the Carousel back in February and ended up all the way here. She should've kept her ice cubes. "And there are a lot of Folk who don't like it—one of them, in particular—and he knows about you." She looked at Monica. "He knows that you're my best friend and what you mean to me, and I don't want him coming anywhere near you." They were almost at the old play-scape with the squeaky swings and the single, sun-bleached slide. "I needed you to know everything, because I don't want anything to happen to you ever again."

The words funneled out of Joy like the last swirl of bathwater down the drain. She felt emptied and cold. The confession had wrung out all the tension inside her. *No more stupid. No more lies.* She wanted to lie down and rest. Her hiking boots and Monica's polka-dot pumps together made the only sound, a harmony of footfalls.

"That's it?" Monica said as she finished her latte and chucked the empty cup into a bin. It was thick, rusty metal with a minimum of forty flies.

Joy nodded, emotionally spent. She couldn't look up, in case Monica had *that* look—the look that said that Joy was dangerous, unstable, not-to-be-trusted, and should be locked away for her own good behind thick, padded walls. Monica was a SADD leader and a peer model; she knew all about drugs, drinking, bulimia and self-delusions. She knew how to look for the signs. Would she see any of them in her? This was the moment Joy had feared her entire life.

"And Mark is...Ink?" Monica said slowly. "This 'Indelible Ink'?"

"Yeah," Joy said. "Ink is Ink. Mark is Ink."

"And this is real?" Joy tried to interpret how Monica said it, but it was hard to tell. Was she going to bolt? Was she quietly dialing 911? Was she careful not to make any sudden moves? Joy simply nodded. Monica kept walking. "And you're not supposed to be telling me this, right? This is what you couldn't promise to tell me before?"

Throat tight, Joy nodded again. She missed the sound of her own heartbeat in her ears. The world was too quiet without the background rhythm that let her know that she was alive—she'd never noticed it before, and now it was gone.

"I promised I'd only tell you the truth."

"But why wouldn't you *tell* me before?" Monica said. "You wouldn't tell me *anything* about what happened!" Was that frustration or fear, anger or hate? Joy couldn't tell. "I was scared, and Mom was scared and you were acting weird and I didn't know why!"

"I didn't want you to think I was *crazy!*" Joy said. "I didn't want you to hate me—to think that I was a freak! That I was dangerous, delusional..." But that wasn't it, not all of it. Joy felt her breath stutter. "I didn't want you to know how badly I'd messed things up, that it was *my* fault you'd been hurt," And the truth blossomed like a briar full of thorns. "I couldn't take it if you left me, too!"

Monica glared, her mouth a small *o* of disappointment.

"Now you're being stupid," Monica said, eyes watery. "I thought we'd agreed, No Stupid."

"No Stupid," Joy said, wiping her eyes with the back of her hand. "I'm sorry."

"Come here," Monica said and pulled Joy into a hug—not a stupid polite hug, but a real hug—the one reserved for family and loved ones and very best friends. Joy wondered what number Ink had given this hug. She squeezed Monica's shoulders, surprised to be shaking; she'd forgotten what it was like to live without the fear of someone finding out, of someone deciding that she was insane—it bubbled out of her like laughter and crying, sounding something like "Thanks" and a lot like "I love you." Joy held on to her friend for all she was worth—which was a heckuva lot.

"You believe me?" she muttered over her friend's shoulder that was damp under her chin.

"I believe *in* you, even if I don't quite get the rest of it," Monica admitted as she patted Joy's back and pulled away. "It's a lot to take on faith."

"I know," Joy said, sniffling. "And I can prove it, but it's a one-way ticket. It's your choice, but you can't ever take it back."

Monica glanced at Joy's purse as if it might hold a gun or a syringe. Joy took out the tiny plastic saline bottle and handed it over. Monica held it up in the sunlight, perhaps noticing that the scintillating liquid inside didn't look normal, or maybe that was something that could be seen only with the Sight.

"Is it a drug?" Monica asked, turning it over, watching the droplets hug the sides. "Some sort of hallucinogen?"

"You read too many pamphlets," Joy said. "It's an elixir. It's made from tears."

"Tears?" Monica said. "You mean like pH-balanced?"

"Not exactly," Joy said. "They are made from tears like mine. It's an elixir that will give you the Sight."

Monica's gaze shifted. "Permanently?"

Joy shrugged. "As far as I know."

"I'd be able to see everything you see." Monica said each word slowly. "This whole Twixt world full of magic, but I can never not-see it again, is that right?"

"That's right," Joy said. "But it's *your* choice. I just wanted you to know everything, to have every option available, in case something bad happens."

"To you?"

"To either of us."

Monica splashed the liquid around. She couldn't know how much that vial had cost Inq or the damage it had done once Aniseed realized what having a Scribe's *signatura* could do. Joy didn't know the consequences for giving a human the Sight, but since the Cabana Boys had all used it, she figured there must be a rule about it somewhere.

"Does it hurt?" her friend asked.

"No more than Visine," Joy said. "And a lot less painful than a broadsword to the face."

Monica nodded. "Fine."

"Fine?"

"Yeah," Monica said. "I'm in. If I've already been smacked

upside the head by something down the rabbit hole, I'd rather see it coming. I want to see it for myself."

Joy shivered halfway between excitement and terror—to drag Monica into the world of the Twixt was unthinkable, but to not be so alone, to share this thing together, was amazing. But to do so might risk them both. She hesitated, barely allowing herself that greedy, selfish hope.

"Are you sure?" she said.

"Honestly? Half of me thinks this'll prove that you're as crazy as you say you aren't," Monica said, which made Joy go cold, but then her friend winked. "The other half of me hopes that you're right, and the world has just been pretending to be normal all this time."

Joy grinned and pointed to a nearby park bench. "Okay, then. Sit down."

"Now? You mean right now?"

"Yeah," Joy said. "I have to go soon, and I want to be sure you're okay."

Monica sat down, tucked her skirt under her legs and put her purse primly to one side, crossing her feet at the ankles and straightening her short-sleeved shirt. She blinked a couple of times in anticipation as Joy walked behind the back of the bench. She popped the saline bottle top and took a deep breath. This was it.

"Are you ready?" Joy asked.

Monica leaned her head back, brushed her stiff hair across her forehead and stared straight up, eyes wide—the scar through her eyebrow pointed straight at Joy, an arrow to the heart that wasn't there.

"Hit me," Monica said.

Joy squeezed out a single drop, sparkling with color. It dangled before it fell and hit Monica's eye in a peppery burst. Joy carefully dripped another droplet into her left eye and capped the bottle. Monica closed her eyes and leaned forward, pressing her knuckle gingerly under her lashes. She wore waterproof mascara.

Monica didn't say anything as she blinked, wide and owlish. Joy didn't say anything as she held her breath.

"Did it work?" Monica asked.

Joy tapped her on the shoulder. "You tell me."

Monica glanced up and saw Ink standing on the path, looking both curious and shy. Without his glamour, he was timeless and otherworldly with his almost-human shape and his fathomless, all-black eyes. Monica frowned, trying to decide whether or not to believe what she was seeing. Joy sympathized. The first time she'd seen Ink, she'd thought he was a Goth kid with Halloween contacts.

"Your eyes are creepy," Monica said.

He smiled. One dimple. "I got them from my mother."

Joy laughed. Monica shook her head, her earrings swinging. "No. I still don't—" she started, her tone growing angry, helpless, as she turned to face Joy. She picked up her purse. "I don't buy it. I'm sorry."

Joy wilted. *No!* She was losing her. *Her best friend.*

"Do you want to see a trick?"

Monica turned and stared at Ink. The question was so ludicrous, it surprised her.

"Sure."

Ink opened his hand, and Joy tossed him the plastic bottle. Ink weighed the thing in his grip as his other hand reached back, tucking the wallet chain to one side and removing the straight razor in one deadly, fluid motion. Monica stiffened, squeezing her purse. Joy leaned closer.

"Watch this hand," he said. "Don't blink."

Ink tossed the plastic bottle high into the air, sliced a rent through the world and stepped through. He disappeared instantly as another hole zipped open a few feet away and Ink appeared, walking smoothly through the fresh door, catching the tumbling bottle in his hand before it hit the ground.

He smiled, both dimples.

"Sweet Jesus," Monica breathed.

"Show-off," Joy muttered as she accepted the bottle back. "And you say Inq's the exhibitionist."

"It is a new sensation," he said. "Being seen as I am."

Joy turned to her friend, holding the elixir close to where her heart should be. She wanted to give Monica time to process, but she needed more than anything for her friend to be okay. For *them* to be okay.

"Do you believe me?" Joy asked. There was no turning back.

"I believe I may have a heart attack," Monica said. "You're sure you're not a street magician? I half expect there to be a flash mob any minute."

"Cameras cannot see me," Ink said. "You can try taking a picture. Inq did. That was what ultimately convinced Joy."

Monica pointed at him. "That's your sister, right? The one dating the Russian hottie with the sweet ride?"

Ink cocked his head. "'Hottie'?" The word sounded ridiculous in his mouth.

"That was Nikolai," Joy said. "He's with Inq. I'm with Ink."

Monica pressed both her hands to her forehead and whistled out a low note. "God, help me, I think this is actually making sense."

"You get why I couldn't tell you, right?" Joy said. "I didn't want to keep secrets from you, but I wanted to keep you safe. Now it's too dangerous for you *not* to know, but it still had to be your choice."

Leaning back against the park bench, Monica scraped her

shoes in the dirt. "Right. So now I know." She fanned her face with both hands. "Okay. What now?"

"First, don't tell anybody," Joy said. "The last thing I ever wanted was to be locked up for being crazy, but a close second is having anything like that happen to you. You'll probably see a lot of strange things that you hadn't noticed before, but they ought to leave you alone. You've been protected under the Edict for over six months, so they should know better."

Monica frowned. "If that was the case, why would I be in danger now?"

"You shouldn't. But there are some who seem to get away with not playing by the rules," Ink said with an irony aimed at both Joy and the Tide.

"We're only really worried about a couple of the Folk. One is called Sol Leander, the leader of an antihuman movement called the Tide. The other is called Aniseed. She's—" Joy hesitated "—bad." *Evil.*

"We do not have to concern ourselves with Aniseed," Ink said.

Joy scowled. "Not yet," she said. "Sol Leander looks like a tall Egyptian guy, older, gaunt, long face with a widow's peak, sunken eyes and a flair for the dramatic," she said, pocketing her vial and fumbling for her keys. "He usually wears a sparkly blue cloak."

Monica frowned. "You're kidding, right?"

"If you see him, remind him that you are under his auspice," Ink said. "He is under an obligation to protect you."

"What?" Monica said, eyes snapping. "Me? Why?"

"You wear his *signatura*," Ink said simply and pointed above his eye. "There." Monica reached up and touched her scar. "Sol Leander watches over those who have survived an unprovoked attack. When the Red Knight came for Joy and wounded you, it placed you under his auspice."

The look of horror on Monica's face made Joy cringe. Joy was at least glad Ink hadn't mentioned that he'd been the one to put it there.

"Whoa whoa whoa!" Monica said. "Is this Red Knight still out there?"

"No," Joy said quickly. "Not anymore." She was very aware that Ink still didn't know what she'd done, but this was not the time, now that Monica was safely in the know. "There's a lot to explain, and I will, but I have to go. Really. I took a big chance coming here, but I had to see you first." Joy smiled, projecting every bit of love and thanks and trust she had into her friend's confused stare. "I'll see you when I get back."

"Get back?" she said weakly. "But you just *got* back!"

"If you can believe it, I have to get ready for my ball at midnight." Joy shook her head and grabbed Ink's arm. "I love you, lady!"

Monica opened her mouth to say something, but then decided against it. She brushed her hair from her face. "Love you, too," she said, her eyes wet with more than runoff elixir. "Just remember—No Stupid."

"No Stupid." Joy nodded and hit the button on the key fob. A white Ferrari 458 appeared parked on the peewee baseball diamond, halfway between first base and home plate. Leave it to Ink to miss the parking lot by a mile.

Monica shrieked. "What is *that*?!"

"That," Joy said, unlocking the doors with a click, "is a killer first impression."

TWENTY

"NICE," RAINA PURRED IN APPROVAL AS THE CAR slowed to a halt. Joy was just glad that her feet could still touch the pedals. She'd set the driver's seat on the farthest setting in order to accommodate the dress. Even with all the carefully placed safeguards, silk ties and padded pillows, Idmona had fretted over Joy's ride, evidently expecting a coach of some kind and not a modern sports car. Joy was conscious of every crinkle as she parked the Ferrari in front of the East entrance, flanked by milling crowds of Folk.

Light speared the entryway, surrounded by sparkles and twinkles and fast-flying things that swept over the throng. Bodies pressed close and conversations were loud as people jockeyed for position, clamoring closer to the gate. The sound was overwhelming, a garble of music and noise.

It was like the Macy's parade on Oscar Night.

Joy could feel the push of a thousand eyes staring through the windows.

Raina unbuckled her seat belt. "Better let me help you out," she said. Joy was completely willing to let the woman play bodyguard—besides the fact that Raina was clearly both competent and fearless, Joy doubted she could stand up on her own.

Raina's Pantene hair shone in the headlights as she crossed in front of the car. The press of Folk backed away, either respectful or repulsed. Raina was calm, composed, professional, mature and obviously had no problem ignoring the weird and wild assemblage. Joy, being Joy, felt like she was going to puke.

The taller woman opened the door and offered Joy her hand. Joy braced herself and tried not to grunt as she leveraged herself forward. Her face felt pinched, powdered in crushed pearls and glitter, and she squeezed Raina's fingers in white-knuckled panic. She wished that Ink could be here but knew he was in position, waiting for her in the Grand Ballroom like Gatorade at the end of the finish line.

"Just breathe," Raina whispered. "You own this."

Raina slipped the silk ties loose and tossed the satin pillows aside. Joy stretched out a toe to get a foothold, feeling completely unlike herself, as the hugging pressure of the crinoline eased off her legs. She remembered Idmona's coaching. *Keeeeep* your head up. *Loooook* confident. *Truuuuust* your instincts.

Joy *had* to trust her instincts—she couldn't see her feet.

Once Joy managed to get upright, Raina circled her with stately grace, lifting the hem of her skirts and fluffing them full of life; the delicate beaded trim tinkled against the ground. Joy stood very still. Clutching the elaborately beaded purse in a death grip, she tried to act like she did something like this all the time.

Joy marveled again at her ever-widening definition of "something like this."

Winks of colors and wings and scales and jewels sparkled like rainbow stars against the dark. Joy tried not to get distracted by the enormity of the place, picturing the map in her head as she walked down the aisle, Folk pressing along the sidelines, fighting for room. The Grand Ballroom must be to her left, down the long entryway that connected the main chambers to one another. She would have to walk down that hall after her presentation in the amphitheater, escorted by the Council into Twixt high society. Ink would be there, waiting for her. She clutched her clutch purse closer. She could do this. She would make it until then.

Raina checked the bustle once more, straightened Joy's pearls, handed her the dragonfly mask and tweaked the hair comb into place, anchoring her real hair to the tumble of false curls attached to the back of her head. Joy was infinitely glad she hadn't needed to sit for the impossible hairstyle—the hairpiece had fit nicely over her scraped-back ponytail and the makeup job had been grueling enough. She twirled the stick attached to the damselfly half-mask, watching it sparkle like the eyes of the crowd. She didn't need a mask, the solid layer of paint on her face was like porcelain, but Joy felt absurdly grateful for the added wall over her features. *Like a shield. Like armor. Ready for war.*

"Ready?" Raina asked.

"Yes," Joy said. She caught the woman's gaze as she tucked Joy's hand into the crook of her arm. "And, thanks. Really, thanks." She meant it, for a lot more than just this. She meant it for Enrique and Ink and the dress and herself.

Inq's *lehman* smiled. "My pleasure," she said, and it sounded as true as if she were one of the Folk. "Now let's get you inside." She winked. "It's showtime."

Joy killed the lights and locked the automatic doors behind her. She was about to drop her keys inside her purse when she remembered *first impressions* and hit the fob's blue button. The car vanished. There was a chorus of "oohs" and gasps and a smattering of appreciative applause. Joy closed her purse with a snap and allowed herself to be led Under the Hill.

The scenery changed from dark to sparkling; the outdoor

concert cacophony faded into the quiet hush of the Council chambers. It felt old and rich and sacred indoors. A chattering of busy voices buzzed in the background, along with the delicate clattering of china and glass. Those, too, faded away as she was led up the stairs to a familiar lobby. Raina removed her arm and Joy felt the loss as she self-consciously rearranged the objects in her hands.

Raina lifted a thin scarf from a podium to the left of the door. She unfolded the sheer material and draped it artfully over Joy's head like a veil, screening everything in shimmery gold. Raina fussed needlessly with the corners, checking the hidden scalpel and the crystal comb as she tugged it into place.

"I must leave you here," Raina said, sounding truly sorry. "Only the Folk are welcome tonight. But you can always call me, if you need anything." She patted Joy's arm. "I texted you my number. Anytime, day or night."

"How about five minutes from now?" Joy said.

Raina smiled. "You'll be fine. You're one of them, remember?"

Yes. I'm one of them, Joy reminded herself. *For now.*

Joy squared her shoulders, and Raina opened the door.

The Council Hall was exactly as she remembered when she'd last stood in its wings—it was different walking through its central doors instead of the side entrance; the floor dipped gradually down toward the enormous tree trunk worn smooth in its center, and her dress was wide enough to brush both rows of seats. The walls of the amphitheater curved overhead like the petals of a giant flower bud, sloping lines drawing the eye upward to the central, star-shaped skylight, reminding her of Enrique's funeral and its floating chandelier of memories. *What did this room remember? Would it remember this?* The Council Hall looked more somber, less like a natural Christmas tree and more like a government building. The stone mosaics did not so much twinkle as loom. She walked toward the Council like a bride.

The natural dais was surrounded by a low wall, which framed a semicircle of white chairs sprouting up from the floor. Five Council members stood, awaiting her arrival—a sixth hung suspended in a large droplet from the ceiling, and a seventh was notably absent. The High Water seat. *Graus Claude.*

She tried not to think about him in a locked cell overhearing this.

Joy steeled her face to appear as neutral as possible, praying the veil and layers of foundation would hide any telling blush. She debated placing her mask over her face, but she didn't need her double strand of pearls to tell her that that would be considered rude. Her hem rustled against the edge of the stump and her shoes knocked against its surface, muffled under the dress. The glass beads chimed, and Joy caught sight of tiny motes of light climbing through the gallery seats, reflected shimmers off her bejeweled gown.

The pearls whispered instructions. She curtsied. The Council bowed. The black crystal figure with molten veins and fiery eyes gave off a series of *pings* and *cracks* as it moved. Whatever was in the water curled itself in a circle over its tail.

The Council Head—Bùxiŭde Zhēnzhū—gazed down at her with his old, old eyes, the scales on either side of his neck expanding and settling like slow, reptilian breathing; the tips of his long moustache danced in a nonexistent breeze.

Remember Graus Claude. Respect him. Always.

The Council looked grim. Even Maia, squat and rubbery, looked uncommonly grave, and the towering dryad's crown of rustling leaves stilled. The dark-skinned, redheaded pixie wore her twin ornamental spears crisscrossed and peace-tied behind her back—their trailing crimson ribbons ran over her shoulders like blood.

Joy didn't trust herself to look at Sol Leander, although his star-dusted cloak teased the edge of her Sight. She could feel his glare—cold and dripping—as it oozed down the side of her face.

There's nothing he can do. He is powerless to prevent this.

"Joy Malone, you are to be presented as one of the Twixt," the elderly Council Head said in his thin, reedy voice. His hands were folded together, hidden under embroidered sleeves. He didn't need a gavel to command attention—his eyes and his tone held authority like a fist. "Your sponsor should have been the one to formally present you, but as that is regrettably not possible, we shall forgo that customary procedure." He bowed from the waist, and the others nodded politely in return. Even Sol Leander dipped his head in acquiescence. The very idea of his kowtowing to anyone raised Joy's hackles. *What's he up to?*

The fact that Graus Claude wasn't here should have been an outrage to his constituents, and, as far as she knew, tradition was *everything* to the Folk. Joy sensed that there were many long histories playing out before her eyes, and without Graus Claude, she was ignorant and defenseless against them. Should she protest? Defend him? Would this make the ritual illegitimate, incomplete? She touched her pearls discreetly behind her purse. They whispered wordless reassurance—this was still within the rules. Graus Claude's wisdom was still with her. *Not completely ignorant*, she thought. *Or completely defenseless.* She was, as Graus Claude said, a wildflower with bite.

Bùxiū de Zhēnzhū focused his slit-pupil eyes on her.

"Turn around."

Joy hesitated for the barest instant, thinking, *I really don't want to*...but she did, gradually turning her back to the Council, her heels echoing off the high walls as she stared out into the gallery of empty seats. She was absurdly grateful that they hadn't silently filled up behind her. Unfortunately, now she was thinking about the Council behind her back, including some who hated her and some who were armed.

She tried not to fidget despite feeling exposed, practically naked in her damselfly dress with its plunging back, her *signatura* laid bare to those with the Sight.

Joy heard the shuffle of many feet, the shush of robes, the clomp of shoes, the *ping* and *crack* of crystalline limbs, a woody creak of shifting twigs and the rapid-hummingbird-flurry of wings. It took everything inside her not to turn around. She clutched her things, her elbows squeezing the hidden zippers and clasps along her sides. She felt surrounded, circled, scrutinized...

It struck her that she was being judged.

Wait. I know how to do this!

Joy fixed her jaw, lifted her chin, breathed in from her diaphragm and out through her nose. This was a *performance*, just like any other—something she'd done hundreds of times since she was six—graded on appearance, showmanship, aptitude, skill. Competing in Level Nine gymnastics meant that she had kept her eye on the ultimate goal, the Olympics, to be the best of the best. Joy was trained as a performer who had no illusions—she knew her strengths and her weaknesses, and her strength was *this*. She knew how to perform. Better still, she knew how to *win*.

So as the Council approached, Joy was still as a statue, and when the first touch happened, she did not so much as twitch.

The sensation took a split second to register: a hand, papery and chapped, pressed flat against her *signatura*, bathing her veins in warm, wispy light. She did not close her eyes, but let the colors of magic swirl before her eyes. Then it was gone. A slimy-soft touch, boneless and wide, sluiced over the same spot on her spine. Joy imagined Maia stretching upward in a single, taffylike motion and blobbing back down in Jell-O-y jiggles. A delicate *pop* and *crackle* preceded a ham-fisted block of stone that pressed against her sigil with all the tenderness of a shove. Her bones filled with a momentary punch of fire; Joy held her breath to keep from gasping and waited for the lava Councilex to move on. A tiny hand tapped once, then disappeared, leaving behind a vague impression like music. A cold, cold wetness pressed against her, trickling down her back like a soaked sponge, impossibly alien, dark and distant, strangely pliant, like a flipper or fin. She pressed her tongue to the roof of her mouth to keep herself from screaming.

The dryad's touch was a relief, rough and warm as cork, and something in it felt welcoming, like the promise of spring. She imagined Graus Claude's hand, his olive-gray skin surprisingly soft along with the prickle of his manicured claws...but he wasn't here. She knew who was next.

Joy tensed, half expecting a knife between her spinal bones, stabbing into her dead heart. She braced for it, wondering if there was something she could do—something she *should* do—or if any of the Councilex would stop him if he tried. But Sol Leander's touch felt no different, perhaps more human than the others, leaving a not-unpleasant tingle behind like mint. He withdrew, leaving her still and statuesque, to all appearances completely unfazed.

She missed her heart's hammer. It would tell her what to feel.

"It is done," Bùxiǔ de Zhēnzhū announced behind her ear. "Walk forward, Joy Malone, and greet your people."

Her feet moved automatically as if performing the opening steps of routine; Joy gently placed one foot in front of the other, imagining an arrow between her feet and up her spine at ninety degrees to emerge unerringly out the top of her head. It gave her a regal bearing, a surety of purpose. At least she wouldn't have to do a split leap in this getup. But thinking of it that way, Joy could relax, safe inside her performance mask. She *owned* this. She did it. This was *easy*!

The veil was whisked off her head between one step and the next with a suddenness that almost made her trip over her skirt. Between blinks, the empty seats were filled to bursting—the entire Hall crowded with Folk, which had been filtered from her Sight, hidden behind the golden veil. The entirety of the amphitheater stood as one and bowed, silent witness to her moment as she continued up the aisle, leading the Council like a train.

Well, she hadn't fainted from fright. *Bonus points!*

Joy entered the Grand Ballroom like a queen. Not a hint of doubt or surprise creased her face as she took in the jumble of creatures who stood awaiting her arrival. The room had grown to massive proportions that ballooned and bowed the walls as the Hill swelled to compensate for the number of guests present. The lights moved as colorful sprites and will-o-the-wisps zipped through the air, reflected in the mirrors and crystal and golden gilt. An enormous chandelier dominated the ceiling, dwarfing the hodgepodge collection at Enrique's funeral; the crystal constellation was made up entirely of perfectly round glowing globes that radiated happiness like sunshine on her skin. The gala was impossibly huge and impossibly beautiful, brimming like a wineglass full of diamonds and pearls.

She touched her necklace and said a prayer.

All eyes turned to her. All conversation hushed. Joy felt the Council behind her and stopped when they did, poised on the precipice, as if they'd rehearsed this introduction a dozen times before. Their voices chorused as one.

"As representatives of our most noble Houses, whose collective oaths constitute this, the Council of the Twixt, we invite all those gathered here to witness the ascension of Joy Malone as a member of our esteem and welcome her to take her place amongst us; which, in accordance to our laws, ascribes and mandates our Decree that she be counted as one of those chosen to uphold the last vestiges of our stronghold and honor as a caretaker of this world onto the next."

Councilex Maia slid forward and held up a glass globe the size of a softball. She placed it in Joy's hand and pressed it between hers. Her fingers squished.

"Place this to your brow," she said. Joy dutifully lifted the orb to her forehead, feeling the cool kiss of glass. "Remember this moment." Joy was unsure what to do. The Earth spirit squeezed tighter and whispered, "Close your eyes, feel this moment, and join us forever."

Her brain balked at *forever*, but Joy closed her eyes, picturing herself in the Hall, the colors, the lights, the alien touches, her fear and fierce resolve—she poured all of the memories into this one moment. Light glowed against her eyelids. She opened her eyes and was blinded by the small sun in her hand. Maia peeled back her fingers. The glowing star rose slowly, climbing to join the thousands of its kin.

Then Joy understood.

She stood beneath the gathered memories of all the Folk who had undergone this ritual, becoming part of the Twixt. It touched something deep inside her that had no name. *I am one of them*, she thought with an unexpected sense of pride and belonging. *Now and always.*

The Council intoned, "Until the Imminent Return."

"Until the Imminent Return!" the room chorused back.

Joy smiled her Olympic-class smile.

Until the Imminent Return—which may be sooner than you think!

The room exploded into babble, and music stirred into song as the crowd surged forward. Joy was careful *not* to step back. Retreat was not an option—she had to be a show of strength. She raised her mask and braced herself for impact.

A dark figure intervened, insinuating himself smoothly at her side. The crowd parted around them, still chattering politely at a distance. Joy turned to her rescuer.

His hair was longer, thicker, swirling over his forehead and tucked softly behind his ear, tied with a black ribbon like some French aristocrat. He wore a long, high-necked jacket, sleek and tidy and made entirely of black feathers, clasped with silver chains over his chest. His pants were buckled with bone, ribbed along his thighs and calves, a parody of bird's legs that ended in wicked claw-toed boots. He wore silver finger talons on both forefingers, attached to thick bracelets by thin chains. He straightened his waistcoat of fitted black-on-black jacquard, touched the beaked half-mask and smiled.

Two dimples, which completely undid her.

Joy took Ink's arm.

"You look nice," she said. She'd meant to say *Thank you*, but she was still recovering.

"You are stunning," he said. "See how they are stunned?"

She blushed, disarmed—Ink was no longer boyish, but handsome. No longer shy, but bold. *Confident. Clever. Rakish. Sexy.*

"Did I say 'nice'?" Joy said. "I meant stunning."

"Are you stunned?"

"A little."

Ink tugged a lock of his hair into place and grinned. "Good."

She curtsied as Folk approached her, matching gestures

and pleasantries, veiled invites and jibes. The pearls fed her appropriate responses as fast as thought. She pursed her lips, tilted her head and offered her left wrist to a feathered snake that burbled in approval, flicked its tongue and slithered off. Joy was once again obscenely grateful to Graus Claude.

She wished that she'd given Kurt and Briarhook her four-leaf clover for luck.

Ink guided her through the masses. There were many faces that she recognized; some, like the snail woman or the young-faced harpy, were Folk she'd seen in the cache at Dover Mill; others, like Filly, stood out in the crowd. The blonde warrior wore her hair loose, resplendent in a long, embroidered dress, a bronze-colored horse mask sitting squarely atop her head—its mane looked like real horsehair and ran like a sheet down her back. It took a moment to find Inq, wrapped in a stiff cape like a jeweled carapace, shining like some exotic beetle that could only be a queen. She caught Joy's gaze, raised her glass and smiled. The Scribe was in her element, but clearly not in the Bailiwick yet.

"How soon?" she asked after bowing to sniff a kitsune's paw.

"We shall know when someone gives the signal," he said. "Which may be somewhat challenging, considering the number of guests." He scanned the room with his fathomless black eyes. "I had not realized that there were so many—I knew their marks, but I had forgotten that each one represents a person, a face."

"Imagine how many more might be behind a locked door," Joy said quietly.

"Do not let it distract you," he said. "This time, *we* are the bait. You must concentrate on being unforgettable." He smiled again. "Have a care for your poor subjects—they have not had an excuse to gather like this for nearly a thousand years."

Joy squeezed his arm. "Don't leave me for a second."

He stroked her hand gently. "If that."

Joy slid her fingers along the double strand of pearls, adjusting the clasp, accessing their wisdom. She hoped that Graus Claude could hear her small successes and know that she was playing her part and more. *Hang on.* She sent the thought like a prayer. *We're coming!*

"Excuse me, Miss Malone." The voice came from her left as a hand gestured to her right. "A small matter."

There was a popping noise, and Joy felt Ink stiffen and fall. She whirled around, staring at the crumpled pile of feathers and chains wearing Ink's face caught in a moment of surprise. Across the room, Inq collapsed into a boneless heap. There were shouts of disgust, gasps of horror and titters of amusement. Joy's thoughts scattered, angry and afraid, but the Tide's representative held no weapon, his empty hands parting the air in a deferential shrug.

And Joy knew even before he could say the words.

He'd shut down the Scribes.

"The gala is exclusive to the Folk, you understand," he said, accepting a wax mask from a liveried dwarf. "And, unfortunately, your escort is not—strictly speaking—one of our ilk, and therefore unsuitable to attend this event." Sol Leander gestured magnanimously to the rest of the crowd. "However, I believe that there are many who would be honored to serve as your escort for the remainder of the evening." He stepped back with a supercilious bow, slipping the boxy mask over his face, his voice curled up from beneath the lip. "It is, of course, *your choice.*"

Joy watched as two masked Folk quickly gathered Ink's unconscious body and carried him swiftly from the room with well-rehearsed speed. They'd been expecting this. They'd known. They'd planned this all along.

"Ink—"

"I'd been informed of the Scribes' safeguards once I'd joined the Council," he confided softly. "But discovering the precise location was a small matter of persuasion." Sol Leander straightened and readjusted his cape. "They will be stored in the coatroom for the interim, along with the other accessories," he added. "Would you like them to check your handbag, as well?"

Joy was speechless. *He's not dead. He's just been...disabled. In public. In the most despicable and humiliating way possible.* She knew it had been done to flaunt her helplessness, her foolishness and the Tide's superiority, pushing the Scribes aside like so many chairs. She could not protest without incident, she could not lash out without consequence, she'd been disgraced, disarmed and neatly played—she didn't even need Pearls of Wisdom to tell her that.

A flick of wild horse mane, and Filly was running, weaving through the crowd, out the door, disappearing down a hall, off to tell the others that the plan was over before it had begun. Inq could not go into the Bailiwick. Ink could not provide escape. No one would be able to find the hidden door, rescue the princess and break the spell. Joy was on her own, outmaneuvered and alone.

Sol Leander and the surrounding crowd waited like expectant vultures, eagerly anticipating her response.

She had to play along. Stall for time. Look for the loophole.

Lifting her mask to her face, Joy raised her chin and her voice.

"Indeed," Joy said haughtily. "I accept."

She offered her arm to Sol Leander.

The leader of the Tide hesitated only a second in surprise. He could refuse her and be the first to publically snub the newest addition to the Twixt in over a thousand years, a changeling that he had personally verified only moments before, or acknowledge that he'd inadvertently included himself as one of the gala hopefuls who curried her favor—and bear the public implications that he did or did not wish her alliance. She almost smiled watching him squirm, thinking of Graus Claude's rumbling approval.

Sol Leander lifted his hand under hers and led her into the gala.

Joy could barely breathe. This was a *dangerous* game.

The crowd parted with squeals and knowing murmurs, and there was an undercurrent of what Joy suspected was Maia's sly laughter. She concentrated on keeping her hand steady. Sol Leaner, too, kept the back of his glove hovering just under her palm—likely both found the idea of actually touching one another physically repulsive, but the question was: Who would flinch first?

Circling the breadth of the room under the strange, lilting music, Joy and her escort carved a path through the dance. Gossipy cliques followed, eager to catch a telling glimpse or a noxious bite. Joy tried to keep her eyes on everything but Councilex Leander and her mind on anything besides Ink. There was plenty to tempt the senses, and she drank in distractions like wine. Fairies flew overhead, perching in rafters or cushioned shelves, sprites stood straight as arrows, their wings folded tight against their backs. The Fire Folk gathered in corners, glowing like cauldrons or flaring across the room like comets, leaving streaks of orange sparks in their wake. Towering Forest Folk preened as they gossiped—tall dryads, short satyrs, smirking brownies, wild-eyed elves and what looked like a bunch of particularly well-tended shrubs rustling with mirth by the ale. Earth Folk gathered together like bouquets of every color; faces bright as bluebells, russet-skinned and monarch-winged, gray and gritty goblins, noble ogres, bent-backed trolls—they all paused and bowed, acknowledging Joy as she drifted past. Strangely, they were all smiling at her, warm and welcoming, unlike the sky-cold thing by her side. She could catch only snippets of conversation except when they passed the fountains, the Water Folk's burbles whispering secrets into her *eelet* ear.

The Bailiwick's playing coy, mark my words.
See her pearls? See her nape?
Why bother, I ask thee? For 'tis all naught but flesh.
Salt water, he said. Sea salt and blood.
Still smells human.
Make her drink.
Sieve the truth!
EEE! Look at his face!

Sol Leander's hand disappeared, dipping down to pluck a fluted glass from a shallow pool of cold water and white river stones. Moisture dripped off its base, tickling the finned creatures that swirled beneath the surface. He offered it to Joy and chose another for himself. She accepted it—as she must—and he took the first sip—as he must, the pearls slipping proper etiquette into her brain. Joy wanted to break the thin-necked stemware and throw it in his face. She could still see Ink's body crumpled like a dead bird at her feet, and here she was playing nice with the enemy. She watched him glare through the eyeholes. He hated this charade as much as she did. *We are both wearing multiple masks.*

She knew that she would have to take a sip; to do otherwise would be to rebuff him, publicly insinuate that he'd chosen poorly or that she did not trust him, suspecting poison or some other trick. And while a part of her wanted to down the whole glass in one swallow, she remembered that one sip of funeral wine, like a sweet hammer to her palate. Joy needed all her wits tonight.

As a lifelong athlete, she was used to going without.

She put down the wineglass, untouched. A dryad adorned in Morning Glories skirted aside as if the glass itself was tainted.

"I find this is not to my taste," Joy said simply.

Sol Leander stood motionless. Had she insulted the wine or him? If he chose to interpret it as a personal slight, he would have just cause to take offense, but if he guessed wrong, she could claim no slight was intended and that the fault lay in the wine—his breach of manners at her own gala would be compounded by his position...or underscore how nimbly he'd been played. Which would he choose? Councilex Leander hovered, holding his now-inferior drink. The closest witnesses practically frothed in delight. Even the pool bubbled in what Joy could hear as tickling, childish laughter.

"Perhaps a dance, then, if that is more to your taste?" a familiar voice interrupted as smoothly as Ink. Joy turned, hoping to see him, but knew the voice was wrong, the face was wrong, framed with its frost-colored hair and ocean eyes flinty behind an elaborate swan mask.

"May I have the honor?" Avery bowed and offered Joy his hand. Stupefied, she took it and let him steer her into the dance.

This is all wrong! This is not *how it goes!* Joy's mind scrambled furiously, but her feet knew the steps as she followed his lead, the pearls instructing her body what to do. She clutched her mask and purse in one hand as his left hand, under his cloak, lay flat as iron against her waist. She turned her head aside, looking properly askance instead of at him.

"That was daring," he said.

"Was it?" Joy quipped. "Are you talking about your master or me?"

Avery kept his eyes fixed on the crowd, professionally distant, more intent on the gala than on her. "Oh, you both managed to provide quite fine entertainment," he said casually. "Although I imagine that you have far more to lose than he—his pride is certainly suffering, but he will make you pay for every dram." He lifted his arm for her to slide beneath in a slow, mincing turn. He reclaimed her as they continued to waltz. "Do try to keep that in mind."

Joy let the tilt of their shoulders act as a nod. "I will."

"Will you?" Avery said, executing a complicated step. "I'd like to see that."

Joy swallowed, trying to ignore the hungry stares swirling by in a multicolored blur. Pixies swooped. Nixies splashed. A horde of minuscule creatures in matching coats tapped ironwood sticks in some ancient rhythm using the butts of their canes and the soles of their feet. Avery propelled Joy expertly along the edge of the waltz under appreciative glances and skeptical stares. He was a good dancer. She clutched her pearls by the clasp. She was on parade for the public, immortal, hungry and bored. She wondered what was the equivalent of a rag mag in the Twixt? She could picture the headlines in splashy, bold font.

"That's a Wendigo on your left," Avery whispered. "Best bare your teeth."

She did. The man showed throat as he swept his partner clockwise.

"Thanks," she muttered.

"Do not thank me, or anyone," Avery sighed, steering her deftly to one side. "You must stop thinking like a human—these are *your* rules now."

Joy bit the side of her cheek to avoid saying something cheeky. She kept her voice down and her eyes straight ahead. "You want me to think like them? Fine. How's this—the Scribes are down," she whispered past his ear. "Filly's gone to tell Kurt, but no humans can come in here, and likely Briarhook will bail. Graus Claude is warded against any who are his friends, so I cannot go find him, and Ink and Inq will be out for several days, which will be far too late since the Bailiwick is set to be condemned after the gala, and I'm stuck playing politics in a party dress under the watchful eye of everyone in the Twixt!" They separated in a formalized bow and switched directions, circling together like petals in a pool. She quietly seethed until they matched up again.

"Well, then," Avery said. "What will you do?"

"I'm thinking," she said, although she wasn't managing to do a very good job. Even with the double strand of pearls, she had to concentrate on concentrating. She could not access the dance as well as stored etiquette and manage to think her own thoughts, too. "It has to be now," she muttered. "Once Graus Claude has been tried and convicted, who knows where he might end up? No one will be able to access the Bailiwick if he's lost. This is our one chance to get him before it's too late."

Avery's mouth twitched beneath the swan beak. "You sound so dramatic."

Her skirts brushed as she turned. "You make that sound like a good thing."

"It *is* a good thing," he said. "I was beginning to wonder if you were more like the furniture than the Folk." Joy frowned, wondering if he was slighting Ink again. "I am not the only one who hopes that your true nature will become evident tonight." He paused, bowing over her knuckles. "In fact, many are counting on it. People are curious. The girl with the Sight? The ex-*lehman*? The third Scribe? The Red Knight's bane?" He listed her faults as if they were titles. "They came to see *you*—the true you. You must demonstrate that, if you truly are one of us."

"You mean whether I am an arrogant, malicious, double-talking cheat loyal only to fulfilling my own, personal agenda?" she asked while turning inside the curve of his arm. She smiled at his wintry gaze. "Well, then, I guess I am."

His lips thinned. His feathered cloak swirled as he turned. Facing her, he gripped her firmly, slamming her against him on the major chord.

"Prove it," he said.

Joy gasped. "You're too close."

His elbows straightened an inch, putting a breath between them.

"What are you doing?" she whispered through clenched teeth.

"Raising the stakes," he said roughly. "If you're going to play this game, then play it to win."

Heat flushed her cheeks, pinking her chest and neck. "Stop it," she said, angry, flustered, uncertain if he was being helpful or rude. "You're in this, too. You've been following me in order to report to the Tide, right? Anything I do right now might reflect badly on you."

"I didn't think you noticed," he said drily. That was when she realized how much he'd been risking following her, informing her, aiding her long before he'd sat with her circle of conspirators in the brownstone foyer. Avery had placed his loyalty to the Twixt above that of the Tide or his master. She refused to feel guilty, but couldn't help being impressed.

"Will you get in trouble?" she asked.

"I can honestly report that my observations did not indicate any evidence of what may yet happen this evening, since, by your own admission, you do not know what you will do next. Your indecision is to my advantage, and I plan to exploit it," he said. "I am certain you understand." The dance was limping to a close. "As far as my intercession earlier, I plan to excuse myself by claiming I'd been willing to sacrifice my honor by placing myself in your dubious presence in order to free my master of obligation on his behalf, which is true." Avery said. "I might even be rewarded."

"Wonderful. Glad I could help," Joy said as they twirled, Avery lifting her body by the waist as she hopped to assist. She came down lightly, but overly conscious of her shoes. She was unused to wearing heels while moving to music. It was jarring in the small way that real things were.

"Honestly, it was no great sacrifice," Avery said, snapping her back to the moment. He avoided her gaze as he glanced over the crowd. "Any ideas yet?"

Find Ink. Find Graus Claude. Find the door. Break the rules.

Joy sighed, thinking fast. "I'm going to cause a distraction."

"I see."

"It will likely get you in trouble."

Avery leaned forward and whispered in her ear, the one with the *eelet* and the drop water opal. The one Ink had first touched with wonder.

"Better make it good, then," he said.

Joy pulled away, disrupting the dance, and smacked him hard across the face.

It was weak and silly, but it had the desired effect. Avery's head snapped to the side, and he backed away stiffly, dropping her hands like lead weights. He stood rigid, flushed, his lips a hard slash. Bowing tightly, Avery glared at her through the swan mask's frosted lashes, although she could have sworn he looked impressed with a reddening cheek. The other dancers stared, the nearby onlookers tittering with horrified delight.

"I probably should say something like 'unhand my sister'!" came a voice from the back. "But I believe that she can take care of herself."

TWENTY-ONE

STEF AND DMITRI STOOD TOGETHER AS THEY ENTERED the Hall—an odd match with the satyr in ornate split-robes and her brother in a trim Armani tux. The Twixt's collective gaze absorbed the spectacle, completely and utterly unable to blink.

Joy would have liked to believe that her heart started beating the next moment, but it didn't. The crowd parted as the pair drew closer, Stef nodding to Joy. Dmitri, neatly combed and curried, grinned like the devil as he fiddled with his tie.

"Well spoken," he said and tipped his horned head at Joy. "And well met, Joy Malone."

It was as if he'd given the room permission to speak, and the Folk began to oblige him all at once. Joy could only tease out some of the words, but she got the basic gist.

"Outrageous!"

"Inexcusable!"

"Abominable whelp!"

"Get *rid* of them—"

"He cannot be here!"

"Where's the troop buck?"

"Mortals cannot—"

"—*strictly* forbidden!"

A gargoyle pushed forward and snarled around its snout. "No human—"

Stef raised a hand. The rings on his fingers looked new.

"I am not human," he said. He looked impossibly calm. Happy. His voice carried. His eyes twinkled. "Am I, Joy?"

She shook her head, eyes teary. "No," she said softly as she crossed the floor to him. "You are my *brother*," she said, adding extra emphasis. "And I am glad to see you here." She smiled with slightly less wattage than her Olympic-class standards, hooking his other elbow and gesturing to the crowd. "You are welcome to the gala as my honored guests!"

And just like that, the room reawakened as if paused and reset—the music swelled, the dancing followed, the food and the wine and the gossip flowed freely, but now pushed to the edges instead of commanding center stage. She had done it. *Her gala. Her rules.* It wasn't magic, but it might as well have been. Now everyone had to welcome them, whether they wanted to or not. And Stef was right—he wasn't human, he was part-Twixt, so he was allowed to be here, as per the rules. *Take* that, *Sol Leander!* She felt an obscene satisfaction at sticking it to the Man.

Joy led the way as Folk parted before her, continuing to bow and kneel, discreetly avoiding her gaze as she passed. She squeezed Stef's arm, trying to convince herself that this was really him and not some sort of *doppelganger* phantom—or maybe to convince herself that it was. Dmitri snagged a glass of something and tossed it back like a shot.

"Who was that guy?" Stef said.

"What are you *doing* here?" she whispered.

"Are you really going to ask me that?" he said, grabbing a cream puff.

He certainly *sounded* like Stef.

"I love you," she said anxiously, propelling them toward the door. "I'm glad to see you—you don't know how glad I am, really. You both look awesome. Very posh. Very happy. I love you. Did I say that? Thank you for coming. Really. Now leave."

Stef exchanged a glance with Dmitri, who was biting into some magenta-skinned fruit with speckled white flesh in obvious delight. The satyr shrugged. Her brother laughed.

"Well, that was quite a mouthful," he said. Joy wasn't sure if he meant Dmitri or her. "I appreciate the sentiment, but I just got here." He was one of the few not wearing a mask, as if he *wanted* to be seen—as if her brother was tired of being hidden. His eyes behind his glyphed glasses were steely and strong. "And I'm not leaving you."

Joy snatched a couple of grapes, then, having a quick flashback, put them down.

"I could have you thrown out," she said.

"I wouldn't do that," Dmitri said after he'd swallowed. "Not that I could, mind you, I don't have the clout, but that's the sort of play that, once witnessed, has long legs, fast tongues and breeds words. I don't think you really want to do that to your brother—or me—since you've only recently gone from persona non grata to Belle of the Ball, and I wager no one will forget the trip anytime soon." He gestured with another glass of wine, freshly emptied. "Tonight is the dry run for how the Twixt might receive those born with the Sight in future days, and you wouldn't want to sully the delicate negotiations that are no doubt taking place, whispered in ears both here and now. Especially since your brother also happens to be a wizard—"

"Apprentice wizard," Stef corrected. Dmitri bumped his shoulder.

"Details." He sniggered. "Wizards already have a fragile peace with the Folk, so you might not want to rock that particular canoe by staging an adolescent snit fit. And, FYI, you wouldn't want to cross me—I'm much too pretty." The satyr peeled another squiggle of fruit. "Especially since I've brought you a present."

Joy paused. "A present?" Somehow the satyr made it sound naughty.

"A little birdie told me you might need a little something now and a little something later," he said, adding a little bow. Dmitri was currying her favor and doing it in full view of the assembled Twixt. She had to admire his moxie. "Unfortunately, security being what it is, I had to leave them in your glove compartment."

Joy frowned. "My glove compartment?"

"In your car," Dmitri said, dropping the rind on a plate and wiping his fingers. "The one parked outside."

"*In* my car? You mean in my *invisible* car?" She glared at Stef, who failed to look guilty. "That thing's warded against all kinds of stuff!"

"I know," Stef said, plucking a blackberry from Dmitri's dish. "Last week, while you were sleeping, I copied your keys." He popped the fruit into his mouth and pursed his lips at the taste. "A Ferrari, Joy? Really?"

While Joy wanted to be mad at her brother, she actually welcomed the snarky normalcy. "I am *not* having this conversation right now."

"Whatever. Not important," Dmitri said. "Bottom line—it'll be there when you need it. You find an opening, get gone—take whomever you've got with you, and we'll cover your hasty retreat."

"Easy for you to say," Joy mumbled behind the safety of her mask.

"Easy for you to do," Dmitri said. "You were well on your way to making a scene before your dear brother upstaged the moment." The faun slid a skewer of melon balls and dark berries into his mouth and chewed. "Just do what you do best," he said. "Cause a little chaos." He winked slyly. "You know you want to."

Something stirred in the hollow of what once was her heart, a tiny flicker like heartburn or hope. She had allies. They were with her. Here. Now. She was standing among the Twixt in the heart of their world, Under the Hill. If she was going to play the game, she was going to play to win. And if the rules were stacked against her?

She'd cheat.

Joy smiled. "I can do that," she said.

"Not a doubt about it," Dmitri said, casually grabbing Stef by the wrist. "We'll be watching from a safe distance, preferably near a door."

"Stef," Joy said quickly, bringing them both up short. He stared at her, and she felt suddenly small in fairy-princess dress-up clothes and grown-up shoes. She was six all over again, their parents screaming downstairs, looking to her older brother to see if it was okay to be scared. But the truth was that she wasn't six, and she wasn't scared—she was about to take charge, and he was the one who looked unsure.

"I wanted to tell you," she said.

"I know," he answered. "And I know why you didn't."

Joy shook her head. "I'm sorry."

"I'm not. I understand a lot more now—*a lot more*—and I get it." Stef threaded his fingers through Dmitri's curls, a familiar gesture as unconscious as breathing. "I'm here for you." He chucked his chin at the crowd. "You can do this."

She glanced at the hundreds of masked faces, sweeping cloaks and gowns, the horns and hooves, the whiskers and wings, the eyes bright as glass, the unseen daggers half-drawn, the sharp smiles full of forked tongues and whispered laughter—a kaleidoscope of creatures waiting to see what the infamous Joy Malone might do. Front-page news. Film at eleven.

They had no idea what she could do.

"I know I can," she said.

"Aaaaand that's our cue," Dmitri said as he snagged a silver tray of truffles as well as Stef's arm. "Don't disappoint me, little lady. I came to see a show!"

The crowd flowered open. Stef and Dmitri hurried past a clique of angry mutterings and accusing glares. It was as if a small circle cleared itself in anticipation of *something*, thrilled by the expectation of what she might do next. They wanted to witness the next scandal, yearned to weigh and condemn.

We dare you, they seethed.

She turned, sans escort, and found herself face-to-face with Hasp.

She inhaled sharply. The crippled aether sprite leered, his football-shaped head tilted and his bulging yellow eyes wide as a smile spread across his face like syrup.

"Greetings, ex-*lehman* to Ink," Hasp said in his sibilant whisper. The sound of it shivered down her bare back. "You look *different* than when we last met. Do you remember?" Joy flashed on her body slapping into the slush beneath the overpass, Hasp holding her down in the icy puddles as Briarhook twisted her arm. She went cold, clammy, uncertain how to respond. Her renewed confidence fizzled. Wasn't he in exile? Was he supposed to be here? Her skin crawled as she watched his extra-long fingers unfurl, remembering how they'd wrapped around her throat. She touched her pearl necklace like a ward. Hasp followed the gesture with growing glee. He bowed, exposing the long pink scars on his back where his wings had been removed, his *locqus* stripped from him by Council decree. His forefinger snaked forward and snagged the loop of pearls. Hasp grinned up at her.

"Pretty," he said, then pulled.

She felt the snap before she heard it as a fortune of perfect pearls spilled over the floor, skidding under tables and bouncing off hooves. There were shrieks as a few dancers stumbled and fell, and more than a few spectators roared in unkind laughter. Guests slipped. Bystanders pounced. Platters capsized. Glasses broke. Folk hunkered down, eager to snatch up the rolling, golden treasure, pushing neighbors out of the way and knocking others prone. Joy staggered back, feeling the pearls spill through her fingers. When she looked up, Hasp had disappeared, leaving her fumbling without CliffsNotes or protections, humiliated, undone.

No. She gritted her teeth. *I got this.*

Joy spun around and pointed at the nearest gawker.

"You!" she shouted. The lanky harlequin froze. She held a single pearl above her head. "Whomever fetches me every single lost pearl will earn a boon! Is it witnessed?" Joy felt a little thrill as many eyes widened behind their lace and leather masks. She'd done this before—she knew the right words. They were *impressed*! The jester nodded. She waved her hand imperiously. "Go!"

And he did. Dozens followed, scattering to the corners of the ballroom.

Joy grabbed her skirts and hurried toward the door, knowing that the inevitable wouldn't take long. She was a teenage veteran of competitive sports and impromptu raves—screw the waltz, *this* was a dance she knew well!

Behind her there were shouts, curses, squeals of victory and protest, raised voices, a single push and then the unmistakable sound of a punch hitting home.

It was like a gong went off, shattering the facade of genteel society.

One of Filly's stouter sisters raised a fist and shouted, *"Victory!"*

The room erupted.

It was a free-for-all punctuated with barks and laughter and mayhem. Dodging behind a column, Joy rifled under her hairpiece for the scalpel, feeling both silly and clever as she slid the weapon out of her curls. There was a scuffle by the harp stand. Someone flew backward, sending dancers sprawling. A table upended. A chair hit the pool. A towering ice sculpture shattered against the floor. There were screams and bellows and a squeaky garble of angry porpoise protests. Joy saw a sheepish-looking girl with woolly hair grab the boy next to her and kiss him. A handsome stag-man with green eyes landed a sucker punch on a basilisk, who bent double, gnashed its black fangs and shrieked. A feathered boarhound, taking offense, charged.

Hugging the column, Joy checked the doors. Everyone was moving to either join or contain the damage; she recognized a few of the Council members darting through the melee and several bird-masked figures acting as guards. She caught the baleful look on Sol Leander's face as he pointed at her and shouted something wordless. She was glad she couldn't hear him and darted quickly around the fountain. Someone thrust a fist of pearls in her face, but it was knocked sideways, spraying the loot like scattershot. Joy ducked and changed direction, getting a splash of something across her back. She was tempted to pull her rip cords, but had to get clear of the hall. There was a horribly familiar cackle, and Joy glanced back, spying Ladybird applauding her with arrogant glee. He spied her across the room and doffed his plumed hat in wry salute. Frowning, she hid behind the next column. The drug lord's approval was *not* a good sign.

Holding her breath, Joy ran for the nearest table, untouched save for a few missing trays and its linens stained with wine. At least, she hoped it was wine. Ducking quickly, she avoided a tangle of bodies hitting the floor just beyond the table's edge. She was about to bolt when she felt a hand close over her ankle. Joy yelped and kicked the knuckles with her heel. A tray *whanged* down hard, and the grip turned boneless. A pair of stalk-eyes appeared under the edge of the tablecloth, winked at her and disappeared. Joy was grateful to keep moving.

The floorboards trembled, jostling her feet. A swelling shape roiled past, smelling of baked air and fear. Joy didn't have the breath to scream—she was too surprised to do much but gawk as Bùxiǔ de Zhēnzhū transformed, his face flattening, neck lengthening, spine undulating as his clothes billowed out as if carried by the winds that had tugged his moustaches into ropy tendrils, and smoke wreathed his head like fur. His smile zippered wide. His nostrils flared. Scales glittered to the surface. Fire churned in his throat. A rosy glow lit his chest from the inside, outlining ribs the size of railroad ties. His massive tail curled. His breathing sounded like distant thunder—the promise of roars.

Joy slammed her back against the wall and reconsidered dashing past the dragon.

The rising volume of voices pressed down, urging her out. The air crackled with tension and madness. The room grew increasingly angry and loud. She squeezed her scalpel in her sweaty fist. *How was she going to get out?*

A howl split the air, becoming a chorus. Joy chanced a look, shocked to see a willowy woman with a sunburst mask and a familiar squiggle on her jaw lift a ceremonial staff as she sang out a long, throaty wail. The men beside her were built like glaciers, wide and hard, wearing all the colors of winter, their male voices combining with hers into a chilling challenge. One man wore a half-moon mask and dark furs, his one arm ended at the elbow, his long hair speckled with stars.

Ysabel. Joy stared. *And that must be Lucius.*

Ysabel LaCombe, her first client, the one whose plea had exposed her power to Graus Claude, had come to repay her debt. The French Canadian water sprite and her werewolf lover were willing to fight for Joy's freedom.

The wolf pack shifted form, split and circled, driving masqueraders together in squealing herds, snapping at their heels. Folk scattered with renewed fury and fear. The dragon's front claws came down like an avalanche. Mirrors shattered. Musicians fled. The chandelier globes tinkled against one another, a sound almost lost in the bedlam...but not completely. Joy stared up at the ceiling while laughter rang from the rafters and complicated curses echoed off the walls. Folk were shouting at one another to *Let go! Settle down! Come quietly! Find Joy!*

She knew she should run, but she watched the glowing orbs wobble like champagne bubbles hugging the underside of the glass. Her memory was now up among them, the memory of this night—her being welcomed as one of the Twixt—but hers was different, not just because she was once-human, but because she was the first to be presented in a thousand years. To the Council. To the Folk. *Not all the Folk, only those left behind.* Joy stared out over the swollen ballroom knowing it should be impossibly bigger, grander; she knew what was missing. There were *thousands* of bubbles hanging in that chandelier, all the memories of those moments when everyone in the Twixt had been presented just like this. *Not like this*, she realized. *They had been presented to the King and Queen!*

Glowing moments, memories, all of them, preserved for all time.

A time before the Council.

Before the Amanya spell.

Joy knew what to do.

She looked for the nearest possible object, but nothing seemed within reach. She glanced about desperately, but then touched her own hair, feeling the crystal comb—the one Maia had given her in protest of Graus Claude. Joy's fingers closed over the sharp stones.

She hesitated. Maia said it didn't *do* anything. No—she hadn't said that. She'd dodged the question, saying it looked pretty in her hair. Joy thought about what Maia *hadn't* said—she'd given her favor, wrapped it with care and whispered a warning: *Wouldn't want t' break it by accident*, she'd said.

What about on purpose?

Joy snatched the comb and threw it hard into the low-hanging lights.

Crystals collided. Light exploded. Glass shattered. Shooting stars cascaded like fireworks, careening off every reflective surface, setting off a flashing chain reaction punctuated by high-pitched whistles and brightly colored sparks. The chandelier collapsed, imploding in a symphony of nova light. Pieces rained down like burning ash, like stardust, like snow. Everywhere they touched glowed a little brighter. Everyone they touched grew quiet and still. Memories flashed in their eyes, mirror-bright, fading in a matchstick instant. The ballroom dimmed, a hushed twilight, the chaos ebbed into silence.

Joy wondered if she'd done it, if they remembered...

"For the Imminent Return!" Her lone voice echoed off the walls.

The entirety of the Twixt turned and stared at her, stunned.

...

"FOR THE IMMINENT RETURN!"

Folk took up the battle cry—the sound of an awakening.

They cheered, embraced, fell to their knees, many screamed, joyous, many more cried. There were shouts of outrage, pointing fingers and claws, bickering, swearing, recrimination, supplication, despair, hope and blame. The Twixt exploded in a mob of rapture and fury. If Joy hadn't been so adrenalized, she'd have stopped to admire her handiwork. Instead, she squinted against the light and bolted out the door.

Now! She grabbed the ribbons at her ribs and *pulled*.

The dress collapsed in half, folding outward like a flower that she stepped out of with ease. Joy kicked off her shoes, tore the feet off her hose and wriggled out of the crinoline, shedding the fabric like a cocoon. She rolled her long, glove-like sleeves inside-out and threw them on top of the discarded half wig, picked up her scalpel and her purse with the keys and left the rest behind like a melted Cinderella corpse.

Raina was right to have had her practice. She was right about a lot of things, but what Joy needed right now wasn't Raina—she needed to find Ink! And then Graus Claude, Kurt, Filly, Briarhook...

One conniption fit at a time. You've just changed the world!

Joy raced down the hall in her GK leotard and bare feet.

Marble changed to hardwood changed to carpeting and stone floor. She remembered the map as if she'd snapped a pic with her phone, but no one had mentioned a coatroom. She hadn't worn a coat. Joy squeezed the handle of the scalpel, hoping she could erase the snooze button when she found them. She sprinted down the hall leading back to the Council chamber and ran up the stairs. There were so many doors, so many winding corridors, she'd be hopelessly lost if she picked a random direction. She needed a map. She needed a plan. But what she *wanted* was Ink.

Joy crouched in the alcove, panting to catch her breath, amazed and disturbed that her heart wasn't slamming in her chest like it should. It made her feel hollow, like something not-quite-real. She strained to hear the lumber of footsteps or the clatter of the ballroom crowd in pursuit. Joy ducked beneath the stairwell and took stock. How long could she search Under the Hill? How long could she last before being found? She wondered if Kestrel would be here, tracking her down. The idea of the alien-faced tracker sniffing her out made Joy press deeper into shadow.

There was a sound—a whisper of a sound—directly behind her.

She whirled, scalpel out.

"Joy."

Ink was there, hands raised, eyes open, whole. Gone was his elaborate coat; he stood in his black shirt, buckled pants and silver-clawed boots, the ever-present wallet chain swinging at his hip. Joy stared, hardly daring to believe it. She *didn't* believe it.

"They shut you off."

He smiled impishly. "Never again." Ink tapped the spot above his left breast. "I created a blockage—you showed me where." He punched his chest. Nothing happened. Two dimples appeared.

Joy shook her head. "I saw you fall—"

"I fell," he admitted. "But deception is not the same as lying."

Biting back a laugh, Joy flung herself into his arms, and he hugged her hard, pressing her to him, smelling of sea and storm. She kissed him, and his hands slid down her bare back, catching on the seam. His thumb hooked into the Lycra and tugged her closer. "I liked the dress," he confessed. His breathing changed, pressing against her. "I like this more." His mouth opened under hers. She clutched his shirt. There was a flare deep in her belly. Ink blinked twice and swallowed.

"This is not the time," he said.

Peeling apart, Joy took his hand, still feeling sparks. "Definitely not," she said and tapped his arm. "Come on. We've got to go."

Ink flicked open his straight razor. The wallet chain bounced at his hip. "We are still within the wards," he said. "I cannot cut a doorway, and we cannot leave without the Bailiwick."

"But they *remember* now! They can open the door—"

Ink shook his head. "Not without the courier," he said. "Aniseed was to locate the door and open it by Council decree. They cannot find it without her."

"Then we'll get Aniseed to tell us," Joy said grimly. "The graftling knows where it is."

Ink checked the hallway. "Perhaps so," he said. "But not soon enough."

He tugged her forward, taking the lead. Joy followed him, leaving the ballroom far behind. "But isn't Inq—"

"They shut her down," he said flatly. "She was stored with me, but I had not told her—" Ink sighed, lips tight. "I should have told her about the fail-safe, and now it is too late." Joy squeezed his hand. She knew *exactly* how he felt. Siblings were hard. Secrets were hard. Ink tugged her around a corner. "She is safer there than she would be being carried out by us. We will have to assume her role." He nodded back behind them. "You may have made things more difficult—if they remember, they will seek out Graus Claude, but will they be looking for a savior or a scapegoat?" Ink glanced at her curiously. "How did you do it? How did you break the spell?"

"The Folk's memories of their own galas predated the Amanya spell," Joy said, matching his pace. "In a paradox, the earlier spell wins out. I took a chance that those stored memories would do the trick, but I didn't expect that response."

Ink led them up a long set of stairs, speaking quickly. "The Folk have just remembered their King and Queen, their lost kin, their broken promises—they feel guilty and overwhelmed, violated and confused. I imagine they are feeling many things at once," he said. "I am beginning to understand that now."

"Really?" she said to cover her worry. "What are you feeling?"

"Joy," he said, squeezing her hand. "Relief, empathy, anger, resolve, compassion, possessiveness, excitement, hope, love." Ink's voice trailed off as he avoided her gaze. "Lust."

Joy felt herself blush.

He stopped to check the next rise, then ducked to the left, leading them on some path with purpose. Joy followed, feeling more unease. She was hopelessly lost—all the upper hallways looked the same, lined with wooden doors framed in gilt and heavy curtains. Joy shifted her grip on the scalpel, expecting one of the Twixt to jump out at every turn. If they couldn't get into the Bailiwick to open the door, they would have to get him out until everything calmed down. Hiding him on the way out was going to be tricky, but once they cleared the hill, they could disappear. Joy would have to leave the car...

Ink stopped and chose a different corridor. "Here," he said and pulled her through a door.

It was a greenhouse. A fractal glass dome arced overhead with massive trees crowded together along a stone path. The air hot and stuffy, perfumed in flowers and mulch. Moisture clung like sweat and beaded on their lashes. Joy watched the silk ribbon in Ink's hair droop. Things danced among the branches. Joy tensed, but they were only enormous-winged butterflies, dancing motes of blue and orange, white and speckled brown. It was like yet another world than the two they'd left behind.

"Lehman!"

Joy stumbled. Fetid breath hit her face, rocking her back and making her gag. The taste of rotten meat clung to her tongue, and she retched, bile burning the back of her throat. Joy swallowed, eyes watering, and held on to Ink. The quilled monster resolved out of the forest patterns. Her arm stung with memory. Her eyes stung with tears.

"Here. Bailiwick." Briarhook spat. "Deal!" Reaching behind him, Briarhook shoved Graus Claude forward. Joy stared. The grandiose toad was a pale, sickly yellow instead of his normal olive hue; his four arms hung loose at his sides, and his eyes looked bloodshot, a bizarre mix of red and ice-blue. The nightmarish hedgehog sneered, his mealy rags replaced with a bizarre sort of uniform, dark and patchy, with spines sticking out in all directions. The edge of the metal plate peeked out from the low collar. Joy saw one of the crusted rivets up close. "Say you, 'break out' but not 'how far.'" Briarhook spat at her feet, a globule of spittle clinging to his lip. "Know you why? Heart mine—not in it. No." He chortled. Graus Claude shuddered. Briarhook's tail struck him with a fat earthworm *thump*. "Bailiwick is, yes. Drugged. Drained. Bled. Broke." The hedgehog raised a single claw. "But free. Yes." His piggy eyes glittered in his shuddery flesh. He sniffed as if he could scent bloodhounds coming. "For now."

Joy grabbed one of Graus Claude's hands in hers. It was dry and chapped and quivering. She tried to get his eyes to focus on her from under his post-orbital ridge, but she couldn't make herself move his head. The indignity of it was worse than the possibility of losing him.

"Where is Kurt?" Ink asked.

Briarhook shrugged. "Not know. Not here. Work mine,

done." He sneered with his mealy, broken teeth. "Go. Enjoy hunt, you. Know you—take message, eh? Make message you take!" Joy tried to ignore the hate that frothed behind her, bristling with black, barbarous quills. Pain stabbed her shoulder, quick enough to make her gasp. She glared up at him. He'd poked her with a claw. "No die, you," Briarhook warned, poking her again. "Not yet! Not till my heart *mine*—" he squeezed the word through rotted teeth as he slithered toward the stairs on the opposite side of the mezzanine. "Then—promise you, I—you *die*," he said softly. "You die *slow*." His voice dropped low as his face faded into shadow, whispering a private threat, bubbling out of the darkness. "So. Very. Slow."

Ink's razor shone a stab of light like a warning, but the hedgehog was gone.

Joy counted to five. Then five again. She forced the sick tremble out of her limbs by squeezing the giant frog's hand. She shook it with force.

"Graus Claude?" she squeaked urgently. "Graus Claude? It's Joy."

There was an answering rumble in the back of his throat, too far away to do much good.

"Mmm," he said. It was a noncommittal sound.

She crossed her mental fingers. "Bailiwick?"

"Miss—Malone?"

"Yes," Joy said desperately. "Yes. You need to get up. We need get out of here." She glanced at Ink, adding somewhat unnecessarily, "Right now."

Three of his hands started to move, arms flexing, fingers twitching, the massive curve of his spine arcing upward, reminding her of the dragon who was somewhere Under the Hill. The leader of a defunct Council? The one who would no doubt be blamed for what had happened? She could just imagine his desire to find her.

The Bailiwick's low-slung head moved to one side, his eyes sparkled dully, jade instead of sapphire. Ink supported much of his unsteady bulk.

"Where are we?" Graus Claude muttered.

"In the Atrium," Ink said. "Briarhook was instructed to use this part of the forest wing as a fallback should the plan go awry."

Graus Claude creaked, "I imagine this means that things have gone awry."

Ink nodded. "Quite."

The Bailiwick frowned at the Scribe. "What have you done to your hair?" he asked. "It looks ghastly."

"Never mind that," Joy said, not wanting to get into the details right now. "Just tell us how to get back to the East entrance, and we can get you out of here."

Comprehension lit a fire behind his eyes full of defiance and rebuke.

"Miss Malone," he groaned while gaining his feet in jerks and spurts like a rusty toy. "I am a prisoner of the Council under my own admission—my crime is both far-reaching and grave, my guilt only outmatched by what is left of my personal honor and loyalty to a forgotten crown, and it does not matter to me if they know that it is a sovereign oath or not. *I* do. And I fully acknowledge that this opportunity to redeem myself is thanks to you." He lifted his massive head as if by sheer will and yawned like a snarl, his teeth closing with a click. He rubbed his limbs and absently plucked at his surcoat, which was missing some buttons and was torn on one side. For the first time in Joy's memory, he looked shabby and unkempt. It hurt to see him like this, but his eyes were impossibly kind. "You have freed me from a terrible curse and given me the choice to make it right—*my* choice and *my* right. I cannot properly thank you for that service, but I will try." Two of his hands fastened on her shoulders with a soft squeeze, like an embrace, before he withdrew, his palsy quiver more pronounced than ever. "I shall abstain from commenting on how horrific you look." He smiled lamely.

"Graus Claude—" Ink said.

"No," he said sternly, but without much steam. "I understand that you must both go. Now. Leave me to the fate that I have chosen—I ask that you please respect me in this." His eyes flickered with embers of their old fire. "I would protect you once more, as your mentor and friend. You must distance yourself from me in all ways. Your time in the Twixt has just begun, as for me, mine is at an end."

"No!" Joy said, far louder than she should—her voice muffled by the thick glass lining the walls. "Graus Claude, *please!* Everyone remembers. The spell is broken. They are looking for you—for the Bailiwick and the door and the King and Queen—but we don't know what they'll do when they find you!"

The shock of it seemed too much for the noble toad. He listed to one side. Ink was there, lifting him up. The Bailiwick's eyes unfocused, refocused and stared.

"All of them?" he whispered. "The Council? The Court? The entirety of the Twixt?" His voice hitched higher. *"Maia?"*

Ink said, "Yes, Bailiwick."

Graus Claude grunted. "Then by all means—" He attempted to stand, but even his enormous feet could not support him. Three arms became table legs as he shuddered on his knees. "I imagine that you cannot avail us of a door, Master Ink?"

"Not while we are within the wards," Ink said. He glanced at Joy. "We must escape from Under the Hill."

The great amphibian groaned and sat back on his haunches. "It cannot be done." The words were chilling, reminding Joy ominously of the Red Knight. "We are too deep within the Hill, and I am too weak." He squatted in the wet grass, looking more like an old frog than ever. "The people of the Twixt have a right to the door, now that they remember. They have a right to see their King and Queen—or banish them, if that is what they decide. I remain loyal, but that loyalty is mine alone. I have made enough of their decisions," he sighed. "Let this one be theirs."

"No! Don't do this," Joy cried and tugged at his arm. Didn't he understand? Without Inq to go in and find the door, they had to get him *out*! She imagined the ballroom, the unthinking, desperate mob fueled by frustration and angry, futile fears. *"Please,"* she begged. The longer they sat, the more certain she was that the dragon would appear—the very idea screamed at her, urging her to run.

The giant amphibian settled with a *hmph*! His four arms crossed. His chest heaved. His eyes sank, half-lidded, looking grim. He was wounded and woozy and yet spoke with stubborn certainty. "I am not going anywhere."

Ink gently withdrew from the Bailiwick's side. He stepped back and took Joy's hand. She watched his fingers thread through hers—the promise of them, together, Ink and Joy.

"It is his choice," Ink said. The unsaid echoed, *Respect him. Always.*

Joy shifted her weight, her feet in the earth. A cool calm crept over her. This moment was bigger than her. Bigger than Graus Claude. And Ink. And the princess. And the Council. And all of the Twixt. It was the future of two worlds, together, and it was just her, being human. And Folk. And not.

"With all due respect," she said. "I can't let you do that."

Graus Claude sighed at her melodrama. "You cannot *make* me comply, Miss Malone."

"But I can," Joy said, dropping Ink's hand and raising her own. "I demand entrance to the Bailiwick of the Twixt."

He hissed surprise, eyes widening in shock—then passed shock into awe as his mouth stretched, growing taller, unhinging, expanding. His eyes misted over, his tongue curled up, his body grew stony and pale as death. Joy watched as she took his choice from him, along with his dignity and free will. She had asked him to respect her choices, and she had not respected his. Joy was as bad as the Amanya itself.

The Bailiwick opened.

Stepping over the sharp teeth, she watched the line of red fire zip past, thinking of Aniseed's golems, the courier's booby trap, knowing the color of the spell matched the coal brightness of their eyes. She was still human. Human enough to set off the alarm warning that humans had breached the Bailiwick, the last stronghold of the Twixt, a trip wire set to protect their greatest treasure—even if they'd forgotten it for a while. Distance wouldn't matter—the homunculi could travel through the earth; tireless, merciless, bound to an ancient spell, they could find anyone who trespassed anywhere in the world. It was a guarantee that no human would threaten the Imminent Return.

When, in fact, this human was here to make it so.

She paused on that first step, able to see just beyond the crux of his upper lip. She could imagine the sounds of the ballroom spilling through the building, searching for them somewhere, chaotic and loud. And somewhere inside the Bailiwick, there was a princess and the answers and a long-lost door.

"I will save everyone," she said to his milky eye, hoping that somehow he might hear her. "Even you," Joy promised. "And me." She turned around and held out her hand to Ink.

He took it and stepped forward.

And together, they stepped down, down, down into the Bailiwick's throat.

TWENTY-TWO

JOY NEARLY RAN DOWN THE DARK STAIRS, THE CLAWED toes of Ink's boots click-clattering behind her as they made their way toward the light. They burst into the meticulous grove, each petal and blade of grass fashioned by one prisoner waiting patiently to be rescued, to be remembered, to be reassured that it was safe to come home.

"Hello?" Joy called out as she tromped through the meadow, crossing the tumbling brook without the sound of a splash—the water didn't feel cold, it didn't feel like anything. Ink turned, leaning into the nonexistent wind that played with the leaves but not his hair.

"Mother!" he shouted.

She materialized over the horizon, the world revolving with dizzy speed until she stood before them. No one's feet had moved. She smiled at them.

"What news?" she asked.

"Joy broke the spell," Ink said. "They all remember—the King and Queen, their families, the hidden door, you."

"And the coup?" she said. "Those who first plotted against us now remember their purpose. Do you know the name of the traitor?"

"It was Aniseed," Joy said. "Aniseed was the courier, and she was the one who tried to overthrow the Council. She probably intended to remove the royal influence that made everyone loyal and then manipulate the Council from within. When that didn't work, she tried culling the number of humans in order to swing power back her way. She's been behind everything, from the coup to hiding the door to casting the—" Joy's throat closed up, and she inadvertently choked on her tongue.

"Aniseed did not cast the Amanya," Ink reminded her. "She manipulated the Bailiwick into casting the spell."

The princess's eyes narrowed, and Joy couldn't tell if she imagined the woman's glyphs growing darker. It may have been the false sun.

"Inq told me that Aniseed was dead."

"We thought so, too," Joy said. "But she cloned herself."

The princess tried the unfamiliar word. "Cloned?"

"Twained," Ink said. "Aniseed made a graftling."

The stately woman sighed, resigned. "I see," she said, smoothing her hands over her dress. "But I asked if you had the traitor's *name*. The graftling will not have the same name as its parent. Without the courier's True Name, we cannot hope to find the door."

"Wait. What?" Joy said. "The Council locked the door, and they have to be the ones to open it unless all of them died. The courier alone knew its location—but why would they need their True Names?"

The princess gestured to the whole of the pocket world. "They will have locked the door with their sigils," she said, pointing to her arms, the glyphs on her skin. "It was the reason for my staying behind, to help the Council develop the system of *signaturae*. My auspice is the written word—it is how I made both Inq and Ink. I Make things with words. I wrote them into being." She placed a hand on his shoulder. "Words are how we made the *signaturae*. Words are how our worlds passed from chaos into order—names, speech, history, time. Words give us worlds, names make things real." She passed a timid hand gently over the tops of the grasses, smudging her world, blending the colors together like charcoal or chalk. It wasn't real. She looked at the breach tenderly. "Names make things true."

Shock sprinkled down Joy's limbs. Her knees turned to jelly. Her brain popped with sparks. She felt the scalpel slide in her slick grip.

"They locked the door with their sigils?" Joy said. *Of course!* Every Council member would have to come in and unlock their *signaturae*, themselves. They couldn't be forged, they could only be given—to an acolyte, a new member of the Council, like the courier. *Like Aniseed.* No one could have known what Aniseed had planned for *signaturae*. They couldn't have known that the whole system had played right into her hands.

"Names are the only key worth having," the princess said. "I gave that skill to my creations, the power of Names. It was part of what ultimately made the Scribes real."

Joy thought about Maia's boxes and chest and shelves of scrolls. She couldn't remember the shape of it, exactly, but then again, Maia hadn't given Joy her *signatura*. In fact, she had only been given one Council Member's *signatura*, albeit unwillingly. *That* had been real.

Joy had been given Aniseed's *signatura*.

And Joy was the third Scribe.

She turned and faced the horizon, lifting her scalpel to the vague memory of sunlight. She drew a line through the sky, curving it like a bow, pausing to draw a giant dot in its center. A nothingness followed, an outline of pale gray.

"What are you doing?" The princess sounded upset at the scratch through her world like unwelcome graffiti; her voice was uncertain, her expression unsure.

"One down," Joy said. "Seven to go."

She carved seven pointy petals of a pinwheel, each bisected with a circle—a star-shaped snowflake, a spiked flower of eyes. *Star anise seeds. Aniseed's True Name.* Joy drew the courier's *signatura*, and it flashed with familiar fire.

An answering *Flash!* flared in the sky.

"There!" Joy pointed, and the world slid beneath their feet, slamming to a stop before a large circle of glyphs—Aniseed's *signatura*, having revealed itself, sizzled and winked out, revealing a circular door. Six sigils remained, faint outlines in the sky; Joy did not recognize any of them except for one at ten o'clock that resembled a stylized teardrop.

"You found it!" the Princess said, tight and eager with hope. "We need the Council."

"No, we don't," Joy said, lifting her scalpel. "This ends now."

I can do this.

Joy traced the first glyph carefully, watching the invisible firework sparks of undoing erase the locks on things that should never have happened, things that should never have been. She remembered Inq's body, a Rorschach bloom on her bed. She remembered Ink's throat gaping open, jagged and torn. She remembered Aniseed's howl as she completed her sigil behind the electric-blue ward and the way Sol Leander's arrow had glowed an unhealthy, angry red.

She remembered tracing, erasing the sadistic *signatura* that had bound Ysabel LaCombe by the throat.

Six marks remained. Then five. Four. Three. Two.

Joy paused above the last one and glanced at the princess, her face rapt.

"Are you ready?" Joy asked.

The princess's eyes shone. She clasped her hands together. "Yes!"

Ink nodded, transfixed.

Joy erased the last *signaturae*.

The last sigil flared. The door unlocked.

Joy opened it with a mix of nervousness, excitement and dread.

There was light—real light—from a real, foreign sun that looked somehow larger and brighter than the one in Glendale, North Carolina. Joy could feel Ink's arms around her as her eyes adjusted to the colors—the vivid green hills that stretched for miles topped with bright banners and long, trailing flags flying high over yellow bivouac camps. The hillsides were dotted with tents and siege machines, battle equipment, liveried animals, smoking armories and strange beasts. Armies upon armies upon armies camped together—a blanket of soldiers standing ready in armor and chain, leathers and furs, tabards and breastplates, wing-shields and robes.

On one hill, a large court spread like a picnic. Two figures in tall chairs got slowly to their feet, their hair streaming behind them like wings.

"Mother! Father!"

The princess pushed past Joy and Ink and plunged through the door. There was a trembling soap-bubble warp as its surface settled back into place. Joy could see the dark-haired woman running over the hills, racing to meet her family, bare feet flying over the grass-that-really-was-grass, leaving Joy and Ink behind in the Bailiwick, in the doorway, alone.

Joy stared into the eyes of the King and Queen. They looked at her and Ink, faces unreadable. Joy smiled. Ink leaned closer and threaded his fingers through hers. Hundreds of Folk gathered together, a thousand eyes staring at them through the void.

DAWN METCALF

The King turned to his Queen, his words, crisp and clean, crossing the miles, slicing through sound.

"It is as you foretold," he said. "Behold the destroyer of worlds."

* * * * *

Thank you for reading INSIDIOUS by Dawn Metcalf.

We hope you enjoyed your journey into the dark and magical world of The Twixt!

Joy and Ink's adventures continue in Book 4,
INVINCIBLE.
Only from Dawn Metcalf and Harlequin TEEN!

ACKNOWLEDGMENTS

HOW CAN I FIND THE WORDS TO EXPRESS HOW profoundly grateful I am to all those who helped make this book possible? Well, since I've managed to write over 125,000 words so far, I might as well keep going and try to do my best.

I want to sincerely thank my editor, Natashya Wilson, for allowing me to continue exploring the world of the Twixt, my agent, Sarah Davies, for joining me on the journey, and my critique partners, Angie Frazier, Maurissa Guibord and Susan Van Hecke, for helping me keep my eye on the prize and my fingers on the keys. Thanks to my amazing beta readers, Jenny Bannock, Nicole Boucher and Shari Metcalf for their insight and savvy, and extra-big hugs to Mark Apgar, Kate Baker, Kurt Boucher, Steve Dunlop and Kate Smith for supportive straight-talk, friendly smackdowns and helping me research crazy questions that might otherwise get me into serious trouble.

Huge, heaping thanks to the Harlequin TEEN Dream Team without whom there would be no ink about *Indelible*, no visibility for *Invisible* and no sneaky surprises throughout *Insidious*—Shara Alexander, Jenny Bullough, Bryn Collier, Ingrid Dolan, Kristin Errico, T. S. Ferguson, Amy Jones, Gigi Lau, Margaret Marbury, Ashley McCallan, Kathleen Oudit, Mary Sheldon, Lauren Smulski, Libby Sternberg and Anna Baggaley of the UK MIRA Ink team. To all of you working behind the pages: thank you so much!

Lastly, writing is hard. Being a mom is hard. Being a writer-mom, not to mention a wife, sister, daughter, auntie, niece, school parent and friend is nigh impossible (which, by the way, will *not* be the title of the next Twixt book)! Therefore, none of this means anything without the love and support of my family, who give me the freedom to be all of these things as well as pursue my lifelong dream. Thanks to my parents, Holly and Barry, my other parents, Marilyn and Harold, my siblings by birth and marriage, Corrie, Richard, Adam, Michelle, David and Shari, and to my beloved husband, Jonathan, my hero and friend for lo these twenty years, and to the two small people who look vaguely like us, S.L. and A.J., thank you for making my every day magic.

And thank you to all my readers—you make wishes come true!

Somewhere between reality and myth lies... THE TWIXT

Some things are permanent.
Indelible.

Some things lie beneath the surface.
Invisible.
With the power to change everything.

True evil is rarely obvious.
It is quiet, patient.
Insidious.
Awaiting the perfect moment to strike.

"This exhilarating story of Ink and Joy has marked my heart forever. More!"
—Nancy Holder, *New York Times* bestselling author of *Wicked*

Don't miss a single installment of *The Twixt*.
Books 1–3 available wherever books are sold!

www.HarlequinTEEN.com

Alexander the Great meets *Games of Thrones* for teens in Book 1 of the epic new **Blood of Gods and Royals** series by *New York Times* bestselling author

ELEANOR HERMAN

IMAGINE A TIME WHEN CITIES BURN... AND IN THEIR ASHES EMPIRES RISE.

Available Now!

www.HarlequinTEEN.com

Is Amanda being haunted by an evil presence...or has she simply lost her mind?

Coming October 2015

Secretly pregnant, 16-year-old Amanda wonders at first if her family's move to the prairie will provide the chance for a fresh start, but it soon becomes clear that there is either something very wrong with the prairie, or something very wrong with Amanda.

AMY LUKAVICS

GOD BLESS THE LITTLE CHILDREN

www.HarlequinTEEN.com

A Dark Power Is About to Rise in Japan...

"The work of a master storyteller."
—Julie Kagawa, *New York Times* bestselling author of *The Iron Fey* series

Own the full *Paper Gods* series!
Available wherever books are sold.

www.HarlequinTEEN.com

THE GODDESS TEST NOVELS

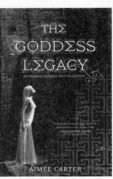

Available wherever books are sold!

A modern saga inspired by the Persephone myth.

Kate Winters's life hasn't been easy. She's battling with the upcoming death of her mother, and only a mysterious stranger called Henry is giving her hope. But he must be crazy, right? Because there is no way the god of the Underworld—Hades himself—is going to choose Kate to take the seven tests that might make her an immortal...and his wife. And even if she passes the tests, is there any hope for happiness with a war brewing between the gods?

Also available:
THE GODDESS HUNT, a digital-only novella.

www.HarlequinTEEN.com